KEEP

YOU

FROM

HARM

KEEP YOU

FROM

HARM

A NOVEL

DEBRA DOXER

ISBN-13: 978-1492381235
ISBN-10: 1492381233

For Jillian

ONE

THE first strange thing I notice when I approach my building is the absence of a crowd. In the two years we've lived here, our front stoop has been home to a revolving bunch of drug dealers and pimps who congregate around one of the biggest underworld purveyors of both services, a guy by the name of Apollo. He lives on the first floor directly below us. Despite his unsavory lifestyle, he's been decent to me since we moved here, and we have an odd sort of friendship.

I climb the deserted concrete steps with my heavy backpack knocking against my tailbone. When I reach the top, I check our mailbox. The floor is littered with the same junk mail I find piled inside. Pulling it out, I bunch it under my arm as I head through the main entrance, a fractured glass door with a useless lock. I've lived in lots of places over the years, but this is by far the worst with its unrelenting bug issues and the stale odor of sweat and cigarettes seeping from the walls. I spend as little time here as possible.

I look toward Apollo's door as I pass. It's cracked open, but there's no sign of him. I briefly consider knocking and asking him where everyone disappeared to, but then I think better of it. I've never just dropped in on

1

him before. The fact is, Apollo is unpredictable, and he can be downright scary at times. I don't want to risk his wrath today.

As I continue past his apartment and begin climbing the narrow stairwell, there's an unsettling prickle on the back of my neck. Something is off. I can sense it. But I move slowly, cautiously rounding the corner and glancing up at our door. It's closed, and there's nothing out of the ordinary apparent on the second floor landing. The burned out fluorescents and the scuffed doorways loom above me, silent and familiar. When I step out of the stairwell, I stand listening as I pull the key from my pocket. The entire building is unusually quiet this afternoon.

The deadbolt turns too easily, and I realize our door isn't locked. Sometimes my mother forgets to lock it despite my constant reminders. I step inside and begin looking around. Our tiny one bedroom apartment seems the same as it did when I said goodbye to my mother this morning and left for school. I shake my head and chastise myself for my paranoia.

Ignoring my unease, I toss the mail and my backpack on the couch that also serves as my bed and head into the kitchen to find some food. I make a beeline for the refrigerator and quickly locate a plate of leftover pasta from last night. When I turn to put the pasta on the table, I freeze. The plate drops from my hand, hitting the floor with a clank as I gasp at the nightmare in front of me. I see my mother in one of the kitchen chairs. Her limp body is draped over the table. Her blonde hair is soaking in her pooling blood.

I'm pinned in place as my comprehension wars with my denial. When the horrific image doesn't disappear, my legs start to tremble, and I fall to my knees before her. My gaze travels over her too still form as I reach out to place my fingers on her arm. Her skin is ice cold, but I grip it anyway. The only sound I hear is my ragged breathing as the floor seems to tilt beneath me. I've feared this moment for so long, but not this way. This makes no sense.

Slowing my breathing down, I draw it in as deeply as I can. I reach inside myself for the familiar energy, but it isn't there. There's nothing. I feel only emptiness. She's gone, and this time it's forever.

'M not sure how long I sat there in the kitchen before finally dialing 911. I didn't want to make that call. I didn't want this to be real. Right now, I can almost fool myself into believing that she's disappeared again and will turn up when she's ready. I want to pretend that's the truth. I want to pretend hard enough that the images of her blood and her lifeless body disappear.

She's been like a boomerang in my life, screwing up and losing me, then returning all bright and shiny with a mouthful of promises. I've spent most of my childhood hating my mother during her absences and fearing her abandonment during her brief stints of sobriety when she regained custody of me, pulled me out of foster care, and pretended we were going to be a family. It fucked me up, the constant upheaval. It forced me to shut down in order to cope. And now I don't know how to react normally to this extreme situation, and the detectives are looking at me like I'm a puzzle they can't seem to solve.

I've been at the police station for hours. I should be grief-stricken. Rivers of tears should be flowing out of me, but instead I feel numb and heavy, like all the gravity in this square, windowless room is concentrated on me.

After answering questions for the entire afternoon and into the evening, the detectives finally ask me if I have any family they can contact. When I shake my head, they talk about calling Social Services, and I'm left alone to wait.

Since I've been here, I've learned that my mother took a blow to the back of her head with an unknown object. I told them that I had no idea who would want to hurt her. It's the truth. Two years ago, when she was still an alcoholic and a drug addict, that list would have been miles long. But she's been clean since she got me back, and no one would know better than me if that fact had changed.

The police seem to believe that her death is the result of her old life coming back to haunt her. I don't doubt that's a possibility. I'm sure that Apollo and the rest of the building tenants know something. I wonder if the police questioned them. If so, I bet they learned nothing. The residents of our building are not the types who believe in cooperating with the authorities.

The door opens again, and the same detective I've spent most of the day with enters the room holding a thick file. His name is Brady. He's very young for a detective, and he's good-looking in a clean-cut *I iron my undershirts* kind of way. His dark hair is neatly trimmed, and his light brown eyes convey the perfect mix of concern and gravity. I get the impression he's been assigned to me because he's closer to my age than the rest of them. They probably think I'll feel more comfortable around him. It's foolish of them to think I'll feel comfortable around anyone tonight. I feel nothing at all right now, and I'm glad for it.

"Your brother is on his way," Detective Brady says.

My weary eyes widen. His non sequitur wakes me up like no alarm clock could. I wonder what kind of a joke he's playing.

"He's flying in from New York. He'll be here tomorrow."

He appears serious. I sit forward in my chair and calmly repeat myself. "I told you. I don't have any family."

His lips press together in a thin line. "I just learned that Social Services contacted him about an hour ago. He said he's willing to take custody of you."

I bark out a laugh and shake my head. He's seriously confused. "I. Don't. Have. A. Brother," I say slowly, enunciating each word so he'll understand.

Detective Brady lowers himself into the chair across from me and sets the thick file on the table between us. He looks almost as tired as I feel. "Actually, you do. He's been petitioning the court for custody of you for the past two years." He places his hand on top of the closed file.

My eyes travel from the file back to him. I shake my head at the certainty in his expression. "There must be some mistake."

"Your mother never told you this?" he asks.

My stomach clenches as doubt starts to seep in.

"Did your mother tell you where she's originally from?"

"Upstate New York," I answer, gripping my hands together under the table.

He nods. "That's where your brother still lives with his family. Your mother left when he was six years old. His father, your mother's husband, still lives there, too. They had no idea where she was until a hospital here in San Diego contacted them about two and a half years ago. She was being treated for a drug overdose at the time and they found ID on her that led them to her husband in New York."

My mind is processing what he's telling me, fitting it into place with what I already know. I knew about the drug overdose and about the subsequent treatment, which finally succeeded. That's when she regained custody of me for the last time. I knew she was from New York and that she was married there. I didn't know she had a baby before me. I didn't know she still had a husband there. I definitely didn't know she was keeping such a big secret. All the goodwill she earned from me over the past two years begins to evaporate.

"It looks like your brother has been trying to gain custody since he found out about you. But because your mother was able to prove she was fit to care for you, they wouldn't consider his petition." He pauses. "You really didn't know any of this?"

While he was speaking, my eyes shifted back to the thick file on the table, which obviously contains this information about my mother and me, information that she never bothered to share. Why didn't she tell me I had a brother? Was that what kept her sober? The fear of losing custody of me to him? This threat was big enough to keep her sober when nothing else could? Suddenly, the idea of this brother feels threatening.

"Raielle?"

My head is spinning as I wrack my brain for anything my mother might have said that would hint at this. But there's nothing. I glance over at the detective and shake my head. "I didn't know."

He eyes me with silent sympathy.

"Do I have to go with him?" I ask suddenly.

He raises his eyebrows at me.

"Do I get a choice?"

His lips form the tight straight line I've become accustomed to over the past few hours. "You're a minor. He's the only relative we're aware of, and he's willing to take you. What are your other options?"

I'm about to say foster care, but I know the system won't want me back when I have a relative who is offering to take me off their hands.

When it's obvious that I have no reply, he continues. "Social Services will be here soon. You'll be placed somewhere temporarily while everything gets sorted out."

I sit silently while a storm brews inside me. The numbness that got me through today is erased by a growing panic. We kept a secret together, my mother and me. But I didn't know she had other secrets that she kept to herself. I was finally beginning to trust her, but she'd been keeping this from me all along. We celebrated my seventeenth birthday and the start of her second year sober just last spring. It was the first time she'd ever bought me a real birthday cake. She had my name written on it in pink icing. Her pale blue eyes shined so brightly in the candlelight as she told me to make a wish and blow them out.

Warm hands press down on my shoulders, startling me. "You're shaking," Detective Brady says. "Maybe you should lie down. I'll get you some water."

His concerned eyes hover before me. I take a deep breath, and I will myself to calm down. I open a drawer inside a familiar cabinet, and I force the breakdown my body craves deep within it. This is what I do. This is how I stay focused on what's important. There are an infinite number of drawers in my imaginary cabinet, and I can only hope that it never crumbles under the weight of what's hiding inside.

"What about a funeral?" I ask, my voice strained but strong now in the quiet room.

He straightens, eyeing me curiously. Then he rubs his hand along the back of his neck. When he answers, I can see he's choosing his words carefully. "Once we're done, you can make arrangements for her. If you don't have enough funds, there are services that can help you take care of things."

I interpret his vague statements to mean that the medical examiner still has her, and she can be buried along with the other indigent people once her body is released.

Then once again, I'm left alone with another cup of water. My muscles are tense. I don't move despite how badly I want to bolt out of here right now. But I just sit, running the detective's words through my head, not sure what they mean for me, not sure how to feel about this brother who has appeared out of thin air. My racing thoughts are a jumbled mess, and my mother's betrayal feels like ice running through my veins. I need it all to stop. I want the numbness back.

There is no clock in here, and I don't know how long I've been waiting before a short, squat woman with dull, dark hair abruptly pushes through the door. This is the woman from Social Services. I've never met this one, but they all have the same characteristics: tired eyes, a too bright smile, and a rushed demeanor which seems to signify that everything they're doing is an emergency.

She sits across from me like a settling wind. She doesn't mention my brother. Instead, she tells me that she's taking me to a facility for the night. The police have brought some clothes for me from the apartment. She has those with her. I stop listening as I follow her out. I've been to this place before. I know the drill.

I passively allow myself to be placed in a car, driven across town, and then shuttled through a building where I'm served a dinner I don't eat, and deposited into a room with four single beds, three of which are already occupied by other silent, sullen girls. I am afraid of the images I might see when I close my eyes that night. But thankfully, I'm so drained that sleep comes quickly, and it's a temporary, but welcome break from reality.

TWO

WHEN I see him, there's no mistaking who he is. The same dark, blonde curls that flow down my back are cropped close to his head. He stares at me with the familiar pale blue eyes that my mother and I also share. His tall, rangy build is the male equivalent of my narrow five foot eight inch frame.

"Hello, Raielle. I've been looking forward to meeting you." He smiles, and it appears genuine, but I nearly cringe when he mispronounces my name the same way most people do.

"Raielle Blackwood, this is Kyle Dean," the social worker says, also mangling my name. "Your brother," she adds as I stand there staring at him. We're in a small room at the Social Services office. The bright morning sun streams in through a single window set high into the concrete wall. My belongings are packed inside a familiar oversized duffle bag, which used to reside in our closet and is now sitting in the corner. The items inside were gathered from the apartment by strangers since I'm not allowed back in. Apparently, the crime scene is part of an ongoing investigation, and it can't be disturbed.

"It's pronounced Ray-elle not Rye-elle," I inform him.

My brother's grin falters, and he glances at the social worker. Her plastered on smile also falls briefly before reappearing. "Well, Raielle" she begins, saying it correctly as she steps toward the door. "I'll let you two get acquainted while I finish the paperwork." Then she promptly leaves the room.

My gaze gradually tracks from the closed door to the stranger standing before me. We eye each other in awkward silence, and I can see that he's noting our similarities the same way I am. "I've been looking forward to meeting you," he says gently, like he's talking to a skittish animal that might dart away if startled.

It hurts to look into his eyes, my mother's eyes. As though reading my thoughts, he says, "I'm very sorry about your mother." When I don't respond, he adds, "Our mother."

"That's funny," I lob back at him, unreasonably angered by his words. "She never mentioned you."

His brow wrinkles, and he studies me curiously. "If you were trying to hurt me, you succeeded," he finally says.

I'm thrown by his honesty. I watch him walk toward a ratty looking couch that's pushed against the wall. He sits down, folding his long legs and clasping his hands together. "I live in Fort Upton, New York with my wife and my three-year-old daughter," he tells me.

I stand in the middle of the room and continue to take him in. When I woke up this morning, a part of me was clinging to the hope that this was all a mistake. My mother would never keep something this big from me. But looking at him now, my throat grows tight. This is undoubtedly my brother, and by the way he reacted to my mean-spirited comment, it seems that even in her absence, she fucked him up, too.

"We're setting up a room for you in our basement. It's been finished. It's carpeted and heated. It's my daughter's playroom. But we can turn it into a nice bedroom for you." He's watching me for my reaction.

"Why are you doing this?" I ask.

He takes a deep breath and exhales loudly. "Because you're my sister. Because I didn't even know I had a sister until two years ago when I found out our mother was a drug addict who had been neglecting you."

I blink at him blandly, purposely not reacting to his words, but not liking his blunt description of my mother, despite its truth.

"Since then, I've wanted to meet you. I wanted to make sure you were okay."

"You wanted custody of me," I clarify.

He nods. "Yes, if you weren't being properly cared for I wanted to become your guardian. I understand you just learned of that yesterday."

"Why do you think Mom never mentioned you?"

He watches me for a moment before answering. "I honestly have no idea. The last time I saw her I was six-years-old. You knew her much better than I did."

His words are spoken calmly now, like he has no feelings about his abandonment. He's right though. I did know my mother well or at least I thought I did. She was a weak person. Generally, when I wondered why my mother did or didn't do something, the answer was *because it's hard*. I can't help but wonder why walking away from her son wasn't too hard.

"I'd like us to leave this afternoon."

I focus on him again.

"I've got your plane ticket and your things. My wife is looking into getting you enrolled in the high school."

I start to feel panicky again. "But I have to bury her. There has to be a funeral."

He nods. "I've already arranged it with a local funeral home. I'm taking care of her burial, but we can't stay to plan the funeral. I have to get back. We can have a ceremony once we're in Fort Upton if you like."

"What did you arrange?"

"She'll be buried in San Marcos Cemetery just outside of town. I ordered the casket and the headstone."

I stare at him wondering how much that must have cost. After the way she walked out on him, I can hardly believe that he's done this so quickly and willingly. I feel the gathering tears burning my eyes. I never could have paid for any of this. "Thank you," I whisper.

His expression turns sympathetic, and I see another emotion that resembles compassion passing over his features.

I know I need to change the subject before I lose it in front of him. "Have you arranged to have my school records transferred?" I ask. "I have to be in the same level classes I'm enrolled in now."

To my surprise, he nearly smiles as he shakes his head. "It's been less than forty-eight hours. I haven't gotten to that yet."

I nod and start listing what needs to be done. "I'm in all accelerated and advanced placement classes. The colleges I've applied to will be making their decisions soon and I need to be in those same classes at my new school to maintain my ranking." I glance up and see him smirking.

"I take it you're a good student," he says.

"Yes," I inform him. Generally, with my background, that comes as a surprise to people.

He sobers at my seriousness. I'm as serious as a heart attack when it comes to school. This is my way out. This is how I know I won't follow in my mother's footsteps. This is my constant. Every time my mother disappeared, and I was placed somewhere new, I diverted my attention to getting all my academic ducks in a row. Right now, I need this lifeline more than ever.

"Okay," he agrees. "We'll get to work on that next. I don't know much about the high school, but our school district has a good reputation."

I offer him a tight, but thankful smile.

"Do you already know what you want to study in college?

12

I answer immediately. "I want to take pre-med courses."

This seems to intrigue him. "You want to be a doctor?"

I shake my head at the thought of that. I could never spend so much time near sick people. "No. I want to do research. Help cure diseases."

His eyes are intent on mine. It looks as though he wants to say something more, but he takes a deep breath and turns away. "Let's see if that paperwork is ready," he says, moving toward the door.

As I watch the tall form of the man who is my brother leave the room, I can no longer hold back the avalanche of apprehension I'm feeling. I'm used to moving. I'm used to strangers taking me in. But my brother is a different kind of stranger. He's already eliciting unwelcome emotions that I hardly recognize. I can only imagine what it would be like to have him as a real older brother, one who watches out for me and feels like family. I wonder if that's what he wants. If so, would I welcome it or would I inevitably push him away? If he doesn't want that, would I be disappointed? I'm surprised when I realize the answer to that may be yes.

I lower myself onto the same couch he just vacated and rub my hands over my face, trying to clear my head. I'll be eighteen in a few months. I won't be in his house long enough for any bonds to form and that's probably for the best. Emotions are dangerous. So are expectations.

THREE

'VE never flown on an airplane before. It's an odd feeling knowing that we're winging our way across the country, putting thousands of miles between me and San Diego. I've never even left the state and within minutes of taking off, California is behind us along with my mother and the chaotic life I've lived up to now.

Kyle seems okay to me. It's hard to get a read on him. I've learned some facts about him while we've been traveling. He's an auditor for the state of New York, which is like an accountant, he tells me. His wife stays at home with their daughter. He volunteered to me that he had a happy childhood. He was raised by his father and his father's girlfriend. They never married because his father couldn't find my mother to obtain a divorce from her. I knew my mother wasn't married to my own father, but she used his last name. I thought it was because she wanted to have the same last name as me. Maybe she was using it to hide the whole time.

It's dark when Kyle pulls into the driveway of a quaint, single story white house. From what I can see, it's in the middle of a neighborhood crowded with other similar homes.

"Are you sure your wife is okay with this?" I ask Kyle for the third or fourth time.

"Chloe is fine with it. She's looking forward to meeting you."

When I step out of the car, I feel an unfamiliar chill in the air. It's early spring, but New York obviously hasn't gotten the memo. Kyle opens the trunk, and I pull out my duffle bag. He's withdrawing his own bag when I hear voices. I look over at the house next door. Three guys are standing in front of a dark colored truck parked in the driveway. They all look tall and athletic. Two of them are horsing around as one pushes the other and then barks out a laugh.

"Those boys are your age. Myles lives there. He's a senior, too." Kyle explains. When he closes the trunk, the one who has been standing silently, apart from the other two, turns toward us. He's taller and broader than his friends are. It's too dark to see him clearly, but rather than glance at us and turn back around, he seems to be staring right at me.

"You'll meet them when you start school," Kyle continues, taking both bags and heading up the walkway.

His shadowed silhouette pulls at me as I stand rooted there, and my heart starts to pump faster. From his outline, I notice wide shoulders that taper down to a trim waist and long, lean legs. His hair is thick with unruly waves that curl down just past his collar. As he watches me, unmoving, I can't help but wonder if his eyes are traveling over me in the same assessing way. I can feel my cheeks heat, and I'm thankful for the cover of night. I'm not boy crazy. I never have been. So, my reaction to this stranger takes me by surprise, and I purposely snap myself out of it. I tear my eyes away from him, and I catch up with Kyle.

The front door swings open, spilling light out onto the walkway. I hesitate as Kyle moves more quickly and embraces the woman who steps out to meet him. She has a round face framed by long, brown hair, parted in the middle and swept back behind her ears. Her chin rests on Kyle's shoulder. Her dark eyes widen when they find me standing behind him. I hear her gasp. She pulls out of his embrace and continues to stare at me.

16

"Raielle, this is my wife, Chloe," Kyle says.

"She looks so much like you," Chloe whispers, her gaze moving over me in shock.

He acknowledges her observation with a tired grin. "Let's go inside."

Chloe seems to realize she's staring at me and rearranges her face into a tight smile. As her surprise settles, her assessing eyes find mine. "It's nice to meet you, Raielle," she says before turning to go into the house.

Warning bells start to go off in my head. The look on Chloe's face, I've seen it before, too many times in too many foster homes. She's wary of having me here, but her reluctance is loosely packaged within a façade of good manners.

I follow them through the front door into a small sitting area with floral couches and bright yellow walls. "I'm very sorry about your mother," she says quietly, looking up at me. Chloe is about average height which means, in my clunky shoes, I tower over her. She's curvy and attractive with round eyes that shimmer in the dimly lit room.

I feel awkward and out of place as I glance around their home wondering if I've just stepped into an alternate reality. This is the kind of overly decorated middle class house you see on sitcoms. "Thank you for letting me stay here," I say politely.

"No need to thank us," Chloe says. "I'm afraid you'll have to sleep on the couch tonight. Our friends have an extra bed they're giving us. But it won't be here until tomorrow."

"That's fine," I tell her, not bothering to mention that I'm used to sleeping on the couch.

"Are you hungry?" She asks like she'll actually make me a meal if I say yes.

I shake my head.

"We got dinner at the airport," Kyle explains.

Chloe clasps her hands in front of her. "Well, you're probably tired."

She points behind her. "The bathroom is right down the hall, and the kitchen is in there. Penelope is sleeping. So, you'll meet her in the morning before I take her to preschool."

"We'll get your school records taken care of tomorrow," Kyle reassures me before I can remind him.

"You can start school whenever you're ready," Chloe says brightly. "You're all registered. The high school is just about a mile that way. Most of the kids in this neighborhood walk, but I can drive you if you like, especially on the cold mornings."

"Could I start this week?" I ask. I'm anxious to make the unfamiliar familiar, to begin a reliable routine.

"Why don't you wait until next week?" Kyle suggests.

I'm about to plead my case when Chloe speaks up. "Let Raielle rest tomorrow and then start on Friday if she wants."

Her support surprises me, and I think it surprises Kyle, too. But as he looks at her, I can see him weighing his decision. At that moment, a realization hits me. Kyle is in charge of my life now. Although my environment has always been out of control, I've been in control of my actions and myself. For the first time though, I may be living with an authority figure who intends to pay attention.

Kyle sighs. "Fine. If you want to start Friday, go ahead. But if you change your mind, you can always start next week."

I smile at his decision and nod my agreement.

Then I watch as Chloe makes up the couch for me. Once that task is complete, Kyle and Chloe smile awkwardly as they say their goodnights. The whole situation is bizarre and uncomfortable. My brother and his wife have just met me for the first time, and here I am living with them. We're strangers, and we certainly do not hug each other despite the pause after Chloe's goodnight when I think she may be weighing that possibility. I'm relieved when she doesn't follow through. Unless I'm reading her hesitation wrong, and she's actually worried about my stealing their stuff while they're asleep. I find myself smiling at that thought. Chloe seems like the typical sheltered suburban girl. Something I'm certainly not. I've been exposed to my fair share of crime, but I've never directly committed any offenses myself. At times, I've been hungry enough to think about stealing food, but I never did. When there was no money to buy notebooks for school, rather than swipe them from a store, I would raid the recycle bins behind the school for discarded handouts or even write on my clothes and make sure not to wash them until after the exam. I've worked hard not to stumble into the typical pitfalls of my situation. Chloe has nothing to worry about, and I wonder if I have anything to worry about where she's concerned.

I could have imagined the grudging acceptance of my arrival in her expression. Even if it's true, and she doesn't want me here, I can't really blame her. I come from a messed up situation. She has no idea what to expect from me.

I pull in a deep breath, surprised by how shaky and disoriented I feel. After slipping on some sweats and a T-shirt, I locate my toothbrush and trudge to the bathroom. When the light comes on, I see lots of blue tile on the walls and on the floor. To my left is a bathtub filled with toys, including a yellow rubber ducky. No doubt about it, this is an alternate reality, a home filled with the clichés. My lips dip down into a small disbelieving frown before I turn toward the sink to brush my teeth.

I slept so soundly last night that I am unprepared for the restlessness that keeps me awake on the couch for hours, watching the hands on the clock inch their way toward morning. It's too quiet here, not like in the city. With only the noise of a ticking second hand to break through the silence, I have to work hard to block out the images that won't be put away so easily tonight. I roll from my left side to my right, feeling the place where the couch cushions meet digging into my side.

I finally doze off just as the sky begins to brighten only to be startled awake by a loud "Hi" directly beside my face. I turn to see a little girl tilting her head at me as though she's trying to decide exactly what I am.

"Hi," I say wearily to her as I sit up stiffly.

"I've got purple marbles," she states, lifting her hand to show me several marbles resting in her palm.

"That's nice," I reply, smiling my amusement through a wide yawn.

"You can have one." She pushes her hand at me.

I reach out carefully and take one from her.

She grins at me before turning to run into the kitchen with her loose hair flying behind her. "I gave her a marble!" I hear the girl exclaim.

"Sit down and eat your breakfast, Penelope," Chloe says. Then she steps out of the kitchen, dishcloth in hand, and looks at me. "Did you sleep well?"

I nod even though I didn't.

"That's Penelope. Her favorite color this week is purple."

I grin. I'm used to living with little kids.

"Would you like some breakfast? We've got fruit and cereal," Chloe offers.

I shake my head. Every time I closed my eyes last night, I saw blonde hair swimming in a pool of congealing blood on our kitchen table. My queasy stomach will definitely protest if I put food in it.

I turn away and grab my duffle bag. I want a shower and then a long walk to clear my head.

Once I'm dressed, I find Chloe still in the kitchen, cleaning up from breakfast. "Is there a downtown I could walk to?" I ask.

"Well, yes," she says, turning from the sink to look at me. "But if you'd like to wait, I can take you after I've dropped Penelope off at school."

I smile politely at her offer, but I don't want company this morning. "I actually feel like walking. I was just looking for a destination."

"Oh," she remarks, seeming unsure before reluctantly giving me directions to the town center, which turns out to be about two miles away.

"Take my cell number with you in case you get lost." She turns to find a piece of paper to write on.

"Okay, but I don't have a phone to call you from."

She turns back around to face me, seeming at first surprised and then worried as she stares at me and chews her bottom lip. Then she reaches into a drawer and hands me an extra house key. Watching her, it almost feels like she's nervous. Uneasiness pricks at me as I wonder what's causing this reaction. A part of me just wants to ask her. Between the graciousness she displayed last night that seemed forced and her strange hesitation this morning, I really don't know what to make of her. But, of course, I won't say anything. Sometimes confrontation works. Other times, it just digs you deeper. I've never gotten in trouble for *not* saying something.

Once I'm outside, I stop at the end of the walkway and glance around the neighborhood. It's a bright morning with no hint of the winter chill from last night. I've never lived anywhere where the seasons change and my slim wardrobe reflects that. I wonder about the possibility of finding a job. Back home I had part-time jobs all over town, and once a week Apollo would pay me to sit on the stoop and collect cash that was owed to him. Familiar people would stop by to hand varying amounts of money to me. I was supposed to check their names off a hand-written list he gave me. I never asked questions, and I always turned in every cent. He once told me I was the only person he completely trusted.

I turn when I hear someone yelling "Hey" from the house next door. The owner of the voice has long, sandy hair that he pushes off his forehead as he nears. An olive-colored messenger bag is strapped across his chest, and it bounces lightly against his khaki-covered hip. I recognize his silhouette as belonging to one of the boys I saw laughing last night, but definitely not the tall one who I think was staring at me. The guy coming toward me could easily pass for one of the surfers that were abundant at my old school.

He stops in front of me. We're about the same height, and I stand perfectly still while he unabashedly looks me over from head to toe. "You are going to be a very popular girl here," he says with a smile that displays deep dimples in both cheeks.

Despite his statement, the glint in his eyes isn't appreciative or predatory. It's closer to intrigued or amused, and I wonder if he's popular or picked on here.

"I'm Myles and you must be the long lost sister I've heard about."

I arch a brow at him. "You've heard about me?"

He shrugs. "Chloe and my mom are friends. What's your name?" he asks.

"Raielle."

"Well, Raielle, will you be attending Fort Upton High School?"

I nod.

"You'll have to let me introduce you around. When do you start?"

"Tomorrow."

He shifts his weight and leans in closer to me. "Did you leave a boyfriend back home, Raielle?"

I tilt my head at him. The way he's saying my name, like he's teasing me, is both endearing and annoying. I can't decide if I want to be genuine with him or shoot him down with sarcasm. The hint of playfulness in his light brown gaze makes me think that he doesn't take himself too seriously. I go with genuine. "No boyfriend back home. What about you? Have you got a boyfriend?"

He lets out a laugh, pretending I'm joking. When he realizes I'm not, his eyes widen and his mouth drops open before he swiftly closes it.

I immediately realize my mistake. "Oh, sorry."

He studies me for a minute before clearing his throat and taking a step back.

Now I feel bad. "Don't worry. I won't say anything."

His brow furrows, and he looks like he's going to deny it, but then he takes a deep breath and asks, "How did you know?"

"I just did," I shrug. "It probably sounds lame to say some of my best friends are gay, but it's actually true." I smile. After realizing that being attractive was a huge handicap in a foster home when the foster dads and foster brothers were often perverts or worse, I started gravitating toward the gay boys. They were generally safer, and if I was lucky, they protected me.

He offers me a lopsided grin that shows his dimples again. "It's not really common knowledge. My friend Lucas knows. I think my parents might suspect, but I'm not interested in having that conversation with them any time soon." He shifts his messenger bag and runs a hand through his hair again. "I think we're going to have to be friends. You know, so you don't get homesick for your old buddies."

I look him up and down, pretending to think it over. "Yeah, that sounds all right."

He grins at me again, a full-on smile this time, and the way it lights up his face makes me feel a little lighter.

I offer him a smile, too, and I take a step back. "It was nice meeting you. I don't want to make you late or anything."

"Meet me here at the same time tomorrow. We can walk to school together."

I agree, and we go our separate ways.

Turns out, Fort Upton's town center takes less than fifteen minutes to explore. There's a diner, a dry-cleaner, a drugstore, a couple of real-estate offices, a little gift shop, a town hall, and a town library. That's it. Feeling disappointed and more than a little claustrophobic, not only is this town landlocked—it's miniscule, I turn around and head back the way I came.

I carry a paperback copy of *Jayne Eyre* in my backpack. I've lost count of how many times I've read it. When I move to a new place, I open *Jayne Eyre* and get lost in the story that's so familiar it feels more like home than any actual home ever has. With an empty day in front of me, and thoughts that I want to keep at bay, the desire to lose myself in its well-worn pages is gnawing at me.

The house is quiet and empty when I return. After a few chapters, I fall back to sleep on the couch. To my surprise, I sleep nearly the entire day away, not stirring until late in the afternoon when Chloe returns with Penelope. It's a shock, waking up here, glancing around, and being hit by the realization of my situation all over again. I ignore the way my stomach rolls as I take a deep breath and focus on Penelope running in circles through the house with a toy airplane. I sit up and try to ignore the nerves I feel at being here in my brother's house. I want to do what I've done in all my foster homes, stay quiet, keep to myself, and go about my business. But this isn't a foster home. This is my brother's home, and I feel like I have more of an obligation here. He's putting himself out by taking me in. He's opened his home to me. I should at least pretend to make some kind of an effort. It seems like I owe him and his family that much.

Soon after I wake, Kyle pulls up with a mattress and box spring tied to the top of a truck. He and a couple of his friends carry it into the basement, and the rest of the afternoon is spent organizing my new room.

The basement is a large open rectangular space with low ceilings, plain white walls, and a beige carpet. Penelope's toys are piled onto shelves on one side of the long room and my bed, along with a dresser and nightstand, are on the other side. There is a half bathroom down here, too. It's actually one of the nicer bedrooms I've had, and I decide to tell Chloe this. Once I do, her eyes light up, and Kyle smiles approvingly at me.

For my first official dinner with the Dean family, Chloe makes meatloaf, and we all sit around the kitchen table. Penelope sits in a booster seat and babbles throughout the meal about Dora the Explorer and the red dress Chloe bought for her after school today. Family dinners are not something I have much experience with. When I glance up, I see Kyle looking at me. He grins before turning back to his daughter and telling her to finish her milk, which she obediently does. I feel like a tourist as I eat quietly and observe them. Their easy interactions cause a dull ache to form inside my chest. I realize that it hurts to watch them, to see their happy family unit. I thought happy families were a myth. If they weren't real, I didn't have to mourn the fact that I never had one. But this one is real, a little too real. I direct my eyes down at my plate and finish my meal quickly so I can be excused. My hasty decision to make an effort getting to know Kyle and his family is going to be more challenging than I expected.

FOUR

CHLOE wants to drive me to school. She's torn between being happy that I already have a friend to walk with and disappointed that she can't take me herself.

"You look really nice for your first day," she says encouragingly.

"Thanks," I say. My first day uniform is my favorite pair of worn low-rise jeans with my clunky brown shoes and a short-sleeved navy sweater that's not too tight or too loose. I know my legs look miles long in these jeans, and this outfit is perfect for intimidating the girls who might already be gunning for me without being too revealing or slutty in a way that could promote unwelcome attention.

I'm afraid my outfit falls short when Myles walks out of his house and whistles. "You're gonna knock them dead today, California girl. You definitely do not look like the girls from around here."

I glance down at my outfit. "The plan was not to call too much attention to myself. Maybe I should go change?"

He winds his arm through mine. "Don't bother. Unless you're planning to put a paper bag over yourself, it won't matter. Besides, I'm going to enjoy being the most envied guy in school."

"You're really full of shit, Myles." I laugh as I reclaim my arm and fall into step beside him.

"I am the most sincere person you will ever meet. By the way, we're picking up my girlfriend at the next corner."

I stop walking. "Your what?"

He shrugs. "All superheroes need an alter ego."

I burst out laughing. "And does your girlfriend realize she's the Lois Lane to your straight Clark Kent?"

He has the decency to look embarrassed. "It's all good. She's a *nice* girl. She took a vow of chastity at her church."

"Uh-huh," I mutter, continuing to walk.

He catches right up. "Listen, she doesn't know…"

"Don't worry. I told you I wouldn't say anything and I won't. It's none of my business."

As we approach the corner, a peppy redhead bounds down the steps of a large brick house. "Hey, Myles," she calls. I notice that her nose is dotted with freckles. The energetic way she moves screams *I'm a cheerleader*. She stops short when she sees me.

"April, this is Raielle. She just moved in next door to me. I told her we'd introduce her around."

April's smile falters when Myles says my name. She looks at him. "You mean she's the one whose mother was…"

"April." Myles halts her with a look before she can finish her sentence.

Her face heats. "Sorry," she mumbles at him before turning to me. "Um, it's nice to meet you."

"You, too," I reply, wondering what she knows about my mother and how many other people know it, too.

April makes a quick recovery and spends the rest of the walk chattering about how great the school is; how friendly everyone is, and how much fun being a cheerleader is. Yes, I guessed right. I do my best to tune her out before my ears start to bleed. Beside me, it looks as though Myles's eyes have glazed over.

When we arrive at the sprawling glass and concrete high school, Myles points out the main office, and he offers to accompany me while I retrieve my schedule. I wave him off, and thankfully, he doesn't argue as I continue inside on my own. The office is quiet when I approach an older lady with grey bobbed hair sitting at the desk closest to the door.

"I'm starting here today. I came to pick up my schedule."

She glances up at me with a friendly smile. "What's your name?"

"Raielle Blackwood."

She nods and turns to her computer. "Gwen!" she calls across the office.

A willowy girl stands and approaches us. "Raielle is a new student starting today. Could you show her to her first class?" The woman hands me my schedule and smiles. Just then, the school bell rings in the hallway. She reaches down for another piece of paper and gives that to me, too. "Tardy pass," she explains.

I glance down at the paper in my hand and see that advanced placement history is my first class followed by advanced calculus and advanced placement English. I'm relieved that the classes I had at my last school seem to be covered here.

"Let me see it." Gwen extends her hand to me. Now that she's beside me, I see that her nose is pierced and both her ears are surrounded in piercings. Her blunt nails are polished black to match her wardrobe and her hair. Either she's the token Goth (every school has one) or she's part of a larger Goth movement here.

"This way," she says handing me back my schedule and leading the way out. "The school is just a big rectangle of hallways stacked over four floors," she explains in a flat, bored voice. The halls are quiet and her words echo softly. "If the classroom number starts with a one, it's on the first floor. If it starts with a four, it's on the…" she pauses and eyes me expectantly.

"Fourth floor," I reply dryly.

She stops in front of a closed door. "This is you. I'll see you later. I'm in your chemistry class." Then she walks back the way we came.

I pause in the hallway, take a deep breath, hitch my bag up higher on my shoulder, and then pull open the door. The teacher stops talking and looks at me along with the rest of the full classroom. I ignore the students and keep my eyes trained on the overweight, middle-aged man who is already reaching for the note I have in my hand. As I move, my shoes click loudly in the silence. He takes my pass and tosses it on his desk.

"Take any empty seat," he says.

I turn and feel curious eyes on me as I zero in on one of the vacant desks in the back. A low whistle sounds as I pass by the first row, followed by the word *hot* not so subtly coughed out on the other side of the room. This results in several giggles. I ignore my second whistle of the day, keep my head high, and move slowly toward the empty desk. Dropping my backpack on the floor, I slide into the seat and give my attention to the teacher.

"Okay, everyone," he says, "let's continue." He begins discussing what I recognize as the Cuban Missile Crisis. I feel heads occasionally turning my way, but I ignore them as I open my notebook and start writing.

When class is over, I shove my books in my bag and glance at my schedule to see that calculus is on the fourth floor. When I glance up, there's a burly guy standing in the aisle blocking my way.

"Hey, new girl." He grins at me. "Do you need help finding your next class?"

I'm about to tell him *no thanks*, but the truth is that I could use some directions. "I know it's on the fourth floor. I just need to find the stairs," I reply.

"Then I'm at your service." He extends an arm, allowing me to precede him down the aisle to the doorway. Once I move around him, I see a few guys congregated at the exit who have obviously been watching our exchange. They keep their eyes on me as I approach.

"I'm Tucker," he says once he's beside me, "and these asshats need to move out of the way if we want to get you to your next class."

"Introduce us," one of them says.

"I haven't gotten her name yet." He eyes me expectantly.

"Raielle," I say, starting to feel sorry that I asked him for help.

"That's an unusual name," another guy says. This one is short and kind of doughy looking.

Tucker starts to push through them. "Cool your jets. We don't want to make Raielle late."

I smile hesitantly at them and follow him out into the hall.

"The first stairwell is down here." He points as he's walking. "What class do you have?"

I glance at my schedule to be sure. "AP calculus."

He nods. "That's at the end of the hall on the far corner. I can walk you."

To my surprise, he grabs my elbow. Instinctively, I pull it away. "I can find it. Thanks."

He's taken aback and maybe a little offended, but he quickly recovers. "Yeah. No problem. Just trying to help."

I attempt to look friendly, trying to offset the awkwardness. "It's okay. I've got it from here." Then I quickly ascend the stairs, dodging the flow of descending students.

I find my next few classes easily and manage to survive my morning without incident. A few other male students introduce themselves to me and one creepy one just leers at me throughout English. Unless they try to talk to me, I don't really notice the other people in my classes.

The back of my schedule has a locker number on it with a combination. Before lunch, I make my way to it. As I'm tossing the textbooks I've collected inside, a shoulder leans against the locker beside me.

"How's your first day going, California girl?" Myles asks.

I smile, happy to see a familiar face. "Like a first day." I shrug.

"Do you have lunch this period?"

"Yeah. But I was hoping to head to the library to get some studying done. Do they let you do that here?"

His eyebrows arch up. "I suppose if someone actually wanted to spend lunchtime in the library, they could." He watches me as I close my backpack and hoist it up. "How about a little socializing? You know, sitting with me and my friends, maybe making some of your own?"

I briefly wonder if one of his friends is going to be the tall, dark silhouette from the other night. But it doesn't matter. I have issues that are more pressing. I shake my head. "Another time."

"Are you telling me that you already have so much work you have to skip lunch?"

I sigh. "It looks that way." The calculus class here is much more advanced than the class I was taking at home. I need to catch up quickly before I fall even further behind. Besides, I don't have a lunch to eat. Back home, we were on assistance. As embarrassing as it was, the state of California provided a hot lunch to me at school every day. But today, I don't have a lunch, and I don't have any money for one.

Myles narrows his eyes. "Another time, then. I'm going to hold you to that, Raielle."

Lunch in the library is quiet, and I get enough done that the calculus panic abates. During the next period, I see Gwen in my chemistry class. She doesn't say hello, but lifts her chin in my direction when she spots me. My last two classes of the day are Latin and art. I breeze through Latin having already taken three years of it, and I use art class to zone out and rest my fried brain.

The school is beginning to clear out, and I'm collecting my books at my locker at the end of the day, when I hear a high-pitched "Excuse me."

I turn to find a petite stranger scowling at me. Thick blonde bangs frame her face, accentuating her pointy chin, the only facial feature that isn't obscured by her mane of hair.

"You need to stay away from my boyfriend," she informs me with a hand on her hip.

My eyes inadvertently dip down to the barely covered cleavage she's puffing out in my direction. I can feel the few remaining students in the hallway turn to watch us. "No problem," I reply evenly. Then I begin piling more books into my bag.

"I'm serious," she bites out.

I exhale loudly and reluctantly give her my attention. "Who is your boyfriend?"

She blinks her disbelief at me. "Tucker Matthews."

Tucker, of course. "Like I said, no problem." I start to turn around again when she grabs my arm to halt me.

Then she gets in my face. "Keep away from him. Do you understand me?"

"Yeah. I think I've cracked your code." I pull my arm from her grip.

"That's enough, Hailey."

We both turn in the direction of the deep, unfamiliar voice. I know immediately, it's him. I recognize the wavy hair, the broad shoulders, and his confident stance. But now I can see his dark blue eyes, and they're shooting darts at the blonde named Hailey.

"But she's after Tucker," Hailey argues.

He angles his head at her. "I seriously doubt that."

She huffs with frustration. "Everyone saw her flirting with him."

My eyes widen at this. His glances at me, then turns back to Hailey. "Everyone saw Tucker walking her to the stairs, and then they saw her blowing him off. He's the one you should be worried about. Not her."

Hailey's mouth falls open and I think mine does, too. I wonder how he knows this because he hasn't been on my radar at all today.

"Were you there, Lucas?" she asks in a small voice.

He nods.

Hailey visibly deflates but she doesn't apologize. She turns to glare at me one last time. "Tucker is off limits. Don't forget it," she warns, before pivoting and stalking away.

"I think you two deserve each other," I mumble under my breath. Then my eyes return to Lucas who is standing silently, watching me with an unreadable expression. I take in his full lips and the firm set of his square jaw. His hair falls in shiny, chestnut brown waves lifting back from his forehead looking like he just ran his hand through it. He's so handsome; it's hard not to stare. He must have girls ogling him constantly, and that thought fills me with a strange disappointment. I felt a connection to him the other night and ever since then his dark image has been lurking in the back of my mind. But now that I see him up close, I realize that it couldn't have been real. He is not the type of guy who goes for someone like me. Even though he's not happy with Hailey right now, she's what guys like him want; popular, aggressive, self-assured, with all her assets on display. He probably goes through them like water.

I wonder if he's going to introduce himself or say anything at all. To my shock, he doesn't. He just walks away. I watch his progression down the hallway until he disappears around the corner. *Weird.*

The remaining students avert their eyes and continue gathering their things. I see Gwen among them. I shake off my uneasiness and head toward the stairs.

"That's Lucas Diesel," Gwen says, slamming her locker closed and falling into step beside me. "Hottest guy I've ever seen in real life." She tics this off on her finger. "Every girl in school wants him." She tics off another finger. "And he talked to you on your very first day." She points a finger at me now. "That's a big deal."

"Since you obviously heard the whole thing, you know that he didn't say a word to me."

She shrugs. "But he knows you exist, and he defended you. That's noteworthy."

"So, is he a complete snob or something?" I ask, still bristling at his wordless dismissal of me.

She pulls out a pack of gum and offers me a stick. I take it to be friendly and to keep her talking. Despite my better judgment, I'm curious about Lucas. "He's not a snob," she continues thoughtfully. "He's just sort of intimidating and unapproachable. And he doesn't have a girlfriend in case you were wondering."

"I wasn't," I reply quickly.

"Uh-huh," she says, not believing me.

We step outside into the cool sunshine, and Gwen continues chatting about him. "He takes plenty of girls out, but he never gets serious. He's a real heartbreaker. If you ever run into a girl crying in the bathroom, it's probably over him. His only girlfriend that I know of was Sophie Becker. They were on and off all last year. But, they're off now despite the way she keeps throwing herself at him."

"Thanks for sharing, Gwen," I say dryly. Now that my assumptions about him have basically been confirmed, I'm ready for a subject change. I glance around the half empty parking lot, wondering if Myles has left for home yet.

Amusement lights in her eyes before she asks, "Do you need a ride?"

Since I see no sign of Myles, I accept Gwen's offer. She leads me to an ancient bright red VW Rabbit. Its front fenders are covered in rust, and they appear to be disintegrating where they arch over the tires. She notices my critical appraisal. "It's not pretty, but it's transportation."

To my surprise, the interior is fairly clean and in much better condition than the shell it's encased in. I tell Gwen where I live, and she pulls out into traffic.

"I was the new kid last year," she says. "Most everyone else, besides us, has lived here all their lives."

I look over at her, and I have the feeling she's telling me that she hasn't made many friends here.

"We moved from Manhattan. Can you believe that?" she snorts out a laugh. "Going from Manhattan to here? My dad got a job in Albany and now here I am….stuck in the middle of nowhere. What about you? Moving to a new place for the end of your senior year must seriously suck."

I close my eyes and take a breath. "Yeah, it does." I can feel her glancing from the road to my face, waiting for me to tell my story since she told me hers. When I don't, she just asks.

"So, why did you move here?"

I glance at her. "My mom died. I'm living here with my brother and his family." I can sense her shock. I can only imagine her reaction if I hadn't left out all the interesting details.

"I'm really sorry," she says softly. "What about your dad?"

I shrug and look out the window, noticing that we're approaching Kyle's neighborhood. "I think he's dead, too." The truth is that he lived with Mom and me when I was little. I remember his scruffy hair and the tattoos that ran up and down his arms. He was an addict, too. One day, he left and never came back. Social Services couldn't track him down the first time my Mom lost custody of me. Over the years, Mom got tired of me asking about him and finally told me that he was probably dead.

Gwen remains silent after that. Whatever kinship she'd been looking for with me isn't going exactly as she planned, and I say nothing to reassure her.

Penelope is playing outside when we pull up to the house.

"So…I'll see you on Monday," Gwen says. It seems like she wants to say more, but she doesn't.

"Thanks for the ride," I tell her. The moment I'm out of the car, Penelope comes running toward me. Her hair is in a purple headband, and she's wearing a white dress covered in purple flowers.

"Hi, Raielle," she yells at me before dissolving into mysterious giggles.

"Hi there. I heard your favorite color is purple."

"No," she says, shaking her head. "My favorite color is purple and pink."

"Oh, sorry. My mistake."

"How was your day?" Chloe asks, coming around the side of the house wearing gardening gloves. Penelope runs up to her and lingers close to her.

"Fine," I reply, eager to get inside.

"Who was that driving you home?"

"Just a girl from school." My backpack is weighing me down, and my stomach is grumbling with hunger. I smile at them and head for the door. I'm assuming it's okay to take food from the kitchen although no one has said as much. I find an apple and a soda in the refrigerator, and I bring them down to the basement with me. I sit down on my bed and bite into the crunchy fruit. Back home, I would come home from school, start my homework, and begin making dinner for Mom and me. I always made dinner because she was too tired to do much when she got back from work. She cleaned houses in the morning and in the afternoon she worked part-time in an insurance office.

The apple gets stuck in my throat when the last image I have of her flashes at me. Before it can unravel me, I quickly try to replace it with another memory, one where she's happy and smiling. I remember my birthday party again, and I wish I had more memories like that. I put the apple down and pull out my books.

37

By the time Chloe calls me upstairs for dinner, I've put my memories of my mother away and most of my history assignment is done. We sit down together at the kitchen table just like last night and probably like they do every night. I feel calmer now that I've been to school and I know what to expect there. That is until I glance up and notice the tightness around Kyle's eyes. He catches me looking at him and changes his expression to a neutral smile. Rather than making me feel better, his grin causes my stomach to twist. I wonder if he's having second thoughts about my being here. I haven't interacted with him much since I've been here, and maybe he's disappointed in me. If he is, will I be sent back to San Diego or will I be turned over to Social Services here? My appetite is gone, and I begin pushing my food around on my plate.

"You're not in the clean plate club," Penelope says, pointing at my dinner with her fork. "Mom says you have to finish all of it if you want to be in the club. Even if it tastes yucky."

Across the table, Kyle laughs. "Your mother doesn't make any yucky food, Penelope."

Chloe doesn't react. She just keeps eating silently.

"She makes green beans," Penelope says. "Those are very yucky."

"Those are very good for you," Kyle tells hers patiently.

"Do you like green beans, Raielle?" she asks.

"Sure," I say, even though I don't like them much. "They have lots of vitamins."

"What's a vitamins?" she asks, blinking her round eyes at me.

"It's good stuff that helps you stay healthy and strong."

"Will it help me run really fast?"

"Yup, and jump really high, too," I answer, smiling at her questions.

"I love jumping," Penelope exclaims. "Can you make me some green beans, Mommy?"

Chloe's fork stops on the way to her mouth. "Of course. I can make them tomorrow."

"Yeah! Green beans tomorrow." Penelope claps her hands.

Chloe and Kyle level expressions of pleased disbelief at me as I try to do a better job of eating my own dinner.

Once Penelope is taken down from her booster seat and told to go play, I stay in the kitchen and offer to help Chloe with the dishes. When Kyle stays behind, I know he wants to talk to me.

"What did you do for lunch today, Raielle?" he asks.

I put my plate in the sink and turn to him. This question isn't what I was expecting. "Um, I just got some studying done in the library. I was told that was okay."

"What did you *eat* for lunch?" he asks.

I feel like I'm in trouble, but I don't know why. "Um…"

Beside me, Chloe clears her throat and opens one of the kitchen drawers. She withdraws a cell phone and a five dollar bill. "I was supposed to give these to you this morning before you left. I'm sorry, I forgot."

"Oh," I say, looking at the items in her hand.

Kyle takes the cell phone from her. "It has texting and a basic phone plan. Actually, the texting is pretty basic, too. So, keep that in mind. The money was supposed to be for lunch today." The clipped way he describes these items, and the tension in the air, make me believe he's mad at Chloe for forgetting to give them to me.

When I don't reach for the items, Kyle takes my hand and places them in my palm.

"You don't have to give me these," I protest. "I'm going to look for a job."

Chloe and Kyle glance at each other. "You don't need to get a job, Raielle," Kyle says.

"But I've always had a job." My gaze travels between them. I've just gone from wondering if they want to send me away to being given my first cell phone and the first five dollars I didn't have to earn myself. As my relief sets in, I can feel my pulse pumping in my ears. I'm surprised to realize how much I didn't want to be sent away.

"I know you've had to be independent for a long time," Kyle says. "But things are different now. I want you to concentrate on settling in. I want you to be a kid for a while and see how it feels."

I don't respond. I can't do what he's asking. I don't know the first thing about being a kid. And all I can think about when he says that things are different, is how they used to be. "Have you spoken to the police in San Diego?" I ask. "Do they know any more?"

Chloe appears uncomfortable and starts washing the dishes. Kyle shakes his head at me. "I called them this morning. They don't know anything else. But she will be buried tomorrow. They told me that. Would you like to go to church or something to say a prayer for her?"

I shake my head. A church is the last place I would go if I wanted my mother to hear me.

FIVE

O N Saturday morning, Chloe leaves to take Penelope to gymnastics. Penelope is beyond excited, leaping around the living room in her pink leggings and purple T-shirt. Once they're gone, Kyle asks if I want to take a ride to the hardware store with him. I know I should go so I can spend time with him, but I chicken out and beg off. I spend the rest of the morning angry at myself and at the inexplicable nerves that overtake me at the thought of getting to know my own brother. I resolve to say yes next time he asks me to do anything with him.

Later on, I go outside to the front porch to get some reading done for school. I've just cracked open my textbook when a black truck pulls into Myles's driveway. Lucas Diesel and another guy climb out just as Myles comes out of his house to meet them. They all have on grey uniforms and matching baseball caps.

I'm thinking about ducking back inside when Myles spots me.

"Hey, Raielle. Come here for a minute," he calls, waving me over.

At this point, I know that retreating into the house would be lame even though it's my preference. I put my book down and walk across the grass to his yard. I can feel all their eyes on me as I approach.

"Raielle, these are my buddies, Lucas and Jake." Myles takes me by the arm and walks me over to them.

I try not to notice that Lucas is eyeing me with that same inscrutable expression he wore yesterday. In contrast to that, Jake smiles and steps right in front me. "I'm always happy to meet a pretty girl," he says. He has a dark buzz cut and thick eyebrows that arch appraisingly over his bright green eyes.

I shake his hand and smile despite the cheesy line.

"Back off," Myles says, jokingly pushing Jake away. Then he snaps his fingers in the air. "Wait a minute. I forgot. You already know Lucas. I hear he saved you from a run-in with Hurricane Hailey."

I raise my eyebrows at Hailey's nickname and at the fact that Myles knows what happened in the school hallway. "Actually, I don't know him. And I didn't need saving yesterday." I turn to address Lucas for the first time. He fills out his uniform quite nicely, and it takes all my willpower to keep my eyes on his face. His presence has an impact on me. There's no denying that. I've never felt anything like this, and I'm trying to tamp down on it. I wonder if he feels it, too. If so, he's giving nothing away. I only hope I'm not either. "But I do appreciate what you did," I manage to tell him.

Lucas is about a head taller than I am which means I have to look up more than I normally would to make eye contact with him. Right now, his cool blue eyes are intent on mine. I decide if he ignores me and turns away again, I'm going to give his back an obscene hand gesture along with a piece of my mind. But he doesn't ignore me. I almost wish he had when his full lips curl into a half smile. Gone is the indifference, replaced by a glint of humor as he takes me in, his eyes roaming over my face and hair. That's when I realize that my messy curls are piled into a bun on top of my head and I'm wearing one of my mom's old concert T-shirts I found in my duffle bag, The Cars written in shiny blue block letters, over torn ratty jeans.

"We're heading over to baseball practice," Myles says, pulling my attention back to him. "Do you want to come with us?"

I continue to ignore the way Lucas is making my heart flutter. "To watch you practice?" I ask Myles.

He nods. "The season is almost over. You should come. Lots of girls hang out in the bleachers to watch us practice."

I chuckle and roll my eyes at him. "As much as I'd love to admire you along with your other groupies, I think I have to wash my hair."

Myles feigns shock, placing his hand over his chest, pretending I've wounded him. I'm pretty sure I hear Lucas laughing softly under his breath.

"Your loss," Myles shrugs, making a miraculous recovery. He grabs a bag from beside the garage door and makes his way to the truck.

I turn back toward Kyle's house. "Good to meet you guys," I call over my shoulder.

"Raielle."

I stop as the familiar voice from yesterday speaking my name sends shivers through me. I swivel my head around to see that both Myles and Jake are in the truck now, but Lucas hasn't moved. "You're welcome," he says.

I watch, rooted to the spot, as he gets into his truck, backs out of the driveway, and pulls away without ever glancing at me again.

TELL me how you're doing," Kyle says, lowering himself onto the end of my bed.

I close my calculus book and place it beside me. "I'm good," I say, and I think it's the truth, considering. I spent the day catching up on schoolwork. My calculus teacher gave me some extra work to prepare for a test next week. I spent most of the day completing it.

"Classes seem okay?" he asks.

I nod.

He runs a hand across the back of his neck and seems hesitant. "My father is coming over Monday night for dinner." He watches me for my reaction.

I'm actually curious to meet the husband Mom ran away from and never wanted to talk about. "Okay," I say.

"Good," he nods. "He'd like meet you. But I told him that he shouldn't talk about Angela if it makes you uncomfortable."

The truth is I'd like to ask him some questions about why she left. I'd also like to ask Kyle about the tension I've felt between him and Chloe. If she made an honest mistake forgetting to give me the phone and the money, why was he angry with her last night? Unless, it wasn't a mistake. Unless he thinks she did it purposely because she's not okay with having me here. But I won't ask him because I don't really want to know the answer.

Sunday passes quickly. The Dean family wants to picnic in the park, and they tell me that my presence is requested. Since I decided to say yes to everything they invite me to do, I go. But once I'm there, I mostly sit quietly, unsure of what to say. They don't seem to notice as they enjoy the sunny afternoon, watching as Penelope runs after other kids and any dogs that happen by. I've noticed that she can't sit for more than a few minutes. I guess that's typical for a three-year-old. Even though I feel like a trespasser among them, they don't act as though I am, and by the end of the afternoon, I'm surprised to find that I'm enjoying myself.

But come Monday morning, I'm relieved to be leaving for school. I've never been with a family that spends so much time together. I understand it's a good thing and that it's probably normal, but I'm used to being alone. The constant company is overwhelming and by Sunday night, it felt stifling.

I shoulder my backpack and stop by the kitchen to say goodbye to Chloe and Penelope. Kyle has a long commute into Albany. He's usually gone before I make an appearance upstairs in the morning.

"Bye, Raielle," Penelope tells me. She has milk dripping down her chin and there are Cheerios all over the table and on the floor below her chair. I wonder how hard it could be to get the Cheerios into her mouth.

Chloe smiles at me and hands me an insulated blue lunch bag with a smiling Dora character on the front. I arch a brow at her.

"I told Mommy you could use that one," Penelope says. "I use the purple one."

"You realize I'm in high school, right?" I ask Chloe.

Chloe shrugs a shoulder. "It's all I've got. I can buy some brown bags next week if you want. I packed you a turkey sandwich, an apple, some cookies, and a juice box."

I thank her and chuckle to myself as I place the bag in my backpack. When I look back at Penelope, she raises her spoon of milky cereal, bypasses her mouth, and dumps it onto the floor. When she's see me watching, she dissolves into giggles.

With a quick wave, I'm out the door. There's no sign of Myles this morning, rather than ringing his doorbell, I just walk on alone. I'm happy to see that April isn't waiting at the corner either.

School is bustling with activity when I arrive. Since this is only my second day, I don't recognize anyone but I notice them noticing me—the new girl. After unloading half my books and my lunch in my locker, I make my way to first period history. There are a handful of students in the class when arrive. I take the same seat I had yesterday. After I pull my notebook from my bag, I spot Lucas strolling through the door. He crosses the room and takes a desk by the windows two rows down from me. I wonder what he's doing here. I didn't notice him on Friday.

Once he's seated, an attractive girl with a pixie haircut moves next to him and starts chatting with him. His eyes move around her and land on me. I quickly look down at my notebook. I can hear my heartbeat thudding in my ears, and my reaction to him frustrates me. It's stupid for me to crush on the most sought after and unattainable guy in school. The last boyfriend I had stole from me. Then he got arrested for stealing money from his fosters and tried to blame it on me. Boys are a distraction I do not need. I have a feeling Lucas Diesel would be very distracting.

I'm not at all surprised when Tucker arrives and plants himself at the desk beside mine.

"Hey, Raielle," he says.

I sigh and turn to him. "Tucker."

"How's it going?"

"So far, so good. Since I haven't been harassed by your girlfriend yet today."

He actually looks embarrassed. "Yeah. Sorry about that. She's a little possessive."

"And a lot psycho," I mutter as I turn back to the front of the room hoping Tucker will stop talking to me.

I can feel that I'm being stared at, and I dare to glance over at Lucas. Our eyes clash. But this time, I don't dart mine away and neither does he. He's just blatantly looking at me. He's not smiling or frowning, just staring. The pixie cut girl flirting with him notices and turns to see what's so interesting to him. When she spots me, her brows knit together, and her mouth closes in a tight line. Thankfully, the teacher walks in and I turn away, breaking the strange hold he has on me. I take a deep breath and decide that I will not look in his direction again.

The history lesson begins, and I stay glued to every word, taking copious notes, never once glancing in Lucas's direction. When class ends, I shove my notebook into my bag and leave as quickly as possible. I can feel Tucker on my heels, but I don't stop when he calls my name.

I'm the first one to arrive in calculus. I take a seat and glance out the window. Then I absently scribble in my notebook as students begin filing in. When someone slides into the desk beside me I look over, and my eyes widen when I see that it's Lucas.

He gives me a lopsided grin that makes his eyes twinkle. "You look like you've seen a ghost," he says.

"Are you in all my classes?" I ask.

He faces forward in his desk and splays his long legs out in front of him. Without looking at me, he says, "Just the morning ones."

I don't respond, but I do wonder how on earth I missed him on Friday.

When the calculus teacher enters the room, I know that paying attention with Lucas beside me is going to be difficult, but still necessary. And I do pay attention, but I'm also very aware of him and everything he's doing, whether it's shifting his legs, taking notes, or resting his chin on his hand. I've never been this aware of a guy before, and it feels like he's just as attuned to me. From the corner of my eye, I notice him glancing at me throughout the class, but I never overtly do the same.

When calculus ends, before I can stand and rush out again, Lucas says, "English next, right?"

I nod as I grab my bag up from the floor. Once I make my way down the aisle, I see that he's waiting for me at the end. We enter the busy hallway together. He doesn't talk as we walk to our next class, and our silent stroll to English is starting to feel awkward. I decide to make a joke as I turn to him and ask, "So is your girlfriend going to accost me and accuse me of flirting with you, too?"

He smirks at me. "If that's your way of asking me if I have a girlfriend, the answer is no."

I immediately realize how my question sounded. His self-satisfied smile makes my face feel hot. "It wasn't. But thanks for sharing," I comment, hoping he doesn't notice my embarrassment. Then I keep my gaze straight and my mouth shut for the rest of the walk.

I'm relieved to finally arrive at English class. I take my seat, and Lucas sits right beside me again. A striking girl walks in and sits on the other side of him. She's dressed in seriously tight, practically painted on jeans, and she has wispy hair so blonde it's almost white.

"Where were you Saturday?" she asks him as she places her pink-tipped fingers on his tan forearm. "Sophie had a ton of people at her house. It was the first pool party of the season and you missed it."

Of course, he's friends with this girl. I'm arranging my pen and notebook while covertly watching this exchange. Lucas casually moves his arm so her fingers aren't touching him anymore. "I was busy," he says.

"Well you're coming next weekend, right? Chad's band is playing over in Ridgeton. We're all going."

Lucas gives her a tight nod. "Yeah. I'll be there."

The girl squeals in delight, and I think I actually flinch at the sound. Class starts, and I get a reality check when the blonde keeps whispering to Lucas throughout the lesson. When class ends, I hurry out into the hallway alone.

Myles is leaning against my locker when I arrive. "Lunch today, right? You promised."

I point at my locker door. "Are you going to let me get in there?"

"Not until you agree to be sociable and come to lunch."

I smile reluctantly. "Fine."

He takes a step to the side, allowing me access.

"I didn't see you this morning." I pile my books inside and pull out my lunch bag.

"Sorry about that. April drove us. She needed to get here early for cheerleading practice. I would have texted you, but I don't have your number."

I reach into my back pocket and place my new phone in his hand.

He starts tapping on the screen. "Your only contact is Kyle?" he comments curiously. "Now you have me, too." He calls himself from my phone and glances up at me again. "And I have you."

I pocket my phone and follow Myles toward the cafeteria I've only seen in passing. The noise hits me first. It's a loud, echoing mix of clanking dishes and raised voices. The sun glares in through a wall of windows, whitewashing the scattered long and short tables that line the airy room. I see the faces of Myles's friends sitting at a narrow rectangular table he's obviously heading toward. Jake and April are there. So is the blonde from English. She's sitting next to an exotic looking girl with almond shaped eyes and shiny, dark hair that flows smoothly over her shoulders. Sitting side by side, the contrast of their coloring is pronounced, especially since their overall style and look is exactly the same. Next to the exotic girl, is Lucas. He doesn't seem to be friends with any homely girls. I spot an empty seat on the opposite side of the table. It's the one farthest from Lucas, and I decide it's safest to sit there.

"You all know Raielle," Myles says, pointing in my direction as he takes the chair across from me. He's next to Jake and I'm next to April. My eyes flick over everyone and I smile, taking care not to make eye contact with anyone in particular.

"No, rude boy, we don't all know her," the blonde from English class says. "I'm Kellie and this is Sophie." She points to the dark girl beside her. I assume that's the same Sophie who used to be Lucas's girlfriend.

I wave a hello to them and start pulling out the sandwich Chloe made for me. I've never had anyone make me a lunch like this, and having it today gives me a warm little thrill that has me feeling foolish. It's just a packed lunch.

"Did you mug a first grader on your way to school today?" Myles asks, smirking at my bag.

"Are you making fun of my insulated Dora lunch sack?" I lob back, acting offended. I'm too pleased right now to actually feel any real embarrassment.

"That's Dora? She kind of looks like an Oompa Loompa."

"Hey," I point at him. "Don't hate on Dora. She's just a post-modern girl trying to find her way in the world. She's an explorer when most girls her age want to be princesses. Let's show her a little respect, okay?"

Myles blinks at me, and I realize that the whole table is staring. Then Jake busts out laughing. Myles shakes his head and grins. "You're a trip, Raielle."

My eyes travel to the other end of the table, and I notice that Sophie and Kellie are looking at me and whispering as they sip their diet sodas. From what I can tell, that's all they're having for lunch. Lucas is peering down at his tray trying unsuccessfully to conceal a smile. I turn back to Myles before Lucas can catch me looking at him. I take a huge bite of my sandwich and wink at a still amused Myles, feeling nearly normal today or what I imagine normal feels like. I haven't used my abilities since I've been here, and when I go for a while without tapping into them, I can almost pretend they don't exist, like they're not biding their time, waiting to emerge and alienate any sense of normalcy I manage to achieve. It's only a matter of time.

Once lunch ends, everyone scatters. I don't have to worry about Lucas trying to walk with me again because he's securely guarded by Sophie and Kellie who are glued to either side of him. As I walk to my locker, I'm determined to stop being so aware of Lucas Diesel.

SIX

'M at Gwen's house afterschool. During chemistry, she asked if I wanted a ride home again, and when we realized how much chemistry homework we were being assigned, she asked me to come over so we could get it done together. I texted Myles to let him know my plans by replying to a text he sent me earlier, offering me a ride with him and April. Gwen quietly snickered at how long it took me to tap out a few words back to him. I'm new to the whole having a phone and texting thing.

"When in doubt, convert to moles," she mutters, staring at the textbook.

"What?" We're sitting on the floor of her bedroom. To my surprise, it's pink. Gwen the semi-Goth girl has a pink room and a white cockatoo. She's not nearly as tough as she wants people to think.

"That's what Mr. Pascorelli said during the first class. When in doubt, convert to moles."

"But that doesn't help at all."

"No kidding. I'm hungry. Let's take a break." She stands before I can respond and heads downstairs.

I follow behind, locating her in the kitchen. Both her parents work, and her older brother is away at college. She has the place to herself every afternoon until six she told me.

"I'm going to cut up some cheese and apple slices. Want some?" She's resting her hip against the granite countertop.

"Sure. Sounds very nutritious," I laugh.

She frowns. "No junk food here. House rule, unfortunately."

I glance around at the stone and stainless steel kitchen while she bustles about, pulling food from the refrigerator. "So, you ate lunch with Lucas and his friends today," she says with mischief in her eyes.

"Correction. I ate lunch with Myles and his friends. He's my neighbor. I think he's taken me under his wing or something."

She shrugs. "So, are you into Myles or Lucas?"

"Neither. What about you? Got a boyfriend? Are you into anyone at school?"

She turns her attention back to the cheese she's slicing.

I sense something juicy and move to stand beside her. "You can tell me. I probably don't know whoever it is anyway."

The knife in her hand pauses. "You can't tell anyone."

"Who would I tell? I talk to you and sometimes Myles. That's it. And I promise I won't tell Myles."

"You talk to Lucas. People saw you in the hallway today," she says.

I throw my hands in the air. "Oh my god. This school is ridiculous. Every time I talk to a guy in the hall it makes headlines."

"Crap!" Gwen yells, jerking her hand back.

When she cautiously holds it up, I see rivulets of blood pouring from her finger, dripping down onto the hardwood floor. I grab a dishtowel on the counter and wrap it around her hand.

"What are you doing?" she asks in a panicked voice. "Those are nice towels. My mom's gonna freak."

Before I can think better of it, I act on instinct. While still applying pressure to her finger with the towel, I place my other hand on the exposed skin of her forearm. I can immediately feel her wound pulling on the energy inside me. My stomach hollows and then seems to shift. It's similar to the feeling you get when an elevator moves down too quickly or when you've gone too high on a swing and you fall through midair for a moment before the swing catches you again. It's an exhilarating and satisfying sensation that vibrates through me but abates quickly when I remove my hand from her arm. Her cut was minor. It probably would have only required a few stitches.

I can see Gwen blinking in confusion. She knows she felt something strange but she's not sure what. My mother told me that when you're healing a person, depending on the severity of the injury, that person can feel almost giddy. She likened the sensation to a buzz you get from alcohol. Of course, she would. With Gwen's minor finger cut, I doubt she felt much.

This is the first time I've healed someone since before my mother died. Every time I give into it, I'm defying her. Her warnings run through my head again now. "Resist using it," she told me time and time again. There are always consequences. She was partly right. I've found that I can heal small cuts and wounds, broken bones, too, without consequence. But more serious issues, life and death injuries, can't be tinkered with. I saw this myself when my mother tried to heal one of her junky boyfriends who had been stabbed and showed up at our doorstep covered in blood. She cared too much to resist healing him, but then his son died from an aneurism the next day.

Gwen gingerly pulls the towel from her hand and examines her finger. I didn't completely mend the wound. That would look too suspicious. But I turned the deep slice into more of a paper cut. "It stopped bleeding," she says, turning her hand over. "I guess it wasn't as bad as I thought."

Just then, my back pocket rings, causing me to squeal in surprise. Gwen points and laughs. "You're such a luddite."

"Look at you with the fancy SAT word," I tease. "For your information, I'm not a luddite. I'm poor. There's a difference."

"Then let me give you some advice, Raielle. If you're going to keep your cell phone there, set it to vibrate. Then enjoy the booty call." She waggles her eyebrows at me, and I grin at her before turning away to answer. It's Kyle.

"Where are you? Chloe is getting ready to put dinner on the table. I told you my dad was coming over tonight."

I mutter a curse under my breath. "I forgot. I'm sorry. I'll be right there." I end the call feeling badly. I turn to Gwen.

"I heard. I'll get my keys."

When we arrive at the house, an unfamiliar car is parked on the street in front. It's a large white sedan. I'm about to open Gwen's car door when I turn back to her. "You never told me who you're crushing on."

She rolls her eyes at me. "I shouldn't tell you because you're not telling me."

"Because I have nothing to tell," I argue. It's sort of the truth. It doesn't matter if I'm interested in someone since I'm not going to act on it.

She closes her eyes. "It's Jake."

I grin. "Jake? Hey, I actually know him."

"I know. You ate lunch with him." She seems envious.

"Where were you at lunch? I didn't see you."

"Because you were sitting in the center of the caf where all the bright shiny people eat. I was sitting in the back, at a corner table where the rest of us peons dwell."

I shake my head. "You're so wrong, Gwen. I am not one of *those* people. I never have been. If it wasn't for Myles, I wouldn't have sat there at all. For all I know, they set him straight after lunch and now I'm banned."

She gapes at me. "Do you own a mirror? How could you *not* be one of those people? Guys literally stop in their tracks when you walk by. I know you seem oblivious to the way you look, but I never figured you actually were."

I rub my forehead. I'm starting to get a headache. "People react that way at first, but when they realize my personality doesn't match, I'm put in the loner column, and I'm left alone."

She tilts her head at me like she doesn't believe me.

"I'll sit with you at lunch tomorrow, okay? I'd rather eat with you anyway."

Her eyes widen. "You're going to purposely torpedo your rep?"

I sigh at her ridiculousness. "Or I could bring you with me to Myles's table, and you can talk to Jake."

She vigorously shakes her head. "No. You can't do that."

Her reaction surprises me. "Why not? Are you shy or something?"

Gwen runs a hand over her jet black hair. "I'm not shy. I'm a realist. He'd never be interested in me."

"Why would you say that?"

She bugs her eyes out like the answer is obvious.

"You have a lousy attitude, but you're attractive and smart. You should let me talk to him for you." I'm not sure why I'm insisting. For some reason, her surprising lack of confidence makes me really want to help her.

"No! Don't you have a dinner to get to?" She huffs at me.

"Fine," I roll my eyes. "Let's make a deal. When it comes to boys, you lay off me, and I'll lay off you."

She gets a weird twinkle in her eye. "No way. I won't make that deal. Because when you and Lucas get together, it's going to be epic, and I want to hear every detail."

"Oh my god. You're deluded." I turn my back on her and climb out of her car.

I hear her giggling behind me before she pulls away.

There's chatter coming from the dining room when I step through the door. After setting my bag down, I walk hesitantly toward the noise. Chloe spots me first.

"You're here," she states. "I'll make you a plate."

As she ducks into the kitchen, my eyes travel around the table, landing on two unfamiliar faces, both of whom are staring at me.

"She looks just like her mother," the older man says. He is obviously Alec, Kyle's father. He has thick grey hair streaked with yellowish-brown patches. It's combed back away from his long forehead. I can tell that he's a tall man even though he's sitting down. Beside him is a weathered looking woman. She has leathery skin, and she's layered in jewelry. Large gold disks hang from her ears matching the thick gold ropes that surround her neck and wrists.

"Raielle," Kyle says. "This is my father, and this is Linda."

I smile weakly. "Sorry I'm late."

Chloe returns, setting a plate down in front of the empty seat beside Penelope, who is engrossed in the task of getting a single pea onto her spoon.

I sit down at the table and keep my eyes on my plate while I settle in. I'm not nervous exactly, but I do feel uncomfortable for some reason. Maybe it's the way Linda seems to squint at me as though I have something wrong with my face.

Alec breaks the awkward silence. "Despite everything, Raielle, I was very sorry to hear about Angela."

"Thanks," I mumble. When my eyes meet his, I feel a strange shock at their intensity. They're a deep green color reminding me of the ocean in winter and looking just as frigid. In contrast, his expression is calm and emotionless. It occurs to me that his eyes would go better with his girlfriend's sour face. Maybe they blame me for the fact that he couldn't get a divorce from my mother. Then again, maybe I'm imagining things. Maybe I want this man to be awful to excuse what my mother did to him and Kyle, because the alternative is too hard to accept.

"How are you doing? You've had quite an upheaval," Alec asks.

I don't want to meet his eyes again, but I do. "I'm fine. I'm lucky Kyle and Chloe were willing to take me in. I'm very grateful to them." As I'm saying those words, I realize they're true. I would have done okay going into foster care again. I always survived. But this is different. This is better somehow, like I'm a part of something rather than a ghost flitting in and out of strangers' homes.

Kyle smiles at me and so does Chloe. "You don't have to be grateful," he says. "You're family. Of course you would come here. We're happy you're here despite the circumstances."

I nod at him while I study my plate again. I don't really do feelings and mushiness very well or at all. I hide my discomfort by helping Penelope scoop the rest of her peas onto her spoon. Kyle must sense my wariness because he changes the subject to work. Apparently, Alec is an accountant, too. A dry discussion of New York State tax law ensues.

I mostly push my food around on my plate throughout dinner. Soon Chloe excuses herself to put Penelope to bed, but only after Penelope smothers her grandfather in goodnight kisses. Once she's gone, I begin to clear the table. I've got nearly all the plates piled on the counter when Chloe returns.

"Go into the living room with everyone else," she orders. "I'll finish in here." She takes the dishtowel from my hand and ushers me out.

In the living room, Alec and Linda are seated on the couch. Kyle sits in a chair across from them. I take the empty armchair beside him. Everyone smiles at me.

"We hear you're an excellent student," Linda says, addressing me for the first time.

"Yes, ma'am."

She purses her lips. "Ma'am? Please, call me Linda."

Across from me, Alec leans forward, resting his forearms on his knees. He's built like an over the hill athlete, with thick arms and a barrel chest. "I understand your mother never said anything to you about Kyle," he states. I glance over at Kyle and he offers me a tight smile. Of course, he would tell his father everything.

"No, she didn't."

"Having a brother must have come as quite a shock."

"Yes, it did." I squirm in my seat. I don't want to say anything negative about my mother.

Alec offers me a gentle smile. Then he leans back into the couch.

Now that Alec has given me an opening, I ask my own question. "Why do you think she never told me?"

He doesn't seem surprised by my question. After a long moment, he shakes his head slowly and sighs. "I have no idea. I couldn't imagine walking away from my son and never looking back."

I don't miss the accusation in his words. "How did she leave?" I ask.

"What do you mean?" Alec tilts his head at me.

"Did she just disappear one day?"

He rubs a hand across his rough cheek. Linda reaches out and touches his arm.

"She did just disappear," Kyle answers for his father. "I was at school. Dad was work. When she didn't show to pick me up, they called him. We came home and she was gone."

I glance from Kyle to his father. Kyle's lingering hurt is obvious. "Was she drinking back then?" I ask. As usual, I'm thinking of ways to excuse her behavior.

After a pause, Alec replies, "I thought she might have had a problem."

I glance down at the carpet. Even if she was drinking, it still doesn't make sense. She always regretted it when I was taken away. She tried to get me back every time. My mother had her issues, but walking away from her child would have been out of character. At least for the person I knew.

"We probably won't ever know the truth," Linda says, rubbing her hand reassuringly over Alec's arm.

"It's all in the past now." Alec places his hand over his girlfriend's smaller one.

"Papa?"

I turn to see Penelope walking into the room, rubbing her eyes and dragging her blanket behind her.

"What are you doing up?" Kyle asks.

Penelope makes a beeline for Alec. "I want Papa to tuck me in," she says in a tired voice. The moment she's within reach, Alec scoops her up and places her on his lap. The adoration on his face when he looks at her makes my throat feel tight.

Chloe emerges from the kitchen. "You're supposed to be in bed, young lady."

"It's all right. I can tuck her back in. Right, puppet?" Alec says.

Penelope nods with satisfaction.

"I want you to stay in bed this time," Chloe warns as Alec passes by with his granddaughter in his arms.

"I will, Mommy," she promises.

I clear my throat and stand. "I have some homework to do. Nice to meet you, Linda. Please tell Alec it was nice to meet him, too."

She waves a dismissive hand at me. "You can tell him yourself next time. We'll being seeing plenty of each other now."

"Goodnight," I tell everyone. I barely make it down to my room before my eyes burn with guilty tears. I hate that I feel jealous of Penelope and the wonderful family she has. Then I realize that they're my family, too.

At least, they could have been.

I lay down flat on my bed and look up at the ceiling where they're all still sitting above me. It was so easy to hate my mother when she was drinking. For the past couple of years, I tried really hard not to judge her on her past mistakes. I wanted a fresh start with her as much as she did with me even if I never admitted that to her. I did love her, and I was proud of her sobriety and the effort she was making for me. But now, I find myself slipping back into that place of bitterness and resentment. I don't want to think about what I could have had, but it's hard not to when it's paraded in front of me this way.

I roll over onto my side and stare at Penelope's toys in the corner of the room. I don't have any homework left to do, and I don't bother getting undressed. I just lay there in the dark, trying to extinguish the spark of anger inside me that threatens to catch fire. But I can't quite manage it.

The last image I have of her won't be ignored tonight. I keep seeing it, like a movie that's paused on one scene, never moving backward or forward. I see the blood. I see her vacant stare. I feel the cold nothingness that is her skin when I touch it. I lay there awake, all night, restless and conflicted, thinking too much, until the first muted signs of morning begin to brighten the dark corners of my basement bedroom.

SEVEN

'M a zombie the next day. I'm running on no sleep, and I still feel choked with emotions that I can't seem to bury. Myles and I walk to school together again. I manage to put on a good face for him. Luckily, once April joins us, I don't have to participate in the conversation because she happily monopolizes it.

I am vaguely aware of Lucas in my morning classes. He offers me his usual tight half-smile when his gaze lands on me, but much to my relief, he doesn't try to walk with me again in the hallway. That could be because I don't answer his grin with one of my own despite the way my pulse kicks up when I see him. I'm just too drained to deal with his silent intensity today.

"I'm going to sit with Gwen in the caf," I tell Myles when he appears at my locker before lunch.

He wrinkles his brow. "Who?"

"Gwen Westfield. She works in the office. She has black hair and always dresses in black."

He squints at me. "You know her?"

"You don't? This school isn't that big."

"She just started here last year," he shrugs. "I never really see her around. Besides, she seems weird."

"I just started here last week and you were more than happy to befriend me." Then I have a light bulb moment. "Did Kyle ask you to be friends with me?"

His eyes dart away from mine.

"Oh my god. He did. Didn't he?"

He holds his hand up. "He didn't ask me to be friends with you. I decided to do that on my own. He just asked me to introduce you around. To make you feel comfortable."

I run my hands over my face. "Did he tell you and your friends about my mom and everything that happened? Did that make you feel bad for me or something?"

"Wait a minute," he says, raising his voice now. "You've got it wrong. Kyle only told me that he found out about you a couple of years ago, and because your mom passed away, you were coming here to live with him. Then he asked me to show you around. That's it. It was Chloe who came by later and gossiped about you and your situation to my mom while April and Lucas were over. That's how they know about it. I never would have said anything to them. I never would have done more than show you where the front office is at school if I didn't actually want to be your friend, which I do. Okay?"

I just stare at him. I'm on emotional overload today. I need to get a hold of myself. "Okay," I finally say. Then I offer him a grin to reinforce it.

"Okay," he mimics with a quick head nod. "Let's go eat."

"But I'm still eating with Gwen."

He stops walking.

"She's my friend, too. I want to sit with her. You can join us."

"Maybe I will," he says, as though it's a challenge he needs to meet.

But when we arrive in the cafeteria, April pats the seat beside her and Myles glances at me apologetically.

"Go sit with Lois Lane," I whisper, pushing him playfully on the shoulder. Then I spot Gwen sitting at a round table in the back with two other people I don't know. I head in their direction pretending not to notice the eyes at Myles's table following my progression past them.

"Hey," I set my Dora lunch bag down beside Gwen.

She smiles up at me, and I notice that under her black sweater, she's wearing a yellow T-shirt today. She has a little color for a change. That's interesting. "Raielle, this is Tyler and Lisa."

Tyler and Lisa practically gape at me when I sit down with them. Tyler has dark shaggy hair that nearly reaches his shoulders. He's cute in a geeky John Cusack kind of way. Lisa's head is topped by a cloud of red hair and her skin is mostly freckles. When my eyes meet hers, her cheeks heat. The poor girl looks like little Orphan Annie. They all eye Dora as I withdraw my lunch items, but they don't comment.

"I have all the *Dexter* episodes on my DVR," Gwen says to them, obviously continuing a conversation they were having before I arrived. "You should watch the ones you missed. The first season is amazing." She turns to me. "Have you ever seen *Dexter*?"

I shake my head.

"Seriously? You need to come over, too, then. It's such an unbelievable show. Michael C. Hall is completely hot in a dangerous psychopath kind of way."

Since the conversation isn't really holding my attention, I find my eyes wandering over to another table. Sophie and Kellie are in their same seats. They're laughing hysterically over something, and I can't help but think it's me when I see both their eyes are darting in my direction. Is the fact that I'm sitting at this table so funny? My eyes travel to Lucas whose face is partially hidden behind Jake's. His attention is on his lunch tray. He doesn't seem to be participating in any conversation at all.

"Raielle?"

I turn back to Gwen who's watching me expectantly. "This weekend?" she prompts. "Do you want to come over and have a *Dexter* marathon with us?"

"Um, sure."

"Cool," she beams at me.

Across the table, I think I see Lisa gulp.

Eating lunch does nothing to wake me up, and I nearly nod off in chemistry. On the way out, I let Gwen know that I'm walking home with Myles today. After his speech about wanting to be my friend, I decide I should make more of an effort to return the favor.

THE endless day is finally over. I'm moving tiredly down the stairs to meet Myles. Hoards of students are passing me in their rush to be free from school when someone brushes hard against my arm. Inside me, the energy starts to build. I stop and grab the railing. My stomach hollows and drops. I clench my abdomen muscles, tamping down on the surge, trying to rein it in. Oblivious to the commotion around me, I sit down while my hand is still gripping the rail. A very sick person just touched me. Their bare arm made contact with mine, and it set the process in motion. The strength with which this is hitting me means whoever it was has an extremely serious illness. Holding in the desire to heal once the energy forms is physically painful. I'm compelled to do it, and when I don't, it turns on me.

My skin breaks out in a cold sweat, and a wave of nausea rolls through me. All my muscles ache. It feels like I have the flu on steroids. My hands are shaking, and I can't even think about moving until this passes. This is my own fault. When I'm in control, this doesn't happen. Lots of people suffer from different ailments. If this happened every time I came into contact with a sick person, I couldn't function. Today, I'm not in control of my emotions. I'm exhausted, and I let my guard down. Now, I'm paying for it.

I don't know how long I sit there, waiting for the shakes to pass. Eventually, the stairwell empties and the commotion fades. Everyone is gone. The only sound I hear is my own harsh breathing. Then a door opens and slams shut on the floor above me, echoing in the silence. Someone is descending the stairs. I stand on unsteady legs.

"Raielle?"

I immediately tense. The unmistakable voice saying my name belongs to Lucas. Of course, it would be him that finds me here.

"Are you okay?"

He's beside me now, hovering over me, trying to see my face, which I'm hiding behind a curtain of hair. I take a deep breath and turn to him, letting my hair fall away. "I'm fine." I try to smile.

He scrutinizes me, and I can see that he doesn't believe me. This is the closest I've ever been to him. His eyes are only inches from mine, and I decide that they're the same color as the sky during that brief magical moment after the sun finally drops below the horizon, when the pink and red dissolve away leaving only a dark mix of blue and violet in their wake.

My phone buzzes in my back pocket and I startle. Lucas startles, too, and wraps a hand around my arm to steady me. The place on my arm he's touching begins to heat, and I can feel my cheeks starting to burn. I hide behind my hair again as I pull my phone out and study the screen. My hand is too shaky to read the text from Myles, but I can guess what it's about. Hoping Lucas doesn't notice that I can't hold my phone still, I pocket it again.

"Myles is outside waiting for me," I explain, not meeting his eyes. When I reach down for my bag, I realize he has it.

"I'll walk you down," he says gently. His warm hand is loose but firm around my upper arm.

I feel like an idiot as we slowly descend the stairwell together. I should make up an explanation. Tell him I'm getting a cold or something, but I can't find my voice. I just let him lead me downward, feeling stronger and more at ease with each step. Having him so close to me, helping me, even as it's becoming less necessary, is mortifying. But it also makes me feel safe and protected in a way that's unfamiliar. It doesn't occur to me to reclaim my arm. Even when Myles spots us coming through the door, and he stalks over, looking annoyed, I don't step away from Lucas.

"I thought you ditched me. I've been standing here for almost fifteen minutes. I texted you. Twice."

I'm about to apologize when Lucas speaks. "It's my fault. I held her up." Then he removes his hand from my arm. I'm steady on my feet now, but I immediately feel the loss, and I can't help smiling at his pun.

Myles cocks a curious eyebrow at Lucas. Then he turns to me. "Let's go. I need to borrow my mom's car so I can go buy April a birthday present."

"Didn't she say her birthday was yesterday?" Lucas asks.

"Yes," Myles replies in a clipped tone.

I turn to Lucas to get my bag from him, but he just shoulders it. "I'll give you both a ride. Come on." Then he walks toward the parking lot without waiting for a response.

I take a deep breath and try not to ogle Lucas's impressive backside encased in weathered jeans that hug him in all the right places.

Myles is gearing up to ask me why Lucas delayed me. So, I distract him. "Did you forget April's birthday?" I ask.

He scowls. "Yeah."

"Why bother with this?" I ask him.

"What do you mean?" He seems genuinely perplexed.

"I can understand if you're not ready to announce yourself to the world, but you don't need a fake girlfriend. Besides, I don't think you even like April."

We're nearly to Lucas's truck when Myles stops and looks at me. "She's the one who wanted to go out with me. I figured, why not? I thought that maybe…" He hesitates and looks down at his shoes. "Anyway, by the time I realized she and I weren't really clicking, I'd let it go on too long. Now there's no way to break up with her without hurting her feelings." He shrugs. "It's senior year anyway. Everyone will go their separate ways soon enough. We'll grow apart and that will be that."

I see the sadness in his eyes, and I feel for him. Despite his cavalier attitude, pretending to be someone you're not can't be good for you. In my own way, I understand it.

"You two coming?" Lucas calls to us. He's standing beside the open door of his truck.

Myles walks ahead of me and starts to climb in on the passenger side when Lucas holds out an arm to stop him. "You think I'm holding this door open for you?"

Myles grumbles, pulls opens the back door, and slides inside while I lift myself up onto the front seat and quietly thank Lucas. He nods and places my bag on the floor in front of me.

"What are you going to get her?" I ask as we're pulling out of the school parking lot.

"Jewelry," Myles answers.

"What kind?"

"I don't know. Maybe a necklace or something," he says absently.

"Put a lot of thought into this, did you?" I ask.

"Okay, help me out then," he says with a challenge in his voice. "What do you think she would like? What kind of stuff do you like to get?"

I huff out a sad little laugh. I don't think I've ever gotten a birthday present. I can feel Lucas looking at me, wondering what my reaction to Myles's question means. "I'm kidding, Myles," I answer quickly. "A necklace sounds like a nice gift."

Within minutes, we arrive at our street. Myles and I both open our doors. I'm about to jump out and call a thanks over my shoulder to Lucas when his hand touches my shoulder. "Hold up a minute, Raielle."

"See ya," Myles yells, already dashing across his yard.

I close my eyes and sigh. Then I sit back onto the seat and look at him. His warm hand still rests on my shoulder. The weight of it is radiating heat down my whole body.

"Do you want to tell me what happened back there on the stairwell?" he asks quietly. His eyes are watching mine.

I don't even bother scrambling for an excuse. I can't tell Lucas the truth but for some reason I don't want to lie to him either. When I don't answer, he asks another question. "Did someone say something to you or do something?" His eyes harden as his question hangs in the air.

I shake my head. "No. Nothing like that."

He relaxes slightly, removing his hand from my shoulder and running it through his hair. At least, I think he's more relaxed. His subtle expressions are tough to read.

"You're not going to tell me, are you?" he says.

"It's really no big deal."

He waits until I'm looking at him before saying, "You can talk to me, you know."

I bark out a surprised laugh.

"What?" he asks. Then he smiles at me. It's a genuine smile this time, not his trademark smirk.

I thought he was good-looking before, but when he smiles, he's devastating. "You're about as approachable as an iceberg," I inform him, trying not to stare too hard at his perfect features.

His grin stays in place. "That's because you've been about as friendly as a Rottweiler."

My eyes widen in disbelief. "You're comparing me to a dog?"

His smile quickly disappears, and he scrubs a hand over his face. "Jesus, no. That's not what I meant."

I chuckle softly, liking the sudden appearance of a more human Lucas. "I'm messing with you. I'm not offended. You're right. I haven't been very friendly, but you were unfriendly first."

"So, you were just reacting to me?" he asks with a skeptical look.

His question surprises me. I tense up, not sure how to answer because I'm not just reacting to his gruffness. But I can't tell him it's because I feel an attraction to him that I don't want to feel. I can't tell him that I have no idea how to deal with my physical reaction to him. I can't tell him anything close to the truth. When I fail to answer another one of his questions, he tries a different approach. "I know you're dealing with a lot right now."

I stiffen even more. He was there at Myles's house when Chloe spilled the beans about my mother's death. I just don't know what beans she spilled exactly.

"So," he continues, his eyes holding mine, "since I'm most definitely not made of ice, if what happened on the stairs today ever happens again, you can talk to me about it. That's all I'm saying."

I blink at him as I realize what he's thinking. He thinks I had some sort of a panic attack. I laugh ruefully and shake my head. He seems confused by my reaction. He's being so nice. I'm not sure how to respond to this sweet Lucas. I just know that this Lucas is far more disconcerting and potentially more dangerous for me than the silent brusque one. "Thank you," I finally say. "I appreciate that." Then I feel the need to bolt. "Thanks for the ride, too," I tell him, grabbing my bag, getting ready to jump out.

He seems disappointed. "Anytime," he finally says.

He stays parked by the curb until I'm inside. I stand in the doorway and watch him drive away feeling a little off kilter. I saw a very different

Lucas this afternoon, and now I'm not sure what to think.

Penelope comes running up to me. "I painted a flower in school today and Mommy let me hang it on my wall. Do you want to see?"

I grin down at her. "Sure."

She takes off down the hallway, and I follow. Then I stand in her purple and pink room, making noises of approval as she shows me her picture. But in my mind, I'm still seeing Lucas. I'm hearing his voice. My skin feels warm and too tight when I think about him. I wonder what effect our conversation will have on how we treat each other in school tomorrow. Will he give me a big friendly hello? Will he try to walk with me to our shared classes again? If that does happen, what kind of gossip will it fuel? Sophie and Kellie will surely have something to say about it. The last thing I want is to bring attention of any kind to myself. After what happened today, I know it's important to keep my emotions in check. "Stay in the shallow water," Mom would say. She told me that was the key to surviving when you were like us, and she taught me from childhood how to turn my healing instinct off. She explained it was like another sense. It was like closing my eyes. I got pretty good at it. I did it instinctively. But since I've been here, it feels as though it's hovering near the surface all the time, just waiting for some event to trigger it. Finally, today, I nearly lost control of it.

"Let's build a block tower," Penelope suggests, sitting down on her floor, dumping out her pail of wooden blocks.

I sit beside her and begin piling blocks atop one another.

"Are you my sister now?" she asks.

I glance down at her wide brown eyes and her wild, unkempt hair. Chloe always has her perfectly put together in the morning, but by the afternoon she's covered in food stains and her hair looks like it's been through a hurricane. "I'm your aunt," I tell her. I realize that I hadn't really thought of myself that way before. I'm actually an aunt. That's pretty cool. "I'm your dad's sister."

She laughs at me as though I'm being ridiculous. "You can't be Daddy's sister. He's too old."

I chuckle with her, wondering how Kyle would take that news. But she does have a point when it comes to age. Kyle is only twenty-five, which is fairly young these days to be married with a three-year-old. Chloe is a year younger than he is. She must have been barely out of college when she had Penelope. I couldn't even begin to imagine being a wife and mother at such a young age, if ever at all.

I'm balancing a block atop the column we're creating when Penelope says, "You can be my sister, and because your mommy is gone, you can share mine."

I release the block, and my hand drops into my lap.

"Okay?" she asks. Her voice is quiet and unsure, like it's our secret.

"Okay," I whisper.

She smiles, and my gaze leaves her round eyes to travel over her upturned nose and her shiny pink lips. Her innocence tugs at my heart.

"YOU'RE coming with us to Atlas, right?" Myles asks after I meet him outside in the morning.

"Doubtful. What's Atlas?"

He gives me a curious look. "Didn't anyone mention it to you?"

"I don't know why you think your friends talk to me, Myles. They don't. Show me what's in the box before we get to April's house." I noticed it in his hand right off, and I'm pretty sure that was his intention.

He holds it out to me. Then he dramatically peels the lid back to gradually reveal a silver pendant shaped like a seashell. It has a round blue stone in the middle of it. He's watching me for my reaction.

"It's beautiful," I smile.

"Really?" He seems pleased.

"Really. You did good." I continue walking, noticing how pleased he is with my compliment.

Myles snaps the box closed and puts it back in his pocket.

"Where can I get a part-time job around here?" I ask him. I know Kyle told me I didn't need a job but not having my own money and depending completely on him makes me uneasy.

He glances up at the cloud-filled sky and thinks about it. "You could try the new ice cream shop that opened downtown."

"There's a new ice cream shop?" I ask surprised.

He nods, distracted now that April is walking toward us.

I decide to make a trip downtown after school to check out this new place. Working around there would be perfect since I could easily walk.

I move ahead of them to give them some privacy. When I hear April squeal in delight, I walk even faster toward the main entrance of the school, but not before turning back to see her jumping up and down with her arms squeezed tightly around his neck.

After a quick stop at my locker, I head to first period. I can't believe how nervous I am at the thought of an imminent encounter with Lucas. To my surprise, he's already there when I arrive. As always, my heart thunders in my chest at the sight of him. My fingers tingle when I notice the ends of his hair are still damp from his morning shower, and I want nothing more than to touch them. I wonder if my physical reaction to him will ever approach something close to normal.

He spots me and smiles. I take a deep breath. Once again, his tight smirk is history. His grin is completely genuine and stunning. It appears things are going to be different between us. I debate the wisdom of taking a desk on the other side of the room. If I do that, I'm showing Lucas that I don't want to be friends or anything else with him. After the way I lost control yesterday, I know that would be the smart thing to do if I want to keep a tight rein on my emotions. But I can't bring myself to actually do it. I answer Lucas's smile with one of my own as I sit down beside him.

"Good morning," he says, turning his whole upper body toward me.

"Morning." I bend down to pull my textbook and notebook from my bag. I slept well last night, and I gave myself a pep talk this morning. I am going to stay in control today. Not even the attention of Lucas Diesel, the object of many a swooning high school girl's fantasy life, is going to break me. I can be friends with him and not have it affect the Zen I'm going for today. I hope.

"Hey guys," Tucker says as he takes the desk behind me.

"Hey," I reply unenthusiastically.

Lucas doesn't reply at all. He angles his body forward again.

"Are you going to Atlas this weekend?" Tucker asks.

Since I know he's speaking to me, I make myself turn around. "That's the second time I've heard about this. What's Atlas?"

His eyebrows shoot up dramatically. "What's Atlas?"

"Is there an echo in here?" I ask dryly.

Tucker laughs. "Atlas is the only all ages club around here. Chad Bleeker's band plays there the second Saturday of every month. You know Chad, right?"

I shake my head.

"He's in this awesome band called Isolation. They had a song on the radio over the summer. It was just a local station, but still. Anyway, everyone goes when they play."

"Sounds interesting." I turn back around and catch Lucas eyeing me. He's about to say something when the girl with the pixie cut who usually sits next to him appears between us.

"Lucas," she whines. "You didn't save me a seat."

A muscle in his cheek tics. "I never save you a seat."

The teacher arrives, and the girl huffs her annoyance before heading down the row to an empty seat in the back. Once class begins, getting through the hour with him so close feels like an endurance test. But I pay attention and take continuous notes, all while I'm painfully aware of Lucas beside me.

I resist the urge to dash out of class when the bell rings. Just because I'm foolishly attracted to him like every other girl with a pulse, I shouldn't take my frustration with myself out on him. If he can be nice, so can I. I take my time gathering my things in case he does plan to wait for me, but pixie girl has a plan of her own.

She appears in front of him and waits until he notices her before she asks, "Do you have practice after school today? Because I was thinking you could give me a ride home after my yearbook meeting."

"If you can be down on the field by five, I'll give you a ride," he replies.

"Great. Thanks." She smiles widely at him.

Since it would be awkward to remain standing there any longer, I pick up my bag and head for the door.

"Are you guys going to make the state playoffs this year?" I hear her ask him behind me.

"Doubt it. I'll see you later."

I feel Lucas beside me now as I enter the busy hallway. When he moves in closer, he asks, "Do you think you'll go this weekend, to Atlas?"

"Um," I hesitate. I wasn't really planning on it. I wonder if he's about to ask me to go with him. Butterflies take flight in my stomach as I start weighing the pros and cons of that possibility.

"You're welcome to go with us. You could ask Gwen to come along too if it would make you feel more comfortable."

To my credit, I don't laugh out loud at myself and my ridiculous thoughts. He's obviously not asking me out. "Who's 'us'?" I ask.

"Didn't Myles talk to you?" He seems ready to become annoyed if I answer no.

"I think he started to tell me about it, but we never finished the conversation." Mainly, because April was strangling him with her birthday present gratitude.

"I'm driving Myles, April, and Jake," he explains. "I can take you and Gwen, too."

I glance up at him. Reason tells me to avoid crowds until I'm sure I have my healing instinct under control. But the part of me that likes the idea of a night out, like any normal teenager would, wants to accept the ride. Lucas's eyes are trained straight ahead as we maneuver through the crowded hallway. "Thanks. I'll think about it," I answer vaguely, still undecided.

He stops suddenly. The students walking behind us curse when they almost run into him. I turn to see him standing there with his hands on his hips, irritation flashing in his eyes. "You'll think about it?"

I blink curiously, not understanding his reaction. "Yes. Is something wrong?" I ask.

He flashes a tight smile. "Nope. Everything is just perfect," he says, his voice flat indicating that it's anything but. Then he continues on to class.

After that, he sits next to me again but he lets Kellie monopolize him. He walks with me to our next class, but he makes no conversation and I don't bother either. We've somehow fallen back into strained silence. I wonder if it's because I didn't jump at the chance to go with him and his friends to Atlas. Maybe I should have cheered when he deigned to provide me with a ride.

I give myself a mental shake and decide that I'm way over-thinking this. I make a beeline to my locker when the bell rings.

I say hello in the general direction of Myles's lunch table when I walk by it to sit with Gwen and her friends. When I arrive, they're examining the suspicious looking hamburger meat on their lunch trays.

"Everyone seems to be going to Atlas this weekend. Are you guys interested?" I ask as I join, still annoyed with Lucas, but blatantly ignoring my better judgment.

Lisa scowls in response, and Tyler shakes his head.

"I guess that's a no for you two." I turn to Gwen.

"Do you want to go?" she asks, putting her half-eaten apple down on her tray.

I shrug. "Lucas said he would drive us. He's already taking Myles, April, and Jake." I don't tell her that he pulled an unexplained mood swing after he asked. So the invitation may be rescinded.

"We would go with Lucas and his friends?" she asks with disbelief, like she's just won the lottery. I know the thought of riding with Jake is mostly responsible for her reaction.

From across the table, I see Tyler roll his eyes. "You should go," Lisa says. "We can do our *Dexter* marathon on Friday night instead."

Gwen slumps in her chair. "What am I thinking? My parents won't let me ride in a car driven by a boy they've never met."

"Really?" I ask.

Her head nods miserably. "They're kind of severely strict about that stuff. Will your brother let you go?"

I shrug. "It never occurred to me to ask him."

"How about if I drive us and we can meet them there?" she suggests, looking a little perkier.

"Um, sure," I answer, feeling both relieved and disappointed at this new development. "Then we can leave when we want to," I add, realizing that Gwen having her car there could be handy in case I lose it again.

Gwen drums her fingers on the table. "This is going to be so cool. Have you met Chad Bleeker yet?"

I shake my head. "No. But I've heard of him."

"It's not surprising that you haven't met him. He's not exactly in any of our AP classes if you know what I mean. But if you saw him, you'd remember. His head is completely shaved and pretty much everything on him is pierced—at least everything you can see." She raises her eyes brows up and down to punctuate her point. "And he has these tattoo sleeves that are unbelievably intricate. He must have sat for weeks for those."

"That's a pretty detailed description," I comment.

"You can't miss that dude when he's around," Tyler says.

"So we're on for Saturday?" Gwen asks.

I nod, feeling a little tremor of excitement. "We're on."

AFTER school, Gwen offers to drive me to the ice cream shop. She's already worrying about what she's going to wear on Saturday night.

"How about black?" I suggest.

"Very funny."

I turn away from the passing landscape and watch as Gwen fiddles with the radio. "What was up with that yellow shirt yesterday?" I ask. "I really liked it. You looked nice and kind of optimistic. It threw me."

She stops on a familiar Disturbed song, "Stupify", turning it up so loudly that conversation is impossible. I reach over and turn it down. "You don't want to tell me?"

She glances at me. "It was just a yellow shirt. It doesn't mean anything."

"Okay," I say using a tone that lets her know I don't believe her at all.

She nibbles her lip while she drives. "I wear whatever fits my mood," she admits grudgingly. "Lately, it's been a lot of black. Yesterday, I didn't feel like all black. That's all."

I grin at her. "That's kind of what I figured. I just wanted to hear you say it."

"I'm sorry you're not riding with Lucas because of me," she says after a moment. "I was thinking I could tell my parents I was going to your house instead. That way we could go with everyone else and they wouldn't have to know."

"No. Don't lie to your parents for me. If you're doing it because you want to ride with Jake though, that's another story."

"Jake is not going to happen," she states.

"Neither is Lucas."

"But Lucas offered to take you. He wouldn't do that if he didn't like you," she argues.

"He's taking a bunch of people, not just me."

She sighs heavily. "He's into you. Stop arguing with me about it, okay? He was watching you all through lunch."

I shake my head as I look out the window. "That doesn't mean anything. I catch him looking at me too sometimes, but then he just acts like a moody ass to me."

"Maybe if you gave him a little encouragement, he wouldn't act that way."

"I don't want to encourage him. Besides, I was being perfectly nice to him today. He was friendly this morning and everything was fine before he did a one-eighty back to jerkdom again."

"There it is," Gwen said, pointing to a small storefront on the first block of the small downtown area.

The place is called Scoops and it has a red and white striped awning. "Is it a good idea to open an ice cream store in a place that's freezing cold most of the year? Do people want ice cream during the winter?"

Gwen parallel parks her car in front of the store. "Ice cream isn't a seasonal thing. The Dairy Queen in Ridgeton is packed all year round. Look, there's a Help Wanted sign in the window."

Gwen waits in the car for me while I go inside. It's a typical ice cream shop with some round café tables and a large counter that lines the entire right side of the store. Beneath a glass top are metal tubs filled with colorful ice cream flavors. Beside it is a topping station table.

The girl behind the counter gives me an application to fill out. When I hand it back to her, she tells me she'll pass it on to the owner. Her complete disinterest doesn't give me much encouragement.

"**S**HE'S not here to be our free babysitting service, Chloe," Kyle says.

"I know that. But we did take her in. She could help out a little. Babysitting so we can go out for a change isn't asking too much of her."

I'm hovering on the landing that leads to the basement. They obviously don't know I'm standing here. I was on my way up when I heard them, and their tone made me pause.

"At least ask her," Chloe pleads.

"I'm not asking her. She's going to feel obligated to say yes. I don't want to put her in that position."

"You're being ridiculous, the way you tiptoe around her."

Penelope comes around the corner and spots me. "We're having pizza for dinner, Raielle. Do you like pizza?"

With that, both Kyle and Chloe turn to see me standing there. Kyle rubs a hand over his face while Chloe moves quickly and starts setting the kitchen table. When we sit down to dinner, everyone is quiet. After a few moments, I say, "I wouldn't mind babysitting."

Kyle sighs. Chloe continues cutting Penelope's pizza slice into tiny bites. "Thank you, Raielle," he says.

"How about this Saturday night?" Chloe asks.

My pizza pauses on the way to my mouth. "I actually have plans this Saturday. But I could do it any other time."

"What are your plans?" Kyle asks curiously.

I glance at Chloe to gauge her reaction, but her attention is back on Penelope. "My friend Gwen and I are going to a place called Atlas. Myles and his friends are going, too," I add.

"Who is Gwen?" he asks.

"A girl from school. She just moved here last year."

"Atlas is an all ages club with live music," Chloe tells Kyle. "My friend Maya used to work there."

"Is this Gwen driving?" he asks.

I nod, wondering where this is going.

Kyle clears his throat. "I'm glad you're making friends, Raielle. Just make sure you're home by midnight. I think that's a reasonable curfew."

I nearly smile at how uncomfortable giving me a curfew makes him. For some reason, his discomfort makes the curfew fine with me.

THE rest of the week passes quickly. Lucas isn't rude anymore, but he isn't exactly warm and fuzzy either. He says hello and sometimes we walk between classes together, but our conversation is limited to homework, as in "did you finish the English assignment". It's awkward, but I don't know how to fix it, and I don't think he does either. For all I know, he doesn't even want to.

I avoid the main stairwell at the end of each day, instead going out of my way to take the back stairs. I don't know who brushed by me that afternoon, but I don't want it to happen again.

There is one piece of good news this week.

"Do your friends get free ice cream?" Gwen asks at lunch on Friday. I got the call last night. The afternoon before, I had an interview over the phone with Stacy, the owner, and the next day she hired me to work three afternoons a week, including Saturdays. I wanted more hours, but that's all she has right now.

I take a bite of my turkey sandwich. "Let me work there for a while before I begin subsidizing your ice cream habit."

"When do you start?" she asks.

"Next week. I work Tuesdays and Thursdays from three to seven and Saturdays from one to five." I haven't told Kyle and Chloe yet. I know Kyle won't be happy but I have a feeling Chloe won't mind my being out of the house more.

"How will you get back and forth?" Gwen asks. "Is your brother letting you borrow the car?"

I shake my head. "I'll walk."

Her eyes go wide. "At night? By yourself?"

I chuckle at her reaction. "It's only a few miles and seven o'clock isn't late. I walked home through downtown San Diego much later than that."

"What if it's raining?"

I shrug, unconcerned.

"I'll pick you up," she says.

"What?" I put down the chip I was about to bite into. "You're not picking me up. Thanks, but no."

"I can't believe he won't let you borrow the car," she says, not letting this go for some reason.

I sigh. "Look, I haven't asked them. I don't have a license anyway. So it doesn't matter."

She blinks at me like what I said doesn't compute. "You don't have a license?" she asks incredulously.

"Who doesn't have a license?" Myles asks from behind me.

"Raielle," Gwen says, turning to look up at him.

"You don't have a license?" Myles repeats with disbelief.

I roll my eyes at them and start shoving the remains of my lunch into my bag. "We never owned a car. So, I never learned to drive. It's not a big deal." I stand up trying to indicate the conversation is over.

He and Gwen follow me out into the hall. "Raielle never learned to drive. She doesn't have a license," Myles muses. I turn around to see who he's talking to. I turn right back when I see that it's Lucas.

"It's a rite of passage. It's a major milestone in a teenager's life," Myles continues as he walks behind me.

"You should sign up for driver's ed," Gwen suggests. "I think it's after school. You'll have to take the class with all the sophomores though," she snickers.

"I'm not taking driver's ed. I don't have time." We're standing at the doors that will take everyone in different directions. I'm about to push my way through them to escape.

"You don't need to take a class. I can teach you," Lucas says.

I turn and practically gape at him.

"That's a great idea," Gwen says with barely contained glee.

Myles places a hand on my shoulder. "You should get your license, Raielle. You may not own a car now, but you'll want to be able to drive someday."

I glance at them. Gwen and Myles smile supportively, but Lucas narrows his eyes at me, like he's daring me to accept his offer.

"Fine," I answer, my eyes on his, meeting the challenge I see in them. I won't admit to them that I've always wanted to get my license. If it were Gwen offering instead of Lucas, I'd be jumping up and down right now. "Thank you," I tell him, not sure why he made the offer in the first place. I'm already regretting accepting it despite the traitorous parts of me that are gleeful at the idea of spending more time with him.

Myles squeezes my shoulder before releasing it. "Are we going to see you guys tomorrow night?" he asks.

"We'll see you there," Gwen replies.

I never got around to telling Lucas I didn't need a ride from him. I'm wondering if he's annoyed about it when he reaches out and touches my arm lightly.

"We'll make arrangements later," he says. Then he and Myles disappear through the doors. Predictably, Gwen bounces on her feet with a huge conspiratorial grin.

"You could have offered to give me driving lessons," I accuse.

"No way. You're not on my insurance. My parents would flip out if I let you drive my car. Besides you got a better offer."

"That's a subjective opinion," I mumble, hoping it doesn't turn into a total disaster.

EIGHT

I DECIDE to wear black corduroy leggings, black knee-high boots with a moderately high heel, and a long-sleeved blue sweater. I feel calm and in control, but I'm exposing as little skin as possible to reduce the likelihood of anyone brushing against it.

"You look nice," Chloe says as her eyes travel over me.

"Back by midnight, right?" Kyle reminds me.

I nod.

"You have your cell phone?" he asks.

I nod again.

His eyes move over me. "Where?"

"Right here." My hands are empty, but my leggings have some back and side zipper pockets. I tap them for Kyle. Earlier, I had to ask him to loan me ten dollars for the cover charge. He handed it over easily enough. But now that I have a job, I feel better knowing I can pay him back, or at least not have to ask him again.

A car horn beeps outside. "I'll see you later," I call as I head out the door.

Gwen rolls down her window and yells "Sexxxy laaady!" at me. I'm thankful I heard Lucas's truck leave earlier. I can only hope that Kyle and Chloe did not hear that.

"Shout a little louder. I don't think they heard you in Albany," I tell Gwen as I climb into her car and try to see her in the dark. "What are you wearing?"

"Black." She cranks up the radio as she pulls away from the house. She's got her iPod plugged into the dash. Again, a Disturbed tune plays, and I wonder if she owns any other music. Maybe something written in the last decade? But I do recognize the song. It's "Remember". I swallow the lump in my throat when the chorus begins. My mom used to listen to this when she was having a rough time. Instead of making me upset though, I'm grateful for the reminder of her. I hardly thought of her at all today and that realization fills me with remorse.

"Do you have some kind of ID?" Gwen asks. "Even though it's all ages, I think that actually means something else when Isolation plays. They say fuck a lot and I think Chad dropped his pants once."

My mouth hangs open. "Are you serious? Isn't that indecent exposure?"

She shrugs.

I shake my head and tell her that I do have ID. I don't tell her my only ID is a fake though. Apollo had it made for me so I could get into clubs to see a band he was backing. The band was actually pretty good. I just hope the bouncers here don't balk at my phony California ID.

Atlas is a mob scene. Cars line the street for blocks as we approach it. A blue and red neon sign with the club's name flashes over the door casting a garish glow over the crowd of people waiting to get in. "Oh my god," I mutter, eyeing the line.

"I've heard people come from all over. Isolation has a decent following around here. Where the heck are we going to park? There!" she yells, spotting a car leaving.

Once we're on the sidewalk, I realize how tight Gwen's black jersey dress is. Though it covers her from neck to knee, it leaves little to the imagination. She's paired it with black combat boots, and she's pulling it all off with her usual aplomb. In my heels, I tower over her as we join the masses by the door.

The night is unusually warm. Heavy rain clouds hang low in the sky, thickening the air with moisture. "Hey, that's Myles up there," Gwen says. "He's waving us over. Come on." She grabs my hand and pulls me toward the front. People shoot us dirty looks as we bypass them.

"You made it," Myles grins at us. April has her hands wrapped around his waist. "Lucas and Jake are already inside. April wanted to wait for Sophie and Kellie, but they're unfashionably late. So, we're heading in."

The bouncer is a tall serious guy with a severe flat-top that's gelled into spikes. He glances at everyone's ID and lets them pass. But he holds up his hand to me. He takes my ID from my hand and examines it. I stand calmly watching him. Finally, he hands it back to me, fastens a green band around my wrist, and lets me pass. Once inside, I pay the cover charge and locate everyone waiting for me by another interior door.

Myles's eyes go directly to my wrist. "You've got a twenty-one and over bracelet. You can get us all drinks."

"I'm not getting anyone drinks." I try to rip the band off but it won't give at all.

Gwen gets my attention and ushers me through the next door. The moment it opens, a driving rhythm assaults me, pulsing all around us. The club is dimly lit, and the people inside are moving shadows as they bounce to the music.

"This must be the opening band," Gwen yells beside my ear.

We make a path through the crowd so we can see the stage better. Once it's in view, I see an overweight guy dressed all in leather screaming his guts out into the microphone. It actually looks a little painful for him. Gwen turns to me and pretends to stick a finger down her throat. "Let's get something to drink," she suggests.

When we reach the bar, Gwen pushes me in front of her.

"Stop manhandling me." I raise my voice to be heard over the din. "I don't have any money for drinks anyway."

"It's on me. Get us a couple of sodas." She shoves some bills into my hand.

I roll my eyes at her and wait to be noticed. It doesn't take long. "What can I get you?" a seriously built bartender in a black Atlas T-shirt asks me. The girls around me, who have been waiting longer, turn to me and scowl.

"A Diet Coke," I reply. He raises his eyebrows in surprise, but quickly pours the drink and hands it to me. I deliver it to Gwen and give her the change.

"Where's yours?" she asks, taking the cold glass from me.

"I didn't want one."

She narrows her eyes. "How about we get some real drinks next?" she asks. "Would you want one of those?"

I shake my head at her and watch as she purses her lips in mild annoyance.

"You're handy in a crowd, California girl," Myles says beside me, flashing his dimples. "We spotted you towering over everyone from across the club."

Behind Myles I see Jake, who has Kellie glued to his side, and Lucas who I'm actually not towering over despite my heels. He is heart-stoppingly handsome tonight in a black long sleeve jersey that fits him like a glove putting an impressive amount of muscle on display. His dark hair is pushed off his face revealing the hard planes of his brow and cheeks. When my eyes find his, I feel a jolt at their intensity. He's like a laser fixed on me, and my whole body starts to heat.

I glance away and take a breath I hadn't even realized I'd been holding. I can't maintain eye contact with him when he looks at me that way, with a hunger I know I must be misinterpreting. For all I know, he's angry with me again for no good reason. That's when I notice Sophie pressed against his side.

"Oh my god," Kellie screeches pointing at my wrist. "You've got a bracelet. You've got to get us some lemon drops. Those are so yummy. Right, Soph?"

Sophie frowns at me. "Yeah," she answers. Obviously, she wants a drink. She's just sorry she needs me to get it for her.

I shake my head. "I'm not getting anyone drinks."

Kellie's mouth drops open. "Why not?"

"Because I don't want to." I'm really starting to regret using my fake ID to get in here, but it's the only piece of identification I have. I'm not completely opposed to drinking. I've had a drink or two at a party. But my experiences with my mom have obviously influenced me. I would never buy alcohol for her when she asked, and I won't buy it for anyone else either.

"How did you even get that bracelet?" Kellie sneers as she begins reaching for it.

Before she can touch me, a large hand wraps around her arm and stops her. "Leave her alone," Lucas says.

Kellie yanks away from him and lets her glare travel between us. Then she mumbles "such a fucking waste" and steps back, dismissing us.

Lucas disengages himself from Sophie and takes my wrist in both of his hands. Gently, he slips his fingers beneath the bracelet and begins to tug it downward. My eyes flick up and catch his. "Make a column with your fingers," he says. His face is only inches from mine.

I squeeze my straightened fingers together and Lucas manages to slide the bracelet down and off. He shoves it in his pocket and rubs my wrist.

I clear my throat and try to find my voice. "You keep saving me from rabid blondes," I tell him.

"You keep pissing them off," he answers.

"Well, thanks…again."

"Why did you get it if you don't want it?" He arches a curious brow. We're nearly eye level with each other. He's still a few inches taller than me but he's leaning down, creating an intimacy between us in the crowded club.

"My only ID is a fake one. Haven't you heard, Lucas? I've got a checkered past."

He tilts his head at me. "Yeah, I've heard. But I think you're a good girl at heart."

I can feel his warm breath on my face. He's looking at me like he knows me, and I smile to cover the nerves that are making me jittery. "Don't tell anyone. You'll ruin my rep," I reply.

His eyes, so dark in the dimly lit club, shift to my lips.

My breath freezes inside my lungs. When his gaze moves up again, what he sees in my eyes makes his nostrils flare. I wonder if the attraction I'm feeling is written all over my face. Suddenly, he squeezes my hand and releases it, leaning away from me.

"Come on guys," Myles says, jolting me back to earth where I realize our friends are standing there watching us. "Isolation is on."

I allow myself to be herded toward the stage again. But my racing heart won't quickly forget what it's like having Lucas so close, looking at me like the connection I feel to him is real, and he feels it, too. Gwen is beside me now, and I soon lose track of him. The place is too packed to get close to the stage, but we stake out a spot in the middle of the crowd and watch as the band strolls on.

A thundering cheer erupts, and I grin as the energy in the room skyrockets. I figure out who Chad is right away. He swaggers up to the microphone, his guitar swinging down past his hips. His tank shirt displays the tattoo sleeves I've heard about, and his bald head reflects the stage lights. He yells a countdown into the microphone and on four the music begins to pound. Chad takes his place in the center. When he opens his mouth, I'm amazed at his voice. Everyone was right. The band is really good.

The crowd begins moving, and fists start to pound in the air. Gwen turns to me expectantly. I smile and nod at her. My gaze flicks from Chad to the rest of the guys on stage. He's flanked by two more guitar players. When my eyes land on the bass player, they widen. I recognize him. His long stringy hair is pulled back into a ponytail. I can only see his profile, but I know I've seen him before. I continue moving to the music, my eyes staying on the bass player until he finally turns in my direction. I gasp and take a step back, bumping the person behind me who gives me a little shove back. I know where I've seen him. But how can it possibly be him? I stand frozen in place not sure what to think.

"You okay?" Gwen yells at me.

I don't answer. I stare at the man I saw talking to Apollo in front of our building in San Diego. But I need to get closer. I need to be sure. Rudely pushing through people, I inch my way forward. I vaguely hear Gwen calling me, but I keep moving, ignoring the dirty looks and the aggressive shoves. I'm only a few feet from the stage when I feel hands on my arms urging me back.

"What are you doing?" Gwen yells in my ear.

The crowd is rougher up here. They're forming a pit, and Gwen slams into me nearly knocking me down.

"Let's move back," she pleads, tugging on my arm.

"Do you know the other guys in the band?" I ask. "Do they go to our school?"

She shakes her head. "I think they're older."

When I get slammed into again, I decide there's no need to stay up here. I can wait until they're done and then try to talk to him.

As we move back, I begin to pick out familiar faces from school. Hailey and Tucker are here with Tucker's friends from history who spoke to me that first day. In front of them is Lucas. He's not watching Isolation though. His eyes are panning the crowd. Beside him is Sophie who is leaning into him. I dart my gaze away from her and ignore the pang I feel. Next to them are Jake and Kellie. Kellie is sitting piggyback on Jake, her chin resting on the top of his head. I glance at Gwen, and her slumped shoulders tell me she sees them, too. It appears we both have crushes on guys who are taken. But while Jake seems perfectly content with Kellie clinging to him, Lucas is paying no attention to Sophie.

I take Gwen's hand and lead her toward the edge of the crowd. I want to be near the door when the band exits the stage. We stand listening to the music for nearly another hour. The room is considerably hotter now. Condensation lines the walls, and my back is moist with perspiration. Finally, after a finale that rocks so hard, the entire clubs shakes, Chad yells "thank you" to the cheering crowd and heads to the side of the stage.

In the sudden quiet, my ears begin to ring. I squeeze against the wall to get to the door before the band disappears through it. The bass player is the last one off. When he passes, I reach my hand out and grab his arm. He's dripping with sweat, and my fingers slide over his skin. Finally, he turns. He glances at my hand on his arm and then up at me. He stops moving, and his eyes grow wide. I can see it in his face. He recognizes me, too.

Before I can say anything, a thick arm wraps around my waist and hauls me backward. The bass player seems to regain his senses, and he quickly disappears through the open door. I struggle to push the arm down and off me. "Let go!" I yell in frustration. I'm carried back to the bar area and unceremoniously dumped on a stool.

"No touching the band," the bouncer says, pointing his finger at my face. "Unless they ask you to." Then he winks and turns away.

I immediately stand. "What the hell was that, Raielle?" Gwen demands. Behind her, I see the rest of the group moving toward me. Most of the crowd is shifting the other way, in the direction of the exit now that the show is over.

"If I was going to throw myself at one of them, it wouldn't be that skanky guitar player," Kellie grimaces.

I ignore them all and start moving toward the stage door again. This time, it's Lucas's hands on my shoulders that stop me. "What are you doing?" he asks.

"I have to talk to the bass player." I try to move around him, but he moves with me.

"Why?" He's leaning down, placing his face in front of mine.

This time, I avoid eye contact with him. I don't know what to tell Lucas. Just saying that I recognize the bass player from San Diego wouldn't justify my reaction. But he reacted the same way to me. His reason for being outside my old apartment building has something to do with me. I can feel it.

"He wasn't interested in you. Get over yourself," Sophie says to me, tugging on the waistband of Lucas's jeans in an attempt to pull him away.

Lucas clenches his jaw and removes her hand. "We are not a couple, Sophie. Please stop acting like we are."

She gazes up at him, and her eyes fill with tears. Lucas sighs heavily.

"Nice going," Kellie snaps at him. Then she puts her arm around Sophie and leads her away.

"I'm going to catch a ride back with them," Jake announces before following behind the two girls.

"Well, this has been fun," Myles quips.

Lucas scrubs a hand over his face.

"You ready to go?" Gwen asks me.

My gaze shifts back toward the stage door. Then I nod. It might be better to find Chad at school and ask him who his band mate is. It's obvious he knows who I am. It would probably be wise if I tried to find out more rather than storming in there and making him talk to me right now.

As we head for the exit, behind me I hear Lucas ask Gwen, "Where are you parked?" After she tells him, he says, "We'll walk you."

Once we step outside, the muggy night air feels cool on my damp skin. My boots click on the pavement. Gwen and I lead the way with the three of them trailing close behind.

"Why did you and Sophie break up anyway?" I hear April ask.

I try to keep pace with Gwen, pretending I'm not listening intently to the answer. After a long silence, I think Lucas isn't going to respond. But then he says, "I was never going to feel the way she wanted me to. It wasn't fair to be with her."

"Wow, that sucks for Sophie," April says. Then she giggles.

I glance back at her wondering if she somehow got her hands on a few drinks.

When we finally reach Gwen's car, she turns and gives them all a little wave. "Thanks for walking us."

As I move toward the passenger side, Lucas steps up beside me. "Are you going to tell me what that was about?" he asks quietly, so only I can hear.

"Kellie and Sophie were rude to me, as usual," I answer glibly.

"You know that's not what I mean."

I reach for the door handle wishing I could tell him. Wishing I had someone I could trust. Knowing all too well that I don't. "Goodnight, Lucas."

He face tightens with annoyance. Once I'm seated, he closes the car door for me. Through the side mirror, I see him standing there, watching us as we drive away.

NINE

"WHERE would I find Chad Bleeker at school today?"

Myles just stares at me.

"What?" I ask.

He runs a hand through his hair. "Why do you want to know? Are you becoming another crazed Isolation fan girl?"

We're almost to April's house. I want to wrap this conversation up before we get there. "Look, I just need to talk to him. I've never seen him in school, and I have no idea how to track him down. I promise you that fandom is the last thing on my mind."

"Fine," he says, shaking his head like it's against his better judgment. "He's probably feeding his nicotine habit down by bleachers."

"Thanks. I'll see you later." I speed up and wave to April as I jog across the street. Once the school is in sight, rather than heading up the front steps, I detour around to the back. Sure enough, down on the field behind the school building, there is a group of smokers congregated on the bottom step of the bleachers.

I spot Chad surrounded by three guys who look similar to him, all wearing a sort of emo-punk fusion style with lots of visible tattoos at their wrists and necklines, and black skinny jeans that disappear into biker boots. They all stop talking to watch my approach. With tunnel vision, I see only Chad, who is eyeing me as white smoke spills smoothly from his nostrils.

I stop in front of him. "Can I talk to you?"

Someone beside me whistles. "Bleek's got another groupie. She's the hottest one yet."

"Talk," Chad orders, looking me over.

"In private," I add. More whistles sound. I roll my eyes at his friends as I wait for his answer.

He tosses his cigarette onto the ground and begins walking around to the other side of the bleachers. I follow behind him, assuming he's not trying to escape me. Once we're away from his smoking circle, he turns to me abruptly.

"If I decide to fuck you, I don't want to hear from you after. Okay? One and done. That's the deal."

I stare in disbelief and then try not to laugh. He's decent looking in a badass way, but he's mostly just an ass with ashtray breath. "That's a really interesting offer," I reply calmly. "But I just wanted to ask you a question."

He slants his head at me like he's not sure he heard me correctly.

"I was wondering if you could tell me about your bass player, the guy with the long ponytail."

Now he's squinting at me. "You mean Rob?"

I nod as though I know who that is. "Yeah, Rob…"

"Jarvis," he finishes for me.

"Right. I know him from somewhere, but I can't put my finger on it."

"Did you fuck him?"

My shoulders tense with the insults I'm holding back. "No," I reply with a hard to maintain neutral expression that is actually hurting my face. "Is he from San Diego?"

Chad barks out a laugh. "Hell no."

"Has he traveled there recently?"

"I'm pretty sure he's never left the state," he replies, growing impatient.

"Are you sure? Maybe he was in California visiting a friend or something. Maybe he was traveling for a job?"

He shakes his head and laughs again. "I don't think janitorial work requires much travel."

"He's a janitor?" I ask surprised.

Chad shrugs. "That's just his day job until we get a record deal."

"Where does he work as a janitor?"

"Don't remember," Chad replies, and his eyes zero in on my chest. "Why are you so interested in him? Maybe we wouldn't have to keep it to one time as long as you didn't get too clingy or expect anything from me."

Chad's outrageous offer barely registers as I'm beginning to second guess myself. Is it possible the bass player is not the person I saw talking to Apollo? "Well, thanks," I reply, "I'll think about it." With that, I quickly walk away, wondering when my next opportunity to take a shower is.

WHEN I arrive in history, Lucas is already there. "Are you free to go to the DMV after school today?" he asks just as I'm sitting down beside him, my thoughts still on my conversation with Chad.

"Go where?" I ask, confused.

He faces me. "The Department of Motor Vehicles, to get what you need for your learner's permit."

"Right, the driving lessons." I nod. "What does getting a learner's permit involve?"

"You need to fill out some forms, get the study book, take an eye test, and pay a fee," he rattles off casually.

"How much is the fee?"

"Around eighty bucks, I think."

I begin chewing on my pen. "I don't think that's going to work."

I see understanding dawn on his face. "I can pay—"

"No way," I interrupt him. "Thanks but you are not paying the fee for me. Once I've gotten a few paychecks, I'll go get it. Okay?"

"You have a job?" he asks.

I nod. "I start tomorrow, at Scoops. The new ice cream place in town."

He thinks for a minute. "Okay, then. We'll fast forward to the driving part after school today."

I agree to that, and all too predictably my nerves send my heart racing at the thought of being alone with him. But my mind is still on other things. I spend the rest of the morning in a state of distraction, still wondering about the guy I now know to be Rob Jarvis, and how I can find out more about him. Whether I'm mistaken or not, I can't just let it drop without knowing for sure.

Luckily, Kellie ignores both Lucas and I in our next class. I assume she and Sophie are still angry with him. When it's finally lunchtime, I'm surprised to find Chad Bleeker standing by my locker.

"Hey," he says, leaning his shoulder casually against the locker beside mine. "I was wondering if you wanted to eat lunch with me at one of the tables outside."

"Eat lunch with you?" I repeat, wondering if I heard him correctly.

"Hi," Myles says, appearing on my other side. His eyes widen when he sees who I'm with. "How's it going, Chad?"

Chad hardly spares him a look. "It's going, Giles."

"Myles," he corrects him in a tight voice.

"Right," Chad says, uninterested. "What do you say, um, sorry what's your name?" he asks me.

"Raielle," I answer, trying not to laugh at him, but failing.

He misunderstands and grins back at me. "Raielle, do you want to eat lunch with me?"

I don't want to eat lunch with him or do anything else with him. "My friend is already waiting for me in the cafeteria," I explain. I'm shocked when I see a flicker of disappointment in his face. "But you could join us," I quickly add.

Chad glances from me to Myles before answering. "Thanks, but I don't really do the caf. Maybe we could do something else another time?"

I can almost hear Myles's mouth dropping open beside me.

"Yeah, another time," I answer awkwardly not sure what's going on exactly. One minute he's being a rude asshole to me and the next he's shyly asking me out with big puppy dog eyes.

"Okay, then. Later," he says before turning and strolling down the hallway.

When I turn around, Myles is shaking his head at me.

"What?" I ask.

"I wouldn't have thought he was your type."

"Please, he's not. I just needed to ask him a question this morning. I guess he read more into it." I shrug.

Myles keeps shaking his head as we walk toward the caf.

"Okay, stop it," I scold. "You're going to give yourself whiplash."

He comes to a halt in front of the cafeteria entrance and faces me. "Look, Raielle. I know you're not naive. I don't know what your issues with guys are, but please don't hurt Lucas. He's a good friend, and he's been through a lot. If you're interested in someone else, don't string him along, okay?"

For a moment, I'm too shocked to respond. "I'm not," I finally say. "I wouldn't do that. Besides, Lucas hasn't asked me out or even acted like he wants to."

Myles takes a deep breath. He seems disappointed. "Don't play dumb, okay? It's not an attractive look for you."

97

Then he goes inside, leaving me standing there.

I'm sullen and quiet during lunch. If Gwen and her friends notice, they don't say anything. I mostly nod as Gwen describes our evening at Atlas. I'm stewing over Myles's accusation, feeling wrongly accused. If Lucas is telling Myles he's interested in me, but he's saying nothing to me, it's not my fault. Lucas is mostly silent and cryptic when he's around me. He shoots me these heated looks occasionally, but I'm not a mind reader. I've done nothing wrong. Have I? It's true that I've been trying to ignore the attraction I feel for him, but Lucas doesn't know that. Does he? Even if he did, what does he expect me to do about it? I'm not going to throw myself at him. If he's interested in me, he should say something. Actually, no he shouldn't because I'm not ready to hear it. My emotions would be all over the place if I let myself get involved with him. Just standing near him sends my pulse into overdrive. I can't imagine what it would be like to actually kiss him. My cheeks grow warm and my palms start to sweat just thinking about it. There's no question about it, getting involved with him would not be smart. What the hell did Lucas say to Myles anyway? What did Myles mean when he said Lucas has been through a lot? I think about him far too much. Yet I know virtually nothing about the guy.

I'm getting too worked up about this. I need to calm down and clear my head so I can keep my emotions in check. I abruptly excuse myself and walk quickly out of the cafeteria, purposely not looking at the usual table where Myles and Lucas sit.

In art class today, our assignment is to use pastels on paper to interpret the way we're feeling. Beside me, Grady, a beefy guy who has never spoken a word in class, is drawing two stick figures who appear to be having sex. He has a creepy little grin on his face as he's eyeing his work. The girl beside me is sketching the beach. I pull out a black pastel and proceed to cover my entire paper in solid black. I'm done in less than five minutes, and I spend the rest of class watching the clock. When the teacher comes around to collect our assignments, she's too astounded by Grady's picture to notice mine.

MANAGE to cool off as the afternoon drags on. But a minor run-in with Kellie threatens to throw me off kilter. "So, it's Chad now," she taunts as she passes me in the hallway. "You do get around."

I don't bother to deny it. I say nothing and hope that Myles is not the one spreading that rumor.

As I'm emptying the contents of my locker into my backpack at the end of the day, Lucas appears beside me. He doesn't say hello. He just stands there waiting for me, his face a mask of coolness. I clench my jaw and decide that Myles has no idea what he's talking about. I zip my backpack closed and automatically head toward the back stairwell.

"I'm parked in front," Lucas says, indicating the front stairs that I've been avoiding.

I nod and turn around. Lucas is behind me as I quickly move down the stairs, careful not to come into contact with the other students who are descending with us. I finally stop and wait once I'm out on the sidewalk in front of the parking lot.

"You in a rush?" Lucas asks, eyeing me with what looks like disdain.

"No," I reply, trying not to sound out of breath.

He walks ahead of me toward his truck. "I thought we'd drive over to the industrial park," he says without looking at me. "There's a section of parking lot there that's usually empty, and there are some private roads in the back we can use." He's the one moving quickly now, not bothering to see if I'm even with him as he speaks.

"If this isn't a good time, we can cancel the lesson," I offer since he seems less than thrilled about giving it.

He stops short and whirls around at me. "Do you want to cancel?"

I rear back, startled by his reaction. "No. You just don't seem like you want to do this. If you've changed your mind, it's no big deal. Just tell me rather than acting like a dick."

To my surprise, his glare softens. Then he nods once. "You're right. I'm sorry. I'm in a shitty mood, and I'm taking it out on you. I still want to do this if you do."

I briefly consider calling it off, but I then I think about Myles telling me that Lucas has been through a lot and decide to give him a break. Finally, I just nod at him and he opens the passenger door for me.

"I'm sorry for calling you a dick," I tell him once we're moving.

He smirks at me. "Sure, you are." After a few moments of quiet he asks, "Are you nervous for your first driving lesson?"

"It's not exactly my first lesson," I say sheepishly.

He turns, raising his eyebrows at me.

"One of the foster kids I lived with for a while liked to jack cars and take them for joyrides. I'd go along, and he'd let me drive sometimes."

His eyes grow round. Then he laughs. "I wasn't expecting you to say that."

I shrug, amused by his reaction. "My checkered past again."

He smiles at me, and I have to look away before I start wishing I could see that smile directed at me more often. "Why are you in a shitty mood?" I ask, watching the scenery out the window.

He sighs, pulling my curious eyes back to him. His fingers open and flex before closing over the steering wheel again. "I'm going to suck it up and be honest with you," he says.

My brows arch up. "Oookay…"

He's looking at the road when he says, "Chad Bleeker isn't good enough for you. He treats girls like dirt. You deserve better than him."

I sink down into my seat and shake my head. This school is unbelievable. CNN's got nothing on these kids. "I'm not involved with Chad Bleeker."

He glances at me. "You're not?"

"I sought him out this morning to ask him a question, and I guess he misinterpreted our conversation. He thinks I want to go out with him or something."

"Or something," Lucas remarks dryly. "Does this have something to do with why you wanted to talk to the bass player the other night?"

"Yes."

"If I ask you again what that was about, is there any chance you'll tell me?"

While I consider my reply, I reach back to lift the hair off my neck. The interior of Lucas's truck suddenly seems hot and cramped. "I know you were at Myles's house when he learned I was moving here. But I don't know how much you might have overheard about what happened before I came," I begin.

Lucas's eyes travel from my exposed neck, to my face, and then back to the road. "I know your mom had some," he pauses, "issues. So you spent time in foster care growing up. I know she died just before you moved here."

I shake my head ruefully. "Did Chloe give my story a G rating or did you?"

"I guess I did." One side of his mouth curls up sympathetically. "This is it," he says, maneuvering behind a brick building and into a large parking lot that has only a smattering of cars. After putting the truck in park, he sits there and looks at me. "I'm really sorry about your mom," he says quietly. He sounds so completely sincere I suddenly feel the threat of tears. I take a deep breath as I try not to cry in front of him.

"Thanks," I answer quietly. I'm still not sure exactly what Chloe divulged that day, and I'm reluctant to explain any more than he already knows. Despite the little voice in my head warning me not to say anything, I find myself doing it anyway. "I recognized the bass player.

Just before I came here, I saw him back in San Diego, talking to someone in front of our apartment building. I wanted to know what he was doing there. That's all." I shrug, pretending it's not bothering me as much as it actually is.

He wrinkles his forehead. "The bass player for Isolation? Are you sure it was him?"

"No. I'm not one hundred percent sure, but…" I glance down at my hands, positive that Lucas is going to tell me I must be mistaken.

"But you think so," he finishes.

I nod.

"Did you find anything out when you talked to Chad?" Lucas asks.

"Chad told me he works as a janitor and that he's probably never left New York State."

Lucas doesn't say anything.

"When I approached him the other night after the show and grabbed his arm, he looked at me like he recognized me, too. Actually, he looked like a deer in the headlights when he saw me, and it seemed like he just wanted to get away from me as fast as he could."

"You shouldn't have gone up to him that way," he says in a serious tone.

I nod even though I disagree. I have no idea why I'm even telling him this much.

"Maybe there's another way to find out more about him," Lucas suggests.

I glance at him, surprised that he seems to be taking me seriously. "I know his name now. Rob Jarvis. I could probably try Google next."

"If you do find anything, don't approach him again. Okay? Call me and we'll figure something out."

I laugh ruefully. We're back to this again. Not too long ago he said he wasn't made of ice, and that I could talk to him. Then he turned all rude and moody the very next day when I told him I wasn't sure about going to Atlas. Right now, his suggestion seems beyond ridiculous to me. "Lucas, I'm not going to call you. Why would I call you?"

He shifts toward me in his seat. "Because I'm trying to be your friend here." His eyes are snapping with irritation now. "Why do you want to make it so hard?"

I flinch at his words and drag my gaze away from him.

I hear him let out a heavy breath. "I'm sorry," he sighs. "I just... I don't know how to talk to you."

Hearing his defeated tone, I immediately regret my words. I look at him again, taking in his eyes, dark with frustration, and his somber expression, which he's not trying to mask for a change, and I note his presence. It's heavy and potent, and it charges the air around me. I'm staring at him so long that his expression softens, and his gaze begins to search mine.

"Myles thinks I'm going to hurt you," I say, not sure why I'm bringing that up now.

A sad resignation flickers across his features. "He's probably right."

"The fact that I could would surprise me."

He offers me a small smile and leans in closer. "I've screwed this up six ways to Sunday, haven't I?"

I study him, but as usual, I find no clue as to what he's thinking. "What do you mean?"

The intensity I've become familiar with saturates his face. "I saw you the first night you came here, Raielle. It was dark, but you were standing under the streetlight, lit from above just like an angel, and I thought you were the most beautiful thing I'd ever seen." His gaze leaves mine, like he's embarrassed by his admission.

My breath grows shallow as his words wash over me, and I remember back to that night when we first saw each other across the darkness.

"Then you were at school." His eyes meet mine again. "I couldn't believe it when you turned up in all my morning classes. I figured I'd catch your eye and smile at you. We'd talk, and I'd ask you out or maybe you'd ask me out. But you never looked my way. Not once," he says with disbelief. "I've never wanted anyone this much before, and you're the only girl in school who doesn't want to go out with me. At all," he adds with a miserable laugh. "I figure this must be karma or something."

I can feel my heartbeat echoing in my ears. I don't know whether to throw myself into his arms or call him a conceited idiot. I do finally know that the way I've felt from the first moment I saw him is not one-sided. This is why the air seems like it's sparking with electricity when we're together. But if I admit my feelings to him, feelings I've hardly even admitted to myself, what will that mean? I'm thrilled and terrified and suddenly paralyzed. And underneath it all, I realize I'm angry with him. That's the one clear emotion inside me right now, and I hone in on it.

I realize that I've been staring at him silently when he finally says, "Anyway…" Then he runs both his hands through his hair. "You don't have to say anything. I just wanted to tell you that. It doesn't have to be a big deal." Then he gets out of the truck, leaves the door open and comes around to my side. He yanks my door open and waits for me to get out. When I don't move, he says, "If you're going to drive, you kind of need to sit in the driver's seat."

He's standing over me with his arm resting on top of the open passenger door. He's trying to appear casual, but I can feel the tension rolling off him.

"This is why you've been acting so cold to me?" I ask. "You were upset because you think I don't want you, *unlike* every other girl in school?"

His jaw tightens when I paraphrase his words back to him. The part of me that was initially overjoyed at his confession is completely overtaken by the part that feels wounded by the passive aggressive way he's handled himself around me. "That first day in school, when you told Hailey to leave me alone, you didn't say a word to me. You just scowled and ignored me."

He rubs a hand over the back of his neck uncomfortably. "I know. I'm sorry about—"

"I don't care. Okay? You're the one who set the tone between us. I'm sorry I didn't notice you in class that first day. I was a little distracted by my screwed up life. When I did notice you, you were a silent, glaring ass to me. So don't stand there and tell me that I don't want you. You don't know the first thing about what I want because your pride was too wounded to ever give me a chance." With that, I jump out of the car and stomp around to the driver's side.

Lucas is on me immediately. "Wait a minute," he demands. "What does that mean?"

"You're a smart guy," I snap. "Figure it out."

When I move to get into the truck, he takes my hand and turns me around. "I think we both know I've got a speed limit IQ when it comes to you. You're going to have to explain it to me."

The suddenly hopeful look on his face chips away at my anger. I sigh and feel deflated as my head of steam evaporates, replaced by nerves and the realness of an uncharacteristically vulnerable Lucas standing before me. My eyes move from our linked hands to his expectant expression. After everything he's just told me, I have to be honest with him. Anything less would be a betrayal.

"I felt it, too. The first night I saw you," I admit, hearing the nervous tremor in my voice. "This thing between us. I feel it every time I'm near you, Lucas."

His hand tightens around mine and my blood heats. "But it doesn't matter," I whisper, trying to reclaim my hand.

He won't release me. "What do you mean? It doesn't matter?"

"Myles is right. I am going to hurt you. And you're going to hurt me, too."

He takes my other hand. "Myles is not right."

I shake my head miserably.

"Even if he is, maybe it's worth it," he says, and I don't miss the subtle plea in his tone.

"You don't understand." I can't drag him into all my crap. I can't have an honest relationship with anyone. I can never tell him everything. He'd think I'm either crazy or a freak, and he wouldn't be wrong.

Lucas sighs in frustration and drops my hands. "You're right. I don't understand."

His pained expression pierces my heart. I need him to know I'm not saying this to hurt him. I recall the way my mother used to describe the way things needed to be. She compared the way we had to live our lives to the ocean and its currents. She told me our preservation depended upon our staying in the calm shallow waters near shore. If we ventured out, we risked getting swept up in the currents and being taken out to sea, losing control, and never reclaiming it again. If I let myself fall for Lucas, I risk losing myself, and I don't know what that might mean for both of us.

"Look," he takes a step closer to me. "Here's what I've got so far. I want you, and it turns out you want me, too." He eyes me expectantly. When I reluctantly nod my agreement, he raises his hand and pushes a lock of hair away from my cheek. "Then let me explain something to you. Now that I know how you feel, there's no way I'm going to forget it or pretend there's nothing between us. I can't think of one good reason why you would want me to."

Then he closes the remaining distance and wraps his arms around me. At first, I don't give in. I remain stiff in his embrace and pretend that being held by him isn't the most amazing thing I've ever felt. I can't remember the last time someone hugged me or touched me in a way that expressed affection of any kind. But it's too hard to resist him, and I decide I'm not going to anymore.

I feel my fists unclench as my arms move down around his sides to his back. I sink into him, resting my cheek on his shoulder. Lucas makes a low noise in his throat when my arms tighten, and I return his hug. I could stand here forever absorbing his warmth and strength, with the ridged muscles of his chest and stomach pressed against me. Then his fingers slowly slide up and down the length of my spine, and our embrace begins to change. I'm suddenly hyper aware of every part of me that's in contact with him. I inhale his clean spicy scent, and I feel a tightening low in my belly. No simple embrace has ever made me feel this way. That has me once again wondering what it would be like to actually kiss Lucas. I'd probably break apart into a million pieces. I would completely lose control. This wakes me up and brings reality down on me. I force myself to pull back. I feel guilty because he really doesn't know what he's getting into with me.

"We'll take things slow," he tells me, as though reading my thoughts.

I disengage from him completely and ignore the fact that I'm already missing the feel of his arms around me.

"Trust me," he says. His eyes travel over me like a soft caress.

I feel a small smile begin because for some reason I'm already starting to trust him.

He answers with a slow, sexy grin of his own. "So, how about that driving lesson?" he asks, redirecting the conversation, taking my silent smile as his answer.

"How about it?" I repeat, and his eyes glimmer with satisfaction. He's just convinced me to see where our feelings take us, and he knows it.

Compared to the preshow, the driving lesson is somewhat anticlimactic. Lucas won't let me do anything interesting like burn rubber on the turns or take the exit onto the freeway. Basically, he has me back up, parallel park, and drive like a little old lady on the narrow back roads behind the office park.

"How about if you let me drive home?" I suggest as the lesson wraps up.

He shakes his head. "Can't. That would be illegal. Although, that fact may not deter the carjackers among us."

"Fine." I pout then open the door to switch seats with him.

Rather than passing me as we meet behind the truck, Lucas pulls me to him. "You did good," he says. Then he kisses the side of my head and releases me.

When my senses return, I join him inside his truck again. The look on his face tells me he knows how his touch affects me, and he enjoys seeing me flustered.

"You want to go again on Wednesday?" he asks.

I take a breath to calm myself. Then I shake my head. It would be so easy to lose myself in him, to forget about everything else, everything I've worked for. As much as I'd like another lesson so soon, I need to keep my priorities in order. "I don't know. I'm pretty behind in my classes. I really should spend some time trying to catch up."

"It's the end of senior year. You should be on cruise control now," he points out.

"Until I get my college acceptance letter, I'm not taking any chances. I heard they can request transcripts up until the very last minute."

"I already got into school. I applied early acceptance," he says like it's no big deal.

I'm so envious that I completely ignore his casual arrogance. "Congratulations. That must feel amazing."

He nods. "My grades can't completely tank now. They still want my final transcript, but I won't lie. It's definitely a load off."

"So where are you going?"

"Columbia."

I laugh at his off-hand tone. "Wow, Lucas. That's an Ivy League school."

He shrugs. "What about you?"

"I want to go back to California. UCLA is my first choice."

He whistles. "That's a good school, too. I hear you can minor in surfing there."

"Shut up." I laugh.

He grins at me, but it soon fades, and I wonder if he's thinking what I am. That if our relationship actually works out, we'll be nearly three thousand miles away from each other next year. But it's seriously premature to let my thoughts go there. We'll probably crash and burn long before that.

"Do you know what you want to study?" I ask.

He thinks for a minute. "I'm not really sure. Maybe journalism."

"Do you have any brothers or sisters?" I ask, changing the subject but not really. I want to know everything about him now.

"A younger brother, Liam," he smiles. "He's in sixth grade."

His easy grin tells me how much he cares for his brother. "Is your family close then? Are your parents still together?"

Lucas doesn't answer right away, and I hope he doesn't think I'm interrogating him. The muscle in his jaw that tenses when he's upset is a tight little ball. "Yes," he finally says.

I think I've just stumbled onto a sore subject, but I don't know why, and there's no time to poke at it because soon we're parked in front of Kyle and Chloe's house.

"I want your number," Lucas says. He pulls out his phone and waits while I retrieve mine since I don't know my number by heart. We exchange numbers. Then he kisses me quickly right on my lips. "See you at school tomorrow," he says.

His kiss startles me, and I can feel my cheeks heat as he watches for my reaction to him. A part of me wants to erase the satisfied smile I see growing on his face. He really can be unbearably arrogant.

"See you tomorrow," I reply, before slipping out of the truck and trying to hide the juvenile blush I know I'm still wearing. My reaction to him strikes me as ridiculous. I'm nearly eighteen, and I've certainly been kissed before. But my god, it's never been Lucas doing the kissing, and the slightest touch from him can't even be compared to the clumsy groping I've experienced in the past.

I've heard the phrase walking on air before but I've never had the need to apply it to myself, until today. As I enter the house, I really do feel lighter and happy and anxious all at the same time. I've never had a real relationship before. I've seen too many girls in my situation try to fill emotional holes with boys and sex. I've also seen too many men force physical relationships onto girls like me. I've somehow gotten lucky, and managed to avoid both. But that makes me very inexperienced. I'm pretty sure Lucas does not suffer from that same problem.

I GOT a job," I announce at dinner.

"I thought we decided you didn't need a job," Kyle says.

"I need my own money."

"What for?" Chloe asks.

I spear a piece of chicken. "For one thing, even if I do get the scholarships I've applied for, I'll have expenses for school next year."

"Raielle, as long as it's within reason, we're happy to pay for those things," Kyle says. I notice Chloe's eyes shoot over to him. I get the feeling they haven't discussed this.

"But it's other things, too," I continue. "There's the fee for a learner's permit, and I need some new clothes. You're doing so much for me already, I can't ask you to pay for those things."

"Learner's permit?" Chloe asks.

I nod. "I'm learning to drive."

"You don't know how to drive?" Kyle says surprised. "What do you mean, you're learning?"

I tense as he puts his fork down, and gives me his full attention. "Lucas, Myles's friend, offered to teach me. We went out today for the first time."

"Lucas Diesel?" Chloe says with raised eyebrows. "He's a very nice-looking boy."

I grimace at the look Kyle gives me, and wish I could sink under the table.

"Raielle, I wish you would have told me these things were worrying you. I could have taken you driving. And of course I don't mind paying for the learner's permit and new clothes. What do we have to do to make you trust us?" He shakes his head. "Please tell me what to do. Help me out here." His expression is filled with disappointment.

There's that word again, *trust*. I feel the weight of Kyle's expectations pushing down on me. I don't know why I'm finding it easier to trust Lucas than my own brother. "There's nothing to do," I tell him. "It's not you. It's me. You were seventeen years too late finding me." With that, I get up from the table and stalk down the stairs to my bedroom.

The guilt I feel for speaking to Kyle so harshly is all I can think about as I stare sightlessly at my homework. I finally give up and close my books when I hear him coming down the stairs. I watch as he stops in front of my bed and sits himself down on the end. "Where is your job?" he asks.

I move my books to the floor and give him my attention. "Scoops."

"The ice cream place?"

I nod.

"When will you be working?" His question is plainly stated. I detect no judgment or censure there.

"Two days a week after school and Saturday afternoons."

He glances down at my textbook on the carpet. "Calculus?"

"Yeah," I sigh.

"I was always pretty good in math. I guess that's why I'm an accountant." He seems to consider his next words carefully before speaking. "I'm sorry for what I said earlier, about trusting us. I should know it's not a switch you can just turn on. I know it has to be earned."

"You don't need to be sorry. I'm sorry for the way I spoke to you," I say, and I mean it. I'm disappointed in myself. I promised I would give Kyle a fair chance. That I would be more open with him, but I have no idea how to actually do that. I'm afraid I can't be the sister he wants. I also worry I can't be the girl Lucas wants. I'm afraid I'm going to disappoint them both.

"I guess we're both sorry then," he smiles. "Raielle, we're still getting to know each other. We've missed a lot of time. We're not going to make up for it in just a few weeks. But I want you to know that from what I've seen so far, I'm very proud of who you are." Then he pats my leg and says, "Goodnight."

I sit there quietly after he leaves thinking about his words. My mother told me she was proud of me sometimes, but it never meant much. She failed at so many things in her life, I didn't think it took much to impress her. But coming from Kyle, it resonates with me, and I feel a twinge of pride at his words.

Several hours later, I've finished my homework, and I'm just turning out the light when my phone buzzes on the nightstand beside me. I see I have a text from Lucas.

I wanted 2b the last person u spoke to before u went 2 sleep.

I smile at my phone and text back. *We're not actually speaking, but you are the last person I'm interacting with today.*

Are u always so literal?

I think so.

Good 2 know. Goodnight.

Goodnight.

I put the phone down and spend a long time replaying my afternoon with Lucas before I finally drift off to sleep.

TEN

DESPITE what he said about taking it slowly, Lucas does not ease me into things the next day at school. After the usual morning walk with Myles and April, I run into Gwen when we hit the schoolyard. With all of us congregated there, Lucas appears. He heads straight for me. Then he wraps his arm around my shoulder and kisses the side of my head. "Morning," he whispers into my hair, and I can feel his warm breath on my scalp just above my ear. My body temperature shoots up as he touches me, and I feel like a spotlight is shining on us. Myles and April are silently staring and Gwen could catch flies in her mouth. Everyone gathered on the front lawn seems to be noticing us.

I glance at Lucas, and I'm not surprised to see his smug face. "We're going to be late," I mumble and then extract myself from beneath his heavy arm and head inside. Predictably, Gwen moves in beside me.

"Oh my god. When did this happen?" she asks.

"Yesterday."

"What exactly went down yesterday?"

I look over my shoulder to see where Lucas is. He's still at the bottom of the steps where it appears Myles is trying to pry the same information out of him.

"Lucas gave me my first driving lesson and we talked."

She squeezes my shoulder. "You talked? What did he say? Did he declare his undying love?"

I chuckle. "Not exactly."

"So, what then?"

I shrug. "He admitted stuff. I admitted stuff. We decided we like each other. That's all."

She snorts out a laugh. "That's the most boring thing I've ever heard. You suck when it comes to dishing out details. Come on. I have to live vicariously through you. You need to give me more."

I feel myself blushing.

"I knew it!" she declares. "I knew there was something good you weren't telling me."

"He sent me a text last night."

Gwen squeals. "Did he sext you? Oh my god, that's so hot."

I roll my eyes. "No, he just said he wanted to be last person I spoke to before I went to sleep." I smile thinking about it again.

Gwen purses her lips. "Hmmm. So, no sexting. But still, kind of romantic. I guess I'll take that."

We split up to head to our lockers. I'm just closing mine when I turn around and see Chad standing there.

"Hey," he says.

"Hey," I repeat, trying to cover my wariness.

He runs his hand over his bald head. His intricate network of tattoos is on display today in a red tank shirt. "So, I was thinking maybe we could hang out after school," he says.

I'm thankful to have a valid excuse. "I'm sorry I can't. I have to work."

He nods quickly and his eyes don't meet mine. "Oh, okay. No

problem. See you later." Then he turns and heads down the hallway.

That was weird and fast. I'm wondering if I hurt his feelings. I'm surprised he even has any after my first encounter with him.

Lucas is just walking into English as I reach the classroom door. I stop for a moment and stare at him, hardly believing all that transpired between us yesterday. I watch as he lowers himself into his desk, folding his longs legs beneath him. Then he turns toward the door. His eyes brighten when he spots me. Butterflies take flight in my stomach, and his gaze follows me as I cross in front of him, taking the desk beside him.

"Oh, Lucas, you have to let me copy your notes from last week. I was completely brain dead on Friday."

I glance behind him to find pixie girl standing there.

Lucas closes his eyes for a moment before turning around. "Sure, Alison," he says, reaching for his notebook. Then she proceeds to monopolize him with inane questions about the notes until the teacher appears. I'm wondering if I should be jealous, but his obvious desire to disengage himself from her mostly amuses me.

When class ends, she's right there, trying to talk to him again. "I'll catch you later," he tells her dismissively as he falls into step beside me. I notice her frowning at me.

I'm about to ask him if he ever went out with her, when he interrupts my thoughts. "I found your guy," he says once we're in the hallway.

"What?" I ask, confused.

"Robert Jarvis. I looked him up."

I stop to face him. "You Googled him?"

He nods. "He works at the Spring Valley Assisted Living Center." Then he hands me a piece of notebook paper with the name written down on it.

I stare at it dumbly. "I can't believe you took it upon yourself to do this," I say.

He puts his fingers beneath my chin and lifts my face. "Of course I'd want to help you."

I swallow self-consciously. "Was he easy to find?"

Lucas shrugs. "I just typed in his name and Fort Upton. Then it took a little digging. I mostly found websites talking about Isolation. There's actually a fan site with personal information about all of them, including Jarvis. This assisted living place is right outside of town, not too far from here. Have you heard of it?"

I shake my head. "We're not going to find any connection between him and me, are we?"

He gives me a sympathetic half-smile. "Not if there isn't one."

I fold the paper and put it my bag.

"YOUR boyfriend just warned me to stay away from you," Lucas states, tossing his lunch tray down onto the table with a clank.

Gwen's eyes widen at his appearance. Tyler and Lisa stare up at him in mute surprise.

"Are you sitting with us today?" I ask even as he's lowering himself into the empty seat beside me.

"Why?" he growls. "Are you saving this seat for your boyfriend?"

I toss my sandwich down. "Okay, I'll bite. What are you talking about?"

He leans toward me. "Chad Bleeker just confronted me in the hallway. He said I'd better stay away from you because you're his."

"What?" Gwen and I both screech at the same time.

"Is there something you'd like to tell me?" he asks.

"Of course not," I reply defensively.

"Then why the hell would he say that?" Lucas snaps, and the people at the tables around us turn to look.

I can feel my cheeks heating. "I have no idea. I've never given him any encouragement and the fact that you think I did and I'm lying to you about it is ticking me off." I begin shoving my lunch back into my bag. Across the table, I spot Tyler and Lisa slinking away, but I'm sure Gwen is glued to her seat. She wouldn't miss this show for anything.

Lucas sits back and sighs heavily. "I know Bleeker's always full of shit. I'm sorry, okay?"

I ignore him and continue gathering my things.

"Raielle," he places a hand on my arm. "He caught me off guard," he pauses, struggling for his next sentence. "This whole thing caught me off guard."

I glance up and realize he's referring to more than just Chad.

"Did you say anything to him?" Gwen asks Lucas.

He runs a hand through his hair. "Yeah. I told him he was mistaken after I slammed him up against the wall."

"Lucas!" I cry.

"What?" he asks, starting to tense again. "Are you going to defend him now?"

I glare at him, and he glares right back. "Gwen, could you give us a minute?" I ask in a calm voice that belies the way my blood is boiling.

"Seriously?" she whines.

I level pleading eyes at her.

"Fine," she huffs.

Once she's gone, I take a deep breath and turn to Lucas. He's leaning back in his chair. The glare is gone. Now he's just staring at me stone-faced. "Chad keeps asking me out," I begin and watch the muscle in his cheek tic. "And I keep telling him no. But I think I hurt his feelings, and I don't believe there's any need for you to bully him or get physical with him."

He barks out a laugh, but he doesn't seem at all amused. "He's the one who threatened me. It doesn't bother you that he's walking around declaring that you're his?"

"Of course it bothers me. There's obviously something wrong with him. But, I don't know. I guess I feel kind of bad for him."

"You feel bad for him? He screws a different girl every night. He has groupies hanging around him all the time. You do not need to feel bad for the man whore of the school."

I roll my eyes at his reaction. "Fine. I'll talk to him. I'll ask him to stop saying untrue things about me."

He sits forward. "No, you won't. You'll stay away from him."

"You're overacting," I complain, annoyed.

"I mean it, Raielle."

I blink in disbelief at him. "What makes you think you can tell me what to do?"

"I'm not telling you what to do."

"Sounds like it to me."

He shakes his head. "I just think that staying away from him is the smart way to handle this. Eventually he'll get the picture. If he doesn't, I'll have to explain it to him again."

"This whole thing is ridiculous," I mutter. "I can't believe we're fighting about it."

Lucas reaches over and takes my hand. From the corner of my eye, I'm aware that most of the cafeteria is watching our display. "Is it wrong that fighting with you turns me on as much as everything else about you does?" His hand tightens around mine because he thinks I'm going to pull away in embarrassment. But I surprise myself by smiling at him instead because I feel the same way, completely alive when we're together, fighting or not.

"So, I was thinking," he begins, my hand still in his. "I could pick you up after work tonight and we could go get some dinner."

"Okay," I answer, letting my irritation dissolve away. Kyle already said he would come get me after my shift, but I don't think he'll mind if I tell him Lucas and I are going out.

We gather our things and leave the cafeteria together.

When I text Kyle to let him know that Lucas is getting me after work and we have dinner plans, he surprises me by texting a short reply back, telling me I have to be home by ten on school nights. I get the feeling he is not pleased.

GWEN is waiting by my locker after school. She informs me that she's driving me to work and during the ride, I'm going to tell her everything about Lucas and me.

"You haven't really kissed him yet?" she asks as we're sitting in traffic, waiting to get out of the school parking lot.

I shake my head. She already dismissed the peck he gave me as nothing more than a preview. "This is barely twenty-four hours old. We mostly just argue so far," I laugh.

She clears her throat and glances at me. "I overheard something today, but I'm not sure if I should tell you or not?" she hedges.

"Tell me what?" I ask, of course.

"I heard Sophie and Kellie at their lockers after lunch. They were basically talking shit about you."

"That's not exactly a big surprise," I reply shrugging it off. Then my curiosity gets the better of me. "What were they saying?"

She doesn't answer.

"Gwen?"

She blows the hair out of her eyes and glances warily at me. "It was mostly Kellie. She said that you're basically a slut, and the only reason you have Lucas panting after you is because you're leading him around by his penis."

"Great," I mutter, resting my head back against the seat. "If Lucas hears this, he's going to go crazy."

"He should," she says.

"How did I get pulled into all this drama? I just wanted to keep my head down and finish my senior year."

"It's high school, Raielle. Drama is a required part of the curriculum." She pulls up in front of Scoops and turns to me. "So, you're all in on this? No more denying it. No more pretending that there's nothing between you and Lucas? You're going to go for it?"

I chuckle at her. "Yeah, I guess I am. I couldn't deny it if I wanted to."

"Smart girl," she says.

"Thanks, Gwen. For being so supportive." I feel badly that Jake is so obviously interested in Kellie and Gwen is pretending that it doesn't matter to her. "What do you think about Tyler?" I ask.

"What do you mean?" she asks, wrinkling her nose at me. "You mean, do I like him?"

I nod. "He's adorable in a subtle geeky kind of way. I don't think there's anything going on between him and Lisa."

She shakes her like it's a crazy suggestion. "No way. Now, go. You're gonna be late."

"Will you think about it? I'm pretty sure he's interested. I catch him looking at you a lot."

This news seems to surprise her, but then she shakes her head resolutely. "Nope," she says, popping the P.

I frown at her reply. Then after thanking her for the ride, I head into Scoops.

"I'm Stacy," the owner greets me. She's extremely short and petite with a mass of dark curly hair that rests stiffly on her shoulders. "It's just you and me tonight. On Saturdays, you'll be working with Jacinda. She's my niece. You guys will get along great."

Stacy has me fill out all the employee forms, and then she proceeds to show me where everything is. She tells me how much ice cream to use for each size cup and cone. Then she demonstrates the cash register to me. What I hadn't counted on was how cold it would be in the store, which of course I should have anticipated. Stacy is bubbly and friendly, and she disappears into the back after my brief orientation.

My first night is pretty quiet. Only a handful of people come in. I'm so cold I'm not even tempted to eat any ice cream myself. I'm actually shivering when Lucas arrives to get me at seven.

"Jesus, it's cold in here," he says. "How was your first day?"

"Good," I reply. I poke my head into the back to let Stacy know I'm leaving. Once we're in Lucas's truck, I reach over and crank the heat up as high as it will go.

He glances over at me. "You need to dress warmer when you're working."

"Yeah, that's the main takeaway from my first day. By the way, Kyle said I have to be home by ten on school nights."

He gives a little surprised laugh. "Okay, then. Well, we're just going to a little place I know in Ridgeton. That should get you back in time."

"Thanks. I'm starving by the way." I reach my icy hands toward the heater vents.

"We can't have you going hungry on my watch. What the hell?" he mutters, glancing up at the rearview mirror.

"What is it?" I ask, turning around to see what he's looking at.

"It's Grady Callahan and one of his idiot friends. They're all over the road back there."

I look back again and see a Mustang close behind us. Suddenly, its engine roars to life, and it moves up to pass us on the left. When the car is even with us, a guy hangs his head out the passenger window and whoops loudly at us before tossing an empty beer can onto the road. The

Mustang quickly overtakes us and speeds ahead, disappearing around the bend.

"Morons," Lucas mutters.

"Dangerous ones," I add. "Grady's in my art class. He drew a lewd picture the other day. I think he freaked the teacher out."

"Did he freak you out, too?" He arches a brow at me.

"Yes," I reply. "The thought of Grady having sex and possibly procreating does freak me out."

Lucas laughs, and it's a deep rumbling sound that vibrates through me. Smiling, I let my eyes travel over the contours of his face, following the defined line of his jaw, darkened by stubble, as it disappears into the shiny waves of his overgrown hair. Then I follow the curve of his shoulder down to where it widens into his bicep and then tapers into a forearm corded with muscle. When my gaze settles on the strong hand that grips the steering wheel, I think of that hand on my skin, of his long fingers touching me. Just then, he glances at me and my eyes flick up to his. Despite the darkness, I recognize the look I see on his face because I'm sure it mirrors my own. *Desire.*

When Lucas turns back toward the road, his eyes widen. "Fuck!" he yells and hits the brakes, throwing his arm out in front of me to hold me against the seat. Startled, I peer out the windshield and see Grady's Mustang sitting across the middle of the road. The front of the car is folded in on itself like an accordion.

Lucas maneuvers the truck over to the side, and I see the guy who stuck his head out the window stumble around the car and drop to his knees. His face is covered with blood. "Call an ambulance," Lucas orders as he jumps out and rushes over to the Mustang.

With a shaky hand, I dial 911 and give them our location, explaining what happened. Then I get out, too, and approach the car. Lucas is on the other side, trying to pry open the driver's side door.

"I smell gasoline. Get back!" Lucas yells to me.

Feeling my body fill with adrenaline, I run the final few yards to the car. When I reach the guy on the ground, a burst of bright energy flows through me, but I continue past him. Peering through the window, I see Grady slumped over the wheel.

"I said get the hell away!" Lucas reaches in through the open driver's side window, trying to get a grip on Grady. The door itself is bent, and I figure he can't get it open. I watch as he gives up and runs around to the other side where I'm standing. The passenger door swings open easily, and Lucas begins to pull Grady out that way. I move beside him and reach in to dislodge Grady's heavy boot, which is wedged beneath the steering wheel. "There's someone in the back, too," I tell Lucas. He grunts under Grady's heavy weight, finally pulling him free and laying him on the pavement.

When I push the front seat forward and reach in toward the person in the back, he moans and begins to sit up. I startle when Lucas's arm winds around my waist and hauls me backward, wordlessly setting me aside as he leans in to grab the last person. I move back to the first guy still in the road. I put a hand beneath each of his arms and start trying to pull him away from the car. The smell of gasoline is strong, and I can hear liquid dripping onto the ground from beneath the Mustang.

I pull with more urgency, and the moment my fingers graze his bare skin, there's nothing I can do to stop the pull his injuries have on me. As we're moving, my fingers remain on the skin of his arms and his bleeding head is lolling across my stomach. I know I'm healing his wounds; the head gash, some broken ribs and internal bleeding. I feel lightheaded and energized as I lay him down gently and release him. He's already sitting up, looking around, seemingly confused.

I turn and notice Lucas struggling to pull Grady away from the car. The third person is moving on his own, looking stunned. When I reach Lucas to help him with Grady, I freeze. Grady is badly hurt. Blood is leaking from his ear. The front of his forehead appears dented in. He's fighting for his life. I know I can't touch him. I can't risk healing someone who isn't meant to recover. Just as I back away, I hear the sirens approaching. I'm fighting my natural instinct, and it's turning on me with a vengeance. I move further and further away, all the way back to Lucas's truck. I lean against the front grill, watching through a haze of misery, as Lucas talks to the paramedics who have just arrived. My skin breaks out in a cold sweat, and I sink down onto my knees. The guy I healed is stomping around now, yelling at the paramedic who is trying to look at him. I hear more sirens and watch as a fire truck arrives. The night is lit with strobing red lights and dense with static-laced voices streaming over radios.

The front of the Mustang emits a loud crack just before it bursts into flames. I hear more hollering and watch as Lucas suddenly appears frantic, his eyes darting around the scene. When his panicked gaze lands on me, his relief is clear. He rushes over, brushing past the firefighters and their heavy gear. I watch as they spray white mist at the car.

Lucas crouches down in front of me. "Are you okay?" he yells over the noise around us. His face is shiny with perspiration, and his grey shirt is spotted with blood.

I nod and watch as his eyes travel over me and widen. When I look down, I realize that I'm soaked in blood. "I'm fine," I tell him.

He lowers himself to the ground and pulls me into a tight embrace. From over Lucas's shoulder, I see them wheeling Grady away on a gurney. Once he disappears inside the ambulance, my body begins to settle down. My senses clarify again as the haze clears, and I lean into Lucas, feeling his arms tighten around me.

"Why didn't you stay away from the car like I asked?" he says beside my ear.

I pull back and stare into his eyes. "That's a seriously stupid question."

He nearly smiles as he cups my cheek in his hand. Then he slowly lifts me to my feet. "They told me the police have some questions for us," he says.

We both turn when the paramedic who was arguing with Grady's friend walks by. "He's fine. I don't know where all the blood came from," he tells the other paramedic.

The same friend then approaches us. "Grady is so dead," he says, shaking his head. "His parents are gonna shit a brick when they see his car."

"Un-fucking-believable," Lucas mutters, taking my hand and pulling me away from him.

Over the next half hour, we stay at the scene and answer questions for the police. Despite the denials of drinking we hear from both of Grady's passengers, Lucas and I tell the officers the truth. We're exhausted when they inform us that we can go.

"Our first date didn't exactly go the way I planned," Lucas frowns as we're approaching Kyle's house. "I guess I lied when I said you wouldn't go hungry on my watch."

"That's okay. I kind of lost my appetite."

When Lucas parks, Kyle storms through the front door, and he marches toward the truck. "I said ten o'clock, Raielle. Do you know what time it is?"

Lucas jumps out and walks around to meet Kyle. At the same time, I open the door and lower myself down. Kyle's eyes widen with shock when he sees us. "What on earth happened?"

"We came across a car accident on the way to dinner. We stopped to help," Lucas explains as Kyle stares at my bloody shirt. I feel like I'm going to jump out of my skin if I don't get these clothes off me soon.

"Are you both all right?" Kyle asks, his gaze jumping between us.

"We're not hurt," I reply. "Just really wiped out."

"Come inside," Kyle puts his arm around me. "Goodnight, Lucas," he says dismissively.

Lucas seems torn, like he doesn't want to leave me. I'm about to protest Kyle's treatment of him, but Lucas shakes his head, stopping me. Then he tells me goodnight before getting back into his truck.

"You could have been nicer to Lucas," I say as we're walking inside. "What happened wasn't his fault."

"We'll talk about him later. Let's get you changed, and then you can tell me what went on tonight."

I stand under the shower watching the red water pool at my feet before it finally runs clear again and disappears down the drain. I think of our kitchen table and the last time I saw so much blood. It wasn't a hard decision not to heal Grady tonight. I have no emotional ties to him. But what if I'd returned home that day just a little earlier, while my mother was still breathing, while there was still time to do something? After all she'd told me about not changing fate and not playing God, I would have disregarded it all to save her. Let the consequences be damned. I never understood why the need to heal would still be so strong when I couldn't use it. If a person was meant to die, why did every part of me still want to heal them so badly?

When I emerge from the shower, Kyle and Chloe are waiting in the kitchen with a cup of tea. I'm beyond exhausted, and the last thing I feel like doing is reliving the evening by talking to them about it. I toss my balled up bloody clothes into the trash before sitting down with them. I don't touch the tea, and I give them the briefest account possible. Finally, Kyle reads my mood and tells me to just go to bed, adding that I don't have to go to school tomorrow if I'm not up to it.

When I retrieve my phone from my bag to charge it, I see there's a text from Lucas waiting for me.

U okay?

I text back. *Yes. U?*

Good. Grady's an idiot but I hope he's ok.

Me 2.

Get some sleep, beautiful. Goodnight.

I stare at his text for a long time before I respond. *Goodnight.*

ELEVEN

"**H**OW are you feeling this morning?" Kyle asks.

I'm surprised to see him still at home when I come upstairs. Down the hallway, I can hear Chloe getting Penelope ready for school. "I'm fine." I see my lunch bag ready on the counter.

"Can I talk to you for a minute?" He sits down at the kitchen table and waits for me to join him.

I have a bad feeling that this is either about Lucas or my job again. "You're seeing Lucas Diesel?" he asks with a frown.

I'm disheartened to have guessed correctly although his obvious disapproval is surprising. "I guess," I answer, not being intentionally vague, just not yet knowing what Lucas and I are doing exactly.

"You guess?" he asks.

"Last night was our first time out."

"It was a pretty eventful night for your first date," he comments. "Raielle, I'm not your parent. I know that. I know that you've had very little parenting and probably very few rules to follow most of the time." He leans forward, clearing his throat, and resting his elbows on the table.

"I've been playing this guardian thing by ear since you got here. But as far as boys go, I think we need to have some guidelines."

He watches for my reaction. Since I have no idea what he's about to say, I don't react at all. I just wait and watch while he tries not to let his discomfort show.

"Are you...?" he begins and then stops. "Do you need...?" He stops again.

Behind me, I hear Chloe release an exaggerated breath. I swivel in my chair, startled. I hadn't heard her come in. "What he's trying to say is, if you're sleeping with Lucas or with any other boy, we hope you're being safe about it."

I turn back to see Kyle wincing slightly. But he also appears to be relieved that it's been said, and he didn't have to say it. I may be lacking in experience, but I learned about sex early on, probably far earlier than most girls. My mother was never shy or discreet about it. That's also how I learned that when sex was about something other than love, it could leave you feeling pretty empty. "I'm not having sex," I state clearly for both of them. "There's nothing for you to worry about."

"Okay. Good," Kyle says abruptly, ready to bolt. He kisses Chloe, Penelope, and then me quickly on the cheek, completely surprising me, before leaving for work.

Once he's gone, Chloe aims a skeptical look at me. "If you're sleeping with Lucas, let me get you on birth control. No offense, but you really don't need to get pregnant right now."

I stand, not surprised, but somehow disappointed in her. "I can't get pregnant if I'm not having sex." I decide not to take the lunch she's made me, and I walk outside to meet Myles.

"Everyone is talking about how you and Lucas were heroes last night," Myles says when I join him on the sidewalk.

"I didn't do anything. It was Lucas."

He shakes his head at me. "I talked to him this morning. He said you were right in it with him."

"Is that how you found out about it? From Lucas?" I'm surprised that he would call people first thing this morning to tell them.

He shakes his head. "April told me last night."

"How did she find out?"

"Her younger brother is friends with Chris Andover. I heard he was in the car, too."

I assume he was one of the passengers. It's unbelievable how quickly news travels here.

Gwen is on me the minute we arrive at school. "I just heard. Why didn't you call me?" Soon, the students, who have only stared at me since I began here, approach me for the first time and ask me for details. Even the person I think must be Chris Andover strolls right up to me like we're best friends. "Can you believe it? I got tagged for underage drinking," he says, laughing. "Grady's in serious shit," he adds, sounding shockingly unconcerned about his friend.

"I know," April chimes in. "I heard he's in a coma or something. Lara told me his room is right down the hall from Derek Hoffman's. He's that junior that was diagnosed with Hodgkin's Disease. Just last week they were both in school and now they're on the same floor at the hospital. Makes you appreciate what you have, doesn't it?" she asks Myles, placing her arm around his waist.

He nods wordlessly.

I realize that this Derek must be the person who brushed against me in the stairwell.

"I heard the car was on fire when Lucas was pulling Grady out? Is that true? He's so brave," a girl I don't know asks me, gripping my arm as she's talking.

I shake my head and try to step away from her, but I bump into someone else on my other side. Too many people are touching me and trying to talk to me, it's overwhelming and uncomfortable, and I need some space. I turn and squeeze through the people crowding in behind me. "Hey," someone yells at me. With my head down, I keep walking toward the school entrance. I'm nearly to the door when a wall of muscle steps in front of me, and two hands land on my shoulders. "What's the rush?" Lucas asks.

I breathe out, relieved it's him. "We're famous this morning."

He nods curtly. "Looks that way."

"I can't believe how quickly everyone found out."

"That's Fort Upton for you," he says, ushering me through the door with a hand on my lower back.

"Weirdoes," Gwen says as she follows in behind us. "They don't say a word to you until today. Now that they want all the dirt, they act like they're your best friends."

"It will settle down soon enough, and they'll find something else to talk about," Lucas says. Then he turns back to me. "You okay today?"

"I'm fine. You?"

His eyes hold mine as he takes a step toward me. "I'm good." Then he reaches out and brushes my cheek with the back of his hand.

Gwen clears her throat. "So, um, yeah. I'll see you guys later."

I give Gwen an embarrassed wave, but Lucas doesn't seem to notice her departure. "I want a do-over," he says.

"A do-over?"

He nods. "For our date. This Friday night. You in?"

He's standing so close, I feel lightheaded. "I'm in," I reply, glad my voice sounds normal despite the giddy schoolgirl screeches of joy going on inside my head.

'M starving once I get home. Not taking the lunch Chloe made for me out of spite was a stupid move. I stayed away from the cafeteria because I didn't want to talk about the accident anymore. People continued to approach me all day. I did my best to ignore them and pretty soon they were eyeing me with disdain and avoiding me again just the way I like it. Lucas handled it better. He obviously wasn't enjoying the attention but he at least provided curt answers and wasn't overtly rude. I can't say the same for me.

At dinner that night, Kyle makes Penelope's day. "We're going to Papa's house on Friday for his birthday," he announces.

"Yeah!" she claps. "Can I help him blow out his candles?"

"Of course," Chloe smiles.

Penelope erupts in cheers again.

Kyle looks at me as his fork pauses in the air. "You're invited, too, Raielle. My father really enjoyed seeing you the other night. He'd like it if you could be there."

I swallow my lasagna. "Um, thanks, but I've already got plans."

"With Lucas?" Chloe asks.

I nod.

"Bring him along," she suggests.

I glance at Kyle for his reaction. He nods his approval.

"Come to Papa's birthday party with us, Raielle," Penelope says. "Pleeeeease," she adds.

"They're having it early for Penelope. There should be time for you two to do something on your own afterward," Chloe suggests.

"I'll ask him," I finally reply. "And…thanks for inviting us."

I call Lucas when I get back downstairs to my bedroom. "I can't believe it," he says when he answers. "Ms. Raielle Blackwood is calling me on the phone."

I laugh at him. We've never actually spoken on the phone before. For some reason, having his voice directly in my ear feels more intimate than it should.

"This is the first time you've initiated a conversation with me," he says matter-of-factly.

"It is?" I pretend not to realize this even though I know it's true. Just calling him took a little internal pep talk.

"True story. I'm hoping it's going to be a trend."

I chuckle before taking a deep disappointing breath. "About Friday night," I begin. "Kyle and Chloe want me to go with them to a birthday party for Kyle's dad."

After a few seconds of silence, he finally replies. "Okay," he says in a flat voice.

I wasn't sure if I was going to extend their invitation to him figuring he'd never want to go, but the subtle hurt tone of his voice changes my mind. "But I don't want to cancel our plans. I'm just throwing a wrench into things. They said I could invite you, but I completely understand if you don't want to go."

"Do you want me to go to the birthday party with you, Raielle?" He sounds unsure.

I close my eyes and shake my head at no one. Now I've made him think that I don't want him to go. I really am terrible at this. "Yes," I reply. Then I hear him laughing quietly. "What?" I ask confused.

"That was really hard for you to admit, wasn't it?"

"No," I say, frowning at the phone. "I'm happy I can amuse you, Lucas." He's so annoying. Now I'm wondering if he was really upset at all. "I have to go and finish my homework now."

"Don't let me keep you. But feel free to call back if you start missing me," he says, his tone teasing.

"Yeah. You should wait by the phone."

He laughs, low and deep. "Goodnight, beautiful."

I sigh. "Goodnight, Lucas."

After another hour of studying, I turn off the light, lie down on my bed, and stare up at the shadows on the ceiling, my mind too occupied to slow down for sleep. I feel the nervous flutter of butterflies lingering from my conversation with Lucas. He called me beautiful tonight in that thick rich tone his voice gets when all the intensity he carries around with him is focused directly on me. I'm still having a hard time believing what's happening between us. Back home, I easily avoided forming relationships with the people around me. They came and went. When they went, it was no big deal. But here, it's different. I'm not sure what it is about his place, but I don't want to push Lucas away like I normally would. I don't want the way he makes me feel to disappear. I know it's risky to be with him, but for once, I want to stop being cautious and start living my life. I don't want to walk away from the people here in Fort Upton. If I had to leave tomorrow, I would miss them. That fact should be scaring the hell out of me. But it doesn't. It feels like a tiny seed of happiness growing inside me. I could ignore it or I could do something really terrifying—I could nurture it. Maybe, I could even watch it flourish.

TWELVE

THE plan is for Lucas to meet us at the house. He and I will follow Kyle in his truck. Alec and Linda live in Fort Upton, but after Kyle tried unsuccessfully to give me directions, we decided caravanning is the best idea.

Penelope is jumping up and down, excited that she gets to wear her new red corduroy dress with the ladybugs embroidered on it. "Do you like my dress?" she asks everyone multiple times.

I hadn't realized this was a dressy affair, and I appear in dark jeans and a black turtleneck. Chloe assures me that I look fine. I don't feel fine though. I feel surprisingly nervous at the thought of spending the evening with Lucas and my newfound family, none of whom I knew only a month ago. It almost feels as though I'm living someone else's life.

The doorbell rings right on time at five o'clock. I open the door to find Lucas standing there looking so pleased and perfect, I can't tear my eyes away from him. His rich, chestnut hair is more styled than usual, but the unruly waves stubbornly remain where the overgrown ends meet his shirt collar. He's wearing faded jeans and a navy Henley shirt that compliments his dark blue eyes. Those same eyes are traveling over me, and they sparkle with mischief when they land on mine, drawing me in with that electricity that always buzzes between us.

"Hey," he says in a quiet voice.

I smile at him just as Kyle appears beside me. "Hello, Lucas."

He sobers slightly as he returns Kyle's greeting. Chloe and Penelope emerge from behind me to say hello. After Penelope elicits a compliment on her dress from Lucas, we all head to our cars.

"Relax, Ray," Lucas whispers as we walk toward his truck.

I take a deep breath and nod at him.

"I called Grady's parents," he says once we're settled inside. "They told me he's in a coma. I guess the rumor's true."

"Oh, no," I reply, sinking into my seat, picturing the way he looked as Lucas pulled him from the car.

"He's got some brain swelling his dad told me. They still don't know if he's going to be okay."

"How did his dad sound?"

Lucas shrugs. Then he slides his hand across the seat and wraps his fingers around mine. "He sounded like you'd expect—not real good."

I move my hand toward him across the seat so he doesn't have to reach so far to maintain his hold on me.

"So this party is for Kyle's dad?" he asks, after clearing his throat.

"Yeah," I nod.

"Your mom was married to him, but you never met him before you came here?"

"No. I'd never met Kyle either." He doesn't seem surprised by this. So, I assume he knew, probably from Chloe.

"How are you getting along with Kyle and his family?" He squeezes my hand reassuringly. I get the feeling he believes I won't want to answer his questions. But, to my surprise, I don't mind.

"We're getting along fine. Kyle's pretty decent. For some reason, I think he really wants to be my brother."

Luke glances at me, surprised. "Why do you put it that way?"

I look down at our clasped hands, and I realize that I feel comfortable with him, safe even. It's so unusual for me to feel this way it takes me a moment to recognize it.

"Raielle?" he prompts when I don't reply.

I put my wandering thoughts aside. "I don't know," I say. "Our mom ran out on him. She never once mentioned him to me. He doesn't owe me anything. I wouldn't blame him if he resented me."

"Resent you?" he asks surprised. "You had nothing to do with any of that."

"I know. It's just all so screwed up. I guess it's hard to know how we should feel or what we should be to each other."

Kyle's brake lights flash at us, and I see that he's parking in front of a sprawling house set back away from the road. "This must be it," Lucas comments, peering out the windshield at the white columned entrance and the circular driveway. The yard has a rolling front lawn filled with perfectly pruned bushes.

As we're getting out of our cars, the front door opens, and Alec steps out. "Papa!" Penelope yells and she runs into his waiting arms. I see several cars filling the driveway, and I wonder if other guests have been invited.

When we meet at the front door, Kyle introduces Lucas to Alec and then to Linda who appears in the entryway, ushering us all inside. "We have a few friends here, too. I think you know them all, Kyle."

We walk through a bright alcove lit by a skylight in the vaulted ceiling. The noise level rises as Linda leads us into a formal living room with a fireplace and two long beige couches that face each other. An older couple stands as we enter, and I feel Lucas grow tense beside me. I glance at him curiously, but he doesn't acknowledge me.

I nod at each person I'm introduced to, and then I immediately forget their names as I ignore the way their eyes linger on me. I imagine there must have been lots of talk about me when word got out that I was moving here.

"We know Lucas," says the woman. Her grey hair is clipped short, and she's wearing thick glasses dotted with rhinestones. "How are your parents?" she asks him.

"Fine, thank you," he responds in that cold emotionless tone he wears like armor. It's the tone he used with me in the beginning and one I hope to never have directed at me again.

I settle beside him on a loveseat in a corner of the room and take his hand in mine. This time I'm the one reassuring him. He offers me an uneasy smile that doesn't reach his eyes.

I watch as Penelope runs around excited to be here, asking when we'll have the birthday cake. Linda explains that she's made a buffet dinner and tells us to go ahead and serve ourselves. "Are you okay?" I ask Lucas once everyone begins to move toward the dining room.

He nods.

"Who are those people?"

"They know my family from church," he answers.

"It seemed like you were upset to see them."

"Not now. Okay?" he snaps, releasing my hand and standing.

For a moment, I'm too shocked to move. But then I stand, too, propelled up by my simmering reaction to his tone. Lucas has undergone another mood transplant. I decide to put some space between us, and I move toward the fireplace mantle where there are several photographs displayed. I see a younger Alec standing with a gangly teenage Kyle who is holding a football. Then there's one of Alec, Linda, and several other people standing behind Kyle who is dressed in a red cap and gown. Beside that is a photograph of Penelope hugging Alec. When my eyes go back to Kyle's graduation picture, I look closer and gasp. I pull the framed photo down to see it better.

"What is it?" Lucas asks, moving beside me to look at the picture.

I'm staring at a smiling blonde woman standing near Kyle. "She looks just like my mother." I turn with the picture in my hand. When I see Penelope dashing by, I stop her. "Pen, do you know who this woman is in the picture?" I point to the blonde.

She glances at it. "That's Grams. I haven't seen her in a long time."

"Grams?" I repeat.

"That's your grandmother, Raielle," Chloe says coming up behind Penelope.

I stare at Chloe and then back down at the photograph again. "When did she die?" I ask, trying to figure out how old she is here. My mother never showed me any pictures of my grandmother.

"Go find Daddy," Chloe tells Penelope. Penelope glances at her mother unsure. "Go on," Chloe prods her. When Penelope runs off, Chloe turns to me. "She's hasn't passed on. But we don't bring Penelope to see her anymore. She's senile, and she doesn't recognize Penelope. It just upsets them both."

"She's alive," I whisper, and it feels like my heart just jumped up into my throat. "My mother told me both her parents died a long time ago."

Chloe purses her lips disapprovingly.

"Where does she live?" Lucas asks.

"She's in a nursing home." Chloe's eyes travel between Lucas and me. "I'm sorry we didn't tell you, Raielle. We didn't realize you thought she was dead. She wouldn't know who you are anyway. Her mind is gone."

"What nursing home?" Lucas asks.

"It's a place called Spring Valley. But I think you should really talk to Kyle about it if you want to see her."

I nod at her, picturing the words written on the piece of notebook paper Lucas handed me in school that day. Somehow, I knew she was going to say that place. Before the words left her mouth, I knew.

Chloe smiles hesitantly and turns to go back to the dining room.

"There's your link," Lucas states.

I shake my head trying to process this. "She lied about so many things," I mutter close to tears. "Why would my mother pretend not to have any family? They've all been here the whole time."

"I don't know," he says softly.

I feel his arm come around me reassuringly.

"So now we have a link, but what does it mean?" I ask. "I need to see her. I want to see her anyway." I turn my face up to his. "She looks so much like my mother. If she'd had the chance to grow old, this is probably how she'd look."

His blue eyes reflect my stunned image back at me. "You should talk to your brother. Tell him you want to meet her," he says.

I nod, feeling confused and betrayed by her all over again.

Lucas nuzzles his nose into my hair. "Have we stayed long enough?" he asks.

He's back to himself again, and I decide not to question it as I take a shaky breath, feeling my body automatically responding to his closeness. I'm startled by the liberties he takes with me now, the way he touches me and stands so close to me. I'm not used to it and somehow even as it's making me uneasy, I'm reveling in it. "We haven't even eaten yet," I say.

He sighs dramatically, but leads me toward the dining room. I don't have much of an appetite, but the food looks really good. Linda can cook, and she obviously went to a lot trouble for Alec. I learn that Alec turned fifty-six yesterday, which makes him almost a decade older than my mother. She was only twenty when she married him and twenty-one when she had Kyle. She was so young when she started her family here and then walked away from it.

We end up staying until after Penelope and Alec blow out his number five and number six candles. Penelope puffs out her cheeks and funnels air through her rounded lips, clapping and screeching when the bright flames dissolve into tendrils of smoke. As the applause dies down, Linda jokes that she couldn't find a cake big enough to hold fifty-six individual candles. After pieces of cake are passed around, Lucas and I say our goodnights and head out into the chilled darkness.

"I had a plan for tonight, but I'm calling an audible," he states once we're on the road.

"Okay," I answer, peering out the window, smiling at his football-speak, wondering if this is some kind of test. My mom dated enough football fans that I inevitably absorbed some useless knowledge, although, it's coming in handy now. "What was the original plan and what's the new one?" I ask.

When he doesn't answer right away, I turn to see his stunning smile. "What?" I ask, innocently.

"You know what calling an audible means," he says, clearly impressed.

I chuckle, figuring I was right about the silly test. "You're such a guy."

He points at me. "Don't you forget it."

"So, those plans?" I ask, rolling my eyes. "Are you going to tell me about them?"

"No. I'm going to save my first plan as a surprise for another time. Tonight, I want to take you somewhere I like to go."

"Where?"

"You'll see." He glances at me and his eyes shine in the darkness. A few miles later, Lucas turns onto a dirt road and comes to a stop behind a chain link fence. When I look out the windshield, I see a field with a baseball diamond. I give Lucas a curious glance.

"This is it," he says. Then he reaches in back and grabs a blanket before getting out of the truck. I'm just stepping down onto the dirt when he comes around and takes my hand.

"This isn't where your team plays, is it?" I ask. I thought the high school had its own baseball field.

Lucas laughs. "No. This is a little league field. This is where I played as a kid."

I glance at the low bleachers behind first and third base and I try to picture Lucas as a child swinging a bat and running the bases. "What position did you play?"

"First base, then and now."

"I didn't get the feeling you were that into baseball," I comment as he leads me down a small grassy hill.

"I love it. We just don't have much of a team here. Hockey is a big deal at our school. Baseball isn't even a close second."

He directs me to the bleachers and once we're both seated on the cool metal bench, he reaches around and settles the blanket on my shoulders. I still beneath it, wondering how many other girls have made use of this conveniently located backseat blanket. But the warmth settling in helps me to push those unfair and unwanted thoughts aside. "Won't you be cold?" I ask as I pull the blanket around me and hunker down.

He seems surprised by my concern, but then his lips turn up. "I don't have your thin west coast blood."

"Hey," I feign offense before offering a sincere thank you. Then I glance up at the canopy of stars twinkling overhead, and I'm drawn in by the quiet beauty of this place. "This is amazing. In the city, you never see stars like this," I say, my voice quiet with reverence.

Lucas inches closer to me so that our shoulders and legs are touching. A shiver runs through me, and I'm hyper aware of every place his body meets mine.

"I owe you an apology," he says.

I turn toward him and look into his eyes. I see the same intensity that always seems to be there, but tonight it's tempered by a gentleness that surprises me. His gaze is filled with a tenderness I know he doesn't display often, and I can't help but wonder why it's there for me. I wonder how I've earned it.

146

"When you asked me who those people were at the party, I shouldn't have shut you down that way," he continues.

"Apology accepted," I say without hesitation. His sincerity is too obvious and the night is too beautiful to wreck it by holding a grudge.

He seems surprised. "Just like that?"

"Just like that." I tilt my head at him. "Am I so combative that you expect a fight on everything?"

He grins at me. "Basically, yeah."

I lean further into him and laugh. "Shut up."

His arm comes around my shoulder, and he pulls me against him. After sitting quietly this way for a moment, Lucas says, "Those people at the party know my parents."

"From church, you said."

"Yeah." He lets out a deep breath.

I sit up again and angle toward him. "Just so you know, I doubt there's anything you could say that would shock me or make me feel differently about you."

He brushes his hand across my cheek. "I don't talk about my family. People in town either know the story or they don't, but no one ever hears it from me."

"It's okay. You don't have to tell me, Lucas." Despite his calm exterior, I see the struggle in his eyes. "I'm sorry if things are rough at home."

He shrugs. "It's fine, usually. But when people look at me the way they did tonight, I fucking hate it."

His sudden disdain shocks me. "What way? I didn't notice anything."

He eyes me intently. "They see me standing beside you looking like I've got it all under control, but in their heads they're calling bullshit because they know exactly where I come from."

I lean back to study his face. "You don't really think that, do you?"

He frowns at me.

"I've seen how fast gossip spreads here, but I haven't heard a bad word about your family."

"You wouldn't," he says. "You're an outsider. Besides, your brother and his wife move in different circles. They wouldn't know anything about my family either. But that's probably about to change."

I give him a serious look. "You know, whatever it is, it doesn't matter to me, right?" I can't help thinking that whatever the heck is going on with his family, it can't be nearly as bad as mine. But still, I wish he'd trust me enough to tell me.

His answer is skeptical silence.

"Besides," I say, wanting to lighten the mood, "it doesn't seem to matter to any of the girls in school. Last time I checked, your stud status was still going strong."

This elicits a sliver of a smile. "There's only one girl in school I'm interested in."

"Really? Who?"

His smile fades as he brings his face closer to mine. "You, Ray. Just you," he whispers.

I can feel his warm breath on my cheek. "It seems like an obvious nickname," I say, my voice quiet now, too. "But no one has ever called me Ray before. I kind of like it."

His eyes travel over my face, stalling on my mouth, and my lips begins to tingle as though he's actually kissing me. "You're my ray of sunshine," he says softly.

With that, I'm rendered speechless. I never would have guessed Lucas could do corny so well, but his words light me on fire. His expression changes as he registers my reaction, and I realize the way I'm feeling must be perfectly clear to him. His eyes turn liquid as he inches his lips closer to mine. I'm still wrapped within the blanket when I feel his arms tighten around me. My breath stutters in my chest as I anticipate the moment his lips will meet mine. When they finally do, their touch is feather soft, barely pressing against me. Our breath mingles as he kisses just the side of my mouth, very slowly before he brushes his lips across mine to land them on the other side where he places another soft kiss. I feel his hand move up over my shoulder and then to the back of my head. His fingers tangle in my hair as he uses his hand to bring my face closer to his. Then his lips slant over mine, applying more pressure now, and all the waiting and wondering is satisfied by the white hot realness of having his mouth firmly on mine.

I'm pressing myself against him now, slowly snaking my hands out of the blanket to reach out for him. When I wind my arms around his neck, his mouth opens, coaxing my lips to follow, and our tongues touch tentatively at first, before they begin a slow, intimate dance.

Lucas is all around me. His smell, his touch, his warmth consume me, and our surroundings blur and fade away. Everything seems to dissolve into darkness and all that exists is us, in this moment. I can say with absolute certainty that I've never kissed anyone this way before, with my whole heart, with everything that I am. Just as I realize this, I know my walls are down. If Lucas has any kind of an injury right now, I couldn't prevent the energy from forming. In the back of my mind, I understand how dangerous that is, but mostly I'm just thankful that Lucas is one very healthy specimen of physical perfection.

His warm hand slides down around my shoulder, and he splays his long fingers across the top of my chest, just above my breasts. My heart continues to pump hard, and I wonder if he can feel it against his palm. He begins to slide his hand down, inside the blanket, and my fingers tighten around the curls at his neck. His tongue is still moving against mine as his hand sweeps across my breast. A shock ripples through me, and I surprise myself when I whimper into his mouth. This seems to trigger something within him, and he cups my breast fully as his thumb begins to circle my nipple through the fabric of my sweater. I arch into his hand craving more. There's an aching need between my legs, and I squeeze my thighs together. My body knows what it wants even as my head is swirling in sensation with the nagging fear that I'm losing control of myself. My hand moves down Lucas's chest until I find the bottom of his shirt. I inch it up and slide my fingers inside it. His stomach muscles jump as my fingers come in contact with his warm skin. I press my hand fully against the ridged muscles of his abdomen, enjoying the way he feels beneath my fingers, when he unexpectedly grabs my wrist to stop me.

Without warning, Lucas disentangles himself from me, gently setting me away from him. We're both breathing hard, and he's blinking at me as though he can't bring me into focus. He mutters something I can't understand before running a hand through his hair. "I needed to stop. That was getting…" he pauses and flashes a sexy grin at me even as he's shaking his head.

The tension in me is slow to ease, and I close my eyes trying to will it away.

"Are you okay?" he asks tentatively. "I'm sorry if that was too…"

"It wasn't," I interrupt him, opening my eyes and taking in his concerned gaze and his disheveled hair. I should be embarrassed at my behavior, but I'm not. My only worry is that he stopped, that he has more self-control than I do.

He scrubs his hands over his face a few times. "It's getting late," he says.

I nod.

"I should get you back."

Neither of us move. I let the blanket fall away. Suddenly, I'm far too warm inside it. Lucas takes my hand and leans his face down to mine. He kisses me again. This time it's soft and tender, but he's holding back now. Then he stands, pulling me up with him, and he wraps his arms around me. I lay my head on his shoulder as I embrace him, feeling the hard muscles of his back beneath my hands. I've never let myself feel this way about anyone before. It's frightening and exhilarating at the same time. I tell myself that it's because I've never met anyone like Lucas. On some level, I'm proud of myself. My inability to form connections has been pointed out to me by several social workers and teachers. If only they could see me now. Well, maybe not right now, I smile to myself.

Lucas releases me, and then he bends down to grab the blanket. My entire body still feels flushed as we walk hand in hand back to his truck. In the silence, my mind is already replaying the night over again, and I think back to how it started. I wish he would have told me about his family. I don't understand what the big secret could be. But I haven't told him everything about myself either. We've both kept our secrets tonight.

"Are you going to talk to Kyle about your grandmother?" he asks, once we're back in the truck.

When he turns to look at me, my temperature shoots up even higher as I remember how his lips felt on mine. Then I realize he's waiting for me to answer his question.

"What is it?" he asks.

"Nothing," I answer, smiling to myself. I recall his question and another one that's been nagging at me tonight. "If my grandmother is so senile, I'm wondering if somehow this janitor is taking advantage of her or something. There's no question now that he's the person I saw in San Diego. Or maybe Kyle met Rob Jarvis at the nursing home and sent him to San Diego to watch us. Kyle knew about us for a couple of years by then, and he had been trying to get custody of me. Maybe he hired him to gather evidence for his custody petition."

"Maybe you can focus on the fact that you have a grandmother that you're going meet for the first time and not worry about the rest right now."

I take a deep breath and smile at him. "I know. It feels bittersweet because of what Chloe said about her probably not knowing who I am, but I am glad that I'll get to see her. Are your grandparents still around?" I ask.

"Yeah. They're all retired in Florida. We used to go visit them when I was kid. We went to Disney World together one year.

"Gee," I laugh. "That sounds sickeningly normal, Lucas."

His smiles wistfully as he watches the road. "It does, doesn't it?"

When we arrive at Kyle's house, I see that the outside lights have been left on for me, and there's a soft glow in the living room window. "I'll walk you to the door," he says. "I want your brother to know I'm a gentleman." He winks at me before getting out and coming around to my side. He opens the door and leads me up the walkway with a light touch to my lower back.

"I had a really nice time," he says.

"Despite having to attend a family birthday party?" I ask.

"Any time I get to spend with you is good, Ray."

I can feel my cheeks flush. When he flashes his mischievous smile, I know he notices.

"Goodnight." He pecks my pink cheek, and I understand it's because we might have an audience.

"Night." I step inside and wait until Lucas is back in his truck before closing the door. The house is quiet. I see no sign of anyone being awake. I turn off the lights and head downstairs to my room. My head is filled with thoughts of Lucas as I change for bed. I never thought I could feel so connected to someone in such a short time. It's as though those empty places inside me that I just accepted as a part of who I am disappear when we're together. I used to look down my nose at girls who gushed about their boyfriends and couldn't stand to be apart from them. That would never be me, but maybe I can understand them a little better now.

I fall asleep with no goodnight text from Lucas for the first time this week. But he just left me, and a goodnight in person is so much better anyway.

THIRTEEN

"**D**ID you have fun at the birthday party, Raielle?" Penelope asks.

"Sure. Did you?" I ask as I sit down on the living room couch behind her. She's lying on the carpet, scribbling in a coloring book with her crayon.

She sits up to look at me. "I helped Papa blow out the candles. Did you see me?"

"I did. You did a great job."

"I can help you blow out your candles at your birthday party, too," she says.

"I would really appreciate the help. Thanks."

"Raielle's birthday isn't until the summer, right?" Kyle says, entering the room.

"June," I confirm. I'm glad to see him since he's the person I was looking for when I came in here.

"My birthday is in October," Penelope informs me.

"Can I talk to you for a minute?" I ask Kyle.

He nods. "Let's go for a walk."

"Finish your picture, Penelope. Mommy wants to give you a bath when you're done." Kyle tugs playfully on her hair as he walks by. She chuckles in response.

It's a bright morning. A warm breeze pushes cottony clouds across the sky. I follow Kyle to the sidewalk, and he begins a slow stroll once I reach him.

"Is this about Lucas?" he asks.

"No, actually, it's about my grandmother. Didn't Chloe tell you?"

He nods quickly. "Right. Yes, she did."

"I'd like to see her."

"Chloe said Angela told you she was dead?" he asks, his distaste for our mother obvious in his grimace.

I nod.

Kyle shakes his head at our mother's lie. "I can take you to see her if you'd like, but you can't really have a conversation with her. She may not even realize you're there."

"I'd still like to go."

"Alright then," he says, watching a car drive past.

"Were you close to her?" I ask, fearing the twinge of jealousy that's waiting if he answers *yes*.

He thinks for a minute before answering. Then he shrugs. "Not really. She's a hard person to get close to. She was never the stereotypical grandmother who baked cookies and sewed sweaters."

"What was she like?"

"She was something of a social butterfly. She had a lot of friends. She always had people around her. Our grandfather died a long time ago, back when Angela was still here. So, Gram lived alone, but she always had her house filled with her friends."

"Has she been in the nursing home long?" I ask.

"About two years now."

"Did she know where Mom was? Did she know about me?"

He sighs. "No. She didn't know any more than we did."

"I don't get it," I say, feeling the familiar frustration welling up inside me. "Why would she make me believe she was all the family I had?"

Kyle stops, and I realize that I've stopped, too. He places his hands on my shoulders. "I don't know, Raielle. I wish I did. I'm sorry for what she put you through."

I take a step back to break our contact. "You don't have to feel sorry for me. She loved me, Kyle. In her own massively messed up way, I know she did."

He rubs a hand over his face. "You don't want to say anything bad about her. I admire you for that, for your loyalty. But you might have to face the fact that she kept you away from here for her own selfish reasons."

"What reasons?" I ask, trying to control my sudden temper.

He eyes me sympathetically. "We may never know the answer to that."

I want to yell at him that he's wrong, but I swallow the words along with the tears that are threatening to form. Kyle has his own reasons for hating her, but somehow, I just think he's wrong about this.

My mother always told me that we only had each other in this world and that we were the only ones that could do what we did, heal people. She said it was important that we tell no one. That was easy enough to believe when I thought it was just the two of us. But now that I know we had a whole family here that she never bothered to tell me about, I can't help but wonder if she lied about our power, too. "Can we see her on Sunday?" I ask.

"Can't on Sunday. Penelope has a birthday party and Chloe wanted a few kid-free hours to run some errands," he replies. "How about Monday night?"

I nod, swallowing my impatience. "Okay. Monday."

"Now, about Lucas," Kyle begins. His serious tone tells me that this topic is not going to lighten the mood much. "I learned some things about his family last night."

I immediately realize that the people from Lucas's church talked to Kyle last night, which is exactly what Lucas had been afraid of.

"Did he tell you about his mother?" Kyle asks.

I shake my head. A part of me wants to stop him because hearing the information this way feels like a betrayal. But I want to know too badly to do that.

Kyle slides his hands into his pockets, and his eyes turn wary. "She's ill, Raielle. That's what Alec's friends told us last night."

I eye him curiously. "Ill? What does that mean? What's wrong with her?"

He exhales loudly. "She's mentally ill," he clarifies. "I understand that she's dangerous. I don't think I want you exposed to her in all honesty."

"What exactly did Alec's friends tell you?"

"That people have seen her wandering around their neighborhood, yelling random things, muttering to herself. She stands up in church screaming that evil is inside her. She hurts herself and she wants to hurt her family."

I'm staring at Kyle but I'm thinking back to last night, and to Lucas's reluctance to tell me any of this. "What do you mean she wants to hurt her family?" I ask.

"She tried to burn their house down with all of them inside it."

My mouth drops open. "What?"

"It was sometime last year, they said. She started a fire in the basement. Then she walked outside and sat down on the front lawn to watch. It was two in the morning. The rest of the family were asleep in their bedrooms."

"Oh god," I bring my hand up to my open mouth. "But no one got hurt, right?"

"A smoke alarm went off before it could spread too far. Lucas's father was able to put it out. They sent her somewhere to get help after that. But she's been back for a while and apparently nothing much has changed."

I look away from Kyle, staring down at the uneven cracks in the sidewalk instead. My heart is breaking for Lucas. I had no idea he was dealing with something like this. He never gave any hint of it. But then it hits me. I wonder if I could possibly help her. I wonder if mental illness is like physical illness. This use for my healing ability is something I've never tried before because it never really came up. The closest I ever came was when I asked my mother if I could heal her addiction. She laughed at me, saying she'd been trying to do that for years and daring me to take a stab at it. I did, but nothing happened. There was nothing torn, or broken, or foreign inside her making her abuse drugs and alcohol. There was nothing to heal. Ironically, we couldn't heal ourselves either. The reason had something to do with needing two energy sources, like some kind of Ying and Yang was required to create the necessary reaction. I never understood it mainly because my mother couldn't explain it coherently, making me believe she didn't actually understand it herself. I also didn't understand how we could be the only people in the world with the ability to heal. That makes no sense. But I couldn't exactly place ads in the newspaper looking for others, and Google was no help at all. But imagine if I could cure Lucas's mother? If there were something in her brain that I could actually heal, simply touching her would tell me.

"I don't want you going over there," Kyle says stiffly, bringing my attention back to him.

I stare at him, slowly realizing that he's giving me an order.

"He can come here and you can go places together, but I don't want you in his house or anywhere around her. Do you understand me, Raielle?"

I want to laugh in disbelief at his sudden laying down of the law. I'm ready to protest and tell him how ridiculous he's being, but then I think better of it. I've been running my own life for a long time. If he wants to think he's taken over the job, I'll go ahead and let him, only I'll know better. "Fine," I say.

His eyebrows shoot up. "I don't want to be unfair to Lucas, but he's not my concern. You are," he continues to explain himself.

I nod. "I get it. If what you've heard is true, I'm sure he's not exactly rushing to invite his friends over anyway."

"You're probably right." He runs a hand over his head before shoving it back in his pocket again, looking uncomfortable. Then he changes the subject. "Do you need a ride to work today?"

"No, it's okay. I'll walk."

When we get inside, I check my phone. I have a message from Gwen, but no one else. I want to call Lucas, but I'm not sure I should. Pretending not to know about his mother doesn't feel like the right approach. But if I do call him, what will I say? In the end, I decide not to call right now and to worry about it later.

JACINDA is a lapsed college student taking a year off to chill. That's what she told me when she introduced herself as the owner's niece and my fellow ice cream scooper for the day. I thought it was some kind of pun when she said it, but her oblivious chattering told me otherwise. I quickly realized that she could make conversation with the wall if I wasn't here.

"My boyfriend is driving down tonight, and I might need to leave a little early if that's okay with you?" she says when we're barely a half hour into our shift.

"Um, okay." I answer, realizing that as the owner's niece, she takes liberties.

"I got a new tattoo as a surprise for him. Would you like to see it?" she asks. She's attractive with long wavy hair that she has pulled back in a loose ponytail. Her skintight jeans reveal the kind of curves that guys go nuts for. Next to her, I probably look exactly like the beanpole people called me growing up.

I hesitate. "That depends. Where is this tattoo?"

She cackles at me. "Relax. I'm not going pull down my pants or anything. It's right here." She approaches me, lifting the edge of her black T-shirt up over the side of her torso. There, looking red and angry, is a scab-encrusted tattoo of a panther spanning her side with its head reaching toward her bellybutton and the tail whipping back toward her spine.

"Wow." I wince even as I'm admiring the artistry of it. "That looks like it hurt."

"Like a bitch," she laughs.

"What's the significance of the panther?"

"It's a hellcat," she says. "That's what my boyfriend calls me."

"Ahh," I nod, not sure I'd want that nickname, but whatever.

"You never got back to me." The door to Scoops swings open, causing the cool air from outside to waft in.

I turn to see Gwen, dressed in what looks like a plaid schoolgirl outfit, walk up to the counter. "I know, sorry. Jacinda, this is my friend, Gwen."

Jacinda gives her a little wave. "I'm going to restock the toppings," she says. Then she disappears into the back.

"So?" Gwen asks impatiently. "How was your date with Lucas?"

Just then, the door opens and a couple of tween-aged girls walk in. They're talking to each other and texting at the same time. Gwen waits while I scoop their cones and ring up their totals. Once they're gone, she eyes me expectantly.

"It was really nice," I say, and I can feel my cheeks heating.

"Oh my god! Look at you. It was better than nice."

I smile at her. I'm sure she doesn't know about Lucas's mother or she would have told me.

"So, what exactly did you do?" she asks, resting her arm on the top of the counter.

"You want me to kiss and tell?" I tease.

"Is that all you did? Kiss?" she raises her eyebrows suggestively.

"Yes. It was our first real date. All we did was kiss."

"And how was that?" she asks, appearing disappointed that more didn't happen.

"It was memorable," I hedge. I've never really had girl talk like this and so far, it's not a great fit for me.

"Uh-huh and if you fell off a cliff, you'd probably say hitting the ground stung a little," she giggles, laughing at her own joke.

I shrug with a smile, thinking that it's a good comparison. Free falling off a cliff is a perfect way to describe how I felt when I was kissing Lucas.

"So, since it's only Saturday, are you guys going out again this weekend?" she asks, lowering her voice as Jacinda reappears with tubs of candy.

"No. I don't think so. I haven't talked to him since last night."

"Want to come over then? We can get a movie or something?" She's eyeing the Oreo cookie topping that Jacinda is pouring into a glass container.

"Sure. Um, would you like an ice cream, Gwen?"

She turns her attention back to me. "What? No, I'd better not. This job of yours could get dangerous if I come in here too much. I'll pick you up later."

DECIDE to call Lucas on Sunday afternoon. I haven't heard from him since he dropped me off on Friday night, but that wasn't so long ago. I really hate that I've been staring at my phone, wanting him to call. My gut is telling me that if everything were fine, he would have called. But my head is saying that's ridiculous. We haven't known each other very long. We're not at the chat every day stage. But I do have a good reason to get in touch with him. I want to tell him that Kyle is taking me to visit my grandmother after school tomorrow. When I get his voicemail, I hesitate for a moment before saying, "Hey, it's Raielle. Hope you're having a good weekend. Call me if you get a chance. I have some news."

Then I go back to studying. The house is quiet. I'm the only one at home. Now, I watch my phone even closer, ready to throw the completely silent piece of metal and plastic out the window by dinner time. This time, I know something isn't right, and with what I know about his mother now, I'm starting to worry. Since I don't plan on stalking him at his house or asking Myles about him, there's no way to find out what's going on until Monday. Best case scenario, everything is fine, and I'm completely paranoid and obsessing far too much about him. This actually makes me smile. Who would have thought that I would be swooning over a guy? I'm usually known as some variation of the term ice queen in every school I attend. But somehow, Lucas has changed that. Then why is my gut churning, telling me that something is very wrong?

On the walk to school the next morning, there is palpable tension between April and Myles. She's spouting one word monosyllabic answers to his attempts at conversation, and he's giving up and giving into the silence as we make our way down the last block. I give them an impatient wave as I speed ahead into the building, making a mental note to ask Myles what the heck happened between them when I see him later. Lucas never did return my call from yesterday, and I'm feeling anxious at the thought of seeing him.

I beat him to first period, and I nearly cheer when Tucker arrives and sits across the room from me with the girl who usually talks to Lucas.

I'm trying not to stare at the door when he comes strolling in. My heart immediately begins hammering when I see him. He glances up, catches my eye, and then looks away when I smile. My grin falters as I watch him survey the room, seeming uncertain about where to sit. Then some kind of resignation takes hold as he finally moves in my direction, taking the empty seat beside me, all without ever glancing in my direction again.

I grip my pen tightly as I realize my instincts were right. Not hearing from him after Friday night did mean something was wrong. Something like regret on his part maybe?

"Hey," I say quietly to him.

His eyes shift toward me. "Hey," he replies in a monotone voice, like he's talking to the mailman.

"I left you a message," I say, confused by his coldness. If he's regretting what happened between us, he should say so, not act this way to me.

He nods. "Yeah, I got it." Then he pulls his pen and notebook from his bag and keeps his eyes trained on them as he sets each one on the desk.

"Is everything okay?" I ask, ignoring the sinking feeling inside me and still wanting to give him the benefit of the doubt.

"Sure. Why wouldn't it be?" he responds, turning to me causally, before dismissing me again. That emotionless tone of voice is back and hearing it feels like a knife is piercing my heart.

I shake my head and laugh miserably at myself. I should have known better. Don't form personal attachments because people always let you down. That's how it works out every time. I should have remembered that before I tossed all my hard-learned lessons out the window for Lucas Diesel. God, I'm an idiot. One amazing make-out session, and I'm ready to jump into a relationship with him. I was actually *waiting* for him to call me. I was *expecting* things from him. Well, if he wants to play it this way, he'll get as good as he gives. He can run hot and cold if he wants, but from now on, ice cold is all he's getting from me.

I spend the rest of class building up my resolve so that when the bell rings, I'm able to gather my things and head to the door as calm as can be. I don't burst into tears when Lucas makes a beeline for the pixie girl, chatting with her, and taking no notice of me as everyone files out into the hallway. That's how I survive the rest of the day, by pretending I'm fine even as the tears swim just below the surface. I ignore Lucas all morning and as far as I know, he never attempts to talk to me either. I sit and laugh with Gwen at lunch, never hinting at the knot of disappointment twisting inside me. I even grab Myles at the end of the day and ask him what's going on with April.

"I met someone," he says with a hesitant smile.

I raise curious eyebrows at him.

"He works at the pet store where we get DJ's food. He started last week."

"DJ?" I ask. "You have a dog?"

"Turtle," he says.

I chuckle, and it's the first genuine smile I've had all day. "You have a pet turtle?"

He appears offended. "I have an aquarium. Turtles are great pets. They're quiet and you don't have to walk them. They don't eat much, either."

"Well, that's great, Myles. I'm happy you met someone," I say, and I mean it. He's a genuinely nice person. Nice people deserve to be happy. Too often it just doesn't work out that way.

"April disagrees."

"What was her reaction when you told her? Did she have any idea?"

"Actually," he hedges, "I only told her that we should see other people."

This shocks me, and I can't help feeling disappointed in him, in all guys for that matter. "You should tell her the truth. If she honestly has feelings for you, you owe her that." I hitch my bag up onto my shoulder, completely annoyed now. That causes me to say something I hadn't intended to. "By the way, the warning you gave me about not stringing Lucas along? You gave it to the wrong person."

He stares at me confused.

"See you later." With that, I begin the walk home. When he calls after me, without turning around, I lift my arm up in a careless wave and continue walking, determined to get my priorities back in order.

THE Spring Valley Assisted Living Center is a squat brick building about ten miles outside of Fort Upton in a town called Springfield. It's a bitter cold night, and I'm shivering miserably in the passenger seat as Kyle parks in the large, mostly empty lot. I follow him into the lobby of the building. It's a small alcove with an attendant at a desk, but it's bright and warm, and I sigh with relief as the chill abates. Glancing around, I wonder if Rob Jarvis is working tonight and what his reaction will be if he sees me.

"We're here to visit Cora Crawford," Kyle tells the older man who is eyeing us both.

My ears perk up at my grandmother's last name. I knew her first name was Cora, but I don't think I'd ever heard her last name. It must be my mother's maiden name, too. How could I not know that? Kyle gives his information, and when the attendant locates something on his computer, he motions for us to go inside.

"Why do they need security here?" I ask as we move into a corridor with an elevator. There's a sharp antiseptic smell in the air.

"Anyone could walk in and try to take advantage of the residents. A lot of these people don't remember their families or who they are. I suppose it's intended to keep them safe." When the elevator door opens, we step inside, and Kyle presses the button for the third floor.

We ride up in silence. When the doors slide apart, I see there's another desk and a lounge area at the beginning of a long corridor. A round, short-haired woman is standing behind the desk, and she seems to recognize Kyle. "We haven't seen you here in a while," she comments as her eyes travel to me and widen.

"This is my sister, Raielle." He gestures in my direction, but he seems wary of her attention.

She nods. "I see the resemblance. I didn't know you had a sister." She narrows her eyes at us.

"How's my grandmother? Is she awake?" he asks. I'm relieved he's not going to bother with the story of my sudden appearance here in town.

"She's awake. I have her sitting in front of her window, like always."

"Come on," he says to me. I begin to follow him down the hallway. I can feel the woman's eyes on my back the whole way.

"Right here," he says before leading me into a small dimly lit room. I glance around and see a hospital bed in front of a large picture window that overlooks the highway in the distance. Outside, white and red lights blur past, traveling in opposite directions. Between the bed and the window is a chair. It's facing away from us, and from behind I can see that the woman sitting in it has thinning straggly hair.

"I have someone for you to meet, Grams," Kyle says. He moves to stand in front of her, leaning back against the window and motioning me toward him. I walk slowly, my eyes on her as I move around the chair.

Once I see her in profile, her resemblance to my mother is immediately apparent. The slant of her nose and the lift of her chin are both familiar to me. But her unkempt hair and her unfocused cloudy blue eyes belong to a stranger. She's slight and hunched as she sits swallowed up by a white nightgown that covers her from her neck to her ankles. She never moves or indicates that she knows we're there, but her eyes seem to watch the lights moving outside her window. I can see their starry pinpoints reflected in her glassy stare.

"This is Raielle, your granddaughter," Kyle explains. We both watch her and note her stillness. He glances at me and smiles sadly.

"This is because of senility?" I whisper skeptically. She looks catatonic.

He shifts uncomfortably. "That's what the doctors tell us. They haven't been able to find anything else wrong."

"Did this come on slowly?" I ask.

"It started with small stuff, like forgetting where she put things, but it got worse in a hurry. Finally, we had to put her here, and for the last year or so, she's been like this."

I stand beside Kyle and stare at her. A few silent moments pass before a shiver of anxiety passes through me. I feel a flutter low in my stomach, but it's not the familiar sensation I have when I'm near a person who's ill. It's something similar though. Suddenly, an overwhelming need to touch my grandmother takes hold. "Could I have a few minutes alone with her?" I ask.

Kyle's eyes widen with surprise.

Those words are out of my mouth before I can think them through. I scramble for a viable excuse. "This is kind of a big moment. I'd like to just be here with her for a little while, on my own. Do you mind?"

He seems undecided as he studies me. "All right," he finally says. "I'll be down the hall by the elevator when you're done."

"Thanks," I reply, relieved but also nervous now.

I watch my grandmother's slow steady breathing as Kyle's footsteps fade down the hallway. Once I'm sure he's out of earshot, I reach my fingers toward her. Her withered hand, dotted with age spots, rests in her lap. I bring my fingertips to her skin with the very lightest of touches, and immediately an intense vibration travels from me into her. I notice her turn her head toward me, and I jump back, snatching my hand away, feeling spooked. But then she turns to the window and stares again, as though the moment never happened.

I eye her curiously, seeing no evidence of any awareness now. Then I decide to try it again, but this time I'm braced for the sensation. Hesitantly, I lean forward, bringing only my fingertips down onto the top of her hand. The vibration begins again, strong at first before settling into a low hum. My face is close to hers, and I see her blink, once, twice, and then several times more rapidly. She inhales deeply and her eyes move until they're on mine.

"Angela," she whispers, and her stale breath washes over me. With my fingers still on her hand, I lean back against the window, putting more distance between us.

"I'm her daughter," I say. "My name is Raielle."

Her blue eyes move over my face. "Raielle." Her thready voice saying my name unsettles me. "What are you doing here? Where is Angela?" Then she looks down and sees my hand on hers. Realization dawns in her eyes. "You're doing this," she whispers.

When I nod, she laughs and it's a rough, wet sound. "You're powerful. I can feel it. More powerful than I ever was. Maybe more powerful than your mother."

"You could do it, too? You could heal?" I ask, remaining outwardly calm as my insides churn with a mixture of disbelief and excitement.

She tilts her head at me. "Your mother didn't tell you?"

I shake my head.

"Where is she?" She glances around the room and then back to me.

"She's not here," I reply vaguely.

She looks down at our connected hands again. "So strong," she whispers. "You must charge a great deal," she says, her gaze meeting mine.

"What?" I ask, wondering if I heard her right.

"Money, my dear. You could become very wealthy with your power, you know?" she says, her lips curving into a thin smile. "I made plenty of money curing silly little colds, but I couldn't do this. I couldn't cure diseases of the mind. I tried, but it never quite worked."

I take my hand back as I'm wondering if I heard her correctly. "People paid you money to heal them?"

"Of course. I had people at my door day and night. But your mother was far more powerful than me. She could rid people of terrible things, illnesses that they would pay mountains of cash to be cured of. But she was always so difficult about it. She didn't want to take money for it. Then something happened and she refused to continue."

"What do you mean? What happened?"

Her watery eyes meet mine, and I see malice in them. Before she even answers, I feel nausea crawling inside me. "She took leukemia from a boy and gave it to his father."

Disbelief is my first reaction.

Noting my expression, she explains. "She had her hands on both of them at the same time. She removed the disease from the son and then the father touched her and it went into him." She chuckles, and I can feel the bile rising in my throat. "He died quickly, about a month later. She was afraid to try to heal him, afraid of where it would go next. The family hated us, those ingrates. She saved their child's life."

She grabs my hand back, and she's surprisingly strong. I can feel her trying to pull more energy from me. "It's no wonder you're so powerful. Your father was the strongest healer I'd ever seen. His energy could cure nearly anything. He had quite a following," she says.

"You knew my father?" I'm practically gaping at her as she caresses my fingers.

"We could work together," she muses, ignoring my question, grabbing my other hand before I can pull it away. "Now that you've cured me, we could work together and make a fortune. Your mother lost her taste for it. Then she met your father, and she ran away with him. Once she was gone, people stopped coming."

168

"No. She met my father in San Diego long after she left here."

My grandmother shakes her head. "He was from Los Angeles. She left Alec and followed him out there. Then they had you."

"You're wrong."

"I'm not," she says in a firm voice. "Alec can tell you. I'm sure he remembers it all. She made a fool out of him."

Could she be telling the truth? I wonder as I stare at her frail form. Alec never mentioned this when I asked him why my mother left. Why would he hold that back? What's difference could it make now? I start to feel tired. My head grows heavy on my shoulders. Somehow, she's drawing energy from me against my will now. I'm fascinated even as I'm trying to pull my hands away.

"We might have to go somewhere else," she continues. "This town might not be so welcoming anymore."

"Does everyone know about us? About what we can do?" I ask. "Does Kyle know?"

"Of course the whole town knows," she laughs at me. "I advertised in the local newspaper. Where is your mother? Why has she kept you in the dark this way?"

"She's dead," I answer, not even considering withholding the truth from her any longer.

She winces, and I yank harder, trying to get her to release me. "She was murdered," I tell her, bluntly. "Did you send someone after her?" I ask, thinking of Rob Jarvis, leaning in closer to her, my voice a low, angry whisper.

Fear begins to seep into her eyes. "No," she replies, shaking her head. "No," she repeats. The truth is, if she's been this way for more than a year, she couldn't have spoken to the janitor here and sent him after us.

"You have to be careful," she whispers. "With power like yours, everyone will want a piece. Take me out of here, and I can protect you."

She finally releases one of my hands and unsuccessfully tries to push herself up from the chair. "Please, help me up. We need to leave. I have so many things I can teach you."

"Tell me how you came to be this way?" I ask. "What's wrong with you?"

She blinks in confusion. Then her eyes widen. "I tried to cure conditions that were too severe. But the money was too good to refuse. I didn't know it could hurt me. It almost killed me." She smiles. "But now you're here. You're here and we're going to be unstoppable. Help me," she grimaces as she tries to stand again.

"I won't work with you. I won't take people's money."

She shakes her head. "You sound just like your mother. You'll do as I say or I'll tell everyone about you and the sick people will begin beating a path to your door. Either way, you can't hide your talents. Why would you want to?"

I strengthen my grip on her. I can't let her leave here. I can't let her tell everyone. Panic builds inside me as she takes a deep breath, like she's getting ready to scream. I focus on the vibration that still travels between us. I concentrate on the feeling, on locating it and harnessing it. Then I use all my strength to force it back in her direction. The disease traveling between us, starting to lose its hold on her as it leaves her body, courses through mine now, and I force it to flow back out again, down my arms and into my fingers, striking out at her like a snake and slithering back inside her. Her fingers fall slack as she releases me. I know the moment I tumble back and hit the window that she's gone. This selfish, venomous woman is lost inside herself again.

FOURTEEN

THERE'S a knock at the door.

"Could you get that, Raielle?" my mother calls from the kitchen. It's after ten, and I'm sitting on the couch surrounded by my homework. I extract myself, careful not to jostle the papers I've carefully organized for my study group tomorrow.

I pull the door open, and Kelvin falls in toward me, landing heavily against me. My knees nearly buckle as I back into the living room, dragging him with me. "Mom!"

"Who is it?" she asks sharply. Then her eyes widen in horror, and she reaches for her on-again, off-again addict boyfriend. "Close the door, Raielle," she demands as she lays a groaning Kelvin onto the floor.

Once his weight is off me, I glance down and realize that I'm covered in his blood. "Oh my god," I whisper in shock.

"Shut the door!" she demands again.

I dash to the door and slam it closed, wincing at the loud sound before I return to them. My clothes are wet and sticky, clinging to me with garish warmth.

"Kelvin," Mom weeps as she lowers herself to the floor beside him. "What happened?"

His answer is a wet cough. Blood seeps from his mouth. Mom gasps and stares up at me. "I shouldn't do this," she whispers. "I shouldn't do this."

Then she inches his soaked shirt up, revealing the sliced skin of his stomach. Slowly, she lays her palms on him and closes her eyes. "I'll take it into myself. I'll pull it into me."

"What?" I gasp. "No!"

"I'm sorry," she whispers, turning her watery eyes to mine. "I'm so very sorry."

I sit straight up in bed, struggling for air. Glancing at the clock, I see that it's nearly time to get ready for school. I try to slow my breathing down and calm my trembling muscles. The dream was so real, every detail so sharp, right down to the leopard headband my mother always wore in her thick blond hair. She was never the same after that night. She healed Kelvin, but the very next day his son died, not my mother. She hadn't been able to take his injuries into her own body. Instead, they had found his son. A brain aneurysm killed him instantly, and Kelvin knew that somehow it was Mom's doing. That's when she began warning me that certain death couldn't be cured, that terrible things happened when you tried. I think of my grandmother's story about the boy with leukemia. Mom probably thought that if she used herself as some kind of vessel, Kelvin's impending death could be contained within her. She was ready to die for him. But it jumped to his son instead. Her assumption had been wrong. It was a deadly mistake.

I scrub my hands over my face. My obviously conscienceless grandmother told me lots of interesting things last night. She cured people like it was an entertaining parlor trick. She advertised her services in the local paper for god's sake, and obviously everyone knew about it. Maybe she wasn't taken seriously? I want to ask Kyle what he thinks about the business our grandmother used to run, but I can't do that without revealing how I know about it. How could I know unless my catatonic grandmother told me? I can't ask about it without revealing myself to him. Never tell anyone. My mother drilled that into me. I need to find out more before I completely disregard it.

What about my father? Had my mother really met him here and followed him to Los Angeles? Obviously, nothing she told me, which was never much anyway, could be believed. Is it possible my father is alive and he has these abilities, too? Nothing I thought I knew can be trusted now.

W HAT do you do when a proverbial earthquake shakes loose more secrets from your past? You go to school like any other day. My mind is still turning over all that I heard last night when I close my locker and glance over to find Lucas standing beside me.

"Did you meet your grandmother? Was that the news you were talking about in your message?" he asks.

What the fuck? Now he's talking to me again like the cold shoulder he gave me yesterday never happened? I stare at him, shocked and annoyed by his nerve. I narrow my eyes. "Seriously?" Then I turn and head for class. Unfortunately, it's the same class he's going to.

"Wait a minute," he says, catching up to me. "I'm sorry about yesterday, and I'm sorry I didn't call you back."

I ignore him and keep walking.

"Stop. Please," he pleads, placing a hand on my arm.

I halt and stare pointedly at his hand. He reluctantly removes it. Then he takes a deep breath and runs the same hand through his hair. "Look, after Friday night I needed some time to think. I guess I needed a little space."

I nearly laugh at that as I stare at him through a haze of hurt. "You needed space after our *one* date?"

His jaw clenches. "Don't minimize that night, Ray. It was intense, and you know it."

"It was intensely disappointing," I say even though I don't mean it. Then I turn and resume walking.

He catches right up to me, positioning himself in front me, forcing me to stop again. "We both know that's not true. I never took you for a liar."

I avert my eyes because he's right.

"Just listen to me, okay?"

His eyes seek mine, and I let him find them.

"After that night, I decided it would be better if I stayed away from you."

I keep my eyes pinned to him, and I don't let him see how much his words are wounding me.

He rushes a hand through his hair again. His face is a combination of frustration and remorse. "I've got a lot of shit going on and with everything you're already dealing with, it didn't seem fair to add to it. I didn't stay away to intentionally hurt you. I was trying to protect you from me. I was trying to be selfless. But I'm not selfless, Ray. I'm the complete opposite of selfless where you're concerned. Because after just a few days, I can't do it anymore. I can't stay away from you, and I don't want to. I never did."

Despite my hurt and anger, a part of me can understand what he's saying, and my traitorous emotions are thrilled that he still wants me. But I don't deserve the way he treated me, and I can't pretend it's okay. He's watching me with uncertainty. I don't want to hurt him anymore than he wants to hurt me. But I do want to try to explain myself, something he didn't bother to do for me.

"You could have talked to me, Lucas," I say, surprised at how calm my voice sounds. "I'm a reasonable person. I would have listened. If you'd explained yourself, I would have been capable of understanding you. But instead, you turned back into the asshole I first met, and you treated me like crap."

His jaw clenches at my words.

"And now I can't be sure you won't do it again, but I do know that I don't have to let you." I step to the side and start to walk around him.

"You know now, don't you?" he states from behind me. "Those people at the party told your brother."

Rage flares through me, and I spin around. "Yes, I do know, and if you think that has anything to do with what I just said, you don't understand me at all. But I guess that makes sense. You always do assume things about me. When are you going to realize that you haven't gotten anything right yet?" With that, I storm off to class.

SOPHIE is practically glued to Lucas again. It's disgusting." Gwen wrinkles her nose in their direction before offering me a sympathetic look.

I don't want to glance over at their lunch table, but I can't help myself. There I see Sophie chatting at Lucas, leaning into him, and he's basically ignoring her, like always. When he looks over in my direction, I dart my eyes away, but not before he notices me staring. "Damn," I mutter, taking a nibble of my sandwich.

"I can't believe it ended before it even got started," Gwen continues.

"I don't want to talk about it, Gwen."

"Fine, be all mopey by yourself then. Sometimes talking about stuff helps, you know."

I sigh. "Did I tell you that Kyle is giving me driving lessons now? I'm going for my learner's permit in a few weeks."

She perks up. "That's great. You know, he keeps looking over here."

I slump in my chair. Of course I know exactly who she's referring to.

"Let's not talk about him or where he's looking, okay?"

"Are you sure *he's* the one who blew *you* off because he really looks like he wants to come over here and talk to you?"

I toss my sandwich back into my bag. Feeling like I'm under a microscope is messing with my appetite. "I'm going to head out. I'll see you in chemistry."

From the corner of my eye, I notice Lucas stands when I do. By the time I reach the door, he's there. "So, that's it?" he says, stepping in front of me. "You don't give people second chances? I'm not allowed to make a mistake?"

I don't doubt his sincerity, and I can clearly see his remorse. There's also fear in his eyes, fear that I won't forgive him. I nearly cave right then. The strange pull I feel when I'm near him isn't gone, not even close. It may be even stronger now. My heart wants me to throw myself into his arms, to feel his warmth around me again. But reason tells me it's better this way. After what he did, I'm afraid to give him another chance to do it again.

"No, Lucas," I reply quietly, calmly, not revealing that what I'm about to say is killing me. "No second chances."

I see anger fill his eyes as they shift away toward the hallway. When they flick back to me, they've iced over, chilling me to the bone, and I walk away from him, not wanting to acknowledge the hurt I've just inflicted.

I sleepwalk through the rest of the day knowing that I've done the right thing, but feeling miserable about it anyway. It only gets worse when Chad stops me the in hallway to ask me out again. Of course, Lucas walks by at that moment and sees us talking. He doesn't look away. Instead, his eyes bore into me as he passes.

When I get home, I do my homework and listlessly sit through dinner. Then Kyle takes me out for another driving lesson. It's the same route we took last night after we left the nursing home. He sensed something was wrong and out of the blue, he asked me if I wanted to drive home. Now we're going to go out a few times a week to practice, he promised. When we're alone, I'm tempted to ask him what he knows about the healing ability our family has. What harm could there be in asking? Then I remember my mother's adamant warnings, and I remain silent.

LUCAS isn't in school the next day. I worry about him, but I don't ask anyone about him. Flyers for the senior prom have appeared all over school and it seems everyone is buzzing about it.

"We'll all go together," Gwen exclaims at lunch. "All four of us since we don't have dates."

Then Lisa clears her throat. "Actually, I do have a date."

This is news to Gwen and me.

"I'm going with Jared from work. I asked him yesterday." She blushes a deep red and glances down at her lunch tray.

"I was going to ask you, actually," Tyler states with surprising confidence.

Gwen levels a stunned expression at me and then transfers it to Tyler. "You're asking Raielle?"

Tyler chuckles. "No. No offense, Raielle, but I'm asking you, Gwen."

Her mouth drops open. "You are?"

He nods and she turns to me, seeming to seek my approval.

"Say yes, you idiot," I laugh at her.

She giggles, trying to stay cool despite her obvious excitement. "Okay, yes," she tells him. "But what about Raielle? She can come with us, right?"

Tyler hesitates, but I don't. "No way. I'm not crashing your party. You guys go and have fun."

"But what about you?" Gwen asks.

"I don't really do dances. I've never been to one, and I don't want to break my record now," I say good-naturedly, trying to make them believe it. It's true that I've never been to a dance, but I can't help imagining what it might be like to go with Lucas. I immediately chastise myself because I decided not to think about him today. Taking it one excruciating day at a time, I am determined to purge myself of all my feelings for him.

They stare wide-eyed at me. "You've never been to a dance?" Lisa says, verbalizing all their thoughts, bringing me back to the conversation.

"Last I checked, it wasn't a requirement for graduation," I joke.

We finish lunch with talk of hiring limos and buying dresses. At least, they talk about it. I eat silently, somehow managing a smile whenever someone looks at me.

LUCAS arrives at school the next day with a cast on his arm and misery in his expression. His eyes are sunken in, and I can feel the pain of his injury the moment he lowers himself into the desk beside me during first period. The room is still half-empty, and after the way he looked at me when I refused his apology the other day, I would have thought he'd be sitting as far away from me as possible. But he's stubbornly sitting beside me even as he's ignoring me.

"What happened?" I ask.

He doesn't move, and I decide he's not going to answer when he finally glances at me and shrugs. "It was an accident. I was fixing a loose shingle on the roof and I fell."

"You fell off the roof of your house?" I ask, incredulously.

"Yeah," he mutters through tight lips.

"You're lucky you only hurt your arm? Is it broken?"

He sighs and turns toward me. "Are we speaking again?"

I hate the anger that sparks in his eyes despite his outward calm. "We were never not speaking."

178

"Just not dating," he says, wincing slightly when his cast bangs again the desk.

"Right," I reply quietly. "Are you taking anything for that? Some aspirin maybe?"

"Not your concern." He faces forward again, dismissing me.

It's his right arm, and I watch as he struggles to take notes with his left hand. I feel the familiar pull toward him, but there's more beneath it now. Empathy for those who are hurting is another part of my power that I try to control. But I know I can't with Lucas. There's no point in even trying. It would be so easy to fix his arm. Fixing a broken bone is like riding a bike for me, easy as can be. He winces again as the teacher hands back our homework assignments from last week and Lucas reaches for it with his right arm, the bulky cast that runs from his elbow to his wrist banging against the desk again, harder this time, emitting a loud thud.

At that moment, I decide to heal it. Consequences be damned. I can't watch him in this miserable state when I know I can do something about it. I've repaired many friends' broken limbs, making them think that it was never as bad as the doctors thought. It's interesting how easily people believed the improbable over the impossible, the impossible being that I healed them.

After the bell rings, Lucas glances at me with surprise as I fall into step beside him on our way to our next class.

"So, what is this? I've got to break something so you'll be nice to me?" he asks with his familiar smirk.

"I never wanted us to stop being nice to each other," I explain without quite looking at him.

He bumps me lightly with his good arm causing me to turn to him. "I really am sorry," he says.

I nod. "I know."

We go through the rest of our morning with awkward, restrained friendliness, and I can tell that Lucas isn't exactly sure where he stands with me. I can't help him because I'm not sure either. I know that I miss him, and I would like to be friends, but I'm afraid to want more.

Before lunch, Lucas stays after class to get the assignments he missed yesterday. I wait by the door for him as the hallway quiets down and students scatter either to class or to the cafeteria. When he's finished, he appears surprised but pleased to see me waiting by the doorway.

"Hey," he grins at me.

"I copied all the notes for you from our morning classes yesterday. I have them in my locker if you'd like them." Actually, I hurriedly did that before class so that I'd have an excuse to get him alone and to touch him.

"Sure. Thanks." He eyes me, unsure. My friendly behavior is obviously confusing him.

We walk together down to my locker. The hall is quiet now as he stands patiently beside me, watching as I enter the combination and pull the metal door open. I can feel his eyes traveling over me, and I try to contain the self-conscious flush coloring my face. I grab the loose papers and turn toward him. When he reaches out his good arm, rather than placing the notes in his waiting hand, I touch my palm to his. Immediately, my stomach flutters with anticipation. The pleasant buzzing sensation begins, and I can feel the energy growing. It peaks inside me before uncoiling and flowing from me into Lucas. He sucks in a breath, and his hand jerks within mine. His forearm is actually broken in two places and those sections fuse back together as I breathe out slowly. But then something else happens. I begin to see a scene in my head. I see a woman coming at Lucas with a baseball bat. Her mouth is open in a scream. Her chestnut hair swings wildly around her face. She raises the bat over her head, and his arm comes up to shield him. When the bat jerks downward, I hear something snap in Lucas's forearm just before his face crumples in pain.

With a sharp inhale of air, I remove my hand from his, letting the notebook pages drop onto his open palm. I know I just saw the truth of his injury. I don't know how, but I did. When I allow myself to look at his face, I see absolute astonishment there. His eyes are wide and wild as he stares at me. When I heal injuries, I know the other person feels the same exhilaration I do, but this time, I'm not sure what Lucas felt. I know his bones are healed, but did he relive their breaking with me? Is that what just happened?

"If you have any trouble reading them, just let me know," I say with a shaking voice, gesturing to the notes resting absently in his hand, trying to return us to normalcy.

Lucas blinks at me as he attempts to comprehend what just happened. He turns his hand, and the papers flutter to the floor. Then he lifts his other arm, the one with the cast, and looks down at it, flexing his fingers and turning it over. His eyes find mine again, and they narrow on me. "Ray," he whispers before holding his arm up in front of him and staring at it. "What the hell just happened?"

"What do you mean?" I laugh, and it's not exactly an academy award winning performance. Then I take a step back. "I'm heading to lunch."

"Wait," he says.

I stand there watching his shock change to confusion. He wants to say something to me, to ask me something, but he doesn't. He just stares at me as though studying me long enough might give him the answers he's looking for.

Finally, I end the standoff. I bend down, pick up the papers, and hold them out to him. But he doesn't acknowledge them. "So, um, I can hold on to these for you," I say, acting like nothing strange is going on. Then I step further away from him as I shove the papers into my bag. "I'll see you later." I flash him a tight smile before I turn and head down the hallway, anxious to put distance between us, to let him think about what happened, and to dismiss it as crazy while he decides to be happy that his arm is no longer broken. That's how it goes. That's how it has always happened before. But I've never healed Lucas before, and I've never had the event that caused the injury play itself out in my head. Knowing Lucas, I'm afraid he won't let it go the way most people do. I don't think I can let it go either now that I know his mother did this to him.

I see no sign of Lucas for the rest of the day. He doesn't make an appearance at lunch, and I find myself nibbling on my lip as much as my sandwich. He may be confused, but I know that physically he's completely fine now. Based on his reaction, a small seed of worry begins to sprout inside me. What if he tells someone? If he does, I'll deny it. The likelihood of anyone believing him is slim anyway. As the anxiety takes hold, I begin to regret healing his arm. Broken arms mend. I didn't have to intervene, and I can only hope that it doesn't blow up in my face. But I never could stand to watch people suffer in even the smallest way. I haven't begun to process the vision that accompanied the healing this morning. That has never happened before, and I don't know why it did now. I have no one to talk to about any of this. The questions are swirling around in my head, and the answers are completely out of reach.

After school, I catch a ride with Gwen to her house so we can finish our chemistry lab. She's wavering as to whether Tyler's asking her to the prom means that he likes her or not, and it feels good to immerse myself in her typical teenage issues for the afternoon.

College acceptance letters will be arriving soon and like me, Gwen nervously checks her mailbox every day. Unlike Lucas, the rest of us are on pins and needles. Gwen wants to return to Manhattan and has only applied to schools in the city. I'm worried that my letters won't find me here in Fort Upton. Kyle assured me that he took care of having any mail addressed to me forwarded here. I took the extra step of calling the schools to give them my change of address. So, the letters should arrive just fine. But so far, they haven't.

THE day is finally over, and I'm heading down to my bedroom, when the doorbell rings. Since I'm the closest to the front door, I pull it open to find Lucas standing in the darkness on the other side.

"Who is it?" Kyle asks, stepping beside me. "Hello, Lucas," he says with a frown.

Lucas offers him a tense smile. "I came by to see if Raielle wanted to go for a drive."

Kyle hesitates and glances at me. I can't read anything in Lucas's stoic face, but I know we need to talk, and as wiped out as I'm feeling, I'd rather get it over with.

"It's supposed to storm pretty hard later. Maybe another night would be better," Kyle suggests.

Lucas is about to say something when I interrupt him. "We won't be gone long." Then I reach for my coat without waiting for Kyle's answer. He stands silently while I slip it on, and since he doesn't appear to be stopping me, I head out the door.

It's a cool damp night. The air is heavy with moisture even though the rain hasn't started yet. As I silently follow Lucas to his truck, I notice that his cast is gone. He opens the door for me, and I get inside, still getting no read on his mood since his face is a mask of neutrality. His silence is probably a bad sign though. Once we leave my neighborhood, I turn to him. "Where are going?"

"Not too far," he says, his eyes on the road.

Soon fat raindrops begin hitting the windshield. Lucas pulls onto a bridge that crosses over a river and parks to the side. In the distance, I can see the glittering lights of a city skyline.

"That's Albany," he says.

"I didn't know it was so big," I comment, peering out the window at the glowing buildings that stretch upward, disappearing into the low hanging clouds. Below us, the rushing water is a moving dark mass.

"We'll have to talk in the truck," he says. "I was hoping to take you down there." He gestures to a grassy area just below the bridge. "There are some benches. On a clear night, the view is pretty amazing."

I take the fact that he wants to share amazing views with me as a good sign. It's not raining too hard yet but the heavy drops ping around us as they land on the truck. Lucas keeps the heat running, and I catch the faint aroma of his spicy scent in the air.

His intense eyes meet mine. They're shining at me in the dim light. I notice that his hair curls more in the humidity, just like mine does. He turns his body toward me, resting his right arm along the back of the seat behind him. "I cut the cast off this afternoon," he says, raising and lowering his forearm. "Since I don't need it anymore."

I quietly hold his gaze, deciding to let him steer the conversation. He doesn't appear angry, or nervous, but he does look determined. "Have you always been able to do that?" he asks. When I don't answer right away, he clarifies himself. "Heal broken bones?"

If I'm going to deny it, now is the time to do it. It will be ugly, and he'll know I'm lying, but that's the smartest course to take here. Instead, inexplicably, I find myself nodding at him.

He doesn't appear to be surprised, but he tenses, and the muscle in his cheek jumps. "Is it just broken bones, or can you heal other things?"

While he waits for me to answer, a part of me wants to jump out of the truck and run away. This is my last chance to shut down and shut him out completely. Instead, I can hardly comprehend how badly I want to let him in. I don't want to be alone in this anymore, but I can't trust him, not completely, not with the way he acted before. I have never wanted to be close to someone the way I want to be close to Lucas. I don't understand it, but every part of me wants to let go and embrace it.

"Ray?" he prompts me, using my nickname in that tender way he has. That alone is enough to weaken any resolve I'm still grasping at.

"It's not just broken bones," I finally say, feeling like I'm stepping off a cliff.

He watches me expectantly.

"It's just about everything, I think."

He leans toward me. "Everything? You think?"

"I don't use it much, my ability," I hesitate before continuing. "My mother told me it was a curse, and that using it always came with a price. That it was safer not to use it. But I've seen her do amazing things and terrible things, too. I know I could do those same things if I let myself."

Lucas squeezes his eyes shut and scrubs his hands over his face. I have no idea what he's thinking.

He lowers his hands and blinks at me in the darkness. "Your grandmother's name is Cora, isn't it?"

I stare at him. "How do you know that?"

He takes a deep, shaky breath. "My father took my mother to see her. Your grandmother claimed she could heal people. This was a long time ago, right after Liam was born. My father paid her five-thousand dollars to cure my mother's postpartum depression."

"What?" I whisper, his words sinking in slowly.

"Nothing could snap her out of it, my dad said. He took her to a bunch of specialists, but nothing worked. People told him that this woman in town, Cora, could help people even when doctors couldn't. That she'd cured them of everything from the flu to cancer. So, he took my mother to her."

I can feel myself sinking lower in my seat, leaning away from him, not wanting to hear what I'm afraid is coming next.

"She got rid of the depression," he states, bitterness straining his voice now. "But she destroyed her in the process. She turned her into what she is now. Your grandmother is the reason my family is so fucked up."

185

His hard eyes zero in on me, and I can see the accusation in them. I begin to sink under the weight of his glare. I can feel the sob building inside me, and suddenly I can't pull enough air into my lungs. I reach for the door handle and close my fingers around it. Then I push the door open and watch Lucas's eyes widen in alarm just before I drop down onto the wet pavement.

I land hard on my hip and catch my upper body with my arms. Sheets of cold rain pour down on me as I lift myself to my feet. The need to flee is strong and without any rational thought, I begin to run over the bridge. I hear the sound of the rain pounding around me, but I now know that my mother's words were the truth. Our ability is a curse, and my grandmother used it to hurt people. This is my legacy. This is what I come from, and I can't accept it. I don't want any part of it.

A hand grips my arm, and I try to pull against it.

"Ray, stop. Stop!" Lucas yells.

And I do. My legs stop moving as my sudden panic flees, leaving behind a twisting knot of misery. I slump to my knees, and Lucas follows me down, kneeling in front me. He's soaking wet. We both are. His warm hands cup my cheeks, forcing me to look at him.

"I'm sorry," I tell him in a strangled whisper. "I'm so sorry."

He lifts my face back to his when I try to turn away. "You have nothing to be sorry for."

When I don't respond, he leans in closer to me. "Listen to me. I shouldn't have told you that way. I only just figured it out myself. I never really believed the story my father told me until I saw what you did today. I wasn't blaming you. I know you're not your grandmother. You're nothing like her."

My heart fills with sorrow for Lucas. I may not have done it myself, but it's the power my family wields that took his mother from him. I can't help but wonder how many other people my grandmother may have hurt, how many lives she ruined for money. I can't hold it in any longer. The sob rips through me as my tears mix with the rain streaming down my face.

Lucas's arms come around me, and he presses me to him, murmuring quietly to me, telling me it's going to be all right. But I'm not just crying for what my grandmother did. I'm crying for my mother and for how much I'm missing her. I'm crying for a terrible legacy that I want no part of. I'm crying because I've been in the dark for so long, and I'm now just realizing how innocent that darkness was. Lucas is holding me tightly. I can feel how much he cares about me, and I can't understand why he would, especially with what he now knows. With that terrible thought lingering in my mind, I'm suddenly all too aware of the cold, wet night, and I start to shiver, my teeth chattering uncontrollably.

"Jesus," Lucas mutters. "Let's get you back inside the truck." His arm shifts around my back and the other winds beneath my knees. I feel him lifting me up, and I want to protest but I can't form the words. Somehow, he gets the driver's side door open and places me inside, following behind me. As I'm sitting myself up on the seat, he reaches in back for the blanket, unfolds it, and wraps it around my shoulders. Then he cranks the heat to its highest setting before pushing his hands through the wet hair hanging down into his eyes.

"What's Kyle going to think when I bring you back like this?" Lucas says, his lips twisting up into a smile that doesn't reach his eyes. "This is not going to get me into his good graces."

He's trying to lighten the mood, and I can't help but appreciate his efforts despite their failure. "My grandmother is catatonic now," I tell him quietly. "Completely out of it. I'm so sorry for what she did."

"You don't need to be sorry for her. I mean it, Ray. Don't do that to yourself."

I pull the blanket more tightly around my shoulders, appreciating his words even if I can't do what he's saying.

"Can everyone in your family heal?" he asks.

My shivering eases as the dry blanket and the warm heat begin to work on me. "I don't know. I already told you about my mother. As for the rest, I haven't mentioned it and neither have they."

"Do you know why you're like this? Where this power comes from?"

I smile sadly. "I don't know very much about it, Lucas."

He reaches out and takes my hand from under the blanket. "Don't you want to know?" he asks.

"Yes…and no." I glance down at my hand inside his. "I touched my grandmother when I visited her. I took away her senility, and I talked to her."

His eyes widen with interest.

"When I realized what she was, what she wanted from me, I gave it back to her."

He furrows his brow at me. "What do you mean?"

"She wanted to go back into business, healing for money with me by her side. She said if I didn't agree, she would expose me and my abilities. So, somehow, I stopped the healing energy that was running between us, and I pushed her own energy back at her. I've never done that before." I tilt my head at him. "Just like I've never had a vision when I healed before. Not until today when I healed you."

Lucas releases my hand. "A vision?" he asks.

I nod. "I saw how your arm got broken. I saw your mother with the bat."

His lips narrow into a straight line. "You what?"

I'm slightly relieved by his angry reaction. I was afraid he'd seen it, too, and I would hate to have made him relive that with me. "Has she ever done anything like that before? She can't be allowed to hurt you. Is she getting any help at all?"

He moves away from me. "I don't know what you think you saw, but..."

"Lucas, don't," I plead. "I'm being completely honest with you. I've never spoken about my abilities this way to anyone before. Please be honest with me, too."

He closes his eyes. Then he rubs his hand through his hair again and nods slowly, as though he's resigning himself to the fact that I know his secret. "The new nurse my dad hired screwed up. She mixed up the medication. That's why it happened. But it's fine now." He runs his hand along his now healed forearm. The tone of his voice tells me it's not fine despite his words. "Visions?" he whispers like he can't quite believe that little wrinkle. "You saw her do it?"

I nod.

"And that's never happened before?"

"No. Never."

"Did your grandmother say anything else?" he asks.

I pull my chilled arm back under the blanket. "She told me that my mom met my father here and not in San Diego like I thought. She said that he could heal, too." I shake my head. "I don't even know if the person who lived with us when I was a kid, the person she told me was my father, really was or not."

"What about Rob Jarvis? Did you find anything out about him?"

I shrug. "I don't know anything definitive, but I'm guessing someone in my family met him at the nursing home and hired him to find us. I know Kyle had been trying to get custody of me for a couple of years. It makes sense that he might send someone to watch us, to maybe get some evidence of my mother's lack of parenting skills."

"We could track him down," he suggests. "Ask him to tell us what he was doing there."

A few minutes ago, I was completely alone, and now the words *we* and *us* are slipping out of Lucas's mouth like it's a normal everyday thing. I feel a sense of relief flood through me. "Okay," I reply. "I'd like to talk to him."

"Can I ask you another question?"

His hesitant tone gives me pause. "It seems there isn't much I won't answer tonight."

He leans in closer. "Why did you do it? Why did you heal me despite what your mother told you and knowing that you'd be revealing yourself to me?"

I pull my bottom lip into my mouth, trying to form my answer. His eyes drift down to my lips, making me very aware of them as I try to explain. "This energy builds inside me when people are hurting. I have this deep need to help. I can't watch you in pain and not want to take it away for you."

Something in the way he's looking at me changes, and I recognize the building heat in his eyes. I recall the taste of him and the feel of him, and I also remember the cold shoulder he gave me afterwards. I can feel myself hesitate. If I give into him, and he turns his back on me again, it will devastate me. I can't lose this closeness we've reestablished tonight. Being friends is safer, and it's better than nothing.

I break eye contact to look at the glowing numbers on his dashboard clock. "It's getting late. I told Kyle we wouldn't be gone long. We should probably head back."

He blinks his eyes, and the heat in them flares once more before fading into something that resembles disappointment. But he quickly shutters his feelings. The feigned indifference he wears like a mask is back in place, and I'm beginning to understand what's beneath it. Right now, it appears to be regret.

"You're not going to tell anyone about me, right?" I ask, needing to make that clear.

He shoots me an annoyed look. "Of course not." He grips the steering wheel and turns the key. "So, when I get you home, how are you going explain the fact that you're soaking wet?" he asks as he backs the truck down off the bridge. "And is there anything you can tell Kyle that won't make me look like a dumbass?"

"I'll say that we went for a walk and got caught in the rain."

He raises his brows at me. "I guess that's a no."

When we arrive back at the house, Lucas wants to walk me to the door, but I convince him to stay in the truck as I dash through the raindrops. Kyle and Chloe are sitting in the kitchen when I poke my head in to say goodnight. Their eyes widen as they take in my appearance. "We got caught in the rain," I say with a shrug because there really is no better excuse, and then I head downstairs to change. I hear them talking to each other as I descend the stairs and I'm pretty sure I hear Lucas's name, but I don't stay to eavesdrop. I continue down, anxious to slip out of my wet clothes.

I have a hard time falling asleep that night as my thoughts continue to tumble through me. I reluctantly recall the feeling I had laying here after being with Lucas that night in the bleachers. I was so sure we were starting something that was going to be amazing. But then he freaked out on me. He decided to end us without consulting me. I understand why he did it, and I know he regrets it, but as much as I'd like to regain that thrilling feeling of jumping into something with him, it's going to take time to trust him again.

I think about those goodnight texts I got from him when we first admitted our feelings for each other, and I reach for my phone. There are no texts tonight. But why would there be? He tried to open that door again, and I basically slammed it in his face. But I can't help the disappointment I feel when I allow myself to scroll through the those early texts, thinking I should delete them, but knowing that I never will.

FIFTEEN

THE next day at school, I turn the corner on my way to class when I see Lucas and Sophie standing by his open locker. There's only a trickle of students left in the hallway, and Sophie's voice carries easily to me. Rather than walking past them, I find myself ducking back around the corner, waiting for them to leave. But they don't leave. They continue their conversation.

"Are you going with someone else?" she asks him, but it sounds more like an accusation.

"I'm not going with anyone right now," he replies, sounding much calmer than her. I feel a bite of annoyance at how unflappable Lucas usually is.

"Then why won't you go with me?" Sophie states with disbelief. "I've talked about the senior prom with you all year. The plan was always to go together. We can just go as friends if you want. We used to be good friends, Lucas." Her voice softens.

"I know, Soph. That doesn't have to change, but other things do."

She harrumphs loudly. "It's because of that new girl, Rachel, or whatever her name is."

"Her name is Raielle," he corrects her, and my pulse kicks up, waiting for Sophie to begin badmouthing me.

"You're making a fool of yourself over her. You know that, right? She's not interested in you."

"And how do you know who she's interested in?" Lucas tosses back. "Last I heard, you two aren't exactly BFFs."

Sophie laughs, but she doesn't sound amused. "If you're planning on asking her to the prom, you're too late. She's already going with Chad."

My mouth drops open, and I only hear silence from the hallway. Then Lucas finally responds. "Who told you that?" he asks, his cool slipping slightly now. I inch closer to the edge of the wall, wanting to hear the answer to this myself since it's news to me.

"It's all over school, Lucas. Everyone knows," she states smugly.

"You're telling me he asked her and she said yes?"

"That's exactly what I'm telling you. She's already got a date. Wouldn't you like to go with me? You know we'll have fun." Sophie practically purrs the last sentence. "Lucas, come on." There's a beat of silence, and I have a terrible feeling that she's touching him now. "It's our senior year," she continues coaxing him. "I don't want to go with anyone else. It's always been you and me. We were friends first. Good friends. Can't we be that again?"

After a long silence that has me clenching my jaw, he replies. "Fine, we'll go," he bites out.

My hands curl into fists.

Sophie does seem put off by his less than enthusiastic agreement. "Of course we will. That's how it's supposed to be," she says with satisfaction. "We can share a limo with Kellie and Jake. I'll get the tickets today. We're going to have so much fun." She sounds giddy.

"I've got to get to class," Lucas states. Then I hear his footsteps echo down the hallway. A moment later, I hear Sophie's heals clicking away in the other direction.

I hug my books to my chest as my throat tightens. Sophie lied to manipulate Lucas into taking her to the prom, and it worked. He believed that I would say yes if Chad asked me to the prom. I have no right to be angry with him. I know that. I gave him no encouragement last night. What did I expect? But I know the answer to that. I'm an idiot because I expected him to keep trying, and I expected myself to eventually begin to trust him and give in. What I failed to remember is that Lucas doesn't need to keep trying to win me when he has so many other options, and at least one of those options is willing to play dirty.

When I arrive in class, I get a tight smile from Lucas as I sit down beside him. If I hadn't overheard his conversation, I'd probably be torturing myself, wondering why he seems so standoffish again this morning. We walk together between classes, and I make a conscious decision to just be normal around him, and not to mope or inform Lucas that I'm *not* going to the prom with Chad.

"I was thinking," I begin before we reach history, still working hard at the normalcy thing. "You've given me an opening to ask Kyle about my grandmother's healing business. If I want to find out what he knows, I can now say that you told me what my grandmother used to do and then see how he responds. Before, I couldn't mention it without giving away the fact that my grandmother told me herself."

Lucas halts me with a hand on my arm. My skin warms where he touches it. When his eyes meet mine, my reaction to him is immediate, and I'm hoping my face isn't as flushed as it feels. My hopes are dashed when his nostrils flare in response. He clears his throat and removes his hand. "I think we should talk to Jarvis before you do that."

It takes a moment for his words to register. "Why?"

"If Kyle hired him, we should find that out first."

I tilt my head at the worry on his face.

Students file by us, going to class, and Lucas waits for them to pass.

"Let's talk about this later, okay?"

I reluctantly agree, and we head inside. I spend class thinking about what Lucas said. He's worried about my talking to Kyle. But what are his suspicions where Kyle is concerned? If Kyle already knows what I can do, does he think Kyle wants me to pick up my grandmother's business where she left off? Is he afraid of Kyle trying to use me in some way or expose me? Before I realize it, the bell rings, and I've just spent the entire class inside my head.

After class, Lucas is all business. "Tell Chad you want to watch his band practice. When you find out when and where the practice is, tell him you'll meet him there, and I'll go with you. We'll talk to Jarvis then."

The last thing I want to do is ask Chad to see his band practice and give him the wrong idea. Of course, Lucas doesn't know that I don't talk to Chad on a regular basis. But I agree to it because it's a good idea, and a part of me is mad at him for agreeing to go to the prom with Sophie.

As we approach my locker, I see Gwen standing there waiting for me. Lucas gives me what looks like a sarcastic salute, and then he nods at Gwen as he continues down the hall.

"What happened to his cast? I thought he broke his arm," Gwen says.

"I guess not," I mumble.

"So, are you guys on again?" she asks. "I can't keep track."

"No, we're friends, I think." I turn away from the mesmerizing view of his retreating backside and open my locker.

"Uh-huh," she says skeptically. Then she punches me lightly on the arm. "Why didn't you tell me Chad asked you to the prom?"

"Because he didn't." I roll my eyes as I toss my books in and slam my locker door closed.

"He didn't?" Her brow creases. "But Sharon told me he did."

I turn to face her. "Who the heck is Sharon?"

"You don't know Sharon? She's a senior. She works in the office with me. She heard it from Hailey."

I reach inside my bag, trying to locate my lunch. "Hurricane Hailey? Did she start this rumor?"

"I don't know. She's friends with Sophie and Kellie. So, it's possible, I guess. It's just a rumor then?" She seems disappointed.

I shake my head, and I can't help my amused smile. "What a tangled web I weave."

"So, if he didn't ask you, why is everyone saying he did?"

"I thought Sophie started the rumor because she wanted to go to the prom with Lucas, but Lucas didn't want to go with her. At least that was the case until she told him I was going with Chad."

A smile lights up Gwen's face. "Lucas wanted to take you to the prom?"

I sigh. "You're missing the point here. Lucas is taking Sophie to the prom."

"Not when you tell him that she's a bitch who lied to him. Then he'll want to take you," she says simply.

I take a deep breath and release it slowly. "But if she wasn't involved in starting the rumor, then she didn't lie." I shake my head. "Anyway, I don't want any part of this. It's too much drama for me."

She reaches an arm out to me. "You want to go with him, don't you?"

"I told you. I'm not into dances," I answer, while inside my head I'm yelling, *of course I want to go with him*! But the reality is, this is not something I ever pictured myself doing. Going to my prom with a boy I'm completely crushing on, who's crushing on me right back. That's not my life. That was never meant to be me.

She purses her lips at me like a disappointed school teacher. "You're all kinds of messed up, Raielle."

I roll my eyes yet again. "Tell me something I don't know."

"I don't blame you for having cold feet after the way he treated you. But don't let your pride stand in your way if he grovels enough and wants another chance."

I snort out a laugh and shake my head.

"What?" she asks.

"He didn't grovel, exactly. But he did already apologize, and I think he's still interested."

"Then what the hell are you waiting for? Go talk to him," she says, her tone serious now.

I glance down at the floor, knowing I don't have the guts to do that. "I'll think about it."

"Hopeless." She points her finger at me.

"What's hopeless?" Myles asks, appearing beside Gwen. I subtly shake my head at her, my eyes pleading for her to keep quiet.

"You," she states, looking him over. "What were you thinking when you paired that shirt with those pants this morning?"

With that, I expel the breath I'd been holding. I really don't need more voices being added to the 'Give Lucas another chance' chorus.

Myles eyes me with concern, and I wonder if Lucas told him what's going on with us or if he's heard the prom rumors, too. Knowing I'm probably in for more coercion at the lunch table, I decide now is a good time to talk to Chad.

"Do you guys know where Chad eats lunch?" I ask since I never see him in the caf.

Their reaction to my question is comical. Gwen narrows her eyes at me while Myles's eyebrows shoot straight up. "Why do you want to know that?" he asks.

"I need to talk to him."

"It's true then? About the prom," he says, with obvious disapproval.

"It's not true," Gwen tells him for me. "I don't see how talking to him solves anything, but he sits behind building A. There are some picnic tables back there."

"Thanks." I avoid eye contact with Myles as I waste no time heading in that direction.

Despite the calendar indicating that it's spring, there's an icy chill to the day, and I wish I'd worn my coat. New York can't seem to decide what season it wants to participate in. I shake my head at the weather here, missing Southern California's mild climate more than usual.

I easily spot a row of picnic tables that have seen better days sitting in the shade of building A. This is obviously where the students who think black is a primary color like to eat. I easily spot Chad's bald head at the most crowded table. He's surrounded by girls, groupies it looks like, gushing over him. One of them spots me and scowls as she warns the rest of the group of my approach.

Chad's head immediately pops up, and he stands. When I reach the table, I ignore the dirty looks I'm getting and keep my eyes on him. "Can we talk for a minute?" I ask.

He nods. "Over there." He lifts his chin toward the empty table at the end of the row.

Once we're settled across from each other, he says, "So, I heard that I'm taking you to the prom." He smiles with amusement.

"I heard that, too."

He rests his arms on the table. "Did you start that rumor so I'd ask you?"

I work hard not to glare at him. "No, Chad. I didn't. I thought maybe you did."

"Nah," he shakes his head. "The prom isn't really my thing. But we could still hang out."

My hand is on the table in front of me, and I realize he's sliding his fingers toward mine. I immediately pull my hand back and watch as he changes from smug to curious. I make myself smile, wondering what the heck I'm doing here. "The prom is no big deal for me either," I say and watch his eyes travel down to my chest where they stall rudely.

My jaw tightens, and I cross my arms in front of me. "But I really love your music." I plaster my slipping grin back on. "I was wondering if I could watch your band practice some time?"

He rubs a hand over his scruffy chin and shrugs carelessly. "Sure, the fans come to our practices all the time. We meet over at Desmond's house on Thursday nights."

"That's tonight," I say, pretending to know who Desmond is.

He nods. Then he squints at me. "Damn, you're frozen over there. Take my jacket."

To my utter surprise, he stands, pulls off his leather jacket and brings it around to me. "No, it's okay," I protest. But he places it on my shoulders and sits down on the bench beside me. "Go on. Put your arms through."

I do it because I'm so flabbergasted by his unexpected concern.

"Have you got a pen? I'll write down the address for tonight." His face is uncomfortably close to mine, and I don't like the way his eyes are wandering down to my lips.

"I'll just put it in my phone." Then I unnecessarily inch away from him to extract my phone from my pocket. I punch in the address and the time he gives me. When I look up, I realize he's moved closer again. From the corner of my eye, I see we have a rapt audience. "Um, Chad, I'm not really interested in getting into anything right now," I say awkwardly, keeping my voice low. For some reason, I don't want to embarrass him.

He chuckles. "That happens to be exactly what I'm interested in doing."

I realize he's leaning in to kiss me. "And also, I'm a lesbian," I blurt out.

This makes him pause. "That's hot," he breathes.

I inch away again and realize my reluctance is finally registering with him.

"Seriously?" he asks, staring at me as though he doesn't believe it.

I try not to cringe as I lie with a nod.

"No shit. I've never met a lesbian before. That's cool." He shrugs. "It makes sense." Then he smiles slyly. "Bring your friends tonight. Okay?"

"Sure." I shrug out of his jacket wondering why he thinks it makes sense. Then I realize he's probably referring to the fact that I keep turning him down. What an egomaniac. And I am planning to bring a friend. It's just not who he's expecting. "So, I'll see you later," I say, standing and watching as his eyes rake over me.

"Yeah. Later," he agrees on his way back to his table.

Once I'm a good distance away, I glance over my shoulder and notice his cronies leveling curious looks at me. I know exactly what he's just told them. I laugh to myself. I've just added another rumor to the pile, and I wonder how long it's going to take before this one gets back to me.

I'm scheduled to work tonight, but I call Scoops and ask Stacy if she's knows of anyone who might want to switch days with me. Turns out, Jacinda is there, and she offers to stay through my shift if I take hers tomorrow. So, now I'm working Friday night, one of their busiest nights Jacinda tells me with barely suppressed glee now that I've taken her shift.

I send Lucas a text telling him when and where the practice is. He texts me back a few minutes later to let me know he'll pick me up at eight.

At dinner that night, Kyle is not happy when I tell him that I'm going out with Lucas.

"It's a school night," he states. "And you just went out with him last night. I think this whole thing is moving too fast."

"Nothing is going on. We're just friends."

He darts a skeptical look at me.

"I'm not lying to you, Kyle," I state, feeling angry at his distrust even though his instincts aren't exactly wrong. The fact that nothing is going on doesn't mean Lucas and I both don't want it to.

This seems to deflate him. "I know you're not," he says.

"Your nose will grow if you lie just like Pinocchio's." Penelope points at my nose.

"That's right. Lying is very bad," I say.

She nods gravely at me.

"Eat your dinner," Chloe instructs Penelope, helping her to spear a bite with her fork.

"Be back by ten," Kyle states.

I nod my agreement and hurry through my dinner.

D A S H outside when Lucas pulls up, and I already have my hand on the car door handle when he appears beside me. "I was going to get that for you," he says. The low, rumbling sound of his voice sends a shiver through me.

He's wearing a long-sleeved black pullover that stops just above the waistline of his low-slung jeans. I'm wearing a black turtleneck sweater with blue jeans, too. I grin as my eyes travel over his clothes and finally up to his strong jaw line and mussed hair. "We must be on the same wavelength tonight," I say, gesturing between our matching outfits.

He gives me a stiff smile. "That would be a nice change."

I study him and wonder whether Myles told him the truth about Chad not being my prom date. If so, I would think he'd be toning down the attitude.

I step up into the truck and let him the close the door after me feeling too tired to play 'Guess my mood swing' with him tonight. "Do you know who Desmond is?" I ask once we're moving.

"The drummer. He used to go to our school. I think he dropped out."

The ride continues silently after that. I turn to watch the downtown area pass by the window.

"I got asked a lot about my missing cast today," he says causing my eyes to land on his toned forearm.

"What did you tell people?" I let my eyes wonder to his face, so handsome in profile.

He glances at me. "That the doctors screwed up and it was never really broken."

"How did you get the cast off?"

"I used my dad's power tools, mostly the buzz saw. Liam helped me."

My eyes widen with worry that he used a saw on himself, but his perfectly fine looking arm stops me from commenting.

His hand opens and closes on the steering wheel. "Can I ask you something?"

I immediately tense up. When he asks permission to ask a question, that's a bad sign. Despite my worry, I nod.

"What does it feel like when you're healing someone? Does it hurt?"

A knot forms in my stomach. After spending my life not talking to anyone about this other than my mother, it feels wrong to do so now. But it's too late to turn back. He already knows my secret, and I know his. Deep down I'm glad. I couldn't handle this alone anymore and for some reason, I trust Lucas with this even if I'm not sure I can trust him with my heart. "It hurts not to heal," I finally answer.

He wrinkles his brow as he chances a long look at me.

"When you found me in the stairwell that day, I'd just brushed against someone who was in pretty bad shape. I think it was probably that student, Derek. Because I didn't use my power to help him and I held it back, I felt sick."

"Sick? That's an understatement. You were shaking like a leaf and could barely stand," he points out.

I nod my head.

"That happens every time you don't heal a sick person you come into contact with?" His incredulous question is understandable. I couldn't live my life if that was how it worked.

"I don't pick-up on all sickness. If someone's illness hasn't progressed enough to affect their health, I won't sense it. But if I'm near a really sick person, one who's hurting, it can happen when I let my guard down. I know how to block it out most of the time so that I don't get inundated or overwhelmed. But when I'm upset or stressed, things sneak in sometimes."

He blinks for a minute as though he's processing something. "Jesus, that's why Chris was covered in blood that night but the paramedics couldn't find a scratch on him. You pulled him across the road to get him away from the car, and you healed him."

"It was inadvertent, but yeah, I did. That night definitely ranked pretty high on the stress scale."

He runs his hand over his cheek and glances at me. I can sense his hesitance. "What is it?" I ask.

"Why didn't you help Grady? He was in much worse shape than Chris. He still is."

I barely understand my own abilities. It's hard finding the right words to explain them to him. "There are rules," I say.

He continues to glance at me as he drives, waiting for me to expound on that.

"The number one rule is don't fuck with death."

Lucas widens his eyes at me, looking too long this time, and swerving at the last minute to stay on the road. He curses under his breath and pulls over to the side, putting the truck into park.

"We need to get to the rehearsal," I protest, looking pointedly at his dashboard clock.

"There's time." Lucas turns his body to face mine. "What do you mean, don't fuck with death?"

My palms are beginning to sweat with his full attention on me now. I shift uncomfortably in my seat. "I'm not supposed to heal anyone that's meant to die, as in die imminently. I can't try to reverse that."

"Why? What would happen? Would they die anyway?"

"No. I could save them, but death would find someone else close to them, usually a family member, a blood relative. I've seen it happen with my mom and then my grandmother told me about it, too. That night, I could feel how close Grady was to death. I knew I couldn't touch him. If I brought him back from the edge or something, death might find someone else in his family instead. I couldn't risk it."

Lucas is slowly shaking his head, and I'm not sure exactly what he's thinking. "You're saying death would actually jump to someone else?"

"I know it sounds crazy, but that's how it works." I rub my wet palms over my jeans.

He shifts towards me. "You have to learn more about this, Ray. You need to find out where it comes from so you can understand why it works the way it does. It can't just be a curse. There must be some rationale to it, some higher purpose."

I stare down at my hands, and I shake my head. "Do you really think my grandmother was meant for a higher purpose?"

He tugs gently on my arm, causing me to look up at him. "People abuse power all the time. That doesn't mean the power itself is evil, just the wielder of it."

I smile at him, so smart and reasonable in spite of all I've told him. "It doesn't matter," I say. "There's no way to find out more. Mom is gone, and I'm not planning on talking to my grandmother again."

I notice him studying me. "But Kyle may know something, and there's always your father. We could try to find out more about him."

I immediately feel resistant to that idea, and I begin to shake my head.

"Don't you want to know more?" he asks.

"I don't want to open a can of worms. My mother warned me away from all this for a reason." I feel tears of frustration burning behind my eyes, and I clamp down on them. I really do not want to cry in front of him again.

"I'm sure she was trying to protect you, but she also left you in the dark. Is that where you want to stay?" His voice is so calm while my blood pressure is skyrocketing, I can't help feeling irritated.

I turn to look out the window at the night beyond it. He's verbalizing all the tiny, whispering thoughts that are already in my head. It's not hard to ignore everything I don't know about my abilities. I've been doing that forever. It's harder to ignore the fact that I know virtually nothing about my father. My grandmother contradicted what my mother told me, and my mother lied about so many things. Who knows what the truth is? There is a possibility that my father is alive somewhere, and that he has these abilities and maybe some answers, too.

"Ray, I'm sorry," he says gently. "I'm just trying to help."

"I know."

"You never answered my first question," Lucas says. "What does it feel like when you heal someone?"

I turn back to him and take a deep breath as mostly inadequate words pop into my head. "It feels pretty incredible. It's like the thrill of riding on a roller coaster and the peaceful calm of a warm breeze all wrapped into one sensation. It starts as a low vibration that fills me and then flows out of me, and I feel completely aware of everything. Then it changes into bursts of light, like fireworks going off inside me, tingling against all my nerve endings." I shake my head, feeling silly. "It's just so hard to describe."

"It sounds like an orgasm," Lucas states.

My eyes widen at him.

"I think I understand what you're saying," he continues. "That's how it felt for me, too, while you were doing it, just how you described. It was amazing. I was completely connected to you, like we were sharing something intimate without actually being intimate. How can something that you're compelled to do, that feels so incredible while you're doing it, be a curse?"

I clear my throat. "I don't know." I can feel his scrutiny of me.

"You've had an orgasm, right?"

I bark out an awkward laugh, and I feel my cheeks catch fire. I can't believe he just asked me that.

"You haven't. Have you?" His voice is quiet and full of disbelief. "You're not a virgin. Are you, Ray?"

This is too much. "That's none of your business. Can we get moving? We're going to miss the practice."

"Hunh, you are," he decides.

I turn my beet red face to him, and see that he's not laughing at me or even smiling. He's just staring out the windshield and shaking his head like it's too hard for him to comprehend me. I don't know why I'm so embarrassed. I'm not the only seventeen-year-old virgin in the world. "So what if I am," I state defensively. "Is that a big deal or something?"

He turns his bright gaze on me, and I see nothing but tenderness and affection there. "Yes, it is kind of a big deal. But not for the reason you think." Then he swings the truck back onto the road and drives on without saying anything further on the subject.

I'm left speechless, staring at his profile.

THIS must be it." Lucas parks behind a line of cars. If I wasn't already apprehensive before we arrived, our conversation on the way here has me all worked up. "We need to get in front of him before he spots me in case he tries to take off," I say, trying to focus on the task at hand.

"Maybe you should wait in the car," he suggests.

"What?" I gape at him. "I appreciate your coming with me, but this doesn't really have anything to do with you. Why would I wait in the car?"

His expression hardens. "Gee, I don't know. In case he's dangerous or something?"

I'm about to lob a sarcastic remark back at him when I deliberately stop myself. I don't want to argue with him anymore. "Thank you for your concern, but I'm not waiting in the car."

"You stay close to me the entire time we're in there," he orders, stepping out of the truck without waiting for my response. Rather than bristling, I keep calm, understanding that his sudden gruffness stems from his concern even though I don't appreciate him taking that tone with me.

I don't know how the neighbors can stand the noise. From two houses down, I can already hear the vibrating bass and the sound of voices being raised over the din. As we get closer, I notice people mingling on the lawn. All the homes on this street are similar, small single-level clapboard boxes grouped close together. Lucas reaches out to take my hand as we near the door. No one notices or cares about our appearance here. It looks more like a party than a practice.

The front door is propped open, and Lucas steps inside keeping a firm grip on my hand. Immediately, I'm hit by the thick cigarette smoke that fills the hot, heavy air inside. Swimming within it are hordes of people gathered inside the small front rooms of the house. The floor hums beneath my feet with the music the band is playing. I know they're close but I see no sign of them.

Lucas is slowly snaking us through the crowd. I notice a few familiar faces from school turn in surprise when they spot us. "Hey, man." An unfamiliar guy claps Lucas on the shoulder as he passes us. Finally, beyond the heads of the crowd, I spot Chad. It looks like the band is playing in an enclosed porch at the back of the house. Lucas stops and leans down to put his mouth by my ear. "I'm going to move us closer. Stay behind me."

I nod at him, the feel of his warm breath on my ear lingers as he pulls me forward.

I'm bumped and jostled, but we finally end up toward the front of the crowd. I remain hidden behind Lucas as my eyes find Rob Jarvis. The playing is loud but much lower key than it had been in the club. I'm able to really study Jarvis. His long, stringy hair is in a low ponytail and his sleeveless T-shirt reveals a tribal tattoo banded around his narrow bicep. He has a wiry, lanky build. I know it was him that I saw back home. I wish I could call Apollo and ask him what on earth he was talking to Jarvis about. But I've never called Apollo, and that's how he liked it. He had a different phone with a new number every week.

"Hey, it's the new girl." Beside me, I notice a couple of the girls from Chad's lunch table.

"Hi," I smile hesitantly back at them, suspicious of their friendliness.

They glance at the people around me. "Chad said you were bringing some of your girlfriends. Where are they?" One of the girls yells to me.

"They couldn't make it. I brought Lucas instead."

She eyes Lucas before turning assessing eyes on me. "You don't look like a lesbian." She raises her voice and some of her spit shoots out in my direction, just missing my face.

In front of me, Lucas starts coughing. *Great.* He definitely heard that.

The girl turns back toward the band as they finish their set and the crowd roars their approval.

"Come on." Lucas wastes no time, moving us through the remaining people on the porch and placing us directly in front of Jarvis who is bending down to unplug his bass. I notice how new and perfect his instrument is compared to the beat-up ones Chad and the others are using. When he stands, Jarvis glances at me casually, and then he zeros in on my face again before clearing his obvious shock.

"We'd like to talk to you," Lucas says. He and Jarvis are about the same height and Lucas moves forward when Jarvis takes a step back.

"I can sign stuff for you after I break down my gear," Jarvis mumbles, concentrating on wrapping wires and moving equipment.

A smiling Chad appears beside me. "Where are your friends?" He has a beer in his hand and his bloodshot eyes tell me it's not his first.

I glance at Jarvis who seems to be the only member of the band so concerned about getting his gear packed away. "They couldn't make it. Lucas came with me."

Chad glances behind me. "Watch out for that one," he warns. "He's got a temper. Have you told him you prefer girls?"

I decide to play along. "No. Do you think I should?"

He nods. "Definitely. He needs to be taken down a peg." Then a tall blonde ambushes Chad from behind, wrapping her arms around him. "Hey, baby," he croons to her.

She sticks her tongue in his ear. "Let's go find a bedroom."

With that, I'm forgotten. Chad turns and leads her away.

Lucas is growing angry as he stands guard over Jarvis with his arms crossed. "If this is going to take a while, we can talk to you here," he says in an unnecessarily loud tone.

Jarvis straightens and releases out an exaggerated sigh. "Fine. Let's go outside."

He turns and heads for the back of the porch. Lucas is right behind him as Jarvis pushes through a door and disappears into the darkness.

I'm afraid he's going to try to run, but when I get outside, I see him standing calmly in the grass, watching our approach. We stop in front of him and Lucas turns to me, waiting for me to say something. I don't hesitate. I've wanted to talk to him for too long. "Do you know who I am?" I ask.

His eyes travel down my body. "Should I?" he responds with a lascivious grin.

I can feel Lucas tense beside me, and I decide to get to the point. "Look, I saw you in San Diego back when I lived there with my mom. I saw you talking to Apollo one day in front of our building. I also know you work as a janitor at the nursing home where my grandmother lives. There is no way that's all coincidence. I don't want to get you in trouble or anything, but I would really like to know what you were doing in San Diego."

Jarvis glances between Lucas and me. "I don't know what the fuck you're talking about. Dude, your girlfriend isn't playing with a full deck."

Lucas gets in his face. "We know you were there. We just want to know why. So cut the bullshit."

Jarvis scowls and pushes Lucas away from him with a hand to his chest. Lucas narrows his eyes at Jarvis, and the tension immediately thickens.

Before Lucas can go after him, I move between them. "Please, won't you just tell me if someone in my family sent you to find me and my mother? I won't say anything to anyone. I promise you. I just need to know."

He looks me over again. "I'm not telling you shit. Your whole family is crazy. Your grandmother, your mother, and from what I see, you're no different."

My blood runs cold. "My mother? What do you know about my mother?"

"I'm done with your family. You need to leave me the fuck alone now." He scowls and tries to walk around us.

Lucas steps in front of him and Jarvis's fist connects with his jaw. I gasp as Lucas's head snaps back. But he quickly shakes it off, and with a roar, he's on Jarvis, slamming him down onto the grass, pounding on his face. People rush past me and begin pulling Lucas off him. As soon as a struggling Lucas is yanked up, Jarvis gets to his feet and stumbles back. He's spitting mad as he stands and wipes the blood off his mouth with the back of his hand. Lucas seems fine, but Jarvis's face is a bloody mess.

Abruptly, Jarvis turns and begins storming away, into the next yard.

"Wait!" I yell. I need to know how he's involved with my family, with my mother. I start to go after him, when Lucas grabs my arm. I struggle to pull away from him as I watch Jarvis disappear. "Let go of me!"

"There's no point. He's not going to tell us anything."

"But he knows something. He's involved with my family somehow."

Lucas grabs my waist with his other hand, trying to turn me around. "Listen to me. We need to talk."

I spin angrily but abruptly stop when I see his bottom lip and the right side of his face are beginning to swell. The fight flows out of me, and I wince at the sight of him. "He landed a pretty good punch."

"And I returned the favor. Come on, Ray. Let's go."

I nod and let him lead me past the curious people still milling around and wondering what the fight was about. We go around the side of the house to get to the main road where Lucas's truck is parked. My adrenaline is still pumping and we both move quickly. "What if he tells whoever hired him that I came looking for him?" I ask breathlessly. Cars still line the road, but it's quieter now. I only hear a dog's bark echoing in the distance as we reach the truck.

Lucas lays his hands on my shoulders and turns me to him. "You're asking the wrong question. You should be asking why Jarvis was so defensive and determined to keep his mouth shut. If he was only sent there to find you or to get information about you, why would he react that way to us?"

My muscles tense as I begin to comprehend his implication. But I don't want to let my thoughts go there. It's too terrible to consider. I immediately begin shaking my head at him.

My denial doesn't deter him. "Just think about it. It's not a crazy conclusion to draw here."

I step away, but he stays with me. I keep moving until my back hits the side of his truck. His hands move down to my arms and I stare into his sharp blue eyes. They're dead serious and intent on mine.

"You think he killed my mother," I whisper.

He doesn't answer. We both know that's what he means.

"But why?" I ask. "Why would he do it? Why would anyone in this town want her dead? She's been gone and out of their lives for almost twenty years."

"What was the result of her death?" he asks.

I blink my eyes and feel the tears trailing down my cheeks. "It brought me here," I reply reluctantly. Even as the words leave my lips, I'm screaming inside that it's just not possible. "Kyle couldn't do that. He couldn't kill our mother. Just to bring me here? It doesn't make any sense."

Lucas's hand reaches up, and he swipes at my cheek with his thumb. "Maybe it wasn't Kyle. Maybe it was your grandmother. Maybe she had a moment of clarity and set this in motion."

"No. She didn't even know I existed."

"What about Alec?"

I immediately rule him out, too. "What would his reason be? He went this long without getting his divorce, and I can't think of any other reason he'd want her gone or want me here."

Visions of walking into our kitchen and finding my mother, her head surrounded by her own blood are all I can see as we argue about her killer. It's the same scene I've revisited many times both awake and asleep, except now, my body starts to tremble as I see Jarvis there, too, his arms raised, ready to land a killing blow.

"I didn't know you were the one who found her," Lucas says, his voice thick with emotion, and I realize I must have said at least some of that out loud as he pulls me to him.

"I tried to bring her back." I reach up and clutch his shirt in my hands, needing to hold on to something. "After everything she warned me about, I still put my hand on her and tried. But her skin was already cold. I was too late."

His fingers run up and down my back in a slow, soothing pattern. "I'm so sorry you had to go through that."

I lean into him. I thought I was okay, but I had no idea how much I needed this comforting. I stay this way, close to him, and I let myself feel my grief, knowing that I'm in a safe place. My whole life, I've never felt as safe as I do when I'm with him. It's okay to let myself fall apart a little, because if I have Lucas, I'll be able to put myself together again when I'm ready. His warmth seeps into me, and I begin to relax in his arms. I'm not sure how long he holds me this way before my soft crying finally quiets. But he doesn't release me. He continues to keep me close as my grief starts to change into something else. I become all too aware of his hard muscles pressing against my chest and stomach. His lips are beside my ear, and I know I only have to turn my head a fraction to receive the kiss I'm now craving. But I can't use him that way. I can't let my emotions unravel me and mislead him when I know I'm not ready to jump into something with him again. I regretfully pull back and try to think reasonably about what happened here tonight.

"Rob Jarvis may be her killer, but there's nothing I can do about it. I can't go to the police with just my suspicion, can I?" I ask, releasing his shirt and looking up at him.

He shakes his head, agreeing with me. "I don't think I want you going back to Kyle's house," he says.

"What choice do I have? Where else would I go?"

He has no answer. He doesn't offer his house, and we both know why.

"Kyle won't hurt me," I reason. "Somehow, I just know that. I feel like we're missing something here. To find out what that is, I need to go back and act like everything is normal."

He lets out a frustrated breath and runs his hands through his hair. "There's a problem with your plan if Jarvis tells them we've just confronted him, and they start to worry about what he might have told us."

"He said he was done with my family. I don't think he'll go running to them now."

Lucas eyes me, seeming torn. "Look, if you go back, I need a way to make sure you're okay." He thinks for a moment. "We'll leave our phones on. We'll keep a call connected all night and if anything happens, I'll hear it."

I appreciate the gesture, but it seems a little extreme. "Leave our phones on all night?"

He nods. "I have to know you're okay, Ray."

Then, unexpectedly, he moves forward, pinning me against the truck. I inhale sharply as his body presses into mine. He leans his forehead against me. I can feel his warm breath on my face. I freeze when his lips whisper across my cheek. He stays this way, crowding me, surrounding me. Every place his body touches mine feels like it's on fire. My heart begins a punishing rhythm. It seems like forever, waiting for his next move, wondering if he'll kiss me, needing him to. Finally, he does, hesitantly at first as though he's waiting to see if I'll stop him. When I don't, the sudden pressure of his lips against mine feels so perfect that I moan softly. He hears it, and now he has all the encouragement he needs. He deepens the kiss, instilling it with all his pent up want and desire as his tongue caresses mine. I'm still braced against the truck, my back digging into its hard surface. But I hardly feel it. I only feel how much Lucas wants me, and underneath it, I also feel a dull pain, his pain. I reach my arms up to wind them around his neck. I gather my energy, letting it build, before sending it out to him. I can feel the moment it reaches him. He stills, and I know the swelling in his face is already diminishing.

"Ray," he breathes his nickname for me, and he kisses me again, but this time it's harsher, more demanding. The weight of his body, molded to mine, is making me crazy. An aching need grows deep within me. His hand moves down my side, and he grasps the back of my thigh, pulling my leg up, and hitching it around him. When he presses his hips against my mine, I fist my hands in his hair and gasp at the pleasure that moves through me. His warm fingers are beneath my sweater now, sliding against my exposed skin, and suddenly it just isn't enough. I want his hands on me everywhere. My whole body is aching for him.

"Get a room!" someone yells. Then I hear peals of laughter pass by.

We both hear it, but it takes a moment to sink in. We're standing in the middle of the street, and Lucas nearly has my sweater pushed up to my shoulders, but I shamelessly continue kissing him. Finally, he has the presence of mind to slow us down. He eases away from me, gently lowering my leg and smoothing my sweater back into place. My breathing is heavy in my ears, and I can see his chest rising and falling as he brings himself under control. My eyes slowly focus on him. Calm and cool Lucas looks as shattered as I feel.

His hand reaches up to explore his now perfectly healed cheek and lip. "Thanks," he says with a disbelieving smile, like he's still getting used to what I can do.

"My pleasure," I grin back, surprised that I can manage a grin after everything that happened tonight.

"Mine, too. That was some kiss," he says slyly, running his fingers over his lips. But then his eyes regain their focus, and they sharpen on me. He takes a breath before he says, "Look, I need to know we're on the same page here. I don't want to see you in school tomorrow and be back to square one. I'm not fighting this anymore. Are you?"

His voice holds a challenge, like he's daring me to deny what's between us. But I can't imagine fighting it now either, not after what just happened. Doing so would be dishonest because he's already won my trust again. It's only my fear holding me back now. But I don't want to give into fear anymore. "No." I shake my head, still feeling overheated.

"Good," he nods, looking relieved.

Then I remember the way he walked up to me in school and threw a possessive arm around me the day after our driving lesson. I recall the unwanted attention it brought me, and then the sympathy I got from Gwen when it ended so quickly. I would really rather not deal with either of those reactions again.

"But in all honesty Lucas, I don't want the drama that public displays of affection will bring us. I'm not really into that anyway. So, maybe we could just play it kind of cool when we're in school," I suggest.

Lucas does not look pleased with my request. But then he smirks at me. "It might also put a crimp on your lesbian lifestyle. You want to explain that one?"

I sigh, still feeling badly for lying. "I wanted Chad to stop asking me out, but I didn't want to hurt his feelings. So, I told him I was a lesbian."

He tries not to laugh, but some chuckles slip out. "And he believed you?"

I nod, unable to prevent my own embarrassed smile.

"About Sophie," he begins, running a hand down his rough cheek as his good cheer evaporates. "She thinks I'm taking her to the prom."

"I know."

He seems surprised at first, but then he just nods. He's probably assuming I heard it through the busy school grapevine. "I'm going to tell her that I can't go with her. I want to go with you if you'll let me take you."

This is what I thought I wanted, to go to the prom with Lucas. But accepting this way doesn't feel right. I spent most of my life with a woman who was incapable of following through on anything. In an effort to be nothing like her, I'm pathologically determined to honor my

217

commitments. I need to know Lucas is someone who believes in doing that, too. Besides, this afternoon I overheard Sophie talking to a group of girls about how she's been looking forward to her senior prom since her first day as a freshman. As much as I would enjoy dressing up and spending a romantic evening with Lucas, the prom itself holds no real significance for me. If I hadn't moved here, I'm sure Lucas and Sophie would be going to the prom together. I'm also pretty sure Hailey started the Chad rumor, not her. If Lucas cancelled on her now, it would be a real slime ball move, and I don't want to be the reason behind it.

I brace myself for his reaction. "You told her you would go. I think you should take her as planned."

He doesn't disappoint me with his incredulous expression. "You want me to go with Sophie?"

"No, of course not. But it's not right to back out."

He blows out a frustrated breath. "I always wanted to go with you. I was going to ask you, but I was still trying to get you to forgive me. Then Sophie told me you were going with Chad, and I was pissed about it. That's when I said I'd go with her. It was never some romantic proposition."

"I was never going with Chad."

His face fills with regret. "I know that now. Both Myles and Gwen told me."

I hold firm. "But still, you said you'd take Sophie. So, you should."

He shakes his head and laughs in disbelief. "Jesus, Ray. Are you seriously this selfless or are you still punishing me?"

I cross my arms and direct my eyes down to the sidewalk. I'm surprised by how much that hurt. It suddenly feels like he doesn't know me at all. "I'm not punishing you, Lucas."

He mutters a curse before his arms come around me. "I'm sorry. I know you're not. You're a good person. You're better than I'd ever be. And that's kind of unfortunate for me right now."

I understand his frustration. "You can leave early and we can do something after," I suggest.

"You're not going to go then?"

He's nuzzling the side of my head, and I can feel his warm breath in my hair. I lean into him. "No. I don't care about the prom." I notice the cars on the street starting to disperse. "What time is it?" I ask.

Lucas pulls out his phone. "Shit. It's nearly ten." With that, he ushers me into the truck, and then walks around to his side to get us on the road.

"We'll start the call before you go inside," he says as we easily navigate the quiet streets. "If Jarvis talked to Kyle, we should know that pretty quickly."

I release a sigh. I was hoping he'd forgotten about this. "Just so you know, I'm not bringing the phone into the bathroom with me." I watch Lucas, expecting a grin, but he's in serious mode.

"Yes, you are. Just mute it if you're embarrassed. But don't forget to un-mute it. If you do, you'll find me knocking on your window in the middle of the night."

I try not to smile at how seriously he's taking this. I know I should be, too, but I can't seem to muster up any fear of Kyle. I hope I'm not being naïve about him.

When we arrive at the house, the outside lights have been left on for me as usual. While we're still inside the truck, Lucas calls my phone, and I leave it on as he walks me to the door. It's been another whirlwind of an evening with him. All the time we spend together seems to be extreme in some way. I wonder if we can be so volatile and still work. I know one thing…we won't ever be boring.

"Goodnight, beautiful," he says before leaning down to kiss me. I expect a chaste kiss, like last time, in case we have an audience. But I get a hungry, demanding Lucas, coaxing my mouth open and plunging his

219

tongue inside. It takes me a second to catch up, but when I do, I eagerly meet his needs with my own. When he abruptly pulls away, he leaves me both stunned and trembling.

After a moment, he raises his eyebrows and gives me an amused smile. I realize I'm just standing there staring at him rather than going inside. "Talk to you later," I mumble, feeling my cheeks grow warm as I turn to go in. Then I can't help but look back over my shoulder and watch him walk away, admiring his long-legged confident stride and the way his jeans hug his narrow hips. He can almost make me forget the turmoil that brought me here and still surrounds me.

The house is quiet, and it appears that everyone is asleep. I turn off the lights and I'm about to head downstairs when I hear Chloe. "You smell like cigarettes." She's standing on the landing above me, dressed in her bathrobe.

"I wasn't smoking."

She squints at me. She doesn't believe me. "I wanted to tell you that Alec and Linda are coming over for a barbecue on Sunday. We'd like you to join us. You don't have other plans, do you?"

I shake my head.

"Good. This is just for family. No other guests." She watches me, waiting for my agreement.

"Okay," I reply, knowing she's telling me not to invite Lucas.

Chloe says goodnight, and I disappear downstairs realizing Lucas heard our conversation. I know Chloe isn't exactly thrilled that I'm here. I've always felt that. I suppose sometimes it's hard for her to pretend otherwise.

"Not a real warm and fuzzy lady, is she?" Lucas's detached voice startles me.

"She's okay," I reply softly. "Are you home yet?"

"Just walking in now."

I hear shuffling and some static from his end. "I'm putting you on mute now; I'll be back in a couple of minutes." I use the bathroom. Then I get changed and brush my teeth. I have a pile of homework waiting for me but I'm too tired to tackle it tonight. I lay the phone on the nightstand beside me and plug it into the charger so the battery won't run down. Once I turn out the light and lay down in bed, I un-mute the phone. "You there?" I ask.

"Right here. Everything okay?" his deep voice asks in the darkness.

"So far. So good. Can I ask you a question?"

"You just did."

I smile in the dark. "You're a wiseass."

"Was that your question? Because it sounded more like a statement."

I giggle. "Yes, that was me stating the obvious." His quiet laugh carries through the phone. "Now, here's the question. You said you didn't know I found my mother. So, what do you know? What did Chloe say when she came over to Myles's house that day?"

"Let's see," he begins. "She said the most beautiful girl I've ever seen is going to move here and she's going to knock me on my ass."

I chuckle softly. I like this playful side of him. "Right. Why don't you try that again? This time don't forget to use your bullshit filter."

"Hey, that was me stating the obvious."

A pleasant warmth flows through me. I'm about to tell him that it goes both ways. But then I realize something. "Are you avoiding the question?" I ask. "What on earth did she say? Was it that bad?"

I hear rustling. "This was before she met you. I'm sure she," he pauses, "you know, sees things differently now."

I sit up. "After that disclaimer, you have to tell me what she said."

There's silence on his end.

"Lucas, please."

"Okay. But she only knew the facts at that point, that you'd been in and out of foster care, that your mother was an alcoholic and a drug addict, and that your life had been pretty unstable. She was afraid you were going to be some messed up kid who would be a bad influence on Penelope. But obviously you're none of those things. She had nothing to worry about."

I bite my lip, but it's not surprising she would assume that about me.

"I think it's pretty fucking impressive," he says.

"What is?"

"That you're not the person Chloe expected. That you're so well-adjusted despite how you grew up."

I laugh. "I wouldn't exactly say I'm well-adjusted."

"Well, you're not the delinquent you could have been. You know, aside from joy riding in stolen cars," he teases.

I laugh softly. With Lucas's teasing and flirting voice flowing over me, my annoyance at Chloe doesn't take root too deeply.

"Are you going to sleep now?" he asks after a time.

"I guess I'm going to try. You?"

"Trying, too. Goodnight, Ray."

"Goodnight, Lucas." The moment those words leave my lips, I start to wonder what he sleeps in. I'm picturing form-fitting boxer briefs. Since I've never seen him shirtless, but I've felt the hard ridges and planes of his chest and stomach, I'm filling in the blanks quite nicely. I roll over and stifle a groan. How am I ever going to get to sleep when it feels like he's right here in my bedroom with me?

Nearly an hour later, I'm still turning restlessly under my covers.

"Ray?" Lucas whispers.

"Yeah?"

"Can't you sleep?"

"No."

There's silence on his end. Then he says. "I have an idea." I hear a

222

rustling noise, and I assume it's him getting out of bed. Then I hear soft music begin to play. I recognize the mellow sounds coming through the phone.

"Did I just make things better or worse?" he asks.

"Is that M83?"

"Yeah. Is that okay?"

I smile in the darkness. "It's nice."

"Let's try to get some sleep."

"Okay." I close my eyes and let the music nudge away the tension. The soft melody flows over me like a gentle breeze. It seems that Lucas is having trouble sleeping, too, and maybe it's because of his awareness of me. I can hardly process the way I'm feeling as I lay there, listening to the same music as him, knowing that he's with me even if he's not actually *with* me. Soon, I can feel myself slipping into slumber.

SIXTEEN

A T breakfast, Kyle asks if I want another driving lesson after work tonight. Chloe woke up early and made pancakes for everyone, which is unusual for a weekday when we're all in such a rush to leave. Kyle even delayed his departure to have some. Everything feels fine, better than fine this morning, and I decide that Lucas's fears have not come to pass.

I offer to do the breakfast dishes. Once I'm done, I head outside and find Myles waiting for me. Since his falling out with April, Myles has been getting rides to school, and I've been walking on my own. My suspicions are immediately raised when I spot him on the sidewalk.

"Good morning, California girl," he greets me.

I arch a cranky brow at him. Even though I finally did fall asleep last night, four hours of slumber do not make for a happy morning disposition. "You're cheery today," I comment.

He shrugs, a smile still lingering on his lips, and he starts heading toward school.

"Why are you walking this morning?" I ask.

"I always walk."

225

"Not for the last few days." I point out. "Did someone ask you to walk with me today?"

Myles glances at me and flashes his dimples. "I'm glad you two worked things out."

I roll my eyes. This is Lucas's doing. I know Lucas would not reveal my secret to Myles or tell him about our encounter with Jarvis, which makes me wonder what exactly he said to him. "Why does he think I need to be escorted to school?" I ask.

Myles shrugs. "He told me you guys were good now but that he's still stuck going to the prom with Sophie. He said he told you last night, and he wanted me to make sure you're okay with it. You know, feel you out. But don't tell him I told you that."

I decide it's a plausible story. "Tell him I'm fine with it."

He eyes me curiously. "Are you really?"

"Yes. I understand the position he's in. Tell him it's fine. Are you going to the prom?"

Myles scoffs at that. "It doesn't look that way. I offered to take April, but she already asked some guy from her church."

"You could bring your new guy."

His eyes widen. "Yeah, right."

"How are things going with that?" I ask.

Slowly, his lips curl upward.

I laugh. "Wow. That good, huh?"

He nods, looking embarrassed. "Yeah, it's good."

I stop right there and look him in the eye. "I'm happy for you," I tell him.

"Yeah, me, too. For you and Lucas." He shifts uncomfortably. "About what I said to you, you know, about stringing him along. I'm sorry. I was out of line."

"Yes, you were." But not necessarily completely off base, I think. "And it's okay."

226

I'm shocked when he gives me a quick hug and then trots up the main lawn to the school.

After parting ways with Myles, I walk inside and go straight to my locker. I'm transferring books and notebooks for my morning classes, when I hear a familiar voice say, "Hey."

My senses are immediately heightened, and the butterflies swarm inside my belly. I still can't believe what his nearness does to me. "Good morning," I grin, straightening and hoping he listened to me yesterday when I told him no PDA in school. I decide he did because he doesn't physically touch me when I close my locker and turn toward him. Although, the way his eyes are drinking me in, he might as well be caressing me.

"Raielle," a hesitant voice calls my name from behind me, breaking the spell Lucas's eyes have cast on me.

I turn to find myself eye-level with a narrow male chest. When I look up, I see a vaguely familiar face peering down at me anxiously. He's on the basketball team here, I think. I recall seeing him in uniform once. A dark cowlick falls over his forehead, and he absently flips it back with a quick neck jerk. I know he's in one of my classes but I can't place him. "Hi," I say.

He's watching me closely when he realizes that I don't know who he is. "I'm Aaron. We have Latin together."

"Oh, right. Hey." Beside me, I hear Lucas snicker.

"Well, um," he glances down at the floor and then raises his eyes to me again. "I was wondering, since you broke up with Chad, if you don't have another date yet, maybe you'd like to go to the prom with me?"

I stare up at him, and I'm too shocked to form a response.

Beside me, Lucas stiffens and takes a step forward. "You see me standing here. Right, Aaron?"

Lucas's reaction has me wishing the floor would open up and swallow me.

Aaron appears confused by the question. "Yeah," he says.

"Now see this." Before I realize what he's up to, Lucas leans into me, takes my face in his hands and kisses me fully on the lips. Then he releases me and turns back to Aaron with a smug grin.

Aaron's shocked eyes travel from Lucas to me and then back to Lucas again. "Sorry, dude. I heard you were back with Sophie."

"You heard wrong, *dude*."

He shrugs at us. "I guess I got my wires crossed."

I finally find my voice. "Thanks for asking me, Aaron. That was really sweet of you." He nods and seems embarrassed. I watch him lumber away, and I feel badly. I turn to Lucas. "You didn't have to show him up like that. I wasn't going to say yes."

Lucas spreads his arms out beside him with an incredulous look on his face. "I was standing right here and he asked you to the prom." His arms drop, and he shakes his head. "That won't fly, Ray. God knows how many other guys are planning to ask you. People need to know we're together."

"Other guys aren't planning to ask me," I scoff.

"Like hell they aren't. But after today, they'll know you're not available." He reaches his hand out for mine. "Let's get to class."

I hesitate, and he watches me patiently. Finally, I relent and place my hand in his. I'm worried that pretending not to be together will cause more trouble than our simply being open about it. Lucas heads down the hallway, bringing me with him. After a few steps, I think about what Aaron said. "What did he mean Chad and I broke up? Where did that come from? When were Chad and I dating? How did I miss that?"

Lucas grins at me. "I guess your lesbian story didn't catch on."

"I guess not. Lesbian rumor fail."

BEFORE lunch, Lucas tells me he needs to stop by the office. When I ask him why, he's evasive, only saying, "I gotta take care of some stuff." So, I walk to the cafeteria with Gwen, as usual.

"Now you're back on again but he's still taking Sophie to the prom?" she asks, her eyes wide with disbelief.

"He wanted to back out on her, but I told him not to." We find our usual seats. Lisa and Tyler are already there.

"Why?"

I shrug and open my lunch bag. "It's the right thing to do."

"It's the lame thing to do. He shouldn't listen to you. He should dump her ass and take you." Gwen pops open her soda and takes a sip.

"What's this about?" Tyler asks.

"Lucas and Raielle are an item now. But Sophie asked Lucas to the prom before that monumental event occurred. So he's going with his ex instead of her. It's a total disaster."

"That sucks," Lisa says, glancing in the direction of Lucas's usual table. I look over, too, and see that he's not there, but Sophie is glaring at me. I quickly return my attention to my lunch.

"Speak of the devil," Gwen whispers.

Lucas is heading for us with his lunch tray and Myles by his side. "Hey," he says, putting his food down and sitting beside me. Myles sits in the empty seat across from him.

Gwen raises her eyebrows at their appearance at our table. "Trouble in paradise, boys?"

Lisa and Tyler look less shocked to be sitting with Lucas than they were the first time it occurred, but they're still overly interested in their lunch items.

"Did you get your stuff taken care of?" I ask Lucas.

He ignores my question. "I got you a prom date," he states.

"What?" Gwen and I both ask at the same time.

229

"It's me," Myles announces.

I swivel my head in his direction. "You?"

He nods and grins at me.

"That's perfect," Gwen cheers.

Lucas can see I'm about to protest. "You can't miss the prom, Ray," he says. "It's not right. This way, we'll both be there, and I'll get to dance with you."

"I don't dance," I say weakly, but I can't help the thrill I feel knowing that Lucas has arranged this for me. Of course, he benefits, too. Once this gets around, he doesn't have to worry about other guys asking me to go with them.

He shrugs a shoulder. "I don't dance either, but I'm sure we can figure it out." He winks.

Then I point out another problem. "I don't have a dress." That is a real problem. I get my first paycheck this week, but I wanted to save it, not blow it on a dress I'll never wear again.

"We'll go shopping this weekend," Gwen says with way too much excitement.

Lucas is scrutinizing me, trying to figure out what I'm thinking. I suddenly get the feeling he wants to offer to pay for my dress. I turn away before he can say anything. "Are you sure you want to do this?" I ask Myles.

"I wouldn't do it otherwise. I was actually kind of bummed about not going. Then Lucas came up with this idea, and I told him I was in. It's a good solution."

"Any girl you asked would have gone with you," I say. I've noticed that he's got plenty of female admirers even though he's oblivious to it.

He shrugs. "But I wasn't going to ask anyone."

I can feel myself caving. Now that it's a real option, I want to go. I'm actually a little bit excited. Bye-bye first paycheck, hello prom night.

"Okay," I say and Gwen squeals as she pulls me into a hug. Lucas grins at

230

me, and I melt at the adorable way his eyes crinkle at the corners when his smile is genuine rather than sarcastic. "When is it again?" I ask.

Gwen rolls her eyes. "It's next weekend, dork."

My own eyes bulge at that. "What? So soon? But they just put the flyers up."

"The date has been planned all year and I'm pretty sure the flyers have been up for a while," she replies. Then she and Lisa start discussing getting a larger limo so that Myles and I can ride with them, but Myles prefers to drive, and I agree with him. I don't want any further expenses for the evening.

The rest of the day proceeds uneventfully for me, but not so much for Lucas. In chemistry, I hear from Gwen that Sophie approached him in the hall and said something that made him go ballistic on her. She doesn't know what that something was.

At the end of school, Lucas appears at my locker and drops his keys into my hand. "A driving lesson and a ride to work. It's a two-fer," he states, looking proud of his idea. Since I really like driving his truck, and it includes being with him, it's an offer I can't refuse.

I adore the interior of Lucas's truck. It's just so him with its soft bucket seats that seem to hug you when you sit in them. The clean spicy scent of him lingers inside making me think of the other night when he had me pinned to this very truck, and all I could feel and smell was Lucas. "Is Kyle picking you up after your shift?" he asks, making me blink back to the present and sharpen my concentration so I can back my favorite vehicle out of its parking space.

I nod.

He waits until I'm out of the lot and on the road before bringing up the next topic. "I think we should keep a call open again tonight."

I shake my head in response. I've been turning the events of last night over in my head throughout the day, and I disagree. "I really don't think I'm in any danger. Everything at home seems pretty normal. I've

231

been wondering if we're overreacting about Jarvis. For all we know he has a combative personality. I think we were jumping to conclusions last night. It's possible he was there to find my mother and me and that's all he did. My mom was no angel. It's more likely what the police thought in the first place. She had a sordid past and it caught up with her."

Lucas doesn't respond. He keeps his eyes on the windshield.

"Besides," I continue, taking the turn that will bring me downtown, "I'm only here for another couple of months. I just need to graduate, and then I'm moving back to California. Nothing is going to happen between now and then."

"You heard from UCLA?" he asks.

"No. But every school I applied to is there. Either way, I'm going back. I turn eighteen in June and then I'll be on my own." I knew I only had a short time with Lucas before we would both be leaving, but saying it aloud causes a lump to form in my throat. I've spent my whole life leaving, but this time will be different. I know I should be protecting myself. I should be holding something back and not allowing Lucas to get to me the way he does, but the effort would be in vain. I can't fight the unexplainable connection that exists between us. Even if I tried, Lucas wouldn't stand for it. He'd be at my door calling bullshit in two seconds flat.

"June what?" he asks.

It's takes a moment for the question to register. "June twentieth. When's your birthday?" I ask as I pull up to the Scoops entrance.

"January twenty-second, which means I'm older and wiser than you." Then he releases his seatbelt and steps out. A few seconds later, he's at my door, pulling it open. When I get out, rather than walking toward Scoops, I turn to Lucas, wrap my arms around him, and hug him close to me. He stands motionless at first, surprised at my gesture. But he quickly adapts as his arms encircle me, and he holds me tightly to him. I'm thinking about how he arranged for me to attend my first

232

prom, and how he took a punch from Jarvis for me. Then he stayed up with me on the phone all night because he was worried about me. He did all this despite what my grandmother did to his mother and all the issues he has going on at home with her. I don't know what I did to deserve having him in my life. I do know that I don't want to leave him. But that's probably what will happen. We'll leave each other because that's how life is. I feel my eyes begin to water, and I take a deep breath, trying to control the tears before they fall.

"Hey, what's this for?" he asks softly near my ear.

"Nothing," I say. "Everything," I whisper a moment later. Then I release him and take a step back hoping my bright eyes don't give me away.

His blue gaze searches mine, trying to figure out what I'm thinking.

"I heard you blew up at Sophie today," I toss out at him, hoping the comment will divert him from the flood of emotion still washing over me.

It works. The warmth in his eyes cools considerably.

"What happened?" I ask.

"Nothing." He runs a hand through his hair.

"You won't tell me?"

"It's not worth repeating." His hands go into his pockets now.

"She said something about me," I state. When he schools his face into the neutral mask that I find so frustrating, I know I'm right, but I decide not to push it. If it was that bad, I don't think I want to know. I might rethink my uncompromising policy for honoring commitments.

"Call me tonight. Before you go to sleep." He plants a light kiss on my lips.

"I'll call you, but no all night call. I need my sleep." I can't have him virtually in my room all night again.

"Why wouldn't you sleep?" he asks with a mischievous smile.

I cross my arms and angle a look at him.

233

"I'll think about it," he shrugs before getting back into the truck, dismissing me before I can argue with him about it.

Once inside, I find my paycheck in the back room inside an envelope with my name written on it. I fold it neatly and slip it into my pocket wondering how much the average prom dress costs.

The first couple of hours are fairly quiet. I'm working with a girl named Sarah who goes to a high school in the next town over. She keeps warning me that Friday nights are crazy, but I don't truly understand what she means until seven o' clock rolls around. Then, out of nowhere, the place is suddenly mobbed and a half hour after that, a line begins to form out the door. No wonder Jacinda was so anxious to volunteer her shift to me.

The next couple of hours go by in a haze of activity. I'm still exhausted from a lack of sleep, and now my hands are numb with cold from scooping gallons of ice cream from the freezer displays all night, not to mention the sore muscles in my arm. Thank goodness Friday night is not my usual shift. By the time Kyle arrives, I'm ready to drop.

"You look wiped," he comments.

My response is a weary grunt, and he laughs at me.

Once I'm in bed, I call Lucas. I'm too tired to do more than grunt at him, too. He says something about picking me up after work tomorrow and taking me out to dinner. I mumble something back about looking forward to it, and then I tell him I'm ending the call and that's that. I'm relieved when he doesn't argue with me, and I'm asleep seconds later.

WHEN my phone rings, I pry my eyes open to find a beam of light, filled with dust particles streaming down from the window high up on the wall. I glance at the clock on the nightstand and realize it's nearly ten in the morning. How did that happen so fast? My phone chimes again, and I grab for it.

"When are we going shopping?" Gwen asks.

234

I rub my eyes. "Good morning."

She ignores my greeting. "There isn't a lot of time to find a dress. Can you go this afternoon?"

"No, I'm working."

"What about tomorrow?" she asks.

"I have a family barbecue to go to."

I hear her breathe out in frustration. "What time are you out of work today?"

"Five, but, Lucas and I are going out."

"Well, then I'll pick you up in half an hour. Looks like we'll have to get it done this morning."

She hangs up before I can protest. I see a text that came in a few hours earlier from Lucas. *Good morning.*

I text back *Good morning,* and then I jump in the shower.

Once I'm dressed, I find Kyle in the kitchen. He has the refrigerator doors pulled open and he's struggling with the grill at the bottom. "What are you doing?" I ask.

He startles and bangs his head on the open door.

"Oops. Sorry." I cringe.

He sits back and looks up at me. "I'm trying to replace the filter on this thing, but it looks like I got the wrong one."

"Where are Chloe and Penelope?" I can still smell the breakfast she cooked earlier.

"At another birthday party for one of Penelope's school friends. What are you up to today?"

"I'm going with Gwen to buy a prom dress."

He smiles at me. "Did Lucas ask you?"

"No. I'm going with Myles."

He raises an eyebrow.

"As friends," I add. "He and April are on the outs. So, we're going as friends."

He seems confused as he processes this. Then he stands and begins to pull his wallet out. "Do you need some money?"

I hold my hand up. "Nope. I got paid last night. I'm good."

"You sure?" he asks.

"Thanks, but I'm sure."

He nods at me then picks up the box the filter came in, turning it around in his hand, squinting at the writing on it.

"I have work today, and then I'm going out after. So, I'll be home later," I inform him.

"Where are you going and who are you going with?" he asks, still examining the filter.

I shrug. "I'm not sure where we're going, but I'll be with Lucas." Then I watch his forehead wrinkle.

"Can I ask why you're not going to the prom with Lucas?"

I hesitate. I wasn't counting on having to explain this to Kyle. "Lucas is going with someone else."

"You and he are still just friends?" he asks.

I shift from one foot to the other. "Well," I hedge. "Maybe more now."

He tilts his head at me. "But he's going with someone else?" he asks confused.

"His ex-girlfriend asked him before he and I became more." I fidget with the bottom of my sweater.

He surprises me when he shakes his head and laughs. "I'm so glad I'm not in high school anymore. Well, it's nice that you're going. And Myles is a good kid. You two will have fun."

"I hope so," I smile, relieved. Then I don't plan to say it. Somehow it just slips out. "Lucas was telling me something about his mother."

Kyle had been playing with a cap on the filter, but his fingers still.

"He said that his father brought her see our grandmother. He said she was rumored to have healing abilities. Did you know that?"

He puts down the filter and gives me his full attention. "I knew about it. She wasn't able to help his mother though, was she?"

I shake my head wondering if he knows the half of it.

"You know," he says, "this rumor goes back even before grandmother. It's said that a member of every generation in our family has had the power to heal the sick. People said our mother had it."

He's watching me so intently now, I feel like squirming.

"Did she?" he asks bluntly, catching me by surprise.

I want to lie, laugh like his question is ridiculous, but doing that won't help me find out what he knows. "She did. And she hated it. It ruined her," I answer.

He's silent for a moment. "Is that why she behaved the way she did?" he asks.

I nod. I know that was at least part of the reason.

"What about you?" He takes a step toward me. "Do you have it?" he asks softly, his eyes studying me.

I nearly stop breathing. For some reason, right now, it feels very important to lie about this. If I don't, I'm afraid everything will change. "No, I don't," I reply evenly. "Do you?"

Something in his eyes shifts, like he doesn't quite believe me. Then it's gone and he smiles. "No."

We stare at each other for a moment, and I can't tell what he's thinking. Kyle looks away first, picking up the filter again and sighing. "Good luck dress shopping," he says before lowering himself onto the floor in front of the refrigerator again.

I release a relieved breath, but I'm not really relieved at all. I'm uneasy.

GWEN arrives and informs me that we're going to the mall. I ask her to stop off at the bank so I can cash my check. I feel jittery, like I've just chugged a couple of espressos. Kyle knew about Mom and I think he knows about me, too. But I don't know what, if anything, that means.

Like a woman on a mission, Gwen marches right into Macy's, which much to my surprise, has a whole department dedicated to prom dresses. There are all kinds in different shapes and colors. I immediately look for the discount rack and start there. Most of them are hideous in awful shades of pink and teal.

"How about this one?" Gwen asks, holding up a deep red floor length dress. It's strapless with a slit all the way up the front.

"You're kidding, right?"

"What?" she asks. "It's sexy."

"It's ridiculous." I shake my head. She returns with a few more ridiculous gowns, looking like she's ready to strangle me as I immediately rule them all out. She's beginning to name other stores we could try when I come across an ice blue dress that I don't hate. It has a high neckline, but it's sleeveless and it gathers in layers at the waist before falling in waves to the floor. More importantly, the price and the size are right.

Gwen follows me back to the dressing room. It's a little tricky getting it over my head, but once I do, it slides down easily. The waist is a bit big, but otherwise, it's a good fit. I turn to the mirror and examine myself. I've never seen myself in a dress like this, and I'm afraid I look ridiculous.

"Come on. Show me," Gwen calls.

I push open the dressing room curtain and step out. Her eyes widen. She just stares and doesn't say anything.

"What?" I ask, looking down at the dress. "Is it awful?"

She chuckles at me. "No, you idiot. You look amazing in that. It's the exact same color as your eyes. It's perfect, Raielle. You have to get it."

I glance back at the mirror, unsure and uncomfortable. "You really think it's okay?"

"I know it is. Lucas is going to take one look at you and go into cardiac arrest."

I smile. I hope he likes it without actually keeling over. "What's your dress like?" I ask her.

"I'm wearing something I found in the city over the summer. It's yellow with all these flowers sewn into the top. I'm so excited to finally have a place to wear this thing."

I run my fingers over the smooth material of the dress. "So, do you and Tyler talk more now that you're going to the prom together?"

She shakes her head, seeming disappointed. "No. No more than usual. I think he just wants to be friends."

"Maybe he's shy?" I suggest.

She laughs. "I don't think that's it. Anyway, it doesn't matter. High school is almost over. I heard from NYU."

I whirl around at her. "You did? When?"

She hesitates. "A few days ago."

Uh-oh. My stomach sinks for her. "You didn't get in?"

"No, I did! Can you believe it?" She jumps up with excitement.

"You stink!" I cry before grabbing and hugging her. "Why didn't you tell me before?"

She steps back from me, looking guilty. "I was hoping you would have heard by now, too. I didn't want to make you anxious or anything."

"I wasn't anxious, but now that you mention it..."

She looks horrified, and I chuckle at her.

"Don't be ridiculous. I'm happy for you, really."

"Thanks. I'm sure you'll get in, too. It just takes a little longer for letters from the west coast to make their way here."

I nod, playing along. But I'm worried that I haven't received anything yet.

"Now, you positively have to get that dress," she says, taking my arm and marching me toward the register. "The prom is going to be a night we'll remember forever."

SEVENTEEN

THE rest of the week passes quickly. I have a huge test in history, and it seems like I'm the only one taking it seriously since senior year is nearly over. Lucas and Myles continue to sit with us at lunch each day and rather than giving me the death glare, Sophie is mostly ignoring me now.

I don't tell Lucas about my conversation with Kyle. In fact, Kyle hasn't brought it up again and just like after the incident with Jarvis, everything seems normal. I almost feel relieved that Kyle knew what he did, about our mother. He thinks he knows something about me, too, but so far, he hasn't pushed it.

Lucas and I had a great date on Saturday night. He took me to a cute Italian restaurant and then we went to see a movie. He offered to see a chick flick, and he was surprised when I wanted no part of that. We ended up at an action film, and he held my hand the entire time. We made out in his truck for a while before he brought me back home, but it wasn't like those other times. He's holding back on me. It's like he knows how easily things can get out of control between us, and he wants to make sure it doesn't happen again. I'm wondering if it's because he knows how inexperienced I am. I'm not ready to have sex with him, but I wouldn't mind if his control slipped a little.

Alec and Linda came over for the barbecue on Sunday. It was a perfect spring day, and I enjoyed watching Penelope play with her grandfather. They really are a nice normal family, and I'm feeling less uncomfortable around them. Although I did excuse myself early, saying I had to study, which was only partly true. The tiny pang of hurt that forms when I see them all together drowns me in guilt, and I hate that their happiness makes me resent my mother all over again each time I see them.

At school on Monday, everyone is talking about the prom. It's being held at a restaurant in Ridgeton that also has a function room. I told Lucas about my dress, and he informed that he's wearing a tuxedo. To my surprise, he's not renting it. He actually owns one.

On prom day, I have to work, but I don't mind. It keeps my mind off my nerves. I'm not sure why I'm so nervous. I guess it's the unknown, having never been to a dance before. It's also going to be unsettling to see Lucas paired with Sophie. The only crimp in the day occurs when I arrive home to get ready and find the house is empty. This morning, Kyle had talked about Myles coming inside so he could take pictures of us. Chloe offered to do my hair and Penelope couldn't wait to see me in my *princess* dress. But now, they're nowhere to be found.

I shower and wash my hair, deciding to let it dry in natural waves and to wear it down if Chloe doesn't arrive home in time to coax it into the up-do she mentioned. Then I apply my makeup, nothing too heavy, and slip into the dress. I have a pair of silver sandals, which were my mom's. I slip those on and go look in the full-length mirror in Kyle and Chloe's bedroom. I hardly recognize the girl I find standing there. I blink at my reflection and for a moment, I see my mother staring back at me. What would she think if she could see me and my new life here? My excitement dims because I don't think she'd be happy about it. She never wanted me to know about my family in Fort Upton.

I turn away from the mirror to check my phone in case Kyle left me a message. Finding nothing, I call Kyle's cell phone, but it goes straight to voicemail. I hang up without saying anything.

Despite the disinterested act I put on, I was excited at the prospect of being fussed over by everyone tonight. Instead, I retrieve my worn copy of Jane Eyre, and I sit alone in my bedroom, waiting for seven o'clock, the appointed arrival time for Myles.

He's about fifteen minutes late when I pull open the door and step outside. At first, he just looks at me, saying nothing. Then he appears confused. "I thought we were taking pictures."

"No one's home," I say, and I can't keep the disappointment from my voice.

"Where are they?" he asks.

"No idea." I shrug.

"My folks are out, too, or else they could take some. Don't sweat it. I'm sure there will be plenty of people taking pictures once we're there. By the way," he whistles loudly, "you're a knockout tonight."

"Thanks. You clean up pretty well yourself." He does look sharp in a classic black tuxedo with a white shirt and black tie. I smile, already feeling better now that Myles is here. He pulls a blue and white corsage out from behind his back and places it on my wrist. "It's beautiful," I tell him as I hold it to my nose and inhale its sweet fragrance.

He has borrowed his mother's Camry for the night, and he escorts me to it. I have a light jacket with me, but it's a clear balmy May evening, and I simply hold it.

"What's your guy up to tonight?" I ask.

"He's at home. He has an apartment in Albany. We're meeting up tomorrow."

"Albany?" I'm surprised. "He's older?"

"He's eighteen, but he's been on his own for a while. His parents pretty much disowned him after he came out to them."

"That's awful."

"That's life," he shrugs. Then he grins at me. "I just heard from SUNY Albany. I got in and I got some scholarship money, too."

"Hey, that's great." I am genuinely happy for him, but I feel myself sinking lower in my seat.

"Have you heard anything yet?" he asks the inevitable follow-up question.

"No."

"You will," he assures me.

I turn to look out the window. It's dusk, and the streetlights buzz to life as we head toward Ridgeton.

The restaurant where the prom is being held is called The Chateau. It's a large white building with a glass front that reveals an oversized chandelier, glittering with yellow lights, suspended over a spiral staircase. Limousines fill the parking lot and students dressed in their formalwear finest are filing inside.

Myles parks the car and turns to me. "Let's do this."

A nervous tremor runs through me even as I'm chuckling at his mock seriousness. He appears at my door and holds out his elbow to me. I'm still grinning as I take his arm. While we make our way to the entrance, I scan the students around us, looking for Gwen or Lucas, but there's no sign of them yet.

Inside, the first thing we see is a photographer taking pictures. "See?" Myles says, grinning at me. We get our photos taken, and then we head into the function room. The lighting is dim with smaller chandeliers hanging over round tables packed together on one side of the room. The other side is a parquet dance floor already filled with people. On a small stage, there's a DJ playing songs. Above him, a large banner reads *Class of 2013*.

"Nice," Myles says over the music.

I nod. It looks surprisingly close to the proms I've seen in the movies. It feels surreal to be here.

"Hey guys!" Gwen runs up to me and pulls me into a hug. Then she tugs on my arm. "We've got a table over there. Come put your stuff down." With no black in sight, Gwen is a vision in pale yellow. Her dress is a full-length baby-doll style, and it looks terrific on her, showing off her slim, willowy figure.

"You look amazing," I tell her while she drags me behind her. Myles follows as we work our way to a table next to the dance floor. Sitting there, I see Tyler, Lisa, and the guy who must be Lisa's date is beside her. "No sign of Lucas and Sophie yet," Gwen informs me. "Come on. Let's dance."

I resist at first, but Myles wants to, and he coaxes me out there. I've been to enough clubs that I can move and not make a fool of myself, but rhythm is definitely not in my blood. Everyone is acting silly, and it's amusing to see the guys from school, who usually look like they just rolled out of bed, all dressed up in their tuxes. The girls' dresses run the gamut from cute to slutty, and there are plenty of the hideous ones I nixed at Macy's apparent throughout the room. But worst of all is Hailey's dress. She's wearing a skintight black lace sleeveless number, and it looks like her bouncing breasts are in danger of popping out at any moment. Gwen and I definitely stand out in our more modest gowns. As I watch Gwen grinning at Tyler and dancing around without an ounce of self-consciousness, I feel grateful that she befriended me, and I decide that I should really tell her that someday.

I spot April standing across the room with a dark-haired boy I don't recognize. Myles sees her, too, and I notice that he keeps covertly watching them.

We dance to a few more songs before heading back to the table. The dining area is filling up, and I notice that waiters are starting to bring food around. I scan the room again.

Myles sees my wandering eyes. "I'll text him and find out where he is."

I pick at my salad and listen with half an ear while everyone chats around me. Myles shows me his phone and shrugs. Lucas hasn't responded. I don't even attempt to eat the chicken that's set down in front me. I haven't heard from Lucas since his usual good morning text, but I figured he was probably busy. And now he's late, really late. Something is wrong. I can feel it. I rub the back of my neck, trying to ease the prickling feeling. By the time dessert is being served, my eyes are pinned on the door and my phone is in my hand.

The principal stands and says a few words about being proud of the class. Then she points to a table where we're supposed to place our votes for prom queen and king. The music picks up again and everyone but Myles and I head back to the dance floor. Gwen tries to pull me up with her, but I shake my head. Once she's gone, I notice April heading for our table. She carelessly bumps into a couple of chairs in her path. Myles stands when she reaches us.

She begins to cry as she points a finger at me. "She's the reason you wanted to see other people, isn't she?" April is slurring her words.

Myles looks stricken as he takes her in. "Have you been drinking?" he asks, reaching a hand out to steady her. But she jerks herself away and stumbles in her heels. "Everyone told me to watch out when she moved in next door to you, but I didn't listen. I trusted you!" She's yelling now, drawing everyone's attention. "You're an asshole, Myles. I hate you!"

With that, Myles grabs her arm and drags her toward the exit with half the room watching them and the other half glowering at me. I sink lower in my seat wondering why I wanted to come to the prom in the first place.

Gwen leaves the dance floor and walks toward me with a sympathetic expression. Then her eyes wander toward the door. "There he is," she says.

I look over and spot him immediately. I vaguely register that he's dressed in his tuxedo and that Sophie, Kellie, and Jake are all with him. But I zero in on his thinned lips and tight jaw. He's upset, and it's written all over his face. I watch as Sophie glares at him and then huffs away. Kellie follows closely behind her. Next Jake says something to Lucas, but soon he walks away, too. Standing alone in the doorway now, Lucas surveys the room.

"What are you waiting for?" Gwen says, nudging me.

I stand and slowly make my way toward him. I hesitate briefly when he clocks me, and his eyes lock on mine. They travel slowly from my face down the length of my body. Then one side of his mouth hitches up. I would be thrilled at the appreciation I see in his expression if I didn't also notice the anxiety that mixes with it.

"Hi," I say hesitantly once I reach him.

His hand reaches to me and I take it into mine. "You're so beautiful it hurts," he says. His voice is low and solemn, and despite the noise in the room, its rich timber vibrates through me.

I feel myself blush at the compliment as he leans in and kisses me on the forehead. "What's wrong?" I ask.

He lets out a deep breath and takes his hand back, plunging it deep into the pockets of his trousers. "There's stuff going on at home. I don't think I'll be able to stay long. I'm sorry."

Stuff? That means absolutely nothing, and I'm disappointed that he doesn't want to tell me. "Is there anything I can do?" I ask, hoping he'll reveal a little more, but he just shakes his head.

When the DJ begins to play a slow song, a small smile appears on his face. "Actually, there is something. You could dance with me." He holds out his hand again.

I take it, watching as his long fingers surround mine. He leads me to a space on the crowded dance floor, and I listen to the song that's playing. It's "Beneath Your Beautiful."

In my heels, we're nearly eye to eye tonight. I feel his arm come around my lower back. Then he shifts our hands, holding them between us, as we begin to slowly sway. My whole body relaxes in his arms as though it knows this is where I'm meant to be. Our connection is even more meaningful tonight because I can sense the sadness inside him. But for a brief moment, I made him smile, and I can be here for him now, just holding him, if that's what he needs.

We move together to the music, not saying anything, just being close to each other. As I'm listening to the lyrics, my heart squeezes. This song could be about us. I shift our hands so they're over Lucas's heart, and I close my eyes as its strong rhythm beats beneath my fingers. We may be surrounded by a room full of people, but right now, no one else exists for me. He turns his face into my neck, and his warm breath fans over the sensitive skin below my ear. I sigh with contentment wishing we could freeze this moment and stay like this forever. The way he's holding me and breathing me in, I sense that he wishes the same thing. It kills me to feel him hurting this way. I want to take all his pain away. I know I'll always want to make anything that hurts him disappear. As the song winds down, our swaying stills, but we don't break apart.

"You should dance with your date at least once."

My eyes pop open. Over Lucas's shoulder, I spot a determined Kellie. She glowers at me before dismissing me. "Especially after you made us wait for you and miss half the prom," she practically snarls at him.

I lean back and watch as Lucas squeezes his eyes closed. When they open again, he gives my hand a light press before releasing it and stepping away from me. I move toward him, wanting to protect him from her. But he just smiles sadly and shakes his head at me.

My heart sinks. I'm the one who forced him to keep his date with Sophie, but seeing how miserable he is tonight, I'm afraid I made a mistake.

Lucas stares up at the ceiling and then back at me once more before walking away. I watch as he winds his way toward Sophie who is surrounded by a group of her friends by the prom voting boxes.

"Got you!" Gwen says, leading me back to our table as she holds my phone out to me. There, I see she's taken a picture of Lucas and me dancing. I place my hand over my mouth when I notice the way Lucas and I are gazing at each other in the photo. We look like a couple in love. I wonder if that's what I'm feeling. Do I love him? Does he love me?

"Where was he?" Gwen asks, interrupting my thoughts. Myles is back now, too.

My eyes reluctantly leave the photo of us. "He wouldn't really say."

"Where's April?" I ask Myles.

"She puked in the parking lot. Her date is taking her home."

I wince at this news. "I'm sorry. It never occurred to me she would think we were an item."

He shrugs. "It's not your fault. I'm going to have to talk to her when she's not drunk and hurling expletives at me."

Another slow song begins to play, and I watch as Sophie drapes herself over Lucas, bringing her arms up around his neck and pressing her body to his. With his hands on her waist, I can see that he's trying to put some space between them.

"Bitch," Gwen whispers.

I can't watch them. I glance down at the picture on my phone one last time before putting it away. When Gwen starts to giggle at something, I look up at her. She points at the dance floor, and I turn to see Sophie stalking away as Lucas talks on his cell phone with a finger held to his other ear, trying to hear better.

"He didn't take any calls when he was dancing with you," she points out.

I'm watching Lucas, and I feel a chill pass through me when his gaze collides with mine. There's something in his eyes I've never seen there before. *Stark terror.*

I stand as he lowers his phone and moves quickly toward our table, but he doesn't look at me. He stops next to Myles.

"Have you got your car here?" he asks.

Myles nods.

Lucas puts out his hand. "Give me the keys."

Myles only hesitates a moment, before standing up and fishing his keys from his pocket. Lucas grabs them and turns for the door.

"I'm going with him," I announce, ignoring Myles's protests and chasing behind a retreating Lucas. I reach him at the main exit to the parking lot.

"Go back inside," he barks at me.

"No," I answer breathlessly trying to keep up with him so he can't ditch me.

He walks a few more yards before wheeling around. "You're not coming with me."

I step around him and continue toward Myles's car. "You're wasting time arguing when you're not going to win. Let's go," I call back over my shoulder. I hear him grunt in frustration before his footsteps quickly follow. When we reach the car, Lucas reminds me of a pot of water boiling over as he roughly unlocks the doors and yanks his open. Once we're seated, he peels out of the parking lot without sparing me a glance.

I don't dare say a word although I'd like to know what I'm getting myself into. The car eats up the dark miles between Ridgeton and Fort Upton. We drive through the town center and then Lucas turns into a neighborhood I've never been to before. At first, the houses are small similar to those where Kyle and Chloe live. But soon the modest homes grow into much larger, obviously expensive ones. Finally, Lucas pulls into a long winding driveway that leads to a towering brick Tudor. I stare wide-eyed at the arching windows and the glossy wooden double-door entrance. This must be his house, and his family is obviously filthy rich. I can't believe I didn't know this.

"Stay in the car," he orders.

I immediately get out. "What's going on?" I ask.

He ignores me as he runs to the front door, unlocks it, and rushes inside yelling his brother's name. I follow closely behind him as he stops at the bottom of a wide staircase and calls Liam's name again. When there's no answer, he races through the living room to the back of the house. I hear a strangled curse as I enter the kitchen a few paces behind him. Lucas drops to the floor at the bottom of a second stairwell at the end of the kitchen. I come around him to find him cradling an unconscious boy in his arms. He's saying Liam's name again and again. There's a trickle of blood coming from Liam's nose, but I can feel that the real injury is to the back of his head. His skull is cracked.

Lucas glances back at me, his eyes wild with fear. "Help him," he whispers. "Please."

I don't say anything, but I move closer to Liam. I can see that he's a younger version of Lucas. They have the same coloring and the same strong facial features. My whole body is pulsating as I give in to the energy building inside me. I'm praying that I can help, that his injuries aren't too serious.

A thud sounds from upstairs causing us both to jump. "My mother." Lucas tenses at the noise, but he doesn't move.

"Lay him down and step away," I instruct.

He hesitates, not wanting to be parted from his brother. I nod encouragingly at him, and finally he shrugs out of his tuxedo jacket, bunches the material together, and gently lays Liam's head down on the makeshift pillow. Then he backs away only marginally.

I place my hand on Liam's forehead and close my eyes, terrified of what I'll find. It only takes a moment for me to understand. Then I breathe out my relief knowing that I can help him. His brain is beginning to swell, but he's not hurt too badly. I place my other hand on his bare forearm, and I let my body do what it needs to. The vibration begins, and I let it grow stronger before I release the coil and send the energy out into Liam. The familiar feeling of falling fills my stomach as my skin begins to tingle. I close my eyes and let myself sink into the sensation.

As the energy passes between us, it happens again. I begin to have a vision. I see Lucas's mother. Her face is a mask of rage as she shoves her frightened son into the stairwell. His arms reach out trying to grab for the banister, but he misses and tumbles backward. There's a landing halfway down the stairs, and he hits it hard, biting down painfully on his tongue as his cell phone drops from his hand. As he's pushing himself up, his mother is there again, standing directly in front of him. This time she shoves him harder, down the remaining steps, toward the tiled kitchen floor below. In shock now, he does nothing to break his fall.

I squeeze my eyes closed, wondering why I'm seeing this, why this is suddenly a part of it. But the horror of the vision fades when the familiar euphoria fills me. Gradually, Liam's skull fuses back together and the injury to his brain recedes. Soon, I can feel him moving. He's trying to sit up.

"Liam?" Lucas says, moving closer, reaching his hand out.

Once the energy disperses, I help Liam up, and I step back so that Lucas can go to him.

Liam stares at his brother, appearing confused. "She pushed me down the stairs," he whispers, like he can't quite believe it. Lucas pulls his brother into an embrace and his body begins to shake. I realize he's weeping. They both are.

As I watch them, I finally understand the anguish Lucas keeps hidden from everyone. I know that the cold expression he wears like armor and the hot temper that flares from within it are products of the turmoil he's been living with for so long. I also know that I can't walk out of here tonight leaving them in a hell of my grandmother's making.

I turn away from them as I pull off my sandals and walk quietly back to the front of the house. Then I move soundlessly up the staircase to the second floor. I stand listening at the top. There are dimly lit hallways on either side of me leading to what I assume are the bedrooms. Only one doorway isn't darkened. That door is open a crack, allowing the light to spill out. I step slowly toward it, my bare feet sinking into the plush carpet. As I'm nearing the room, to my right is the top of the second stairwell that leads to the kitchen. It turns halfway down, just like in my vision. I can't see Lucas and Liam at the bottom, but I can hear Lucas whispering an apology to his brother. He's apologizing for leaving him alone with her tonight.

I move past the stairwell, and now I'm standing before the open door. She's in there. I can feel her there, and I can feel something else, too, coming from inside the room: confusion, darkness, hopelessness. I reach my hand out and slowly push the door open wider. I can see inside the bedroom now. On the floor, there is an overturned nightstand and scattered pill bottles. Lucas's mother is sitting on the bed, facing away from me. Her shoulders are rolled forward, and from the back, her huddled form appears small and still. Her hair, the same chestnut color as Lucas's and his brother's, sticks out wildly around her head while the back is matted down flat.

I slip into the room, stepping around the bed, wanting to get in front of her so I can see her face. As her profile comes into view, I see the same woman from my visions. Her skin is pale, and her eyes are focused on the wall in front of her.

The energy gathering inside me is familiar. Even though Lucas's mother has no physical injuries, she is sick and my own body recognizes that. The same way it recognized my grandmother's illness. I know I can help her. I'm certain of it as I step nearer to her. She doesn't move or acknowledge my presence, and soon I'm standing directly in front of her. Her dull blue eyes stare past me as I lower my hands to her cheeks. With this contact, the energy grows. I'm watching her face when her eyes suddenly open fully and locate me standing before her. I smile, and she blinks with surprise. I'm concentrating on moving the energy between us when her arms shoot out, pushing me away, causing me to stumble back, and breaking our connection. Before I can understand her intention, she's on her feet pushing at me again with surprising strength. I teeter for a moment before I go down hard on my butt. Then she's on me.

She straddles my body as her fingers close around my neck, pushing me down to the floor, and starting to squeeze my throat. My air is immediately cut off. I try to sit up, but I can't budge her. I bend my legs and try to ram my knees into her back, but it does nothing to stop her. I start to panic, uselessly pushing against her, trying to roll her off me.

I can't scream out. I can't seem to make any sounds at all. Even if I could, the last thing I want is for Lucas to find us this way. In trying to help him, I've made things so much worse. My vision begins to blur at the edges, and I close my eyes, not able to watch her as she's killing me. My muscles stop listening to me and struggling becomes more than I can manage. Tears begin slipping down the sides of my face.

Then I feel something, a dull vibration, and my eyes flutter open. The energy is returning. With her hands on my neck, we have contact again. I lift my heavy arms and reach for her, knowing I don't have much time I wrap my fingers around her wrists, concentrating again on moving the energy into her. I can feel myself start to tremble. Somehow, my power is building even as my body is fading. I dig down, pushing it toward her with all the strength I have left, shaking with the exertion. I know her body is absorbing it, drinking it in. I feel her taking it from me. I milk the last drops of energy from within me, and I pour them into her. After a moment, it seems like her grip is loosening. I think I hear Lucas's panicked voice saying my name just as his mother's hands release my throat and everything goes black.

"You're much stronger than I was," my mother says.

We're sitting on the couch in our apartment. I glance down, and I'm surprised to see I'm wearing my prom dress. "What's going on?" I ask her. I notice that she looks better, healthier than I remember.

"I couldn't have healed that woman. Not the way you did."

"What woman?" I ask, leaning forward. "Lucas's mother? Did I heal her?"

"You did. You nearly got yourself killed in the process."

I glance down at my dress and then back at her again.

"You decided not to stay in the shallow end," she muses. "Now you must learn how to swim. But you have to be careful, Raielle. Everyone wants a piece of you. You need to be smart."

I glance around the apartment. "Why am I here? How can we be sitting here talking like this? Am I dead?" I ask.

She smiles at me. "No, despite your reckless behavior, you're not. You were meant for great things, sweetheart. You need to be more careful. Don't let people use you for their own purposes," she says, ignoring my question.

I bark out a laugh. "Will you please tell me what's going on? Am I dreaming?"

Her smile turns sad. "You never did listen to me."

My confusion quickly solidifies into anger. "That's not true. I always listened to you, and I never lied to you." I look into her pale blue eyes as they grow wide at my accusation. "Why didn't you tell me I have a brother?" I demand, my body suddenly trembling with fury. "Why didn't you tell me you had a husband and a son in Fort Upton. You lied when you said we had no other family."

She folds her hands in her lap and stares down at them. *"I left Fort Upton to save myself, and I lied to you about it to keep you safe."* Her eyes find mine. *"You've met your grandmother. I'm sure you understand."* Then she has the audacity to smile.

I point an accusing finger at her. *"But you walked away from your son."*

"He had Alec. You only had me."

I laugh at that. *"You've got to be kidding me? I didn't have you. I didn't have anyone."*

She acknowledges me with wary look and a nod of her head.

"My grandmother said you met my father in Fort Upton and left Alec for him. Is that true?" I ask.

She turns away from me.

I reach out to her. *"Is that true?"*

Her face falls. *"Don't ask about your father."*

"Why not?"

Her eyes fill with tears. *"Because he destroyed me, and he'll destroy you, too."*

I bolt upright, and my throat burns with pain.

"Shhh. It's okay," Lucas says. His image is hazy before me. I feel his hands on my bare arms easing me back down. I realize I'm lying in bed in a strange room. The walls are navy blue, and there are trophies lined up on a tall dresser against the wall. My pounding head is filled with questions, but my throat is too raw to ask them. "Water," I manage to croak out.

"Get some water," Lucas calls toward the door. Then he smoothes the hair back from my forehead. Liam soon appears with a glass of water. Lucas helps me sit up carefully so I can sip from it. The cold liquid slipping down my throat hardly makes a dent in the raw pain, but continue swallowing it anyway. I realize I must be in Lucas's room. I also know that I'm not dead, even as my conversation with my dead mother runs through my head. *Speaking of mothers....* "Where is she?" I ask, searching my surroundings for a clue.

A dim smile appears on his face and then it grows before he finally laughs and shakes his head in what looks like disbelief. "She's waiting in the hall," he says. "She's not here because she was afraid seeing her would frighten you. But she's good. She's better, Ray. You made her better."

I sit up straighter. "Better?" I ask, wanting clarification. Lucas exchanges a look with his brother, and his brother leaves the room. A moment later, Liam returns with Mrs. Diesel. She's sheepish as she approaches me. Her hair has been smoothed down, and her eyes are clear. There is no sign of the menace that once darkened her features.

"Hello, Raielle," she says.

I gasp, holding a hand over my mouth. I look back at Lucas, and he starts to blur as my eyes fill with tears. They slip down my cheeks as I take in his mother and brother both standing before me. Mrs. Diesel slowly approaches the bed. She's holding a bottle. As she stretches her hand out to Lucas, I notice that it tremors slightly. "You should rub this on your neck. It will help with the redness," she advises in a clear, but soft voice.

My fingers go to my neck and the skin there feels sore.

"My mother used to be a nurse," Lucas says. "I would have called an ambulance, but she said you'd be fine. We can still go to the hospital if you want."

There would be too many questions if we did that, and Lucas knows that, too. I shake my head at him. Once he takes the bottle, his mother and Liam leave the bedroom. He uses his thumbs to wipe my wet cheeks. "Thank you," he whispers, his eyes shining with unshed tears. He turns his face away and blinks. Then he opens the bottle and squeezes some clear lotion into his hand. "It's aloe," he says as he raises his fingertips to my throat and gently smoothes the ointment on.

"Where's your father?" I ask after a few moments.

"He's away on business. It was a last minute thing." He takes a deep breath and releases it. "That's why I made everyone late for the prom. I never leave Liam home alone with her. I wasn't sure if I should even go, but Liam kept insisting he'd be fine." He closes his eyes for a moment, seeming to silently berate himself. When he opens them again, regret swirls within their depths. "Finally, I decided to at least wait until her sedative put her to sleep. It took longer than usual, and then I guess it didn't work because she woke up and went after him. He called me while I was dancing with Sophie."

I nod and then try to keep still as his fingers softly move across my neck.

"Dad's in for a surprise when he gets home and sees her." He licks his lips and hesitates before asking his next question. "Do you think it's permanent?"

"It is," I state with confidence. Knowing that what I removed won't return. "The damage in her brain is gone. For good."

He nods, relieved. But he sobers quickly, closing his eyes and shaking his head at me. "I can't believe you took a chance like that. She could have killed you." His eyes widen. "*I* could kill you for what nearly happened."

I won't tell him that I was scared to death, that I thought I was going to die. Instead, I use my raw, scratchy voice to say, "But it turned out okay. So, you won't."

"It didn't just turn out okay. Nothing you do is *just* okay." He pulls me into a hug. "Thank you isn't enough. It's not even close."

"You shouldn't be thanking me at all," I say.

He pulls back to look at me, eyeing me curiously.

"I set things right," I explain. "I undid the damage caused by my grandmother. I wish I could turn back the clock and undo all the pain she's caused your family."

"It's not up to you to make up for what she's done. I don't see it that way."

"I do."

We look at each other and the silence is heavy with the weight of what happened here tonight. "What will you tell people?" I ask. "What will your mother say?"

"I don't know. We'll think of something, and I promise you'll be left out of it. She's umm…She's been mostly crying since I found you both." He rubs a hand over his face. "Seeing you lying there like that. I thought—" He stops talking but his Adam's apple bobs as he works his throat.

I place my hand on his arm.

He takes a deep breath and blows it out again. "She remembers everything she did to us," he continues, "but she says she couldn't stop herself. Honestly, I don't know how we're going to deal with any of this, but it's got to be easier than what we were dealing with before."

I nod my understanding. Then I ask something that's been on my mind. "You've mostly taken care of your mother and Liam, haven't you? Your dad leaves all this responsibility to you?"

Lucas's lips form a tight line. I recognize his stubborn set of his jaw. This is how he looks when he doesn't want to tell me something.

"Lucas?"

He sighs. "Dad checked out a while ago."

I wait, but that's all he says.

"How were you going to go to Columbia next year and leave Liam here?" I ask.

"I wasn't. He was coming with me. I convinced my father to enroll him in a private school in the city. But that might not be necessary now. He never wanted to leave his school anyway."

I didn't think I could care for Lucas any more than I already did, but the affection growing in my heart for him doesn't seem to have any boundaries. I wonder what he's had to give up for his family. He pretends baseball doesn't matter, but maybe he couldn't let it matter. He maintains this unapproachable aura at school, but maybe he uses it to keep people at a distance because it's safer that way.

His fingers brush my neck again. "That's not going to go away so quickly. Can you heal yourself?"

"No. Ironic, huh?" I shrug.

"Why can't you—"

"I don't know," I interrupt him before he can finish. "I'll just wear scarves for a while."

He leans in closer to me. "Tell me the truth, Ray. You've healed both my brother and mother one right after the other. Does that drain you?"

I shake my head. "Just the opposite. I'm already starting to feel better. What time is it? I should probably be getting home soon."

Lucas glances at his watch. "Nearly midnight."

I don't need the help, but Lucas insists on steadying me as I step out of his bed and test my legs. I wasn't fibbing when I said I felt better. I do. Other than my sore throat, I feel perfectly fine, better than fine, and I feel thankful that I was able to help his family. Lucas's gratitude, though, doesn't sit well with me. I don't think I deserve it.

Lucas checks in with Liam before we walk out to Myles's car. Then, during the ride home, he calls Myles, and they make plans for him to drive Lucas back so Myles can have his mother's Camry sitting in the driveway before she wakes up in the morning. I hear him tell Lucas that he got a ride home in Gwen's limo.

Myles is sitting on his front steps waiting for us when we pull up. "What happened?" he asks, standing at our approach. He's still in his tux but with his bowtie undone, hanging to one side. I'm in no mood for a heavily edited recap of the night, and I'm craving some alone time. I turn and hug Lucas as I say goodnight, releasing him quickly.

"Wait a minute," Myles says. "Here's the picture we had taken when we got there." He hands me the glossy photo. I can feel Lucas peering at it over my shoulder. It's hard to believe this was only a few hours ago. Beside me, Myles has his arm at my waist and his deep dimpled smile is typical Myles. My grin is more hesitant, but my eyes sparkle with anticipation.

Lucas is silent, staring at the photograph, and I wonder what he's thinking.

Myles clears his throat before glancing down at the ground. "I should probably tell you that April is the one who started the rumor about you going to the prom with Chad. She confessed it to me tonight. She did it because she thought I was going to ask you. Turns out, it didn't have anything to do with Lucas."

This news surprises me. "It's okay, Myles. Don't feel bad," I say. The truth is that I'm way beyond caring about this.

Beside me, I know Lucas feels the same when he hardly registers a reaction.

"I've got some good news," Myles's face brightens, "Our boy here won prom king."

"Really?" I muster the energy to grin at Lucas. "Prom king? Congratulations."

Lucas grins at me as he rushes his hands through his hair.

"Sophie got prom queen," Myles adds. "She wasn't pleased to be standing in front of everyone without her king."

I feel a hand on my back. Lucas is worried that I care about this, but he has no reason to. I shoot him a weary smile. "I'm going to head inside," I say.

"I'll walk you."

I shake my head. "No, it's fine. Let Myles take you back now. If I look half as exhausted as you do, I don't know how you're even standing."

Lucas pulls me in for another hug and again, the need to flee, to just be alone right now, rises up in me. I move out of his arms, and I thank Myles for taking me to the prom. Then I walk across the lawn to Kyle's house. His car is in the driveway and the outside lights are on as usual. Quietly, I unlock the door and step inside.

"Did you have a good time?"

Kyle's whisper startles me. He's sitting at the top of the stairs in his pajamas.

Telling him anything close to the truth is out of the question. "Yeah, it was okay," I reply. "You didn't have to wait up for me."

"We just got home, too. Sorry we weren't here when you were getting ready."

I stare up at him, wondering where they were tonight.

He sees the question in my eyes. "We'll talk in the morning. Goodnight, Raielle." He stands and disappears down the hallway.

Back in my bedroom, I slip out of my dress and fold it neatly away in a drawer. After the intense events of tonight, it seems strange to be standing in the bathroom brushing my teeth and washing my face like always. I pull on an old Chargers T-shirt one of my mom's boyfriends left behind and somehow ended up in my duffle bag of stuff, and I lay down on my bed, knowing sleep is far away. The house is quiet, and I let my mind wander over every part of this night, including the worst part, the part that nearly got me killed.

I replay the dream I had about my mother. I can remember every detail so clearly, more sharply than I should. She told me things she would never have talked about when she was alive. She gave me a warning. One I'm not ready to think about right now.

Finally, I let myself focus on Lucas. The despair he felt when he asked me to help his brother was like a living thing threatening to destroy me in that kitchen tonight. What if his brother was too close to death for me to help? Could I have refused? But I answer my own question quickly. Most definitely, yes. I would have refused if I knew healing Liam meant possibly harming Lucas. I would not have taken that chance, and Lucas would have hated me for it. The overwhelming gratitude he feels now could have easily been a loathing he would feel just as strongly. Maybe that's why his gratitude makes me uncomfortable. If Liam had hit his head any harder, the rest of the evening would have gone very differently, and a relationship that means everything to me may have been severed irreparably.

I swallow and wince at the pain it causes. My mother's reluctance to use her ability is starting to make more sense. Once people know what you can do, it changes things.

EIGHTEEN

BY morning, the bruises on my neck have faded some. Since the forecast calls for a warm day, I dismiss the scarf idea and cover the marks with makeup before heading upstairs. I can hear the family moving around above me even though it's barely eight in the morning on Sunday. I wonder if Penelope has another day filled with birthday parties for her school friends.

"Raielle's awake," Chloe says when I appear at the top of the stairs. Everyone is in the kitchen eating breakfast.

When I enter, Kyle stands. "Let's go outside and talk for a minute."

I glance at Chloe. Her eyes are red and puffy. She averts her gaze as she sits down beside Penelope. "Is everything okay?" I ask, confused by my strained reception.

"Come outside," Kyle says, walking past me.

As I follow him out the front door, a feeling of dread begins to take hold. There's no way he could have heard about what happened last night, is there? My stomach tightens as I watch him sit down on the front stoop and wait for me to join him. Whatever this is, it's not good.

We sit beside each other in silence for a few moments. I'm trying not to visibly squirm while Kyle is staring out at the quiet street, saying nothing.

"We were at the hospital last night," he finally begins. "We had to take Penelope in."

This is not what I was expecting. She was sitting inside at the table just now, and she seemed fine. Although, she was unusually quiet now that I think about it. "What happened?" I ask.

Kyle grips his hands together, wringing them slowly. "She came out of her room yesterday afternoon saying her face felt funny. We noticed that the left side was drooping. It wasn't in sync with the right side. So, we rushed her to the emergency room."

I stare at his profile as he looks off into the distance. I realize he's not talking about some accident she had.

He glances at me quickly, before looking away again. "The tumors in her neck have grown back."

My heart stops and then starts hammering inside me. "Tumors?"

"They were discovered a little over a year ago. She had similar symptoms then. There was a surgery to remove them, but the doctors told us they could grow back."

I stare at him shocked, not sure what to say. I can't believe he's talking about the happy little girl I've come to know.

"She has a disease," he continues. "It causes her body to grow tumors along her nervous system and in her brain. They're always benign. Sometimes they're a nuisance and easy to remove, but other times, depending on where they appear, they can be debilitating, even fatal." He rubs his hands over his face and abruptly stands up. He walks a few steps before turning around to look at me.

I know what he's going to say now. I recognize the anguished plea in his eyes. How could something so terrible happen to sweet Penelope? realize that I've purposely kept my distance from her. I'm not sure if I've ever touched her. If I did, I didn't feel anything. I know for certain I've never hugged her. Her family is everything mine wasn't, and the pang of jealousy I felt when I watched her carefree life made me feel guilty. So, I kept myself apart from her.

Kyle is standing in front of me now. "I've never been able to do what our mother and grandmother could do, but if you can, if you were afraid to tell me the truth before, please tell me now." He crouches down. "Can you help her?" he asks. His eyes fill with tears that spill over onto his cheeks. I can't help but think of all the tears I've seen shed in the past couple of days.

"I can try," I answer softly.

Kyle remains still for a moment, before he finally nods at me, wiping at his wet face with the back of his hand. "Thank you."

"But, Kyle, you should know that I can't always help," I'm quick to add. He needs to prepare for this just in case. "There are certain situations where there's nothing I can do." I hope like crazy this isn't one of them.

"What situations?" he asks.

I bite my bottom lip. I don't want to say the words out loud to him. "It depends," I hedge. "I'll know more when I touch her."

He nods at me. "That's how grandmother did it. She needed to touch bare skin. We brought Penelope to her after her diagnosis, but she was too far gone by then. We couldn't communicate with her."

That statement causes my thoughts to go running in an unwelcome direction. When Penelope was diagnosed, Kyle already knew where Mom and I were. "Did you think about asking Mom for help?"

His red eyes meet mine, and he nods. "Yes. We did ask her, and she refused."

"You spoke to her?" I ask, completely stunned by this.

"No. She wouldn't speak to me. Alec flew out to talk to her. He tracked her down at her job, and she basically told him to go to hell." He grimaces. "Her own granddaughter needed her and she couldn't have cared less."

I'm not sure how to respond to this news. Mom never told me this, but she didn't tell me a lot of things. I can understand her hesitation, but to completely ignore the situation was heartless, even for her. I glance up at him. "Why didn't you ask me when I first got here?"

He runs a hand over his short blond hair. "I didn't want you to think we had ulterior motives for having you here, because we absolutely didn't. I also thought I had time. Penelope has been having regular MRIs and they showed no new growths. These appeared very quickly, and the doctors say they're more aggressive than the last ones." He pauses. "When would you like to try?" he asks.

I wonder if the tumors cause Penelope pain. I can't stand the thought of that. "Is now a good time?" I ask.

He blinks at me, surprised. "Yes," he breathes out. "Now is good."

I follow him inside. When we find the kitchen empty, Kyle turns toward Penelope's room. "In here," he says.

He's already inside when I step through the doorway. Her little girl room is dark with the shades drawn. Penelope is lying on her bed, and Chloe is sitting at the edge, running a hand over her daughter's forehead.

"She wants to try now," he tells Chloe.

"Right now?" she asks, looking both shocked and afraid.

Kyle nods.

Chloe turns wide eyes to me. Her apparent reluctance doesn't surprise me. She doesn't move from her spot next to Penelope.

"I need to be the only one touching her," I explain.

Chloe only blinks at me.

"Stand over here," Kyle instructs.

She hesitates before finally standing and backing away slowly from the bed. Kyle moves her beside him and takes her hand.

I sit down, filling the spot Chloe vacated, and look at the peaceful face of a very sick little girl. Her dark, wavy hair fans out around her head on the pillow. My guard is down, and I know I should feel the energy building by now, but I don't. That's my first sign that the disease Penelope has is different. I'm already fearing the worst.

I take a calming breath and pick up her small hand. Then to my great relief, it begins. It's only a shiver running through me, not the usual burst of vibration that causes my stomach to drop. I concentrate on the tendril of energy and try to build on it. It takes more concentration and brute force than usual, but it does grow, and I send it down my arm into her tiny hand. I know it has reached her when her eyes slowly open. Their dark depths roam from the ceiling downward until they land on my face. I notice that her left eye doesn't open as wide as her right. I smile at her, and I can feel our connection. Her pink lips turn up in a small grin. I focus on the energy coiling between us again, and I locate the tumors at the base of her skull. I can also feel the scar that runs vertically there. I never noticed it because Penelope's hair is always worn down. Now I know why.

I move over the rest of her spine and find no other growths there. Then I go in the other direction, up toward her brain. The coil hitches suddenly, like a guitar string being plucked, and I jerk back in surprise. For a moment, I'm confused, receiving no input at all from Penelope's body. I aim my focus at her brain again, and I hold back a gasp, suddenly very aware of Kyle and Chloe at my back. I feel a tumor there, too, a large one. I know immediately that I can't heal it. The energy is already trying to disperse and retreat. I've never felt this before, but I understand it's meaning with a strange clarity. I wonder if this is what my mother felt when she healed her boyfriend in our apartment that night or the boy with leukemia before she left Fort Upton. I can't cure the disease inside Penelope, but if I push a little harder, I can remove it. It will leave her body, but it won't go away entirely. This killer will find someone else if I take it out of her. It will find someone close to her, someone with similar makeup for it to cling to. I don't know how I know this, but I do.

Slowly, I remove my hand from hers. I hold my fisted fingers to my chest as I watch her eyes lose their focus and gradually close.

"Is it done?" Chloe whispers behind me. "Is she cured?"

Turning to face them is the hardest thing I've ever had to do. I'm struggling with my remorse as I meet their hopeful, expectant stares. Then I shake my head.

"No? Why not?" Kyle demands, taking a step toward me. Chloe raises her hand to her mouth and begins to sob.

I don't want to talk in front of Penelope. So, I stand and walk out into the hallway and then down to the living room. Kyle is right behind me and Chloe hesitantly trails behind him. His angry demeanor belies the truth in his eyes. He's terrified of what I'm going to say.

"I can't help her." I let the tears trail down my cheeks now. "I'm so sorry."

Chloe begins to whimper before loud sobs wrack her body.

"Tell me why!" Kyle grabs my arm.

I bear Kyle's anger quietly, knowing that what I'm about to say is going to devastate him even further. But she's his daughter. He needs to know. "There's a tumor in her brain."

His rage turns to shock as his grip on my arm loosens.

"It's too large. I can't remove it."

He releases me and backs away looking dazed.

"I'm sorry," I repeat helplessly.

"You're lying!" Chloe screams at me. "You don't know what you're talking about." She turns to Kyle. "What your family can do, it's unnatural. It's evil, and I don't want it in my house anymore!"

Kyle reaches out to her and pulls her shaking body to him. I don't want to upset her any further. Slowly, broken-hearted, I retreat to my bedroom. Once I'm downstairs, I lie down on my bed and curl into a ball, waiting for more tears to flow. But they don't come. Instead, I feel lost. I feel like I've been fooling myself for seventeen years, pretending I could be normal, thinking I could ignore the healing power my body so easily wields and then withholds. I want to talk to my mother so badly it's an ache twisting inside me. Now, when I can finally understand what she went through her whole life, she's gone, and I'm drowning.

I'm not going to tell Chloe and Kyle that I could remove the disease from Penelope, but then one of them could be afflicted with it. I'm betting they would be perfectly fine making that sacrifice. But I wouldn't be. I'm not going to knowingly give this disease to someone no matter how difficult it is to think of Penelope's suffering. I won't impose a death sentence on someone else.

I spend the rest of the day hiding in my room. I don't know how to face them, and I know Chloe doesn't want to see me. I need to leave, but I have nowhere to go. I receive texts and calls throughout the day, but I don't pick up my phone. I don't even check to see who's calling. I'm sure it's Gwen, wanting to talk about the prom and why Lucas dashed out in the middle of it. And Lucas is probably calling, too. But some part of me just can't handle hearing about how well his mother is doing when there's nothing I can do to help Penelope.

Late in the afternoon, I'm still laying listlessly on my bed when I hear the doorbell ring. A few moments later, Kyle comes downstairs looking for me.

"I didn't know if you were down here or not," he says. He looks pale and tired.

I sit up and push the hair out of my eyes. "Do you want me to leave?" I ask.

He shakes his head wearily. "Of course not. I'm sorry about Chloe. She didn't mean any of that."

I don't believe him, and he knows it.

He sighs. "Chloe knew you might be able to help Penelope when I told her I was bringing you here to live. But you need to understand that's not why you're here. You needed a home, and you're my sister. You'll always have a place here. Please forgive Chloe. That was her grief talking, not her."

After remaining dry all afternoon, my eyes finally start to water.

"Lucas is here," Kyle says, coming further into the room.

I close my eyes and wipe away the tears. When I open them, Kyle is studying me. I see can see that he wants to ask me something.

He hesitates a moment longer before his question comes. "Was there ever a time when our mother couldn't heal someone?"

I try to read between the lines, and I think he's wondering if Mom was more powerful than me, if she could have helped Penelope. "I don't know. She didn't like to talk about it. That's why I don't use my healing much. She always told me not to use it, and I listened for the most part. But she did tell me that there are times when we can't heal people because the illness they have can't be reversed."

"This is one of those times?"

I nod, feeling more tears spilling down my face.

Kyle presses his fingers against his bloodshot eyes. Abruptly, he removes them and takes a deep breath. "Should I send Lucas down?"

My throat is too tight to talk so I only nod and watch him quickly retreat.

I stand there waiting, but I don't bother straightening my matted hair and my wrinkled clothes before Lucas appears at the bottom of the steps. He fills the doorway with his broad shoulders and his powerful presence. His concerned eyes travel over me as he approaches. "I've been calling you all day. I was worried about you."

I wonder why I've avoided him today when just his being here already seems to give me some comfort.

"Have you been crying?" he asks, standing before me now, pushing a lock of hair behind my ear.

I throw myself at him, wrapping my arms around his strong shoulders, and burying my face in the crook of his neck.

"Hey," he whispers gently. His arms encircle me and he presses me to him. "What is it?"

I don't answer. I just let him hold me as his warmth seeps inside me, easing the chill of this terrible day. He doesn't question me again. He just stands there, holding me safely in his arms, patiently waiting me out. When I finally do release him, I'm ready to explain myself. I find that I want to.

"It's Penelope," I begin. Then I tell him everything that's occurred since this morning.

WE'RE sitting on my bed. Lucas is leaning back against the pillows, and I'm lying between his legs with my back pressed to his chest and his arms around me.

"That's what you were afraid of when I asked you to help Liam. Wasn't it?" he asks.

Beneath me, I can feel the rumble of his voice inside his chest. "Yes."

"If you couldn't have helped him, do you think that would make me feel differently about you?"

My response is immediate. "I know you would. How could you not?"

He sighs heavily. I feel his warm breath on my neck. "You don't know anything, Ray."

I know he wants to believe it wouldn't change his feelings, and I'm glad that we won't have to find out if it's true. "How is your mother today?" I ask, running my hands over the back of his, which are splayed out over my stomach.

"She's doing better. She wanted to stay inside today, but we convinced her to go shopping to buy some new clothes. My dad got home this afternoon and nearly keeled over in shock. I have my family back, Ray. You did that. You did an amazing thing for us. I'm sorry you can't do that for your family. I truly am. But that doesn't make any of this your fault. You know that, right?"

I shrug. "I know it, and I don't know it."

He picks me up and sets me beside him so we're face to face. "You need to know it," he states with a determined look. "The news about Penelope is devastating. But not being able to heal her doesn't make you responsible for what's happening to her. You have to learn how to deal with this. It won't be the last time this happens."

"But this time, it's Penelope," I say.

"Next time it could be someone else who's close to you. Your healing has limits. You have to find a way to deal with that. A better way than your mother did."

My spine stiffens at his warning and at his implied criticism of my mother, but then I nod. I know he's right.

He cups my cheek and leans into me for a kiss. I sigh when his soft lips touch mine. Our breaths mingle as he tenderly massages my mouth with his, never deepening the kiss, knowing this closeness is what I need now. I couldn't handle more. "I don't want to leave you like this tonight," he says when he finally breaks away.

I glance around, surprised to find that it's already dark. "I'll be fine." I lay my head on the pillow and gaze up at his handsome face. His square jaw is covered in the dark stubble I felt tickling my skin just a moment ago. "I bet this is more drama than you've ever had in a relationship. You probably weren't expecting this when you met me," I comment dryly.

His eyes flicker with humor. "Ray, you blew up all my expectations the moment I laid eyes on you. Nothing about you is what I expected. Do you know what the most unexpected thing is?"

I shake my head, having no idea what he's going to say.

"Knowing that everything we do, you're doing it for the first time with me. No one has ever made you feel the way I want to make you feel every time we're together. When I'm finally inside you, I'll be your first, and I'll know that no one has ever done the things I'm going to do to you. You're not what I expected, and I wouldn't want it any other way."

I stare silently at him. I'm speechless. He's never talked about those things before. I didn't think I was ready to hear them until he used the words *finally inside you* with a burning heat in his eyes, a heat that I sparked to life.

He chuckles at my shock, running a finger down my cheek, before sitting up. The path his finger took tingles as I raise myself up beside him. When he puts his feet on the floor, getting ready to leave, his good humor evaporates. "Be honest. If you don't want to stay here, you can come home with me," he states, looking over his shoulder at me.

I finally find my voice again, knowing that leaving here now would be sending a message to Kyle that I don't want to send. "I'm going to stay, but thanks."

"If you change your mind, you call me." He picks up my phone from the nightstand and hands it to me. "When I call you, you need to answer or at least call me back. Don't go silent on me again, okay?"

"Okay," I reply. Then I clear my throat and ask the question that's nagging me. "How many girls have you been with, Lucas?"

He pauses on his way to the door. The look on his face first shows his surprise, then his reluctance to answer. He must have known I would ask this question after what he just said to me about being my first. "Would I need more than two hands to count them?" I finally blurt out, worrying when he doesn't respond.

He moves back toward me with a sly grin. "I've been pretty busy in your imagination, haven't I?"

I can feel the blush rise on my cheeks even as I glare at his smug expression.

His smile turns tender. "You couldn't even fill one hand," he says.

I feel slightly relieved at first, but when I think of him being intimate with any other girls, my stomach clenches. "Did you sleep with Sophie?" I ask. I know the answer must be yes, and I'm not surprised when he slowly nods. Then his eyes flick down to my neck. He reaches up and lightly trails his fingertips over the marks that must be visible again. "But I've never felt like this before. In a way, you'll be my first, too," he whispers. Then he leans down and places a kiss right at the base of my throat. When he rises up and looks at me, his eyes gleam with affection.

I reach up and run my fingers through the soft waves of hair that have fallen over his forehead. He closes his eyes and hums with satisfaction. I knew he wasn't a virgin. But now I realize that what he did before he met me doesn't matter. I want to be with him in every way. I only hope my inexperience doesn't make me a disappointment for him. With just over a month left before the end of school, before the beginning of uncertainty, I want it to happen before I lose my chance. I want him to be my first.

I walk him to the door, and we embrace again before I watch him walk out to his truck. It's late. I hadn't realized dinner time had come and gone. The house is quiet now, and I go into the darkened kitchen. My stomach growls at the lingering scent of food. When I pull open the refrigerator door, I see a plate wrapped in cellophane. I heat it up and sit down by myself to eat. As hungry as I am, after a few bites, I'm done. The lingering tightness in my stomach is squelching my appetite. After cleaning up, I peer down the hallway to find everyone's bedroom doors closed. I go back downstairs and lie awake in the dark for a long time before sleep finally comes.

NINETEEN

K	**YLE** and Chloe are in the kitchen when I come upstairs dressed for school. Chloe hardly spares me a glance before retreating to her bedroom. Kyle notices her avoidance of me and his lips press into a tight line.

"I made you a lunch," he says. "It's in the refrigerator."

"Thanks for saving me dinner last night." I walk past him to grab an apple off the counter for breakfast. "Are you going to work today?"

He turns to me with a cup of coffee in his hand. "No. We're taking Penelope in for more testing."

We both know what the tests will find. At least I know. I think Kyle is hoping I'm wrong. The desire to hug him is strong. Just like Penelope, I've never embraced Kyle either and I know that's my fault. In the end, I lay a hand on his arm and squeeze it gently before leaving.

I move through the day unable to focus, going through the motions of being in school while my brain is swimming in a fog. This morning, Lucas told me we're going to say that he left the prom because of his mother's sudden and unexpected recovery. Liam called him with the news and he had to get home to her. I guess it's a believable story, and it introduces that fact that his mother is well now. I don't worry too much about it as I regurgitate the details nearly verbatim to Gwen when she meets me at my locker.

"His mother was sick?" she asks as her brow wrinkles with confusion.

"Yeah," I mutter, forgetting that she was out of the loop on that.

She can barely contain herself when she tells me her news. "Tyler kissed me in the limo when we got to my house. More than just kissed actually." Then she frowns. "But I haven't spoken to him since. I thought he might call me the next day, but nope. Not a word."

"This was just Saturday night. I wouldn't worry about that yet."

"But look what happened when Lucas didn't call after you guys made out?" she points out.

"Thanks for reminding me," I reply dryly.

"I'm making a point here."

"I know. But don't worry. He's into you. It will be fine," I assure her. I can't work up much genuine angst for her situation, but I'm trying to be sympathetic. As her friend, she deserves more from me than I can give her today.

At lunch, I watch Tyler sit down next to Gwen instead of taking his usual seat. I grin at her as her face lights up and her doubts disappear. Myles and Lucas sit with us, and I hear about the prom aftermath while we eat. Myles says that Sophie is still pissed and wants nothing to do with Lucas. "About fucking time," Lucas murmurs upon hearing this. Apparently, April was mortified at her behavior and apologized to Myles. He accepted her apology, but he still isn't sitting at his old lunch table.

During this discussion, Lucas keeps finding a way to touch me. His knee presses against mine beneath the table. His hand brushes my arm and then my leg. I want to break out of my funk for him, to show him that I took his words from last night to heart. I pretend as hard as I can, even inserting myself into Gwen's enthusiastic conversation about th last season of *Dexter*. But Lucas's sympathetic attention reveals that he can see right through me.

Finally, the excruciating day ends. At my locker, Lucas and Gwen both appear with offers of a ride home. Since I've hardly given Gwen any attention all day, I feel too guilty to turn her down.

"I'll call you later," Lucas promises, signaling his understanding.

Gwen squeezes my arm in excitement as we head down the stairs. "He's taking me out tomorrow night. He just asked me."

"See? I told you he was into you."

"What should I wear?" she asks.

I notice that she's back to all black today. "Well, is he taking out happy Gwen or maudlin Gwen?"

She rolls her eyes at me. "I could wear the dress I wore to Atlas. He wasn't there. So, he hasn't seen it."

We step outside into the warm afternoon and start to walk toward her car when I spot Alec standing on the sidewalk. He's obviously waiting for me. I stop short but Gwen doesn't notice until she's several steps ahead.

"You coming?" Her eyes travel between Alec and I.

"I can give you a ride home, Raielle. I'd like to talk to you," Alec says. He looks like he just stepped off the golf course in a green short-sleeved Lacoste shirt and khaki shorts.

"Um, sure," I reply, wondering if he's here to talk to me about Penelope. "This is Kyle's dad," I explain to Gwen. "I'll get a ride with him. Talk to you later, okay?"

Gwen eyes Alec, and gives me a hesitant little wave before heading across the parking lot.

"I'm right over here," Alec motions to his car. I walk over and pull open the heavy door, sliding into the leather seat and reaching for my seatbelt.

"Could we get some coffee rather than going straight home?" he asks once he's seated beside me.

I hesitate for a moment, before nodding my agreement. I'm uncomfortable being alone with this man I hardly know, who has so much history with my mother. But with what this family is going through, I can't find it in me to refuse having coffee with him.

We drive in silence with me mostly staring out the window. Alec pulls into the diner on the main road in Fort Upton, just a couple of blocks down from Scoops. We go inside, and I follow him to one of the many empty booths that line a wall of windows. There's only one other customer here seated at the bar. I notice that Alec has chosen the booth farthest away from him.

Once we're settled in, he orders coffee, and I do the same. "Would you like anything to eat?" he asks.

I shake my head.

Alec waits for our coffee to arrive before introducing the subject he wants to discuss. When the waitress places our mugs on the table, the hot liquid steams in the air between us. I take a sip and feel the burn run down the length of my throat.

"Penelope had another MRI today," he says. He watches me carefully now. "They found exactly what you said. There's an inoperable tumor in her brain. It's pushing down on the area that controls her respiratory system. Her prognosis isn't good."

I put my hands around the warm coffee cup. I knew this. I didn't know the exact details, but I knew she might not have much time. Alec's jaw is tight and despite his cool, concise description of Penelope's condition, I can see he's making an effort to hold himself together. When I don't say anything, he continues.

"She could have a few months, maybe less. I want you to help her."

I meet his eyes, and I can see the pain there. I know how close he and Penelope are. "I wish I could," I reply.

His spoon clatters to the table, startling me. He leans in close to me

"I know more about you and how your healing works than Kyle does. I've seen what both your mother and grandmother can do. I understand when it's this bad you can't get rid of it. But you can still help her."

My eyes widen in shock as I begin to lean away from him, pressing my back into the booth.

"I've been preparing myself for this possibility. I want you to give it to me," he says. His pleading eyes drill into mine.

I blink at him, wondering if I'm understanding him correctly. "I can't do that," I tell him carefully.

"Yes, you can. I've seen your mother do it. You only have to be touching us at the same time. That's how it works."

I slowly move my hands into my lap. I rub my sweating palms against my jeans. "You want me to give you a deadly disease," I state, not quite believing what I'm hearing.

"Yes. I'm volunteering for it. Surely, you don't think Penelope should die instead of an old man like me?"

Even as I'm resisting the idea, I can understand it, and I admire him for his sacrifice. But I still can't agree to it.

"We'll do it tomorrow," he continues. "I've already told Kyle and Chloe."

This surprises me. "They're okay with this?"

"They're accepting of it. It's better than the alternative," he states, sitting back now, taking a sip of his coffee.

My heart starts to pound as I consider what he's asking me to do. He's basically telling me to kill him. How can I possibly agree to that? "I'm sorry. No," I say, averting my eyes, staring down into my coffee.

"Are you saying you can't do it or you won't," he snaps.

"Both."

He pushes his coffee away. I watch as the remaining liquid sloshes over the side onto the table. "I know you're capable of doing it. That just leaves the fact that you're refusing to."

281

As I'm watching him, his cheeks begin to flush.

"Why?" he demands.

I take a deep breath and grasp my hands in my lap. "You're asking me to kill you. I can't do that. Even if you're volunteering for it."

He stares at me. "I could pay you."

My mouth drops open. "No," I say firmly.

He barks out a laugh that startles me. "You're appalled at the thought of taking money? You're nothing like your grandmother. But you will change your mind." He runs a hand over his neatly slicked back hair and leans in over the table again. "Listen to me closely, Raielle. Kyle told you that I went to talk to your mother about helping Penelope. What he doesn't know is that when your mother refused to help, I started thinking about you. So I hired someone to go to San Diego and watch you."

My eyes widen at this.

"He saw something interesting one day. A boy on a basketball court jumped up to the hoop, sunk the ball, and came down hard, twisting his leg. He couldn't stand up again. He was obviously hurt, and you were there watching. When the other kids went to get help, you walked over and touched him. A few moments later, he stood up as though nothing was wrong."

My mouth goes dry. He's describing the day I healed Ritchie's leg. Ritchie and I were fostered together for a while. He played basketball near our apartment. This happened only a few weeks before my mother was killed.

Alec narrows his eyes. "That's when I realized I didn't need your mother."

My breathing grows shallow, and I push back even further against the booth.

"But I knew she would never agree to let you help us."

I can feel the few sips of coffee in my stomach turning sour an working their way back up. "You killed her," I whisper.

He nods gravely at me. "I had her killed."

"You hired Rob Jarvis," I mutter, as the room seems to tilt.

He narrows his eyes even more, seeming surprised that I know this. "That's right. I met him at the nursing home where your grandmother lives. I caught him stealing medication when he thought no one was looking. I figured he wouldn't turn down some extra cash. So I paid him to watch you. When I realized you'd inherited your family's special talent, I paid him more to kill your mother. I knew that would bring you here. By then Penelope showed no other signs of her illness, but the doctors said it would be back. Having you here was my insurance. I was hoping I would never have to collect on it, but the time has come. Surely you can't feel any remorse about what I'm asking you to do now."

My throat is too tight to respond. I'm wondering how soon I can get away from him and call the police.

As though reading my mind, he says, "If you go to the authorities, they'll arrest me, and I won't be able to help Penelope. Kyle will lose us both. There's no reason for that to happen. Kyle and Chloe had nothing to do with my actions, and I haven't told them the part I played in your mother's death. Kyle is a good man. He would never approve of what I've done." He eyes me with renewed hope. "You must see the justice in this. I'll be paying the highest price for my crime. Why would you refuse to let me?"

I look into his determined face, and I'm repulsed by him. How can this man be capable of loving his granddaughter so fiercely that he's willing to die for her, but also be responsible for so callously having my mother killed? Now he's handing me his fate on a silver platter and providing me the means to save Penelope at the same time.

I can't stand to look at him anymore. He's the reason my mother is dead. I stare down at my fisted hands, at war with myself as my insides twist into knots. Can I stand by and watch Penelope suffer and die when this evil man is giving me a seemingly righteous way to stop it? I'd rather watch him suffer and die. I realize I want him to. I uncurl my fingers and reach up to pull on my hair, mindlessly reacting to the terrible building pressure inside me. When I feel Alec touch my arm, I flinch back, spilling my coffee across the table.

"Everything okay here?" the waitress asks, placing a stack of napkins in front of me.

I stare down at them as Alec tells her we're fine.

"Okay," I hear myself saying once the waitress is gone. When he doesn't respond, my eyes flick up to his face.

His eyebrows are raised. "Okay?"

I nod and dart my gaze away from him again.

"Thank you," he says. I can hear that he's relieved, not scared or regretful, just satisfied to be getting what he wants. "Tomorrow, then. I'll come to the house."

I offer a single nod in response. The need to get away from him is too strong to resist. "I'm walking home," I announce. I stand and rush out of the diner as quickly as I can. I keep walking all the way down Main Street until I'm able to turn a corner and disappear behind a wall of bushes. I pray he hasn't followed me. As I glance around me, my body is so tense my jaw begins to ache from clenching it. The anger inside me is a like a fire that wants to consume me. My throat is too tight to scream out my rage. So instead, I take my foot and kick at a tree trunk beside me. I ram the tip of my shoe into the rough bark again and again. I hardly register the pain vibrating up my leg as I continue to assault the tree until I'm too exhausted to continue. Then I slump to the ground and just sit there breathing hard, staring down at the dirt.

I'm not sure how long I stay this way before I hear my phone ringing. At first, I don't want to answer it, but then I think of Lucas and hi concerned instruction about not ignoring his calls. When I pull it from my pocket, I feel relieved to see that it's him. "Hi," I answer, knowing I don't sound like myself.

"Hey, beautiful. Want to do something tonight?"

His good cheer is so misplaced that I can't form a response. Soon I'm crying, and I hear Lucas asking me what's wrong. When I don't answer, he begins yelling over the phone.

I'm more trouble for him than I'm worth. Here I am, having another crisis. He's going to get tired of this, tired of me, and I won't blame him when he does.

I make an effort to calm myself down enough to talk. "I'm on the corner of Main and Hillside. Please come get me," I whisper.

"Don't move," he orders, sounding panicked. "I'll be right there."

I rub my eyes and pull in a shaky breath as I realize that I'm covered in dirt. Brushing myself off, I move out onto the sidewalk. I've hardly waited at all when his familiar truck appears down the road. It screeches to a stop in front of me, and Lucas jumps out. His eyes grow wide at the sight of me.

"Damn it, Ray! What the hell happened?" he yells, coming toward me.

Once he's standing on the sidewalk in front of me, I'm so relieved to have him here; I just want to burrow into his arms. Instead, I release a lungfull of air. "I think I had a little breakdown," I answer feeling both drained and foolish, hoping none of this is real but knowing it is.

His brows furrow as he grabs the tops of my arms and leans down to look into my eyes. "What do you mean you had a little breakdown?"

I stare into two blue pools filled with concern for me. "Alec just told me he hired Rob Jarvis to kill my mother," I say, hearing the odd monotone sound of my voice.

His startled gaze searches mine. "What? He told you that?"

I nod. "Your instincts were right about Jarvis. Alec asked my mother to heal Penelope. When she wouldn't do it, he had us watched to find out if I could heal, too. Once he knew I could, he had her killed so that I'd have to come here."

He leans back from me and runs a hand through his hair. "Jesus," he breathes out.

"He told me for a reason, Lucas. He wants me to give her disease to him. He's willing to sacrifice himself to save her. He only confessed to me when I refused to do what he was asking."

I can see the shock tightening his face as he processes this new twist.

"You should have seen his cold eyes when he told me," I say, shaking my head. "Remorse was the furthest thing from his mind. There was absolutely none."

He places his hands on my shoulders. "Am I understanding this right? You wouldn't give him a death sentence. So he confessed this to you so you'd believe he deserves one?"

"Yes," I reply, watching his reaction.

He looks up at the sky. I can see he's trying to make sense of all I've told him. Then he zeros in on me again and pulls me to him. "What do you want to do?"

I hesitate before answering, worrying what he'll think of me. "I told him I'd do it."

He pulls back to look at me. "You don't have to. You could go to the police."

I nod at his suggestion. "I will go to the police, after I've cured Penelope."

"Are you sure? Can you live with that?" he asks.

"Would it make me a terrible person if I said that I could?" I ask fearing his response almost as much as I'm fearing myself right now and the fact that I think I can live with this decision if it means saving Penelope.

"If I were you," he says, "I'd do it in a heartbeat." His tone is one of absolute certainty.

His confident answer surprises me even as it lifts some of the heaviness inside me. But I'll be crossing a line by doing this. I can't help but wonder if my grandmother was always so evil and selfish or if she crossed a similar line at some point. Did that turning point make the next time easier and the time after that until she completely lost her way?

"When does he want to do it?" Lucas asks.

"Tomorrow."

He begins to usher me toward his truck. "I'm going to be there with you."

"No!" I stop and turn toward him. "I don't want you near Alec. He's obviously dangerous."

Lucas's hands go right to his hips. "Are you fucking serious? You just made the perfect argument for my being there."

I open my mouth to protest again.

His eyes close as he fights for patience. "Please get in the truck, Ray. I'm going to be with you when this goes down, and I'm not arguing with you about it."

I lose steam when I see his resolute expression. Then I seal my lips together and let him help me inside. I really don't want him there. I've never done this before, and I'm afraid something unexpected could happen, like the disease not going where I tell it to. I'd rather no one but Alec and me be within one hundred miles of Penelope when I try this.

"Kyle and Chloe don't know what Alec did," I warn him on the drive back. "Please don't say anything."

The muscle in his cheek tightens. "You really believe that?"

"Yes, I do."

"Kyle should know what his father did to his mother. What he's doing to you." His hands tighten on the wheel.

287

"He has enough to worry about."

"And you don't?" He shoots back at me.

"Please, Lucas." I sink tiredly into the seat.

"Fine," he bites out. "But I think you're wrong."

Kyle and Chloe are surprised to see me arrive home with Lucas. "He's staying for a while," I tell them. "You don't have to edit yourselves. He knows everything."

Kyle appears stricken when he looks at me. "My father just called. I'm sorry he was the one who spoke to you about this, Raielle. I wanted to talk to you myself. I wanted to make sure you're really okay with this and let you know you have a choice here."

Lucas grunts his disbelief from beside me. "Let's get you cleaned up," he says, starting to lead me away.

"What happened to you?" Chloe asks, speaking for the first time.

The muscle in Lucas's jaw ticks.

"I fell," I explain quickly, before Lucas can say anything.

"*Right after* she talked to your father," Lucas adds.

Kyle's expression sinks even further. "Raielle, no one wants him to have to do this. I wanted it to be me when he told me how this works. But I also want to see my daughter grow up too badly to fight him on this. I can't tell you how grateful we are that you're agreeing to do it."

"Why didn't you tell us?" Chloe asks, but it's more like an accusation. "You didn't say anything about this possibility."

Lucas pulls me closer to him. In this moment, her feelings are completely transparent. She's afraid of me and of what I can do. She's always known about it, just like Kyle, and it scares her. If she had a choice she'd have nothing to do with me. I don't even bother answering her.

"Come on." Lucas turns me away from them and leads me toward the bathroom.

I stand there like a statue while he runs my hands under warm water and gently soaps the dirt from my skin. I could do this myself, but I don't stop him. We eye each other in the mirror while he takes care of me.

"The marks on your neck are gone," he points out.

My eyes travel down to the area where the bruises once were. That only reminds me of how my grandmother's healing powers went so wrong with Lucas's mother. "You shouldn't come tomorrow," I tell him, watching his reflection.

He pauses for a moment. Then he turns off the water and hands me a towel.

"Lucas."

"What?" he asks on a tired sigh. Then he turns from the mirror to look me in the eye. "If the situation were reversed, would you stay away if I asked you to?"

I glance down at my now clean hands. "Probably not."

He places his fingers under my chin and lifts my face to his. "Then how can you honestly think I would let you do this alone?" His eyes search mine. "What am I to you, Ray?"

I blink in confusion at his question.

"Am I just a casual fling?" he asks.

I pull my chin away and stare at him defiantly. Why would he ask me this now? He knows better. "No," I reply.

"We're more than that, aren't we?"

"Yes," I whisper, hating that after all we've been through, this simple truth is still so hard for me to admit.

"Good," he nods. "So quit acting like you're in this alone. I know you've always only had yourself to rely on, but that's not the case anymore. Stop pushing me away. One of these days, I might actually think you mean it."

I back away from him. "I'm trying to protect you, you idiot."

He puts his hands on his hips. "Well cut that shit out. It just pisses me off."

We stare at each other for a moment, the fact that we've just admitted our feelings run deeper than the typical high school romance dances in both our eyes, but it's overshadowed by the turmoil that surrounds us.

Lucas relents first, gradually leaning toward me and kissing the side of my head.

I still wish he wasn't going to be here for his own protection, but I'm also grateful I'll have him with me.

"We ordered pizza," Kyle says when we make our way back to the living room. "Alec will be over around seven tomorrow night. He said he had some things to take care of first. Personal business to see to."

The simple act of ordering pizza seems incongruous in light of what's gone on tonight. "I don't think it will be instant," I say, understanding what Kyle is implying about Alec's personal business. "You won't lose Alec right away. At least I don't think so." I don't know this for sure, but I believe he will have however much time Penelope has left.

Kyle sinks his hands deep into his pockets and disappears into the kitchen. The next hour passes slowly. Lucas calls his brother to let him know he's having dinner at my house. We all sit and pick at our pizza in strained silence. Chloe feeds Penelope cut up pieces. Penelope is subdued and her listlessness breaks at my heart.

After dinner, Lucas reluctantly goes home after I assure him, multiple times, that I'll be fine. Then I disappear downstairs, hoping that Kyle won't seek me out for another conversation about their monumental decision. I'm relieved when he doesn't make an appearance. In the silence of my room, I have all night to spend alone with my anxiety. It makes for miserable company as I toss and turn restlessly, fearful of what tomorrow may bring.

TWENTY

THE tension in the room is so thick, it's hard to breath. Getting through this interminable day has been excruciating. Although now, I hardly remember any of it. I know I went to school, and I know that Lucas found several opportunities to get me alone, to make sure I was all right, and to let me know that he would help me talk to everyone and call off what's about to happen tonight if that's what I wanted. But I've purposely not dwelled on what's coming. Kyle and his family have lived this day with renewed hope. I couldn't imagine taking that away from them now.

"Where do you want everyone?" Kyle asks. "I think Penelope will need to lie down on the couch."

"That's fine," I agree. "Alec and I could sit in front of her in a couple of chairs and the rest of you could maybe go outside."

"I'm not going outside," Lucas predictably says.

"Why outside?" Kyle asks.

I let out a deep breath. "I've never done this before. I don't know what's going to happen."

"What does that mean?" Chloe asks. "What could happen? How much worse could this get?"

"She's saying she doesn't know," Lucas answers for me. "She's just trying to keep everyone safe."

"We're staying, too," Kyle says. Then he walks into the dining room to retrieve the chairs.

A loud knock sounds just as the front door opens. Alec lets himself in and finds us in the living room. The moment I see him I can feel my body tensing. I glance at Lucas, and he looks like a volcano about to erupt.

"Are we ready?" Alec asks, glancing around the room. He appears anxious, but undeterred.

"Does Linda know?" Chloe asks.

Alec shakes his head. "I saw no need to upset her."

I nearly scoff at his reply. He can have my mother killed, but he doesn't want to upset his girlfriend?

"You don't have to do this, Dad," Kyle says

Alec gives his son a sad look. "Yes, I do." Then he turns to me. "How do we start?"

Before we begin, Kyle and Chloe take turns hugging Alec and thanking him. Lucas embraces me. "You can still change your mind," he whispers. When I shake my head, he says, "You'll do fine. Trust yourself." Now that the moment is here, I'm ready for it. And I do trust myself. I have a strange confidence that I can't explain.

Kyle carefully places Penelope on the couch. "Do I sit here?" Alec asks me, pointing to the chairs.

I nod as I walk out of Lucas's arms and take my place in the chair beside Penelope. Alec lowers himself into the chair next to me. Behind me, I can hear Kyle's erratic breathing, and I know he's heartbroken. He's getting his daughter back, but losing his father in the process.

I take a deep breath and close my eyes for a moment to both calm myself and focus my concentration. I wait for everyone in the room to settle. I can feel the anxiety in the air, and I try to block it out. Once I'm ready, I pick up Penelope's small hand at the same time I hold out my other hand for Alec's. I try not to wince when he grips it.

The feeling is the same as the first time I touched Penelope. The energy is there, but it's weak. I have to fan it like an ember. I focus my attention on the tiny spark, and soon it begins to build inside me. The coil of energy swirls and gains momentum before it gradually unwinds and travels down through my hand and into Penelope's. Like before, she becomes more alert, and her curious eyes find mine. I direct the energy up to her brain, but before it can hitch and try to turn back, I force it along her entire nervous system, down her spine and out to the tips of her fingers and toes. I fill her with it, sensing it flow through her. The energy resists my commands. It tries to return to me. The feeling that this is wrong, seriously wrong, permeates me, but I ignore it. Instead, I dig deep and push harder, until my entire body vibrates with power. I've never felt it this strongly before. All my nerve endings seem to spark inside me.

I squeeze my eyes shut as I chip away at the tumor inside her brain, dislodging its hold on her. Even as I'm focused on it, I can feel the rest of her disease lying in waiting, sealed inside her, planning to grow new tumors that will steal more of her away from us. And I push harder, going after every last bit of it.

When I hear a gasp, my eyes open causing my focus to return to the room. I suck in a breath when I see that Penelope's body is several inches off the couch. She's suspended in the air, and I'm holding her there. I pray that I'm not hurting her, that this is working as it's meant to. Once I know the energy has touched every part of her disease, I start to bring it back to me. There is no exhilaration in this healing. There is no euphoria. Everything about the way this feels tells me not to complete the process. The energy doesn't want to remove this terrible thing inside her. I pull harder on it, feeling the sweat begin to trickle down my back. My body starts shaking so violently the chair legs beneath me bang against the floor. I vaguely register Lucas's worried voice, and I'm not sure how much longer I can keep this up, when the coil suddenly snaps back at me, retreating from Penelope's body and burrowing deep inside me.

Penelope drops down onto the couch cushions. I grip Alec's hand firmly as I try to push the energy toward him. But it's fading, slowly smoldering, as the disease spreads inside me, crawling under my skin and drifting down my spine. My body is absorbing it too quickly. I can't harness it. I have no chance to grab it and move it out of me. Suddenly, something becomes very clear. I'm Penelope's family. She's my niece, and I am the place where the disease has found its new home.

I release both Penelope's and Alec's hands.

"Is it done?" Chloe asks, hovering behind me.

I slowly nod.

Penelope turns her head toward her mother. Then she slowly sits up and smiles brightly. "Hi, Mommy," she says.

Chloe cries out in relief, dashing to her daughter, and pulling her into a hug. Kyle's there, too, embracing his family with tears in his eyes. "Can I have some milk?" Penelope asks, and I hear Chloe laughing softly at this simple request.

Lucas crouches down in front of me. "Are you okay?"

I don't answer. I turn to look at a confused Alec.

"That's it?" he asks, peering down at his hand.

In that moment, I decide not to tell him. He doesn't deserve to know. Then I decide not to tell anyone. "It's done," I say. When I try to stand, my knees buckle. Lucas grabs me, his face sharp with worry. "You're not okay," he states.

I feel the need to wipe his concern away. I push at him as I straighten my legs and show him that I can stand. I'm shaky, but I'm doing it.

Kyle approaches us, and he wraps his arms around me. "Thank you, Raielle. Thank you for giving her back to us."

I don't say anything, but I return his embrace. It's the first embrace we've given each other. When he releases me, Chloe surprises me with a quick hug of her own, before once again gathering her daughter to her.

"How are you feeling?" Kyle asks Alec.

"Okay so far," he replies.

Lucas is hovering over me, and I just want to be alone. "I'm tired," I tell everyone. "I'm going to lie down."

Kyle appears unsure as he thanks me again. I can see that he believes his words are wholly inadequate for what just happened. Alec also offers his appreciation even as I'm turning away from him.

Lucas walks me down to my bedroom. He pulls me close as we stand in the darkness, not bothering with the lights.

"You're amazing," he says. My head is resting on his shoulder. I can hardly believe how calm I am. Already, I can feel something inside me pressing against my lower spine.

"She was in the air. You had Penelope levitating. It was un-fucking-believable," he laughs softly, and I can feel his warm breath in my hair. He leans down and kisses me. When he tries to deepen it, I pull away.

"I'm sorry, I just want to lie down," I say, backing toward the bed.

His brow furrows, but he quickly smoothes it out. "Of course," he says. "After what you did tonight, you've earned some rest. You're still okay with this, right? You don't have any regrets?"

I smile and shake my head because it's true. I don't have any regrets about saving Penelope's life. Considering what I had planned to do, this outcome is the right one. I'm not a killer. I'd been fooling myself because I wanted to help Penelope so badly. Now I believe things worked out as they were meant to.

When Lucas leaves, I change into my pajamas and sink down into my bed. My hands tremble as I pull the covers up to my chin. I'm frightened of what might be happening inside me, of what tomorrow will bring, and if I'll even wake up in the morning. My lower back aches too badly to get comfortable, and I close my eyes, attempting to use my energy to assess the damage. My eyes pop open in surprise when I feel it ignite. I've always needed the touch of another person to build the power inside me. I've never felt it on my own. I've never been able to muster anything when I had cuts or bruises that I tried to heal. But my power has been changing. I've felt it change. Somehow, it's been getting stronger. Without questioning it further, I push the energy toward the tumors in my back. When I immediately feel them start to shrink, I laugh softly, confused but overcome with sweet relief. I release a sigh into the night.

Just as my exhausted body begins to fade to sleep, I hear someone padding down the stairs. I don't open my eyes. I don't want any more gratitude tonight. Somehow I know that it's Kyle standing there watching me. I can feel him breathing quietly in the room. I can sense his bittersweet joy. After several heavy, silent minutes, he turns around and slowly heads back upstairs.

MY eyes open gradually to the sunlight streaming into my room. As I slowly come aware, the events of last night hit me all at once. Penelope is cured. I smile at that. Alec is not going to get his punishment in the form of her disease. My smile fades when I think of him. Today, I'm going to call the detective who interviewed me back in San Diego. I'm going to make Alec pay the right way, at the hands of the law.

I rub my eyes and take a deep breath. Then I sit up slowly and grunt in pain. It's my lower spine again. My chest tightens at the realization that the tumors grew back overnight. I didn't heal myself. Not only that, I can feel two more lumps under the skin of my arm just before my wrist.

I've grown new tumors. I try to slow my breathing to staunch the panic. Then I lie back down and repeat what I did last night. I concentrate and try to call up the familiar energy inside me. Once I feel it, I send it out to the pain. It works again. The tumors fade, but now I know, it's only a temporary fix.

I sit up in bed and stare sightlessly across the room. I don't understand what's happening. I don't know how long I can do this. I don't know how fast the disease will progress. Will it get so bad that I can't control it anymore? I have no idea what this means for me. I sit there listening to the morning routine occurring in the rooms above me. I know I can't just stay in bed all day. The last thing I want is for Kyle to learn what really happened. I need to survive the next three weeks, to finish school, and then leave with everyone still believing it all worked as planned. I want Penelope to have her happy family. I want that so badly for her. So I do the only thing I can. I get ready for school, deciding to stick to my routine until I can figure something else out. When I go upstairs for breakfast, everyone is there. I pause in the doorway.

Kyle notices me first. "Sit down. Chloe made pancakes."

"Mine have chocolate chips in them," Penelope says, craning her neck around to look at me.

I sit down and take a sip of the juice that's already been poured for me.

"I know our gratitude makes you uncomfortable," Kyle begins. "So, we'll just say this one more time as a family. Thank you, Raielle. "

"Thank you," Chloe smiles at me.

"Thank you!" Penelope screeches, holding her fork above her head. Then she drops it and giggles when it clanks on the floor.

I smile at her mischievous antics, and I can feel the tears building. "You're welcome," I say. Then I take a deep breath and eat a few bites to appease them before heading out the door.

At school, I'm able to act as though nothing is wrong around everyone but Lucas. Somehow, he always sees through me. At lunchtime, I tell him I'm going outside to call the police in San Diego. When he insists on coming with me, I blow up at him. He's been scrutinizing my every move all day, and I finally lose my cool.

"I can make a phone call by myself. Will you please leave me the fuck alone for two minutes?!" I yell at him. The hallway is filled with students, all focused on me now.

His jaw clenches. He opens his mouth to say something. Then he snaps it shut again and storms away.

I'm a wreck when I finally make it outside. First, I look up the main number of the police station. When I call it, I ask for Detective Brady. Then I get transferred to his voicemail. I leave my name and number and the reason I'm calling. Then I stay outside by myself for the rest of lunch. Just as I'm heading back in, my phone rings.

"Ms. Blackwood?"

I immediately recognize the voice that spoke to me on that traumatic day not so long ago. "Hi."

"I'm putting a recorder on. I want you to repeat everything you said on your message. I might interrupt you with some questions, but I need to tell you I'm recording this conversation."

"Okay." Then I tell him everything I know about Rob Jarvis and Alec Dean. Of course, I leave out the motive. I can't mention my ability to heal which is the reason my mother was killed. He listens quietly, asks more questions about my mother's relationship with Alec, which, unfortunately, I don't know much about. I make sure to stress that Kyle was not involved and knows nothing about this. Detective Brady answers noncommittally and tells me he'll look into everything I've told him.

Since I'm now late for my next class, I do something I've never done before. I skip. I start walking home. On my way, I call in sick to Scoops

I'm going to blow off the rest of my day to lay around in bed and wallow, or try to think of a solution, a possible loophole to my problem.

When I get home, I'm relieved to find the house is empty. The mail is spread across the entryway floor below the mail slot. I scoop it up and find a large white envelope hand-addressed to me. I gasp when I recognize the messy block letters as Apollo's handwriting. I recall it from the scraps of paper he used to give me with the names of the people who owed him money.

I carefully open the envelope to find another envelope inside. This one is addressed to me at our old apartment. It's from UCLA. My heart rate kicks up. They sent it to the wrong address, and Apollo forwarded it to me. How on earth did he know my address here?

It's a large envelope and that seems like a good sign. I rip it open and read the very first line before giving a little yelp and jumping up and down. Faster now, I start thumbing through all the paperwork that came with the acceptance letter. I quickly see that I got a full tuition scholarship. It's everything I wanted, everything I've worked for. But finally receiving the news today feels like a sucker punch to the stomach. I sink down to the floor with the letter clutched in my hand. I used to imagine myself moving to LA, finding an apartment, starting a new life, a life of my own that no one could take from me. Now, the image is blurred with uncertainty. It truly feels like the dream it always was, a dream that's more out of reach than ever.

TWENTY ONE

CHLOE and Penelope come home to find me still sitting on the floor holding my acceptance letter. When I show it to Chloe, she smiles brightly and tells me congratulations.

When Kyle gets home, he picks me up and whoops loudly. I'm completely flustered by his enthusiasm, and I find myself giggling. Before dinner, we sit down at the kitchen table to go through all the paperwork together. As my legal guardian, he needs to sign some forms and so do I. I let myself enjoy my dream for a while, signing my name with a flourish, laughing and accepting my brother's praise and attention.

Kyle and I are alone when we finish filling out the last form. Chloe is down the hall giving Penelope a bath. "We're a lot alike, you know?" He smiles, putting down his pen. "We don't express our emotions much. Chloe says that giving birth was easier than getting me to talk about my feelings." He chuckles to himself before taking a breath and turning more serious. "But there are some things I really want to say to you, and it's long past time I did that. Raielle, I'm proud to have you as my sister. I want you to know that. I'm so glad that after all this time, you're in my life. Once you leave for school, I don't want us to lose what we've started building here. I want you to come back for your holidays and breaks. I want you think of this as your home, too. We're your family. You have a family now, and your family loves you."

He reaches out to me, and I meet him halfway. My eyes tear up as he squeezes me tight. I'm overwhelmed by his words. *You have a family now. Your family loves you.* I know Chloe and I are not family and will never be, but Kyle and Penelope truly are my family, and do I love them. But when Kyle discovers what Alec did to my mother, and that I turned him in for it, I don't know how he'll feel. Despite that, I am glad for this moment with him. Right now, for however long it lasts, I have a brother.

When Kyle pulls away, he notices my tears, and his smile falls just a little. Just then, a screeching, naked Penelope comes dashing through the kitchen dragging a bath towel behind her. She's giggling as she avoids Chloe's attempts to catch her. Kyle and I burst out laughing as the heavy mood immediately lifts, and Kyle stands up to make a grab for Penelope. When he misses, I shake my head at them as I begin gathering up the school forms scattered over the table. A call from Lucas interrupts me, and a still grinning Kyle signals that he can finish the cleanup. I accept gratefully as I take the phone outside with me searching for some quiet.

"I went by Scoops to talk to you, but they told me you called in sick Why didn't you tell me you weren't feeling well?" he asks when I answer

The last time I talked to him, I used a choice word to instruct him to.leave me alone. His tone implies that I'm already forgiven. "I feel fine I'm just," I pause, not sure what to tell him.

"Just what?" he asks.

"Just hiding out for a little while I guess. I talked to the police in San Diego. They had me give a recorded statement over the phone. They could be picking up Alec and Rob Jarvis any day now. I haven't told Kyle

Lucas is silent on the other end. "I'm sorry about today," he finall says.

302

"You don't have to be sorry. I'm the one who blew up at you."

"Yeah, well. I guess I was hoping everything would finally get back to normal. But when it was obvious you weren't back to normal, and you wouldn't talk to me, I didn't know what to do. I kept waiting for you to tell me what's going on."

I close my eyes and take a shaky breath. Normal is something I'll never be. "It's not up to you to fix everything, Lucas."

"But I'll always want to try. Talk to me," he says, his voice gentle and persuasive.

But I won't talk about it. I just can't. "Hey, guess what?" I ask, trying to sound upbeat.

Through the phone, I hear him release a frustrated breath. "What?" he asks after moment.

"I got into UCLA."

"What! Really?" he exclaims, and I can hear the smile in his voice.

"Yeah. I got the letter today. Full tuition scholarship, too."

"Congratulations. That's great news. It's what you wanted."

"It is," I agree, and real enthusiasm tinges my voice. Even if I don't end up going, this is an accomplishment.

"We have to celebrate. Let me take you out tonight."

I glance back at the house where Chloe has already started preparing dinner. "Tonight?"

"Yes, tonight," he laughs. "Is that okay?"

I grin at the phone. I can't refuse him. "It's more than okay."

I go back into the house to tell Kyle and Chloe that I'm going out with Lucas. Their easy agreement on a school night tells me that I can pretty much get away with anything now.

I take my time showering. Then I pull on snug jeans and a low cut tank top. It's a more revealing outfit than I usually wear. Pretty much everything is on display, but I feel reckless. After pushing Lucas away all day, tonight I'm craving his closeness. Tonight, I need him.

He pulls up almost exactly an hour after our phone call, and I rush out of the house to meet him, my hair flying behind me in long, loose waves. Lucas comes around to open the passenger door of his truck when his eyes land on me and nearly bug out of his head. He takes me in, whistling soft and low.

"I've never been more grateful for warm weather," he says with blatant appreciation.

I give him my own perusal as my eyes wander over his form-fitting T-shirt, which is the same dark blue color as his eyes, and the soft, faded jeans that mold to his narrow hips and wrap around his long, lean legs. His hair is pushed carelessly to the side, and I can see the impressions his fingers have left in it. The look in his eyes tells me we're both feeling the same thing tonight. We need to relieve the stress that has been running our lives for so long, and we plan to help each other do exactly that.

He lifts me up into the passenger seat, letting his hand graze the bottom of my breast. As my skin heats, I immediately know that was no mistake. When he seats himself beside me, he asks, "What do you feel like eating?"

I just turn and give him a look.

He grins wickedly at me. "I really do mean food."

"I don't want food. Take me back to that bridge. The one you said has an amazing view of the city."

He stares at me for a beat, appearing indecisive, before he gives me a nod. "The bridge it is."

Once he pulls out onto the road, I offer my hand to him. He wraps his fingers around it and we drive toward the place where I revealed my secrets to him on that rainy night.

"How's your family doing?" I ask.

He glances at me with a hesitant smile. "They're good." I watch as h thinks for a moment before deciding to elaborate. "We're getting used to each other again," he continues. "Liam is obviously glad our mother's better, but I think he doesn't quite trust her yet. I'm relieved to have her back, but I'm impatient. I want everything to just be normal again. For her though, it's been rough. What she did to us is eating away at her. You can see it. She needs to deal with that before she can move forward. My dad wants her to see a therapist, and she agreed to it. She's trying. She even went to Liam's basketball game yesterday. He played it pretty cool, but he was practically bouncing off the walls when they got home. He's never really had this before, a mother who cares, a mother who wants to be there for him. Even though it's hard for her, she is that again."

I squeeze his hand and smile reassuringly at him. I'm not sure what to say. His mother may be better, but she's not bouncing back the way he wants her to. I hope she just needs some more time.

"I've been wondering about something," he says.

I study his shadowed face, thinking I see hesitation there. "What?" I ask.

He glances between me and the road. "Why did you only apply to schools in California? Why do you want to go back there?"

His question catches me off-guard. I'm about to automatically say that it's my home, but before the words are out, I know they're not true. I may have lived in California all my life, but it never signified home in any real sense of the word. I suspect that's what Lucas is getting at with his question, and if so, he has a good point. I guess I want to go back because it's all I know. Or maybe I really am a California girl at heart. Although I'm not the carefree, laid-back stereotype, it is a part of my identity, and I suppose I want to hold on to that since I'm still figuring out so much of the rest. But now that I have this disease, everything is uncertain.

I glance at him from under my lashes. "I just do," I say simply. I don't think I could ever make him understand.

Once I answer, he looks at me for a long time. It seems like he wants to say something, but instead, his lips curl up in mild acknowledgement before he looks back at the road. Neither of us has brought up the fact that our time together has a finite ending. But that thought is always with me. Before I got sick, I assumed we would talk about it at some point. But now, I want to avoid it. Now, I want to enjoy my time with him, understanding that my happily ever after may be tonight, not some future fantasy, but this moment. The one I'm living right now.

I draw in a deep breath and glance out the window, needing to focus on something other than Lucas for a moment, needing to stop the direction of my thoughts before they travel too far in a dark direction.

When I spot the bridge, calmness settles over me, followed by nervous anticipation once the truck comes to a stop. As I push open the door and step down onto the ground, I'm welcomed by a symphony of crickets. Lucas grabs the blanket he always keeps in the back seat, and he takes my hand to lead me down a short hill to a landing just below the bridge. I easily spot the benches he mentioned before, but he walks past them to a round, sheltered clearing and spreads the blanket on a patch of grass.

Water rushes below us as the day fades behind a black curtain dotted by pinpoints of light. The city skyline sparkles in the distance. I couldn't dream up a more romantic setting if I tried. I sit down on the blanket and watch as Lucas lowers himself beside me. We take in our surroundings for a moment before he begins running the back of his hand along my bare arm. I can feel the goose bumps forming beneath his fingers. Just that light touch has awoken all the butterflies inside me.

"How are you really feeling?" he asks. His voice is quiet and intimate beside my ear.

"I'm feeling happy to be here with you," I reply, turning my head and leaning into him so that our lips are only inches apart.

His eyes darken in response. He moves his hand from my arm up to my neck and finally around to the back of my head where he slides his fingers into my hair. My whole scalp tingles, and I'm already breathless when he finally brings my mouth to his. He brushes against my lips at first. Then he lingers there, nipping at my top lip, running his tongue along my bottom one.

I lift my arms up over his shoulders and wrap them around his neck as I press myself against him wanting to deepen the kiss. Our mouths open together, and his tongue touches mine. I make a happy sound in the back of my throat at the contact, and he shifts our bodies, angling himself above me, laying me down on the blanket, and nudging my legs apart so he can lower himself between them.

I run my fingers through his thick hair before moving them lower, down his back, until I find the bottom of his T-shirt. Then I slip my hands inside it and slide them around to the warm skin of his stomach. His muscles contract beneath my touch as he groans into my mouth. I feel his hands doing the same to me. With our lips fused together, he lifts the bottom of my tank top and presses his warm fingers against my bare skin. I begin to writhe in his arms as the muscles low in my belly contract and tighten. He tilts his hips forward into mine, and an aching need blooms inside me. This is escalating quickly, but I'm not nervous or afraid. I just want more.

When I feel a sudden chill, my eyes pop open to see Lucas leaning back, pulling off his shirt. My breath halts in my lungs as I stare at the defined planes and the deep ridges of his chest and abdomen. His skin is smooth and gleaming in the moonlight. I reach my hands up to touch him, but he shakes his head.

"Let's take this off," he says, pulling up on my tank top.

I obediently sit up and stretch my arms over my head so he can lift it up. My hair slides through it smoothly and falls back down over my bare shoulders and black lace bra.

Lucas just stares for a moment, his eyes wandering over me. "You're so fucking gorgeous," he whispers before crashing his mouth to mine, pressing me back down onto the blanket. This time his kiss isn't slow or gentle, it's urgent, filled with desperate emotion. He sucks on my tongue as he grinds up against me. I gasp, and my fingers grip his shoulders. The tension building inside me tightens when he pushes down the cups of my bra and draws my nipple into his mouth. My head rolls back as I moan loudly and arch up against him.

"You like that," he murmurs. Then he removes my hands from his warm skin and stretches my arms above my head, holding them there. "If we don't stop now, we won't, Ray," he says.

He hovers above me, blocking out the sky, shielding me from the world. He is my world tonight. His hooded eyes search mine, and I can see the haze of lust clouding his thoughts. They're clouding mine, too, and I don't want to stop. There's no way we can stop now. "I want this, Lucas. I want you," I manage to say. My voice sounds breathless in my ears.

He doesn't hesitate. Still watching me, he releases one of my arms to reach his hand down between us. He unhooks the button on my jeans before slowly pulling down the zipper. I shiver as his fingers slip inside, pushing down beneath the top of my panties, and he lightly touches the skin just above my pubic bone. His eyes continue to hold mine. He gives me a slow sexy grin before returning to my lips again, taking my breath away with his deep, passionate pulls on my mouth. Then he starts kissing his way down the side of my neck, lingering at my breasts while his fingers slip further inside my panties, moving downward, and cupping me now. I gasp, and my inner thighs tense at his touch. I feel him push his thumb inside my folds and apply pressure as he begins an intimate massage. I'm not self-conscious like I thought I would be. I'm not embarrassed. This is Lucas. This is perfect.

Something is building inside me. It's so intense, it's almost uncomfortable. My muscles are quivering with tension now. I try to roll my body away, but Lucas is holding me securely beneath him. I feel him move a finger inside me, and my muscles contract around him. When he presses the heel of his hand down hard and slips another finger into me, curving it forward, my hips buck at the jolt of pleasure that rips through me. My head tilts back as my muscles grip his fingers and sparks ignite behind my eyes. My body bows stiffly while he murmurs the word "beautiful" in my ear. I can hear my own quick pants of breath as the ripples flow through me, going on and on before gradually receding, turning my muscles to liquid and spawning a new understanding. A smile curls my lips. When I finally catch my breath, I tell him, "You were wrong."

His eyes gradually focus and curiously find mine.

"I understand the comparison," I explain. "But healing isn't even a close second to what you just did to me."

Lucas throws his head back and laughs. I've never heard him laugh so freely before. The rich sound of it is positively musical. I reach my hands up to caress his gorgeous grinning face.

He closes his eyes and smiles with satisfaction as the fingers that were inside me slowly paint a trail of moisture across my stomach and up the length of my body. All my senses seem magnified as I register the gliding of his fingertips against me. Heat is radiating off him, and I want to pull him down to me so I can immerse myself in his warmth. I can also feel his unsatisfied desire pressing against me.

"Your turn," I say, reaching my hands down toward the top of his jeans, hoping I can give him half as much pleasure as he just gave me.

He grabs my wrists and shakes his head at me. "Thanks but that's not what I want right now." His glittering eyes question mine.

Without hesitation, I nod and watch as he leans back to pull his wallet from his back pocket. He opens it, and withdraws a condom crinkling inside a foil wrapper. Placing it on the blanket, he reaches behind him for my foot. Then he proceeds to take off my shoes for me. He puts them neatly on the blanket beside us before leaning over me, hooking his fingers under the tops of my jeans, and waiting for me to lift my hips so he can pull them down. As he inches them over my legs, I watch his progress with fascination. "I never knew you were so methodical," I say.

He looks down at me. "This is your first time. This is *our* first time. I don't want to rush it."

He's so adorable and so completely off base. "Lucas, I'm really ready. Feel free to hurry it up just a little."

He grins. Then he swiftly tugs my jeans down my legs and has them off in no time at all. Now I'm only wearing a bra that's still askew and black panties.

When he reaches for his own jeans, I place my hands on his. My fingers are itching to touch him. "Let me."

He lowers his hands, watching me as I lift myself to my knees and position myself in front of him. I get the button undone quickly. Then I make sure to brush against him as I slide his zipper down.

He hisses at the contact, and the sound makes my heart beat faster. Under his jeans, I can see a grey waistband circling the taut muscles of his stomach. I push his jeans down to reveal his boxer briefs and what's barely contained inside them. I just stare for a moment, taking in this intimate part of him. I want him so badly, I can hardly comprehend it. I've never felt anything this strongly. I never believed I could.

I place one hand on his chest over his heart, feeling its rapid rhythm, knowing it's in sync with my own racing pulse. Then I reach out my other hand and smooth it over his warm length. He sucks in a breath as I gently circle my fingers around him, gripping him through the thin fabric. His breathing quickens, and his long fingers lift my hand from his chest, bringing it up to his mouth. He shifts his hips, pushing himself more fully into my hand as he places a soft kiss to my other palm. When I look up at him, his tender eyes are lit with passion. He runs his fingers up and down the inside of my arm, making me shiver. I try to reclaim my hand so I can remove his remaining clothing, exposing all of him to my hungry eyes, but he only grips me harder.

My eyes flick up to find him studying my arm. "Lucas?" I ask, confused as I try to pull my arm from his grasp.

He whispers a curse as he runs his fingers over the inside of my wrist. "What are these?"

His harsh grip tells me there's no turning back now. I don't need to look to understand what he's found. I close my eyes and exhale my regret. For a little while tonight, he helped me forget. My body, which had been swimming in desire moments ago, sinks slowly down to the blanket.

Abruptly, he releases my arm and pushes himself to his feet. He's standing over me now, glowering down at me. Under his scrutiny, I self-consciously pull my bra back into place and reach for my jeans. Before I can grab them, he bends down and takes my arm again, turning it so that we can both see the three small lumps running vertically along the inside of my wrist.

"You didn't give it to Alec. You gave it yourself!" He hollers so loudly it makes me cringe. Dropping my arm again, he turns away and rakes both his hands through his hair.

I pull on my jeans and curl my legs under me, waiting for his fury to pass.

"Why?" he finally asks. Then he drops down to his knees before me. "Why would you do this?"

"I didn't knowingly do it," I reply, staring down at my hands rather than at him. "Once it was inside me, I couldn't get it out."

He grabs me by the shoulders and shakes me, forcing me to look at him. "Tell me what you mean. Don't make me drag this out of you."

I blow out a shaky breath. I never wanted him to know. I never wanted to see that anguished look back in his eyes. It's the same look I took away when I helped his mother. The last thing I wanted was to be the cause of its return.

"If I'd thought about it more clearly," I begin hesitantly, "I could have predicted this might happen. I didn't actually think I could give it to myself. I'd seen my mother try, and it didn't work. But what was missing when she attempted it was the family connection. That wasn't missing this time. Once I'd taken Penelope's disease into me, I couldn't push it out again. It wouldn't leave my body."

He's staring at me. His eyes are wide, and I can't tell what's going on behind them. "This is so fucked up!" he snaps at me. "You didn't say a goddamned thing. You let everyone believe it worked."

"It did work."

His expression turns fierce. "Trading your life for your niece's wasn't the plan. I never would have encouraged you to do it if I'd known this was a possibility. You have to give it back to her."

My eyes widen at his suggestion, and I begin shaking my head. "No, Lucas, I can't. I can't cure myself. Besides, even if I could give it back to Penelope, I wouldn't."

His jaw clenches so tightly I wonder why his teeth aren't shattering. "We have to fix this. There has to be some way to get it out of you."

"I'm able to dissolve the tumors as they appear. They grow back, but so far, I can control them. Maybe it will be okay," I tell him, hoping I'm right, but not really believing it.

His eyes narrow in confusion. "Wait, you can control them, but not cure them? I don't understand."

"I don't either. I think it has something to do with the nature of this disease. These tumors, somehow they're different. My energy works on them. But they come back, just like they did with Penelope."

"What if they get worse? What if they get so bad that you can't control anymore?" he asks, voicing my own fears.

I pull my legs into my chest and wrap my arms around them. I have no answer to his question. It's a possibility. I can't deny that.

"We're going back and telling Kyle," he states, standing now, and buttoning his jeans.

"What? No?" I quickly uncurl myself and stand up to face him. "Why would we do that?"

He pulls his shirt over his head before turning back to me. "Because I want him and his wife to know what really happened. They can't go around thinking everything's sunshine and rainbows while you're slowly dying right under their noses."

When he turns, I grab his arm and place myself in front of him. "You can't do that. It's not their fault. Don't ruin this for them."

"Finish getting dressed," he orders. Then he steps around me and starts back up the hill toward his truck.

I yell at his retreating back. "If you tell them, I'll never forgive you, Lucas!"

My words stop him in his tracks. He stands there for a moment before turning and stomping back to me. "So what do you want to do? Bury your head in the sand? Keep quiet and act like everything is fine? Just hope for the fucking best?! If that's your plan, it sucks ass."

I try not to let his anger get to me. He has a right to it. The fact is I have come up with something of a plan. It's been building in the back of my mind since I got the envelope from UCLA. But I haven't had time to really consider it, and if I follow through with it, I'll be completely disregarding the warning my mother gave me in that strange dream I had.

"That is my plan until graduation," I say. "Then I want to go to Los

Angeles and try to find my father. If he has this power, too, and if he's as powerful as my grandmother said, maybe he can help me."

Lucas stares at me, and I can see the wheels turning in his head as this sinks in. Then he gives me a single nod. "That plan doesn't suck ass. But your time frame does. We should go now. We shouldn't wait."

We? His statement startles me. He wants to go with me, and I'm so surprised by that, a tremor of relief runs through me. But I'm still not leaving now. "I'm not running out on my high school career when I'm so close to graduating," I inform him.

He narrows his eyes. "Dead people don't need high school diplomas," he says in a tight voice.

My mouth hangs open. I know he's going for shock value to prove his point, but I can't let it change my mind. "This is what I'm doing. I don't want to argue about it."

"It's three weeks. That's too long to wait. You don't know how long it's going to take to find your father. You don't know anything about him."

"But Alec might. I want to talk to him before the police pick him up."

He closes his eyes and pinches the bridge of his nose. "Okay, fine. We'll talk to him together." He steps closer to me. His eyes are burning with hurt. "I'm furious at you for keeping this from me. Why didn't you tell me? Were you trying to protect me again?"

I'm feeling tired now, and the tumor in my back is making it hard to stand. I shrug my answer, wordlessly acknowledging my guilt.

"Didn't I tell you to cut that shit out?"

I cross my arms over my breasts. I still haven't put on my shirt, and it dawns on me for the first time that anyone could stumble upon u and see me. I can hardly believe how little I cared about that just a few minutes ago when he was touching me. Then his words sink in. "I've go news for you, Lucas. I might not always do everything you tell me to."

"No kidding," he says. I watch as he pulls in a deep breath and h wrinkled forehead smoothes out. "You have to stop this, Ray. You have to start talking to me. I can't stand that you still won't talk to me." He reaches out for me, and I go to him, wrapping my arms around his back, feeling like nothing can hurt me when he's holding me close.

"I'm sorry," I whisper.

"I know," he says quietly next to my ear.

I'm not sure how long we stay this way, just holding each other, before he pulls back to look at me. "I don't like waiting three weeks," he says. "You realize that puts your deadline right around your birthday. We have to make sure you see your eighteenth birthday. I want you to consider taking it one day at a time. If things get worse, we'll go earlier. No arguments."

With all that's going on, I've hardly thought about my birthday. It makes me happy that he remembered. I nod my head because I'm too tired to argue. "About what happened tonight, what we almost did," I say sleepily, feeling warm again just thinking about it. "Should we talk about it?"

"What did we almost do?" he asks innocently.

I laugh. "If you don't know, that's going to make it tough to get a rain check."

His hand cups my cheek, and his eyes narrow in on mine. "Believe me. I'm on it. You'll get your rain check." Then he lowers his lips to mine and our mouths open together, breathing each other in, melting into one another until I break away in pain when his hand inadvertently pushes against my spine.

His eyes question mine before realization sharpens them. Glancing from me to his hand, he frowns, but he holds back the curses I know are on his tongue. "As much as I enjoy looking at you this way, we should get your shirt on," he says. Then he picks up my tank top, hands it to me, and watches while I pull it over my head. When he reaches down to button my jeans for me, I suck in a breath as his fingers brush my bare stomach. I wish more than anything that we hadn't stopped. But as I watch Lucas, and see the deep furrow back in his brow, I know his thoughts are elsewhere.

"Let's talk to Alec now," he says, glancing at his watch. "It's still early."

"Now?" I just settled on this plan. I'm hardly ready to put it into motion.

"We need to be prepared if this thing starts to hit you harder. Once the police pick Alec up, we might lose our only source of information."

I take in his determined tone and nod warily, figuring he's probably right. "So what? We just drive over to his house and hope he's there?"

"Pretty much." He takes my hand, and we climb the short hill together. "Let's not tell Alec he isn't dying though," he says. "We'll tell him you want to meet your father. That's our only reason for being there as far as he's concerned."

"Okay." I'm clenching my jaw now. I need to start dissolving these tumors. Lucas pulls open the door for me, but I just stand there. My back feels like it's on fire. I don't think I can climb in.

"Ray?"

"Can you lift me inside?" I have to ask.

His mouth is a tight line as he effortlessly picks me up and gently sets me down on the seat.

"I need a few quiet minutes," I say, hoping he'll give them to me without starting the argument about leaving earlier again. When he nods and leans against the door to watch me, I close my eyes and try to relax. It takes less than five minutes to direct the energy around my body and shrink the tumors. When it's done, I open my eyes and smile weakly at him. Then I reach my hand out for the door handle. His mood is unreadable as he reluctantly steps aside so I can pull the door closed.

I'm glad Lucas remembers the way to Alec's house because I certainl don't. When we arrive, it looks much the same as it did the night we came for Alec's birthday. I see his white sedan in the driveway, and I'm both apprehensive and relieved to find that he's at home.

"Ready?" Lucas asks.

I look over at him and notice that the muscle in his jaw is a tight little ball. I realize the tremendous effort it took to remain silent when I couldn't even climb up into his truck.

"Ready," I reply, with more enthusiasm than necessary, trying to show him that I really am okay now. But as Lucas steps out of the truck and comes around to get me, I don't move. I don't want to go in there and face Alec again. The thought of being near him makes my skin crawl.

Lucas pulls open the passenger door and immediately appears worried as I continue to stare at the house without moving. I can tell he's misunderstanding. He thinks I'm unable to move myself. His hand touches my arm. "Why don't you wait here?" he suggests.

I shake my head and force myself to get out. Lucas is on edge as he watches me slowly descend. Once I'm beside him, he takes my hand and gently presses it, like he's trying to give me some of his strength. Then he leads the way up the walk.

When Linda opens the door to us, her mouth forms a silent O of surprise.

"Hi, Linda. We'd like to talk to Alec," I say, determined to appear calm and strong while we're here.

"He's in the study. Is he expecting you?"

"No," Lucas answers and begins to move forward when Linda doesn't immediately invite us in.

"Oh," she laughs, putting a hand to her chest. "I'm sorry. Come in." She stands aside so we can step into the large entryway.

"Alec!" she calls down the hallway.

From down the hall, his face pops out of a doorway before his entire body follows. "Raielle, this is a surprise," he smiles widely. "Hello, Lucas."

"They say they want to talk to you," Linda explains with obvious curiosity.

Alec looks carefully at both of us. "Come into the study, kids. Linda, I don't think we'll be needing anything," he tells her, subtly dismissing her. She seems like she wants to protest, but then thinks better of it, offering us a hesitant smile before retreating into the other room.

Alec watches as we file past him into his study. But I don't look at him. Instead, when I enter the room, I notice the large picture window that fills the opposite wall. Because of the darkness beyond it, I see only my transparent reflection hovering before me. It mesmerizes me, looking like an apparition, growing larger as I approach it, taunting me with my own wide and anxious eyes. I squeeze those eyes shut, making myself turn away from it. When I open them again, I focus on a glossy wood desk against another wall—on it are a monitor and keyboard. The monitor is set to a screen saver of Penelope laughing as she sits on a swing at a playground.

"I still feel perfectly fine," Alec comments as he motions us toward the couch beside his desk. He pulls over a chair and sits down across from us. "Maybe the disease is gone. Maybe you're even better than you think." Then he winks at me.

"It's not gone," Lucas says.

I swivel my head in his direction.

"Raielle has it," he states, and I can tell he's seething. I'm stunned. can't believe he just told him this after we agreed not to.

Alec stares at me. "What?"

"Something went wrong. How lucky for you." Lucas's eyes are shooting darts at Alec.

Alec's gaze is still on my face. "You mean I'm not going to get sick I'm going to be all right?"

My loathing for him twists inside me. Its takes all my self-control to swallow my rage and nod reluctantly, confirming the hope that brightens his face. When he begins to smile, Lucas is up like a shot.

I push myself up, too, and grab Lucas's arm as Alec stands in reaction to us. Lucas looks like he's ready to pummel him. "That's not why we're here," I say, trying to calm him.

With his eyes still on Alec, he clenches his jaw.

"We're here for information," I say to Alec. He turns quizzical eyes on me. "I want to find my father. I need you to tell us everything you know about him."

His eyebrows arch up. "Your father?" Then his expression fills with understanding. "I see. You're hoping he can help you." He absently runs his hands over his face, and I can see the relief that washes over him as our news slowly sinks in.

When he gives us his attention again, his eyes are red with suppressed emotion. "I'm happy to tell you what I know, but it isn't much," he begins. "His name is Rainard Blackwood and back then he was a businessman from Los Angeles. He owned a small trade publishing company, I think. I don't remember what they published." Alec notes my surprise at his name. "Yes, you were probably named after him."

But that isn't all that surprises me. "She took his last name," I say, completely astonished. "I really do have my father's last name."

"You didn't know?" Alec asks.

I shake my head.

"Is that it?" Lucas demands. "Is that all you've got?"

"It's an unusual name. That should be enough to locate him if he wants to be found," Alec says.

"Fine. Let's go." Lucas takes my hand.

I don't move. "Alec, please don't tell Kyle and Chloe what really happened. Let them believe what you did at first, that I got rid of it completely, that no one has it now."

He studies me for a moment. "You really are an extraordinary young lady. Don't worry, I won't say a word."

"Thank you," I take a breath, feeling tired again. "You should also know that I called the police."

He nods, seeming unconcerned. "I thought you might."

"Come on," Lucas urges. This time I allow him to lead me to the door.

"Raielle," Alec says, halting us with Lucas's hand on the knob.

I turn back to him.

"I do wish you luck."

Lucas snorts his disbelief as he pulls open the door and nudges me out into the hall.

"I can't believe you did that," I hiss at him once we're back in his truck. "You were the one who said we should keep him in the dark. Instead, you went and made his day."

He bangs his hand against the steering wheel. "I lost it, okay? The prick winked at you. He fucking winked!"

I lean my head back against the seat feeling too tired to continue this. "Please just take me home," I say. Even though my eyes are closed I know Lucas is staring at me. Finally, I hear him put the keys in the ignition, and I'm asleep before he even turns onto the next street.

TWENTY TWO

THREE days later, I wake up to terrible pain. It's shooting through my body, but the spots at the base of my neck and in my right wrist burn the strongest. I try to relax my muscles. My right hand is fisted in the sheets, but I force my fingers to uncurl. I begin to take steady, even breaths. Finally, the coil of energy begins to form. I unravel it, sending it out, letting it flow through me. It takes longer than usual this time, but gradually, the pain eases. I maintain the energy until the burning sensation fades completely. Then I sigh in relief. My relief is so strong that I just lie there, listening to my own ragged breathing, as my heartbeat returns to its normal rhythm.

Beside me, my phone vibrates. I reach for it, and my hand bangs against the nightstand. I quickly become alert as I sit up and stare at my right hand. Then I grab it with my other hand and gasp. I can't feel my own touch. My right hand is completely numb.

Using my left hand now, I press on my fingers, massaging them along with the rest of my hand, trying to bring some sensation back. But there's nothing. From my wrist down, I feel absolutely nothing. Staring at my hand now, I try to move it, and I release the breath I've been holding when it obeys me. It's awkward, but if I concentrate, I can use my hand. I can make a fist, and wiggle my fingers.

I pick up my phone again with my left hand, and I place it in my right. My fingers close around it, but I can't maintain my hold on it. The phone drops onto the bed. The tumors are gone again, but this time they left some damage behind. I cradle my hand and hope this isn't permanent. I really may not have the little over two weeks that are left.

Since I'm a righty, getting through my morning routine is difficult. I end up wearing my hair down because I can't manage anything else, and I throw on a little print sundress with no buttons or zippers that I haven't worn since living in San Diego. I'm only holding myself together right now because I'm in deep denial. I don't want to accept the fact that I'm running out of time.

When I hear Kyle and Chloe chatting about Alec's continued good health, I skip breakfast and make the walk to school with Myles. Obviously, Alec has not told them what really happened and for some reason, I'm not surprised that he's kept his word about that.

I know from checking in with Detective Brady that Alec has been called into the local police station here in Fort Upton for questioning twice. Apparently, he's denying everything. I was told that eventually I'd have to go down there, too, to give a statement in person. So far, Kyle and Chloe are blissfully unaware that this investigation is taking place. They know nothing about Alec's guilt, and no one has told them. If he's ever arrested, it will come out. I'm not surprised that Alec is denying all involvement. I'd be more shocked if he admitted to it. Detective Brady assures me that Rob Jarvis will make a deal that includes testifying against Alec. At least, that's their plan. I appreciate that he's willing to keep me informed.

Lucas meets me on the front steps of the school and gives me morning embrace along with a kiss that lasts a little too long and begins drawing cheers. I break away embarrassed, but he just smiles, unbothered by the attention.

"Friday night," he says, reminding me. But I need no reminder.

I smile, looking forward to it. The other day, Lucas told me that Liam asked why he was never home anymore. After some insisting from me, we agreed that he would spend the next few nights with his family. I know he needs the distraction. Watching me each day is an excruciating waiting game for him. He tries to pretend otherwise, but he can't hide the dark circles beneath his eyes or the quiet concern that keeps him uncharacteristically subdued. Somehow, I'm able to deal with my condition better than he is. I guess that's because it's happening to me. If anything ever happened to him, I would undoubtedly be a complete mess. But we're both happily anticipating Friday night. Friday night, he told me, he has something special planned. I'm pretty sure I'm collecting on my rain check.

There's a pop quiz today in history, and I'm soon regretting that Lucas and I sit next to each other in class. I can almost feel his scrutiny as I awkwardly try to write out my answers. Since my left hand writing is about as legible as one of Penelope's scribbles, I switch to my right hand. I'm actually doing a better job with my right when the pen isn't slipping out of my fingers and clattering onto the floor. When this happens for the third time, Lucas bends down, beating me to its retrieval. As he's handing it back to me, he asks, "What's going on?"

"*Nothing,*" I mouth, returning to my test.

The rest of the morning goes smoother since there's no writing required beyond taking notes. But Lucas hasn't forgotten history class. Before lunch, he appears at my locker. "Let's go outside and talk."

Since I know I can't avoid this conversation, I agree. When he takes my right hand in his, and I feel nothing, I find myself on the verge of tears. I never thought about this consequence.

He leads me to a patch of shade beneath a tree. We both sit down on the grass, and he takes my hands in his. He turns them over, examining my wrists and forearms. I know he's looking for lumps. "I don't see anything," he says, running his fingers along my skin. "Why couldn't you hold your pen?"

I bite down on my bottom lip. His eyes are searching mine for answers. It feels like he's bracing himself for bad news. "My right hand is numb," I say.

His brow wrinkles as he takes my hand in both of his. "You can't feel this?"

I shake my head.

"Since when?" he asks.

"Since this morning."

He rubs his hands along both sides of mine. "Nothing?"

"No. When I dissolved the tumors this morning, I lost all feeling in it. I'm not sure what's going on."

"It's getting worse," he states. "That's what's going on."

I nod, and look over at the other students sitting on the grass nearby. They're talking and laughing like they don't have a care in the world. I feel a pang of regret as I watch them, missing something I never had in the first place.

"I still can't find anything on your father. You get nothing when you type his name into search engines. I called around to all the business organizations I could find in California, and he's not known anywhere. I can't link him to any publishing company that's located out there." He pauses, shifting on the grass. It looks like he's building up to something. "We could try talking to your grandmother," he suggests too nonchalantly. "She might be able to tell us more."

I immediately begin shaking my head. I can feel my stomach churn at the thought of it.

"We should go see her," he states firmly, no longer being delicate about it.

"No, Lucas."

"Even if she doesn't know anything else about your father, maybe she can help you."

My eyes widen in horror. "No!"

"Ray, please..."

"You have no idea what you're talking about. She can't help me. Her power isn't nearly strong enough. Even if she could, all she would do is pass this on to someone else. There's no way I'll agree to that. I don't know how you can even suggest going to her."

He leans toward me. His eyes pierce me with their intensity. "Because I'm desperate. I'd do anything to help you," he bites out. Then he stills. "Wait a minute. You could give it to her. That's perfect. She's a blood relative. Maybe that's why it didn't work with Alec. He's Penelope's blood, not yours. Maybe that's why once it was inside you, you couldn't give it to him. I bet you could give it to your grandmother though."

I lean away from him shaking my head again. I see the logic in what he's saying, although there's no way to be sure it would work. But it doesn't matter anyway. I can't knowingly harm someone, not even her. I've gradually come to understand how relieved I am not to have passed this disease onto Alec no matter how much I loathe him. I would never tell this to Lucas, but I'm grateful the healing backfired. I think about the selfishness of my grandmother, and the horror she inflicted on Lucas's family. I remember the way my mother buried her pain and lost herself in addiction. Now I think I can understand the self-loathing she felt after what happened with the boy who had leukemia, and then again with Kelvin's son. I don't need any more examples of how misusing my healing power could change me, and twist me into someone I would never want to be.

Lucas reaches out and grips my arms. I can tell he's gearing up for a monumental argument about this. I need to make him understand.

I pull his hands off me and grasp them tightly. "I won't use my power to cause harm to others, not even to my grandmother, not even to save myself, especially not for that reason."

When he opens his mouth to protest, I reach for the back of his neck with both my hands, and I get right in his face. He needs to know exactly how serious I am.

His frantic eyes settle and then focus on mine.

"Listen to me," I begin. "If I cross that line, I might as well let this disease destroy me now, because I would cease to exist. In my place would be a monster who is no better than my grandmother."

I stare into his blue depths, trying to silently communicate my unwavering stance, watching closely as his desperation reluctantly changes to understanding and then gradually to pain.

He takes my hands from around his neck and lowers them, holding them in front of him. "What if we find your father and that's all he can do?" he asks. "Move your disease into someone else? What then? Will you refuse his help?"

I'll have to refuse it. Lucas must be realizing that now. If he knows me at all, then deep down, he knows my answer. "Let's just find him first. Okay?" I ask. I can hear the plea in my voice. I need him to leave this alone. I won't talk about worst case scenarios with him. It won't do us any good.

I watch as he struggles against his need to change my mind and purposely calms himself down. His jaw clenches and then relaxes as he reclaims his hand and runs it over his rough cheek. "Okay," he finally says softly, glancing away from me after a long silence.

When he turns back, his neutral mask is firmly in place. For once, I'm relieved to see it there, but I'm afraid he's only decided to table the argument for now.

"There are local records kept when businesses apply for any kind of a license or permit," he says. "If your father owns a business in Los Angeles, his name and the business exist on a register. If we're there to do the legwork, it's going to be easier to track him down .We need to leave now. We need to be there."

I find that I'm resigned to leaving now. I nod my agreement.

"We'll go tomorrow. I'll get us some plane tickets." He waits for my argument. When he receives a tremulous, but grateful smile instead, the tightness around his eyes eases. He exhales softly and places his hands on either side of my face. My cheeks warm when he gently rubs his thumbs over them. Then he leans in and kisses me tenderly.

I can still hardly believe he's in my life. I've never had anyone care about me this way. I never imagined anyone would. I only wish I wasn't the cause of so much worry for him. He deserves happiness and normalcy. I don't think he'll ever have those things with me.

His lips leave mine, and they move up to my ear. "I love you," he whispers.

I pull in a sharp breath as his words trigger silent tears that begin to roll down my cheeks. When he sees them, he softly kisses them away.

Since I first saw that picture of us on my phone, dancing together at the prom, I've understood that I'm in love with Lucas. The way he looked at me in that photo, like I was the most precious thing in the world to him, had me wondering if he felt the same way. But I was afraid I was reading too much into it. I was afraid to really believe it. Never did I imagine that I would hear those words from him or want to say them back. After all Lucas has been through with his family, after all the baggage I've unloaded on him, I'm amazed by his willingness to lay his heart on the line for me. I'm stunned by his bravery.

I lean back and wait until our gazes meet. "I love you, too," I say softly. "So much."

His eyes lock on mine, and it feels like he's trying to see inside me to confirm my feelings. I hope he sees the truth. He deserves to know it as surely as I do. Then he kisses me again, and I can taste my salty tears on him.

"I didn't know how I was going to tell you goodbye when you left," he says, stroking my face, watching me closely. "Now that we're going to California together, once you're well, I'm going to stay for a while if that's okay."

He's apprehensive, waiting for my response. I wonder how he can doubt what my answer will be. My only doubts are not about him. "Of course it's okay," I say with a grin spreading across my face. "Stay until classes at Columbia start," I add optimistically, wanting to reassure him.

He doesn't return my smile. "You're going to be fine. You have to believe that." His tone is one of determination. But I know him too well now. I see it in his eyes. He fears for me, but he's working hard to appear confident. We both know that a happy summer together in California is much more of a wish than a certainty. That fact hangs heavy between us. As the bell rings, I'm afraid Myles got it right. I probably will hurt Lucas in the end. When I do, I wonder if he'll think it was worth it.

Lucas stands and reaches down to help me up. Things are different between us now. I've never felt this close to another human being. It's overwhelming, how strong my feelings are for him.

"I need to take off," he says once we reach the main door. "If we're going to leave tomorrow, I have some things to handle."

"Do you think they'll still let us graduate?" I ask.

"I just have one paper left to turn in. What about you?"

"I have my chemistry final next week," I answer, feeling my shoulder slump. Lucas can still turn in his paper, but I'm not sure what missing final will mean.

"Talk to your teacher," he says. "See what you can do."

I nod. I have no other choice.

The heavy school door swings open, nearly hitting me. Chad pushes his way out, smacking a cigarette pack against the palm of his hand.

"Watch it, asshole," Lucas scowls at him.

Chad stops and turns to him. "What did you say?" he asks, narrowing his eyes.

"You heard me," Lucas replies aggressively, looking too pleased at this unexpected opportunity to challenge Chad.

Then Chad notices me standing there. His gaze shifts between Lucas and me before something occurs to him. "Hey," he says to both of us. "You didn't get into it with Rob again, did you?"

Lucas and I glance at each other. "No, why?" I ask.

"Because the little shit disappeared. He didn't show up for practice this week. He isn't answering his phone. We've got a gig on Saturday and he fucking fell into a hole or something."

My muscles fill with tension as I hear Lucas answer. "We haven't seen him."

Chad withdraws a cigarette and lights it. "I'm gonna kick his ass when he turns up." Then he moves past us muttering angrily, his annoyance with Lucas forgotten.

"He ran," Lucas says once Chad is out of earshot.

"Maybe." I pull out my phone. "I'm calling the police to see if they have him."

I scroll through my list of recent calls, find Detective Brady's number, and dial while walking around to the side of the building for privacy. I feel Lucas move beside me as I lean back against the warm concrete. When his line rings for the fourth time, Brady abruptly picks up and gruffly says his name, startling me with his tone.

"Um, hi. This is Raielle Blackwood." I glance at Lucas. His eyes are intent on me.

"Oh, Raielle," Brady says. "What can I do for you?"

"I just heard one of Rob Jarvis's friends say that he's disappeared. I was wondering if you've arrested him."

He sighs into the phone. "We got a match on some DNA found in your apartment. We can put him there now. We could make an arrest, but we're having trouble finding him."

I close my eyes. "So, he did run." I feel the weight of Lucas's hand on my shoulder.

"Looks that way. We had some uniforms watching him. So, I'm not sure how he did it. But we'll get him."

I open my eyes and squint against the brightness of the sun. "What if you can't find him?"

"We will," he replies. His voice is tight and clipped, filled with the confidence of authority. "In the meantime, we're going to have to talk to your brother. We need to know more about his father's relationship with your mother."

I shoot a worried glance at Lucas. "I told you. Kyle doesn't know anything. He wasn't involved."

"We have to talk to everyone, Raielle," Detective Brady says.

I push off the wall, wondering if Kyle would ever tell the police about my healing power, and if he did tell them, would they believe it? Maybe I've been fooling myself thinking the police would be able to get justice for my mother. They'll either have no motive if everyone keeps my secret or they'll have a motive that's simply ludicrous to them.

Brady tells me goodbye and ends the call. But I still stand there holding the phone to my ear.

"This doesn't change anything for us," Lucas says, squeezing my shoulder to draw my attention. "We still need to leave now."

I put the silent phone away, thinking about Kyle and Penelope, and imagining the police arriving at the house. Then I picture the foundation of their happy home crumbling beneath them. "Maybe we could wait a day or two?" I suggest, barely finishing the sentence before his jaw sets stubbornly.

"No."

"This feels like running away now," I protest.

He brings his face close to mine. "This is running to something, Ray. This is fighting for your future. You seem to think your life isn't as important as everyone else's."

I look into his stormy eyes, and I'm afraid he's right. When nobody gives a shit about you for most of your life, you begin to believe the hype, or lack of it. But that's not the case anymore. I know I need to fight. I owe it to both Lucas and myself. I want a future with him more than anything. "Get the tickets," I tell him.

My answer seems to satisfy him. "You go talk to your chemistry teacher. I'll come by your house later after school, and we'll figure out what we're going to tell our families about our trip."

Then he pulls me into his arms and gives me a scorching kiss. It takes me by surprise. It's overwhelming, the way his mouth is suddenly devouring mine. This kiss is filled with desperation and laced with promise. He won't say that he's afraid of losing me, but his kiss is telling me it's true. When he finally breaks away, we're both breathless.

He takes my hand and releases it slowly as he turns away and walks toward the parking lot.

WALK out of school with a heavy heart. I waited until Gwen left the classroom. Then I told my chemistry teacher I had to go back to California to deal with some family issues. He told me he'd be happy to accommodate me with a make-up test or even a take home exam after speaking with my parents. But I don't yet know what I'm going to tell Kyle about my leaving. So, that may not be a viable option.

It's early afternoon, and I beat everyone home. I head downstairs to begin organizing my things. I can't believe that after all these years of making school my number one priority, I'm going to miss the last couple of weeks and possibly not graduate. My UCLA acceptance is dependent upon my obtaining my high school diploma.

I can feel my pulse speeding up, and I close my eyes, putting a stop to my panic, deciding to handle one crisis at a time. Trying to get well needs to be my priority now. If I can't manage that, nothing else is going to matter.

I sit down on my bed and rub my hand. It feels so strange, like it doesn't belong to the rest of my arm. I use it to carefully pick up my copy of *Jane Eyre*, which sits on my night stand, and I place it beside the other items I've gathered.

When the doorbell rings, my heart flutters figuring it must be Lucas. I'm dismayed as the exhaustion that's my constant companion forces me to trudge slowly up the stairs. I pull open the front door and stand frozen in place. I'm stunned by who I see there.

"Aren't you gonna let me in?" Apollo asks.

He shaved his goatee, and his hair is longer, but he's still skinny as a rail in his too-tight jeans and black button down shirt.

"What are you doing here?" I ask, wide-eyed when he steps past me into the house.

I stare up at his six foot six frame. He glances around, checking the place out, before turning back to me again. "Sorry about your mom," he says.

His comment throws me, sending me back to that terrible moment. "Your door was open. Were you there that day?"

"No. I wasn't around," he offers dismissively, liked he missed the bus instead of my mother's murder. "Congratulations on UCLA by the way." He smiles without any humor, and his fleshless face reminds me of grinning Halloween skeleton.

"Thanks," I reply hesitantly, remembering his prickly personality and how carefully I used to tread around it. "Thank you for sending it to me."

He shrugs like it was nothing. Then he places his large hands on his narrow hips. "Your father sent me to get you."

I blink in surprise. "What?"

"You heard me. He knows you've been looking for him. He knows," Apollo pauses, "you're not well. He wants to try to help you."

"How do you know my father?"

One side of his mouth lifts. "Me and him. We go way back."

I stare at him confused, my mind reeling. "What do you mean? Did you know him when we lived above you?"

He tilts his head at me and raises skeptical eyebrows, indicating how stupid he thinks my question is.

My blood runs cold. Does this mean my father was keeping tabs on us?

Apollo can see my questions building up. "Look, I know you're on your way to find him, and he's saving you the trouble. We don't have time for chit-chat. I'll answer all your questions later. Now go pack a bag. The woman and her kid will be back in less than half an hour. We need to be gone by then." He stands staring at me, and his booted toe begins to tap.

I don't understand any of this. I cross my arms and stare down my nose at him. "I'm not going to just leave with you."

Apollo remains silent.

"I need to talk to my boyfriend before I agree to anything," I insist, hating that I'm using that word for the first time with Apollo of all people.

He only blinks at me.

His calm is fueling my anger. "Apollo!" I scream in frustration.

He takes two long strides toward me and bends down so that his nose is only inches from mine. "Your boyfriend. That's the kid whose been phoning all over LA looking for Rainard Blackwood." He chuckles.

"That was never really your daddy's name. That's why he let your mother keep it. You need to forget about him. And we need to get moving. You have ten minutes to pack or you'll have to leave with nothing."

His words slowly sink in. We didn't even have the right name. We were never going to find him on our own, but I still don't move. "I'm not going to forget about him, and I'm not leaving without him."

He squints at me and shakes his head. "What? You think you love him?"

"I do love him."

"Well, that's too bad," he frowns.

"Why is that?"

"Because he can't come with us."

"Then I can't come with you."

His cool doesn't melt at all. "What happened to you, Raielle? The girl I knew wouldn't let herself get attached to a goddamned puppy dog, never mind some high school boy. You've changed, kid."

He's right, and I know why. "I've found my family, Apollo." And I'm including Lucas in that category.

He nods. "Yeah. You've found some of them. But your daddy is your family, too. If you want to be cured of this thing you've given yourself he's the only family that counts right now. His condition for helping you is that you disappear quietly. You can't tell anyone, and you can't bring anyone with you. Now, you can come with me or not. It's up to you. But we both know your chances aren't real good without his help. In fact, I'd say they're pretty fucking dismal."

I clench my jaw in frustration. "Why is my father doing this? He never bothered with me before. Does he even care if I live or die?"

Apollo lowers his dark gaze to mine. "He's does care. That's why I'm here. He's been staying away to protect you. To keep you out of his life so you could try to have a normal one. There are people out there wh would come after you if they knew you were his daughter. Dangerous people, Raielle. I'm the only way you're going to get to him."

I don't know what to think. Am I supposed to believe everything Apollo is telling me and just go with him? "How long would we be gone?" I ask.

He hesitates before answering. "I don't know."

I balk at that.

He shakes his head at my reaction. "You need to trust me. Have I ever lied to you?"

"No," I concede. "But you sure left a lot of shit out, didn't you?"

He seems amused by my comment. But he soon grows serious again. "Do you think your brother or your boyfriend would want you to pass up a chance to be cured?"

We both know how I'll answer that question. So, I don't bother. I tilt my head at him instead. "Let's say I do go with you, and my father cures me. How will he do it? Will he transfer this disease into someone else? If that's the best he can do, I'm not interested anyway," I toss out at him with more bravado than I feel.

He chuckles at my statement, like my sudden spunk is amusing to him. "To be honest, I've got no clue how that shit works. I've never wanted anything to do with it. The only way to know that is to come with me."

I study him, but I'm not sure if he's telling the truth or not. "If I don't like what I see when I get there, then what? I'm free to go? I can come back here?"

Apollo's dark eyes watch me. "No, probably not," he says bluntly. "Once I bring you to him, people will eventually figure out who you are. After that, you'll need stay to close. You'll be under his protection. Coming back here would be putting yourself and anyone you care about at risk."

"Under his protection?" I laugh. "Who does he think he is the mafia or something? What does that even mean? Will he lock me away somewhere? Why on earth would I agree to that?"

A small smile curves his lips. "No, that's not what it means. You've always been under his protection. Do you think you've stayed safe all these years because you're lucky? You've lived with drunks and abusers. You've been surrounded by thieves and junkies. How many times have you walked home alone at night through some pretty dicey neighborhoods? Yet, not a hair on your head has ever been harmed. You must think you're the luckiest damn girl in the world."

As I stare at him, I nearly forget to breathe. My chest feels tight as my gaze lands on the floor. The truth of what he's saying is too obvious to doubt. I did think I was lucky. But he's right. No one is that lucky. My father has been protecting me all along.

"This was going to happen eventually," he says. "Your daddy's been hoping to meet you for a long time. If he can cure you, what you do after that isn't up to me. I can't make you any promises about what comes next. I can only tell you that if you don't come with me, you have no future with your boyfriend or anyone else. If this boyfriend really cares about you, I'm sure he wouldn't want that."

Apollo's point is too sharp to dismiss, and I actually start to consider leaving with him. But if I do, Lucas won't understand. He's going to despise me for disappearing like this without a word. He's never been confident of my feelings for him, and I know that's my fault. But if I stay here and risk my life for more time with him, he'll blame himself for my fate. I know he won't be able to live with that, and I could never put that burden on him.

I look up at Apollo, finally understanding what's happening, and it feels like all the air has been sucked out of the room. If I don't want this disease to kill me, I have to go with him. If I choose to go with him

I have to walk away from Lucas without saying goodbye and without explaining anything. I don't know how long it will be before I can see him. If my father can't cure me, I may never feel his arms around me again. Only a few months ago, I didn't even know Lucas, and now I feel like he's a part of me. He thinks I'm his ray of sunshine, but somehow, without my even acknowledging it until this moment, he's become my center. All my strength is sourced from the love he gives me. I hold my hands up to my mouth as the reality of my situation barrels into me, flaying me to the bone.

"Now go get your stuff," Apollo says. His voice has gentled in the face of my despair. But I still can't seem to move. "Dammit," he mutters, pushing past me, heading down the stairs.

In a daze, I follow behind him and watch as he shoves the clothes that I've already put out on my bed into the duffle bag I have sitting on the floor.

"Still reading this," he states, holding up my frayed copy of *Jane Eyre*. He tosses that into the bag, too. "Is that everything?" he asks, pulling out my phone charger and placing it on the table beside my phone. "You need to leave that here. It can be traced."

I'm watching him silently, too emotional to pay attention. But when I realize he's taken my phone, I break out of my stupor, knowing I can't be so cruel as to leave Lucas in the dark this way. I turn on Apollo. "I'm calling Lucas. I won't have him wondering if I'm alive or not. I can't do that to him. It's just one phone call, and I'm willing to die for it if you make me." I reach for my phone and silently dare him to stop me. When he doesn't immediately object, I start to head upstairs for privacy.

"Oh, no you don't." Apollo grabs my arm, and I can see he's wavering. "Fine. You can make your one call, but I need to hear it. Just keep to the facts. No details. Short and sweet."

I yank myself from his grasp. "You haven't told me any details."

"For good reason."

I glare at him. He remains silent as I clumsily manipulate the phone. I tap Lucas's number and listen to it ring, but the sound is nearly drowned out by my hammering heart.

"No." A frustrated whisper leaves my lips when I get his voicemail. Then I try to slow my thoughts down. I need to think clearly. I need to tell him how I feel in case I don't get this chance again. I try to keep my voice steady so I won't worry him. When I open my mouth to speak, I'm still not sure what I'm going to say.

"It's me," I begin, hearing the hitch in my voice. I draw a deep breath into my lungs before continuing. "My father knows we're looking for him. He sent someone to get me. We had the wrong name, Lucas. We were never going to find him ourselves." I dart a look at Apollo to see if he's angry at what I've just revealed, but he only looks bored and disinterested. So, I continue.

"My father says he can heal me, but that I need to come to him alone. And I need to go right now. I'm so sorry I have to leave this way... without you, without saying goodbye. But please don't worry. I'm going to be fine." I pause after my lie. I don't know that I'm going to be fine. While that lie slips easily from my lips, I won't lie about seeing him soon. I don't want him waiting for me if I can't come back to him. That would be too unkind.

I take another breath before continuing. "I love you," I whisper, tightening my throat against the emotion that threatens to steal my voice. "I promise to never stop loving you. 'All my heart is yours, Lucas, it belongs to you.'" I end the call, finally releasing the sob that's been building inside me, reciting the rest of the quote I know so well silently to myself... *and with you it would remain, were fate to exile the rest of me from your presence forever.*

I feel Apollo removing the phone from my grasp. "Very nice. Now come on. This is just a high school romance. Believe me, you'll get over him. You're meant for bigger things. If everything works out, your life is about to get good and interesting. And all this? Soon, this place will be the definition of dull. I can promise you that."

When I stand there silently, trying to staunch my tears, not showing the immediate recovery he obviously expects after his little pep talk. He sighs impatiently. "You ready to go?"

I glance up at him. "No."

His voice softens. "Come on. We're driving, and we have a lot of road to cover."

"Where are we going?" I ask.

"We're going home, Raielle."

He ushers me outside, carrying my bag for me. I turn to look at Myles's house as I walk toward the small hatchback Apollo has parked on the street. I recall the first time I saw Lucas standing there in the darkness. The way we connected to each other from the very beginning. The way we fell in love. Loving Lucas has irrevocably changed me. I can never again be the closed-off, focused girl who tried not to care about anyone. I regret not telling him that. I worry that he doesn't understand how deep my feelings for him run. I'm afraid he'll despise me for disappearing this way.

I stumble, and Apollo catches me. "Let's go, kid," he says gently. "You're gonna be in good hands. Your daddy isn't gonna let you die if he can help it."

But I know he's wrong. If I do survive, a part of me will die anyway f I'm without Lucas.

Thank you, thank you, thank you for reading.
Yes, the story will continue! When I have information available, I'll
post it to my blog debradoxer.blogspot.com.

ALSO BY
DEBRA DOXER

Wintertide
Sometime Soon

ACKNOWLEDGEMENTS

To my early readers, your enthusiasm for my initial drafts energized me and kept me going when precious time for writing was scarce. My sincere thanks to Jennifer Bolduc, Annemarie Donovan, Melanie Turano, Caryn Feldman, Deb Goodman, Diedre Heck, Karen Larochelle, Vicki Malver, Sue Panioli, Lori Seller, and Amie White.

I owe a second shout out to Annemarie Donovan, babysitter extraordinaire, who gave me those final quiet hours I needed to try to get the story as right as I could.

Lots of extra Xs and Os to Amie White. You've been a major wiseass since I met you in fifth grade. It feels like you've been making me laugh forever. Now, you're inspiring me, too.

At the eleventh hour, when I hit the panic button, I'm so grateful to Caryn, Scott, and especially Dad for coming to my rescue. When it's crunch time, I can always count on my family. You too, Mom. Mobile devices may not be your thing, but unwavering support is. Love you.

This paperback interior was designed and formatted by

www.emtippettsbookdesigns.blogspot.com

Artisan interiors for discerning authors and publishers.

Made in the USA
Charleston, SC
20 September 2013